Traditional Music
of
South Africa

The Drumcafé's

Traditional Music
of
South Africa

Laurie Levine

JACANA

First published in 2005 by Jacana Media (Pty) Ltd.
5 St Peter Road
Bellevue, 2198
Johannesburg
South Africa

ISBN 1-77009-046-0

Cover design by Triple M

Design and layout by Marlene Willoughby-Smith

Printed and bound by Pinetown Printers

See a complete list of Jacana titles at www.jacana.co.za

Acknowledgements

Anthony Caplan's contribution to this book has been substantial. With a degree in music and a deep theoretical, as well as practical, understanding of African music, he has guided the process and shared his knowledge. He co-researched the material and helped bring it all together in the initial stages of the process. He also played a big role in compiling the CD attached to the book. The Drumcafé thanks him for his dedication and hard work.

Professor Andrew Tracey of the International Library of African Music made an invaluable contribution to this book. Throughout the process he was generous with his time, making himself available to answer the many questions we grappled with, clarifying certain issues. He edited the entire manuscript, drawing on his extensive knowledge of the field to ensure that all our facts were correct and our approach appropriate. The Drumcafé thanks him for sharing his knowledge and time, and for supporting the project.

The Drumcafé extends its gratitude to the following individuals for their general support and assistance in particular areas:

Jaco Kruger, David Coplan, Nothembi Mkhwebane, Sarah Mahlangu, Daniel Mguni, Ronald Levine, Diane Levine, Maisie Barrow and Kevin Bloom.

It also extends its gratitude for the permission to use photographs from the following sources:

Janine Dunlop and the manuscripts and archives department at the University of Cape Town for the use of Kirby, Paff and Bleek photographs and illustrations, Kathy Brooks and Museum Africa, International Library of African Music for the use of photographs from the ILAM archives, Bert Woodehouse, Robert Hart for the use of photographs from the Duggin Cronin collection housed at the McGregor Museum, Dawn Taylor, Marius Coetzee and the Wits Archives at the University of the Witwatersrand for the use of photographs from the John Blacking and Thomas Johnston theses as well as photographs from their archives, Veronica Klipp and the Wits University Press for the use of plates from the Percival Kirby publication, *The Musical Instruments of the Native Races of South Africa*, Dr Yvonne Huskisson and Deborah James.

The attached CD would not have been possible without the licensing of material from the following sources:

The International Library of African Music and Andrew Tracey, David Alexander and Tequila Records, Music Energy Loud Truth (MELT) and Robert Trunz, 3rd Ear Music and David Marks, The !Xun Traditional Council and The South African San Institute (SASI) and Dave Dargie.

South African Tribal Distribution

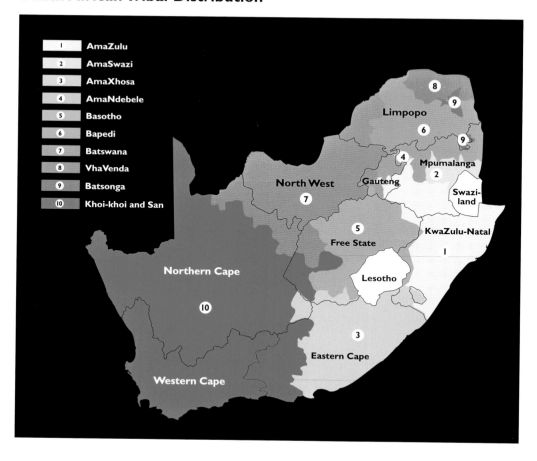

1	AmaZulu
2	AmaSwazi
3	AmaXhosa
4	AmaNdebele
5	Basotho
6	Bapedi
7	Batswana
8	VhaVenda
9	Batsonga
10	Khoi-khoi and San

Foreword

Far from the centres of power as they are – the homestead, the village, the fields, the 'great places' – it is high time in fact that a little support was shown to them from outside their own realm. This book, drawn from many sources, places the traditional musicians back in the centre, by focusing on what we should have known all along about our original music.

The traditional musicians know their own music intimately, as only they can. A few musical academics and enthusiasts 'know' it too on another level, from research which started slowly from about the 1930s. In the broad middle, however, there is little beyond ignorance, clichés and misapprehensions, even on the part of many urban blacks, and certainly on the part of most whites and others. We may be happy to hear that Ladysmith Black Mambazo have just won a Grammy award but who knows where Isicathamiya comes from? Where can we learn? This book is the first broad attempt to provide the source material on ourselves, as South African musicians.

It is a poor nation that does not know its own culture. Ghana showed us the way, the first African colony to gain independence, way back in 1957, followed by every other African country down to us, last of all; we came late in turning the psychological corner towards self-knowledge. Others who showed the way were the early researcher P.R. Kirby, and the great collector Hugh Tracey, who showed us what was there. Since our own 'independence' in 1994 more African researchers have started to come forward. I hope that this book is just the first edition of others to come until we have a whole library of our own musical self-knowledge. All credit to Warren Lieberman, Laurie Levine, Anthony Caplan and their flourishing international Drumcafé, first for introducing many people to the fundamentals of African musicality through drumming, and now for giving us this book about our own music.

– ANDREW TRACEY (PROFESSOR)
International Library of African Music, Rhodes University

South African traditional musicians are pretty tough. They have had to be, to have survived this long in the face of all that has been thrown at them for nigh on two hundred years …apartheid, poverty, migrant labour, ignorance, disdain, as well as the intense competition from the multifarious musical forms supported by the prosperous recording industry, the church, the schools, the media.

2136

2736 1233 1643

Some explanations

When the Drumcafé began the preliminary research on South African music, we soon became aware that there were a number of academic issues, bigger than our project, and larger than our understanding, that have been rotated within academia for many years. As we delved into the research and writing in the field, we started teasing out numerous philosophical issues that are dug up when studying cultural heritage. One might spend years coming to grips with the difficulties posed by such research, but we had a clear sense of what we wanted to achieve and who we wanted to reach, and we decided we could not tackle them in a substantial way, as this is not the focus of the book. Nonetheless, it is important that one is aware of some of the bigger questions, and so we have outlined them below on the most primary level.

On the term 'traditional'

Many ethnomusicologists have grappled with a core philosophical issue that is raised when categorising a cultural art form under the banner of 'traditional'. The term is problematic for a number of reasons. Firstly, in the new South Africa, terminology is imbued with political weight, and often becomes the site of conflict and misunderstanding. One therefore needs to take a sensitive approach when using terminology that might raise associations with the past. Among academics, this term is seen as a static expression of something that is fluid. Cultural expression shifts with social context. New forms bleed into older forms, social contexts change, and art continually evolves and shifts position. Music, like every other art form, moves with the continual forces of change.

When one unravels the notion of tradition, a number of questions with no definitive answers are raised. Where does one draw the line between traditional and modern? Do styles of music that are influenced by the past fall under traditional? Do traditional art forms belong only to the past? Does traditional date itself to pre-colonial contact? Does everything that comes after colonial contact fall under the banner of modern? The questions are endless; the answers are limited.

Some ethnomusicologists have found alternative terms for concepts that are seen as problematic in academic circles. Robin Wells rejects the terms 'traditional' and 'modern', replacing them with 'established canon' and 'emergent styles'. He argues that art belonging to the established canon is located in the past, and is often performed as 'self-conscious references to the past'.[1] Emergent styles, on the other hand, are styles that have evolved over the last 150 years, are part of modern performance contexts, and usually have foreign influences. Wells is in essence distinguishing between styles that have been embedded in a culture with little or no external influence, and styles that developed with modernity and its accompanying developments. Rosemary Smith describes the traditional music of the Zulu as "the indigenous music of the Zulu people as it continues to be performed in a primarily Zulu cultural setting."[2] Smith excludes the music that has developed out of contact with the Western world, although she does not claim that traditional music has remained entirely untouched by outside influences.

For the purposes of this book, and with a full awareness of the problematic nature of such broad concepts as 'traditional' and 'modern', we have stayed with the original terminology. Taking into account both Wells's and Smith's understandings of the term 'traditional', we have covered the musical styles that Wells understands as belonging to the 'established canon'; and we have covered the 'emergent styles' which might have been influenced by the outside world, but which make a strong reference to the past, and are still performed in traditional settings.

On ethnic/language groups

One of the most important decisions in writing an overview of South African music was how to structure the material. The division of the South African ethnic groups into strict categories might be regarded by some as a colonial methodology, and a simplification of the diverse cultures of South Africa. As Hammond Tooke argues, "ethnic classifications were used by colonial authorities to divide and rule."[3] In writing an overview, however, some kind of structural system needed to be designed, and we decided to divide the book according to language groups, in order to provide the most comprehensive perspective of South African music. We are fully aware that we have not accounted for or represented every South African group; there are tribal groups that fall between categories, and given the nature of this study, they are too numerous to be included. The book is divided into the black language groups, which include the Nguni languages, namely isiZulu, isiXhosa, SiSwati and isiNdebele; the Sesotho languages, namely Sesotho, Setswana and Sepedi; the Tshivenda and Xitsonga language groups; and the Khoi-san language group – the San and Khoi. There are numerous similarities in musical traditions among these groups, and we wanted to use these similarities to thread together the content of the book. For this reason we have not included Afrikaans, English or any offshoots of the black languages. These will be covered in the next edition of the book.

By using the language groups as an overarching structure, we were able to represent South Africa's main black ethnic groups. The notion of equating South Africa's language and ethnic groups is explained in an article on South Africa's languages:

"Despite the diversity of these language groups, it is nonetheless possible to begin to understand this complex society by viewing language groupings as essentially the same as ethnic groupings. This is possible because, in general, most South Africans consider one of the eleven official languages, or a closely related tongue, to be their first language; and most people acquire their first language as part of a kinship group or an ethnically conscious population."[4]

On area or district

The details of customs and practices may vary considerably from one area to the next. Many academics have devoted their studies to particular clans in particular areas. Owing to the nature of our study, we have not been able to represent every existing group or focus on specific areas of South Africa. Whereas the Xhosa people of the Lumko district have a long tradition of beer-drinking songs, we will find that the Gcaleka (a Xhosa clan) of the Whittlesea district do not, as just one example. Using the available research and writing in the field, we have made broad assumptions. Please consult the reference section for more detailed research focusing on specific areas.

On songs and dances

Although there are some songs that are known over a large distance from community to community, there are often different versions of one song. The songs that we have included as examples on the attached CD are just one version of many.

Songs and dance gatherings often share the same name as they are inextricably linked. As in most African cultures, songs and dances cannot be separated one from the other. In dance, movement produces a fundamental part of the song's structure, rhythm and overarching sound.

On the CD

At the back of the book is an enclosed CD. The CD contains short clips of music. Readers should look out for references to these clips in the text marked by, for example, *Refer to Track 15*. Please consult the appendix for a listing of the tracks.

On instruments

There is little agreement among ethnomusicologists on one particular spelling or name of an instrument. With time, spellings and instrument names have changed. Thus each researcher used the spelling or name that was relevant at the time he or she conducted the research. For the most part, we have stayed with Percival Kirby's spelling used in *The Musical Instruments of the Native Races of South Africa*. The instruments that were not included in his book, but were later accounted for by researchers who came after him, have been taken directly from later works. We have used our endnotes to account for discrepancies in spelling and names.

If one meets up with musicians, one will find that many of the original names of the instruments have been replaced with new names. Consequentially, one must be aware that the older names recorded by Kirby might in fact no longer be recognised or might no longer exist.

When working through Kirby's book, we noticed that many different instruments are given the same name. For example, the AmaZulu possess at least two different kinds of whistles and flutes that are called by the same name. The table of comparison near the end of the book is an effective means for plotting out the similarities and differences of the cultural groups.

On Ndebele and Tswana chapters

There are large gaps in research on Tswana and Ndebele music in South Africa. The Drumcafé approached many specialists who agreed that the literature on the music of these two groups is almost non-existent. This chapter was based on research that mainly focused on Tswana music in Botswana and Ndebele music in Zimbabwe. The Tswana were all originally living in South Africa before the 19th century. When certain Tswana groups started migrating to Botswana, they took with them their musical traditions. One can thus conclude that there are some similarities between the cultures, although the people are separated geographically. The same can be said of the Ndebele of Zimbabwe and South Africa.

On ceremonies and rituals

We have only included those aspects of ceremonies that relate directly to music. We have not covered all the rituals that are attached to various ceremonies. Our choices of what to include and what to exclude were governed by the musical elements of each ceremony.

On traditional music today

We have not provided a comprehensive update on which musical instruments are still played and which songs and dances are still performed today. We hope to cover this area of research in the near future.

Contents

Introduction

In South Africa there is an idea that is shared by many cultures; a way of thinking that approaches the essence of the African character. In isiXhosa, people express the idea with the saying "*Umuntu ngumuntu ngabantu.*" In Sesotho, the same idea is evoked when someone says "*Motho ke motho ka batho ka bang.*" Such proverbs embody the belief that the individual identity is a function of the collective relationship. It is only through sharing a common humanity that a person becomes fully human.

Music, by its very nature, nurtures the idea of *ngumuntu.* The young are taught music so that they can participate in group activities – so that eventually they can become valued members of their communities. Children are exposed to musical activities from the moment they enter the world. As they learn language they learn to sing; as they learn to walk they learn to dance. Singing, playing instruments and feeling rhythm become as natural as the ability to speak or walk. From everyday activities to sacred ceremonies, from morning to night, through winter and summer, music forms the pivotal core around which a community is structured.

As a matter of course, then, music in South Africa has always lived in the realm of myth and legend – it has been passed down through oral tradition, affecting belief systems and reaffirming the centrality of ritual. Rock paintings of the San, dating as far back as 20 000 years, show people playing musical instruments and dancing. Within this ancient milieu, one of music's roles has been protection, as in the legend of the 'magic drum', which was carried by Venda chiefs when they travelled to southern Africa in the late 18th century so that enemies would be repelled by the immense power of the beat. There is also the enchanted Tsonga 'flute of heaven', which is blown by a diviner during a thunderstorm to drive away the *ndlati* bird – the creature responsible for the lightning. Through such myths, musical practices have been woven into the fabric of southern African societies.

So music retains its relevance in traditional societies through ritual. The Bantu and Khoi-san use music not only to express the values attached to their traditions, but to communicate with the ancestors. Their music reaches beyond the earthly realm and connects them to the spirits, who cast a protective eye over the living. In certain rituals music also has healing properties. In many African

"All art aspires toward the condition of music."

– ARTHUR SCHOPENHAUER
(1788-1860) GERMAN PHILOSOPHER

societies, illness is a function of both physical and psychological distress. It is for this reason that music is used as an effective therapeutic tool; it elicits a positive response in the body and mind of the listener.

The rhythms, it is said, can transport one yet further onto the metaphysical plane. Through drumming and dancing, an individual can experience altered states of consciousness, where evil spirits can be exorcised and benevolent spirits can enter. Certain instruments are said to represent the voices of the spirits, and are thus regarded as sacred. In many cultures the dialogue between the living and the dead is facilitated through song. People use rain songs to pray for rain, and clan anthems to thank their ancestors for good fortune. Music is the centre around which religious practice spins.

Music also cements identity during the initiation into a new phase of life. Before an individual is granted the status of an adult in a community, through an initiation rite, it is essential that he or she be given a strong education in the skills and responsibilities that come with adulthood. Song and dance is seen as a powerful means to hand down these skills. Within this context music becomes the site of power: the initiates learn secret formulae through song, and only those who have been initiated have access to the secret 'language'. Music is, equally central to the African wedding, another rite of passage that changes a person's status. Numerous cultures use music to structure the marriage ceremony so that participants are guided from one phase to the next. As in many other contexts, music during the marriage ceremony is also the most effective means of communicating with and ensuring the presence of the ancestors.

There is also an important political element to music-making within some of the cultures covered in this book. Music is used to reinforce the role of chiefs and kings, and to create loyalty amongst subjects. While the reed dance in Swaziland reaffirms the power of the queens, the reed-pipe dance of the Venda enhances the status of chiefs. In recent times, the music of many South African groups has been a powerful force for social cohesion, binding communities, and reinforcing a common identity. When South African men were forced to join the migrant-labour system during the mid-1900s, music and dance were the most effective means of healing and unification. Similarly, a century before, music had been a site of struggle when the missionaries began the process of mass conversion. Music, as this book will argue, is a form of resistance and solidarity.

But beyond the functional significance of music is the sheer pleasure and joy that is derived from making it. Children sing as they play, and adults hum as they work. Traditionally, people gathered around fires at night to sing and dance. The elderly would narrate folktales to children that were dramatised through mime and song. And today, on any given weekend anywhere in South Africa, groups of people can be found dancing, singing and playing instruments. Where there are no instruments to be found, tins are turned over and beaten with sticks, and cans are filled with stones and shaken. Teams of dancers compete with one another, taking pride in their unique heritage: Zulu dancers wearing animal skins and holding shields execute the ndlamu stamping dance, while Pedi performers don their Scottish kilts to perform the dinaka reed-pipe dance. Although the catalogue of music in these societies is communal, there is always a time and place for solo music-making. Herdboys make flutes out of reeds, and whistle while herding cattle, and women compose love songs on their musical bows.

Of course, where a group dynamic pervades a culture, music is generally characterised by choral singing and group dancing. There is a fluid relationship between song, dance, mime and praise poetry among the Bantu and Khoi-san peoples of South Africa. These art forms are integrated in musical performance to such an extent that they reject Western methods of separation and classification. Dance creates the foundation of the song's rhythm, mime is part of the visual performance, praise poetry can be central to the lyric.

Although the songs have an overriding structure, their patterns leave space for improvisation and creativity. Most consist of repeated cycles, usually with two major parts, the leader section conveying the melody, and the follower section introducing layering through the device of spontaneous response. This gives rise to polyphony – a technique that is widespread, particularly among the Bantu-speaking people. Songs have multi-layered vocals, and there are always at least two voices coming in at different times, singing different texts. When the song cycles are repeated – usually with numerous responses built into each cycle – the various parts overlap, and the singers may add their voices at any point. The followers' responses are often made up of seemingly meaningless and unrehearsed syllables; they emerge as expressions that capture a specific moment. A song's pitch also changes as the performance develops. As it builds to a crescendo and the excitement rises, so the pitch level rises. The performances are invigorating for all these reasons, but a key element is that the same song is never performed in the same way. The tradition is to continually create and recreate so that each performance is unique.

In the past the beauty of this process, as well as the fundamental value of South Africa's indigenous black music, was completely overshadowed by various misconceptions. The first observations on African music occurred in the mid-16th century with the arrival of Portuguese explorers, but it was not until the mid-19th century that the first missionaries introduced the music of their cultures to the indigenous people of South Africa. From then on, any music that did not conform to the norms of the West and did not have a religious slant was regarded as primitive and crude. The assumption was that African music was by nature inferior.

Over the last few years, arts and culture organisations have started to place emphasis on reviving traditional art forms through research programmes and projects. With the overarching objective of preserving and promoting South Africa's cultural heritage, their investments have started to pay off, and the positive impact on a number of communities is evident. Further, university music departments specialising in indigenous music are being set up all over the world, and young musicians are becoming familiar with many previously marginalised art forms. New and established artists are looking to the past for the exciting creative possibilities offered by merging the traditional with the modern.

This is the backdrop against which the concept for this book was born. Warren Lieberman, founder of the Drumcafé, recognised that sponsorship of an overview of traditional South African music could contribute to the knowledge already being circulated within the country. Like many organisations, the Drumcafé acknowledges the need to preserve South Africa's rich heritage through promoting a deeper understanding of our cultural legacy. When we began our preliminary research we discovered that while there is a wealth of material on indigenous South African music, no one has yet collated the disparate elements into one reader-friendly overview. Ethnomusicologists and social anthropologists have compiled invaluable and detailed academic texts, but these are not always easily accessible to the wider public. This book is an attempt to bring the richness of our musical heritage to the interested layman.

The book is divided according to the main black language groups of South Africa. Nine of South Africa's official languages belong to the family of Bantu languages, a branch of the Niger-Congo language family that is represented through much of sub-Saharan Africa. In South Africa these languages are made up of four major subgroups: the Nguni, Sotho-Tswana, Tsonga-Shangaan and Venda. The Nguni is the largest, encompassing the AmaZulu, AmaSwazi, AmaNdebele and AmaXhosa. The broad Sotho-Tswana grouping accounts for a third of South Africa's Bantu-speaking population, and includes the Basotho, Batswana, and the Bapedi. The VhaVenda and Batsonga, who live in close proximity to one another, make up a smaller percentage of South Africa's Bantu-speaking peoples.

Before the Bantu-speaking people arrived in South Africa, the land was inhabited by the San and Khoi. Together these peoples are known as the Khoi-san, a general term used by linguists to designate people with 'click' languages, and by anthropologists to distinguish the aboriginal people of southern Africa from other black inhabitants. Although the San and Khoi languages are not officially recognised in South Africa, both groups have had an enormous impact on the Bantu peoples, who were all directly or indirectly influenced by the Khoi-san culture (one example being the Bantu's adoption of the Khoi-san's characteristic click sounds). Accordingly, the book places appropriate emphasis on the music of this ancient group.

An overview of musical instruments serves to introduce the reader to the black South African instrument groups and categories. Thereafter, each chapter focuses on one group, of which there are eleven. The content includes a brief overview of the group's history, short descriptions of the musical instruments, and an exploration of the musical activities that are included in the ceremonies, rituals and daily lives of the people.

It is simply not possible to cover everything in one book, and knowledge is continually expanding as new research is undertaken both within and outside of South Africa. Our hope is that this first edition leaves the reader with a strong appreciation of (and perhaps even love for) the indigenous music of South Africa.

– LAURIE LEVINE
Johannesburg, March 2005

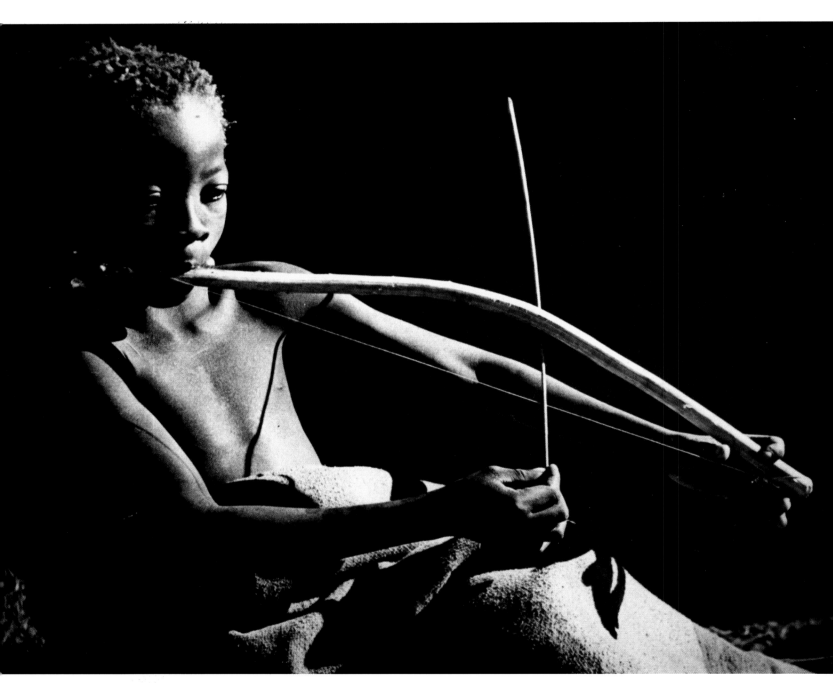

Playing the umrhubhe

An Overview of South African Musical Instruments

The availability of materials also determines the type of instruments that are made and played in any part of the world. In the past, before man-made materials became easily available, the indigenous instruments of South Africa were constructed mainly from natural materials. People made, and to some extent still make, bows from sinew and wood, leg-rattles from fruit or cocoon shells filled with seeds or stones, and drums from animal skins and wood.

Musical instruments belong largely to the category of solo music-making in South African black indigenous communities. Although musical ensembles do exist, such as the reed-pipe ensembles found among the Venda or the horn ensembles once found among the Tsonga, most musical instruments are played solo and are used as a form of self-expression. Percussion instruments are an exception, being used as accompaniment to dances. The majority of musical performances allow the individual to temporarily step out of the community and express what cannot be expressed within the confines of the group.

Owing to the close proximity of South Africa's indigenous peoples and the sharing of land and resources, many musical instruments are the same from one group to the next. People have shared and exchanged ideas, borrowing instruments from each other and adapting construction and playing techniques. One must always remember, however, that despite the uniformity across groups, each musical instrument is unique because it is hand-made. Musicians often make their own instruments to serve their personal requirements. Furthermore, because most traditional instruments are made from natural materials, there are no standard sizes.

Throughout the world, there are four distinct categories of musical instruments, and these can also be applied to the instruments of Africa: membranophones, idiophones, aerophones and chordophones.

Traditionally, the majority of South Africans who played instruments lived on grassy plains, and their economies and socio-political lives were closely linked with cattle.

A similar situation existed in other parts of Africa, such as the plains of Tanzania, southern Angola, and the West African savannah, which meant that personal instruments tended to be simple and portable, with the greatest musical effort being put into singing in groups.[1]

Membranophones (Drums)

The sound of a drum is produced by the vibration of a membrane, such as an animal hide that has been stretched across a body. The body acts as a resonator, amplifying and sometimes modifying the sound of the vibrating membrane.

According to Percival Kirby, every race inhabiting South Africa has played drums at some stage, from the early Khoi playing on wooden milk jugs or clay pots, to the Venda playing on elaborately decorated wooden drums. South African drums vary in shape, size and material. Playing techniques also vary, depending on the dimension of the instrument and the desired effect. Whereas a player uses a stick to rub the head of a friction drum, she beats the skin of most other drums with her hands. Among the South African black ethnic groups, the most common materials used for the body of a drum are either wood or clay. Drums made from oil and tin containers are also widely used today. The drum membrane is made out of local animal skins, mostly goat, cow and antelope.

Drums in traditional societies provide much more than mere recreation and entertainment. They are one of the most important channels used to express a society's shared values, knowledge and experience. The feeling generated by the sound of the drum enhances group identity and becomes a vital healing and unifying force. Drumming provides a strong rhythmical foundation and is also used to assemble a group of people, involving them in communal activity.

Certain South African drums are difficult to find nowadays, and some have disappeared from the musical map altogether. However, these traditional instruments have been replaced with modern substitutes. The drum, seen by many as the most representative African instrument, has retained its popularity in South African communities. As was aptly observed, "Even when the drum itself is physically absent, its presence is reflected by hand-clapping, stamping, or the repetition of certain rhythmic onomatopoeias that are all artifices that imitate the drum beat."[2]

Idiophones (Self-sounding instruments)

Idiophones are self-sounding instruments that vibrate within themselves when struck or shaken. This means that the sound is produced without the addition of a stretched membrane or a vibrating string or reed. The sound of idiophones is one of the most characteristic features of African song and dance. In South Africa, idiophones are an essential aspect of percussion in the context of communal music. They are usually a required part of the instrumentation of an ensemble, enhancing the rhythm of the music. In addition, they create ambience during rituals and ceremonies, and evoke emotional responses from people. Idiophones are sometimes used to scare away birds or control the movements of cattle.

There are three main categories of idiophones:

Shaken idiophones

The most commonly played idiophones are rattles and shakers, used to create percussion in dances. Rattles are either held or worn on the ankles as part of a dance costume. In South Africa ankle-rattles are usually made from cocoons, fruit-shells, goat skin or palm leaves tied up and filled with stones or seeds. Ankle-rattles emphasise a dancer's leg movements, and add their own rhythm to a dance. Today, rattles and shakers are made from any kind of empty container filled with objects such as seeds, rice or small stones.

The bull-roarer is included in this category. It is sometimes referred to as a spinning disc. Attached to a string and held in the hand, the instrument is swung around in circles, producing a roaring sound. Higher and lower tones can be created by altering the speed at which it is swung.

Struck and concussion idiophones

This group of instruments includes objects that are struck together.

Hand-clappers are usually made from flat slabs of wood, animal bones, or sticks, and are knocked together to enhance a song's rhythm.

Tuned idiophones

This group includes two kinds of instruments that are tuned: the *mbira* (thumb or hand piano) and the *marimba* (xylophone).

The *mbira* is believed to have originated in the Zambezi valley and is so widespread in Zimbabwe that it is accepted as the national instrument of the Shona. The instrument is found only in the northern parts of South Africa, where it has been adopted by the Venda, Tsonga and Pedi, and is used largely for recreation. The San of Botswana also adopted the *mbira* when metal became available to them. Outside Africa the instrument is known as the thumb piano, because the metal keys are plucked with the thumbs and/or index fingers. The instrument consists of a wooden soundboard onto which a number of keys made from tongues of metal are attached. The length and thickness of each tongue determines its pitch. The instrument is sometimes placed in a large container such as a calabash, which amplifies the sound. Buzzers made of various materials such as snail shells or metal bottle-tops are often attached to the soundboard and/or resonator to enhance the sound. *Mbira*-playing techniques are complex. The thumb or forefinger of the left hand plays the left side of the instrument; the thumb or forefinger of the right hand playing the right side. The other fingers move across the keyboard to create contrasting rhythms that cut across each other. When one hears the *mbira* being played, it often sounds as though more than one player is performing. In South Africa, this instrument is no longer as widely played as in the past, although it still plays an important role in some of the rituals of the Lemba, the Venda's neighbours.

The *marimba* is most highly developed in Mozambique, where it plays an important cultural and social role. The *mbila mutondo* of the Venda is the only traditional *marimba* of South Africa. It consists of a set of wooden slabs connected to a frame, each tuned to a certain pitch. Long gourds are attached to the underside of the instrument below each note and serve to amplify the sound. Three players strike the keys with rubber-tipped sticks to create a melody. Although this instrument has been adapted by many South African cultures and has become popular over the last few years, the original Venda *mbila* is now quite rare.

Aerophones (Wind instruments)

Aerophones are wind instruments through which air vibrates to produce the sound.

Aerophones fall into three groups:

The flute/whistle family

In South Africa, whistles and flutes are made from natural materials like small animal horns, wood, hollow bones and river reeds. Occasionally metal tubing is used as a substitute for the bamboo flute. Generally only boys play whistles and flutes, which are constructed and played in different ways. The simplest type of whistle found in South Africa is a pipe made from any of the above materials. It is stopped on one end and produces a single note. The player usually creates the sound by laying the instrument against the tongue and blowing air over the embouchure at an angle. Sometimes the player whistles as he inhales, thus producing other notes. Nowadays bought whistles and flutes have replaced hand-made ones.

Some end-blown flutes are open on both ends, and the player produces a variety of notes by closing and opening the bottom end with one finger, and selecting high or low pitches of the harmonic series according to how hard he blows. Transverse (side-blown) flutes are common among the Tsonga, Venda, Pedi, Swazi and Zulu. Ocarinas (round or oval-shaped instruments with finger-holes and a mouth-hole) also belong to this family, and in South Africa, are found only among the Tsonga and Venda.

Whistles and flutes are mainly played as solo instruments. They serve a number of purposes: herdboys use them to signal to their cattle or to each other from a distance; and diviners often prepare their whistles with medicine, blowing them as a signal to the spirit world.

Reed-pipes

Reed-pipes are made from reeds, bamboo or metal tubing. The player inhales and exhales through the embouchure on one end. The Khoi played in reed-pipe ensembles and the Batswana/Bamalete people also adopted this practice. Today the Batswana/Bamalete, Bapedi and VhaVenda all play reed-flute ensembles. The pipes are tuned to a seven-note (VhaVenda), four-note (Batswana/Bamalete) or five-note scale (Bapedi). The VhaVenda and Bapedi have a set of drums in the centre of the circle of dancers/pipers.

Horns and trumpets

Animal horns are sometimes used as musical instruments in South Africa, depending on which animals live in the area. Horns are generally blown through an embouchure in the side, and are played mostly by men. The pitch of the horn is determined by its size. In the past horns were blown as battle signals and were generally used to summon people to the chief's kraal. Horn ensembles are rare in South Africa, although they were once common among the Tsonga. The horns were tuned to different notes and were usually accompanied by drums.

The Zulu play a trumpet made from a tube of bamboo or other modern materials. This instrument is usually end-blown.

Chordophones (String instruments)

This is the generic term used for string instruments, sounded by bowing, plucking, or striking a string that is stretched between two fixed points.

According to Percival Kirby, South Africans possess eleven types of stringed instruments, the majority being one-stringed bows.[3] Bows enjoyed widespread popularity in pre-colonial days, but many are no longer made or played. However, there are still individuals in certain areas who uphold bow-playing traditions, but they are few and far between.

It is generally believed that many of the South African string instruments originally descended from the San hunting bow, which was also used as a musical instrument. Some string instruments were copied from European instruments, such as the violin and guitar, which were popular during the first two centuries of colonial contact among the Khoi, and are still found among Coloured and other South African communities today. String instruments are generally played solo, for instance during solitary activities such as herding, but also accompany soft singing by small groups.

South African bows are made mostly from natural materials. The stave is made from wood, and the string from twisted fibre, sinew, hair or wire. A bow can be either braced or unbraced. When a bow is braced a small wire cord is tied around the string and the stick in the centre of the bow, dividing the string into two parts. The musical bow needs a resonator of some sort. This may be a gourd attached to the stick, or the player may use the mouth as a resonator. The uncommon South African earth bow uses a hole in the earth as a resonator. All bows use the principle of creating melody by selecting harmonics. With a mouth-bow the pitch is altered by changing the shape of the mouth. If the bow has a gourd resonator, the player moves the gourd towards and away from his/her chest for the same purpose. All bows are able to produce at least two fundamental notes, often a whole tone apart, but other intervals are used in some parts of the country.

Bows can be plucked with the fingers, struck with a light stick or grass stem, rubbed with a small hair or a dry stick, and even activated by blowing, as in the case of the Khoi *gora*. The player breathes in and out across a quill that is attached to the end of the string, causing it to vibrate. This was once played countrywide but today is played only by the Basotho. The *lesiba*, as it is called, has become the national instrument of Lesotho.

Nguni

AmaZulu

AmaSwazi

AmaXhosa

AmaNdebele

One cannot speak of the Zulu nation without conjuring up the image of the great King Shaka. It was with the rise to power of this much-revered and feared figure that the Zulu nation came into being. Shaka created a powerful royal dynasty that is still in existence today. His lasting impact on the Zulu nation has been imprinted in history and carried forward through generations of Zulu people staking a claim to their proud heritage. The strength of the Zulu nation is reflected in its large numbers, which makes isiZulu the most spoken language in the country. [1]

KwaZulu-Natal, the Zulu heartland, is located on the east coast of South Africa. It was created in 1994 by the merger of Natal, one of the former South African provinces, and KwaZulu, a former 'bantustan' created for the Zulu nation during the apartheid period.

AmaZulu

History of the AmaZulu

Malandela: the 'father' of the AmaZulu

The first Zulu chief recorded in written history is Malandela, who lived in the 16th century. Before the 19th century, however, the Zulu kingdom did not exist as we know it today. It consisted of many disparate clans, and Malandela headed one of these. Malandela ('the one who follows') and his supporters found a fertile piece of land on the Mandawe Hill, on the southern banks of the Umhlatuze River. The chief had two sons, Qwabe and Zulu, who because of their constant bickering were sent off by their father to rule over their own clans and build their own chiefdoms in different areas. Zulu ('Heaven') and his followers, the AmaZulu ('People of Heaven'), settled in the Mkhumbane River basin where Zulu established his own small realm – the first KwaZulu ('Place of Heaven').[2] Zulu arrived in the region with only two other people – his mother and a manservant. These three people were the first members of the mighty Zulu nation of today.[3]

A struggle for supremacy

By the late 18th century, the most powerful group in the region was the Mthethwa, and smaller chiefdoms, such as the Zulu, paid allegiance to the Mthethwa leader, Dingiswayo. Dingiswayo responded to the growing tensions over scarce resources and land by building a powerful army. In order to protect the Mthethwa against the threat of the Ndandwe, a clan whose power base was increasingly threatening, Dingiswayo amalgamated all loosely structured groups into one powerful, organised society, and absorbed all the clans he defeated in battle into the Mthethwa.

In order to build his power base, Dingiswayo formed an allegiance with Senzangakhona ('He who acts with good reason'),[4] a young chief of the relatively small Zulu clan. He secured Zulu territory as a buffer zone against his enemies, the Ndandwe. In exchange, Dingiswayo offered Senzangakhona a freer reign and military expansion. Senzangakhona died in 1817, a year before his allies, the Mthethwa, were defeated and Dingiswayo was killed. The Ndandwe, under their leader Zwide, were close to achieving complete dominance, their only competitors for leadership being a small Zulu state under Senzangakhona's son, Shaka.

Shaka Zulu's rise to power

Nandi was one of Senzangakhona's illegitimate wives, who had fallen pregnant before her official recognition as his wife. Her pregnancy was dismissed as an affliction caused by an intestinal beetle known among the Zulu as a *shaka*. Shaka was regarded as an illegitimate child, and with his mother spent many years of his childhood moving from clan to clan. According to one version of

"When a musical instrument yields sound, it is said to 'khala', using the verb normally meaning 'cry' (as humans or animals). The verb 'shaya', normally meaning 'strike', is used for playing an instrument."[5]

Shaka's history, he was indeed not illegitimate, but owing to his extremely aggressive nature was detested by all. Shaka and his mother eventually found acceptance in the Mthethwa tribe, under Dingiswayo. Shaka served for a number of years in Dingiswayo's army, and distinguished himself as a courageous warrior and an exceptional military strategist. One day when Shaka's father Senzangakhona came to pay homage to Dingiswayo, he found that his son had become a leader in the Mthethwa group. He promised Shaka the chieftainship of the Zulu clan after his death, but later bowed to the pressure of his wives, and after his death Shaka's younger half-brother, Sigujana, became chief of the Zulu clan. When Shaka heard the news he broke into a great rage and killed the new chief in battle. So Shaka became king of the AmaZulu.

The Zulu warrior spirit is manifested in song and dance

Shaka reigned as king from 1816 to 1828. Over a period of 12 years he expanded his army by incorporating smaller neighbouring clans into his growing kingdom. He introduced new military tactics, which enabled him to conquer all enemies. The Ndandwe, Shaka's most powerful enemies, were forced to flee northwards. In 1819, Shaka completely destroyed the Ndandwe kingdom so that he could possess the land they had occupied. He waged a series of wars that lasted many years, resulting in the dislocation and decimation of the population over a wide area. Leaders who posed a threat to Shaka's reign were killed, and the majority had no option but to submit to his conquest. By threat or force he built his people from a small, rather insignificant clan of 1 500 people into a mighty nation of 50 000 warriors. The Zulu wars are known as the *mfecane*, a Xhosa term derived from the word *ukufaca* meaning 'to be weak' or 'emaciated from hunger'.[5] These cataclysmic events have been described as one of the formative events in African history. As one historian explained, "The first great tragedy of South African history was that in the early years of the 19th century the Bantu-speaking communities began to tear each other apart in what was generally assumed to have been one of the bloodiest conflicts ever to have affected Africa in historical times."[6]

Drums

The *ingungu* is a friction drum made by stretching a piece of goat-skin over any hollow object, such as a clay pot, calabash or iron pot. The player kneels on the ground with the *ingungu* in front of her. She first wets her fingers in water, and then, holding a piece of reed vertically on top of the skin, runs either hand alternately along the reed, causing it to vibrate. The drum produces a low-pitched, roaring sound. In the past the *ingungu* was played in a variety of contexts. It was played to mark a young girl's first menstruation, during the *omula* ceremony, at which a young woman is initiated into marriage by her father, and it also accompanied certain dances.[8]

The clash of two cultures

Although Shaka's kingdom was expanding, opposition to his rule within the royal house gradually increased. On 24 September 1828, Shaka was assassinated by his half-brothers Dingane and Mhlangana during the absence of his army. Soon after Shaka's assassination, Dingane in turn killed his brother, Mhlangana, thus ensuring his ascension to the throne. He took over as chief, but lacked the power to keep the Zulu nation together. Lesser chiefs began to split from the kingdom, but Dingane did not have the credibility or power to force them back. In 1837 the first white Voortrekkers or 'Boers', a group of white farmers escaping British rule in the Cape, began arriving in Natal on their Great Trek. The Voortrekkers wanted to create an independent Boer homeland, and

sought land from Dingane. Feeling threatened by their presence, Dingane killed Boer leader Piet Retief and 101 of his followers on 6 February 1838. The Voortrekkers exacted their revenge at the historic battle of Blood River on 16 December 1838, where 3 000 Zulu warriors lost their lives. Dingane's army was finally defeated when, with the assistance of the Boers, his half-brother Mpande attacked him near the border of Swaziland. Dingane tried to flee into Swaziland, but was killed before he got there. Mpande ruled over the Zulu nation until his death in 1872. During his reign he appeared to be no threat to the white settlers of Natal, and although not as powerful a warrior as Shaka, he ruled for thirty years. During this period, the Boers claimed two-thirds of the Zulu Kingdom.

The Anglo-Zulu War

Cetshwayo became the new Zulu king in 1872. He resembled Shaka in his military approach more than any of the leaders preceding him. The British high commissioner in South Africa believed that the self-reliant Zulu kingdom, now further strengthened by Cetshwayo's leadership, posed a threat to the British policy of expansion in and domination of South Africa. In the belief that the Zulu army, only armed with shields and spears, had no chance of surviving British imperial might, the British attacked the Zulu. This led to the outbreak of the Anglo-Zulu War of 1879, an episode which remains one of the most dramatic in both British and southern African history.

War broke out when King Cetshwayo ignored an ultimatum that he disband the Zulu military system. The British invaded the Zulu kingdom in January 1879, and suffered a humiliating defeat at the Battle of Isandlwana. In the same year, the Zulu military headquarters were destroyed at Ulundi and the British used their power to take control of Zulu administration. They dismantled Zulu national unity by dividing the Zulu nation into thirteen chiefdoms, giving equal power to a number of chiefs. This imposed structure created friction among the chiefdoms, which led to civil war. It gave the colonial office an opportunity to intervene in Zulu affairs, thus exerting more control over them. Meanwhile, Cetshwayo had fled north with his son

Dinuzulu, but was captured and imprisoned in Cape Town. Having agreed to maintain peace with the British, Cetshwayo was allowed back into KwaZulu-Natal in 1883. When he arrived, he was dismayed to find that the civil war had worsened. He went into hiding to avoid attack, and died in 1884, possibly poisoned. His son Dinuzulu was declared his successor.

The British annexed KwaZulu-Natal in 1887 when the entire area was brought under the control of the Colony of Natal's Native Law. The following year, Dinuzulu suffered the same fate as his father, Cetshwayo, when he came into dispute with the British and was imprisoned. From this time onwards, Zulu kings held no real power. In 1910, with the formation of the Union, the status of Cetshwayo's son, grandson and great-grandsons was that of a ceremonial king without any real authority. Some of the kings attempted to reinstate the old system of Zulu kingship, but to little effect.

The Zulu monarchy in the 20th century

King Solomon, Dinuzulu's successor, set up the first Inkatha movement in the mid-1920s, but the movement was ineffective. During the late 20th century, however, certain Zulu leaders were instrumental in the process of recovering Zulu power and pride. From 1968 onwards, Chief Buthelezi fought for the rights of the disempowered Zulu. In 1975, he founded a second Inkatha movement, using it as a platform to oppose apartheid policies. With the help of the reigning monarch of the Zulu, King Goodwill Zwelithini, Buthelezi encouraged the revival of the rituals that belong to the Zulu cultural heritage, and created some new rituals to encourage the maintenance of Zulu tradition.

Only in 1994, with the birth of a democratic South Africa, was Zulu unity reborn, and the monarchy of KwaZulu-Natal recognised and reinstated. The reigning monarch, His Majesty King Goodwill Zwelithini, lives in the Nongoma district of central KwaZulu-Natal.

The modern isigubu

The Zulu imitated the British marching band drum, calling it *isigubu*. This was first a wooden drum made from a hollowed tree trunk sculpted into a cylindrical shape, but is now always made out of a section of an oil drum. Cow- or goat-skin is stretched across both sides of the instrument, and the player beats the skin with sticks or pieces of hosepipe.

Doctor playing imbande

Music in performance

The Zulu warrior spirit in song

Song and dance reinforce and reaffirm Zulu history. Every time a war dance is performed, Zulu men are in essence paying tribute to, and recollecting the heroic past of, their ancestors. Men and women use the collective voice of the community to re-enact their past. When Hugh Tracey came into contact with the Zulu on his recording trips through South Africa, he compared the sound of Zulu voices to "the lowing of a great herd of cattle."[17] Others have likened them to "the waves of the sea pounding along the shore."[18] With a strong choral tradition, the Zulu have a unique style of singing that captures the spirit of their nation. Women explore their full vocal range, sometimes shrieking expressively, while men use the rich Zulu vowel sounds to express the raw emotion behind the song (*iculo*).[19]

Zulu song

With little drumming and instrumentation, the Zulu range of vocal expression is broad.[20] Zulu song is not confined to singing in its narrow definition. People use their voices as instruments of expression. Sometimes they sing (*hlabelela*) with rich harmonies and warm, heartfelt tones that poignantly echo through the land. Sometimes they use their voices to capture the strength of their worldviews, the idiosyncrasies of their ritual landscape, and the conviction of their histories. The Zulu are renowned for their battle cries (*izaga*), which were introduced into their culture during Shaka's reign. They were originally used to enthuse and excite warriors, and are now incorporated into Zulu performances in many contexts. Through repetitive chanting, people are energised and empowered. Typically, the battle cry consists of a leader and a chorus, and takes the form of call and response. As a battle cry reaches its climax, the words become more powerful and the volume rises.

Recitation complements and enhances the texts of one type of female

Rattles

The Zulu wear two kinds of ankle-rattles.

Amafohlwane are made out of small boxes woven from palm leaves (*ilala*) and filled with small stones. These are strung onto a cord and fastened around the dancer's ankles.

Imifece are made from cocoons and are tied in bunches onto a plaited fibre.

The *iselwa* and the *khenqekhenqe* are hand-rattles. The latter are shaken by children.

Imifece

puberty song (*ukubhina*), which contains explicit sexual references. These songs often express incredulity and shock, and the heightened, stylised speech captures the emotion that drives the message. Similarly, wedding songs use recitation to convey strong emotive messages to the bride, preparing her for married life:

Leader: *You start out from over there*
   At your parental home, that of the (Mbatha) family
   (or whatever name is appropriate)
   And then you arrive here (at the bridegroom's home)
   You come and play with us (or at our expense)
   But you will find trouble!
   But you will find trouble!

Chorus: *Geqe, geqe!* (ideophone implying 'empty, nothing',
    i.e. 'It is finished for you!')[21]

In this song the new bride is warned that married life has its troubles. The leader introduces the piece with his solo phrases, after which the chorus joins in, repeating the phrase against the leading part, which is repeated over and over again.

Praise poetry

Praise poetry (*izibongo*) is a vital art form among Zulu men, who use it to assert and affirm their masculinity and their lineage.[22] It is generally regarded as a musical form of expression because of its inherent musical characteristics, such as the influence of pitch upon the speech patterns used by praise poets. Further, as one academic explains, "the praises are acclaimed as part of a total performance which includes song."[23] *Izibongo* may be interwoven in a song: a man initiates the singing of chants (*izigiyo*) which are associated with his praises. He leads the singing and at one point in the performance breaks into *ukugiya*, a solo dance movement, while the other men in the group chant his praises.[24] As is evident, *izibongo* contain an interactive element. This poetic mode often has a fast tempo, with a dramatic, energetic, stylised delivery.

Men break into praise poetry at any point in a performance and in many ceremonial contexts, often as a means to secure and consolidate their sense of belonging in a group.[25] They use praise poetry to narrate the stories of their lineage. Individuals are given praise names through which the entire history of their ancestors can be recalled:

> *"In the rendition of Zulu songs, the singer must praise himself, praise both his parents and the local chief, and mention the rivers that identify his area of residence. People meeting a walking musician do not interrupt him by greetings, but rather wait for the musician to introduce himself in the accepted form. The weight of the praises reinforces the belief that a person is not a 'mushroom'. A person does not emerge from the ground; he is the product of society and his presence is appreciated. Being human is measured by one's ability to relate to other people, without losing one's individuality which is expressed in individual praises."[26]*

Praise poetry is a form of oral literature. The role of the praise singer/poet (*imbongi*) is a specialised one, and these individuals are highly respected in Zulu culture. Every headman has his own *imbongi*, and the most accomplished praise singer is appointed to the royal kraal to praise the king.[27] He uses a web of imagery to retell the story of the king's origins and his role in the formation of the nation. He sometimes plays the part of a community jester, adding a theatrical element to his art. He takes part in all the royal dances, disguising himself in an array of costumes.[28] It is interesting to note that the Babylonian and Egyptian kings surrounded themselves with praise poets as far back as 1450 BC.[29]

Zulu dance

Virtually all Zulu communal songs include dance. With few musical instruments to accompany movement, Zulu dance forms the backbone of the

Bones

Amatambo are usually made from the rib-bones of cattle, and are used as a rhythmical accompaniment to singing.

Bull-roarers

The Zulu call their bull-roarers *mampembe*.

A male dancer breaks out of the group to perform a solo

song's rhythm. So impressive and distinctive is this traditional art form that it has captured the imagination of audiences across a wide spectrum of cultures. Today's audiences resemble the original gatherings of the community, spellbound by the dance. They huddle around Zulu dancers, tapping their feet and clapping their hands more vigorously as the excitement mounts and the dancers' energy explodes. The Zulu dance affects people from all walks of life, and renews a sense of pride in those who have common roots with the performers.

The Zulu apply different terms to the two main dance moves that they use. *Ukusina* is applied to dance movements that accompany the majority of Zulu choral songs. These moves are usually performed by the group in unison. The notion of uniformity in Zulu dance embodies the principle of community. Indeed, in certain Zulu dance competitions, absolute precision and symmetry are among the most important markers of a team's ability, and teams are penalised if they do not meet this standard.[30] The value in this principle is emphasised when it is juxtaposed with solo dance. It is not unusual for a man to break out of the group formation to display his individual prowess. In Zulu society, the individual is given the space for self-expression, but always remembers that he is an important link in the chain of the group. The term *ukugiya* is applied to the body movements of a male soloist simulating a warrior attacking his enemy in battle.[31] When a dancer performs this movement, the other men participating in the dance use the opportunity to chant his praises, and hence to affirm his identity. The energy inherent in *ukugiya* is captured in the description below:

> "... *suddenly one of the young braves, fully accoutred with stick, shield and feathers, will jump up, rush into the arena before the crowd, and there perform all the pantomime of actual Native warfare at its hottest. Working himself into a perfect frenzy of murderous fury, he will charge down on the invisible enemy, with tails and feathers flying, dealing death to right and left as he goes, parrying with his shield, stabbing with his assegai, retreating backwards before the overwhelming odds, leaping into the air with the agility of a leopard, the crowd the while roaring out his praises* (izibongo), *till, the*

Boy playing the umtshingo *flute*

45

foe finally demolished, the warrior will come to a sudden standstill, fierce of mien, with feet wide apart, but plumes still flying, as proud as a gladiator after his victory in the Roman arena: the perfect mimic! So inspiring do the on-looking youths find this thrilling display, that one or more of them immediately follow suit, springing out into the showground, emulating and even surpassing the other's feats of bravery and marvellous antics.[32]

The female equivalent of *ukugiya* is *ukugqashula*, which is "a highly virtuosic display of physical prowess."[33] It consists of two movements that are interspersed between vigorous kicking and stamping movements: the first consists of "two hops followed by two quicker jumps landing heavily on both feet;" in the second the woman "leaps into the air, kicking her feet together at one side as she does so."[34] The soloist breaks away from the group as an individual, but always returns to the group formation as a member of the community. The Zulu individual never forgets that on a micro level he belongs to a team, and on a macro level he belongs to a community.

Ndlamu: *the stamping dance*

The Zulu dance that most strongly embodies this principle is the *ndlamu* dance.[35] Traditionally, Zulu people held organised dances that in early times were described by white settlers as military or war dances. The dance they described was in fact the *ndlamu*, which served to unite men into a cohesive group.

All Nguni perform the *ndlamu*, but the Zulu are the leading exponents of this dance form. It evolved over time, and was adapted into different contexts during the 20th century. The Zulu performed the *ndlamu* in the South African Defence Force and in municipal hostels. They held competitions, and the dance teams were judged according to the symmetry and coordination of the dance steps.

The *ndlamu* dance is still performed in many contexts today, and has become strongly associated with Zulu culture. The synchronised stamping of the feet into the ground is its most distinctive feature. Like many other Zulu dances, it is characterised by the way men hold shields in their left hands and sticks or spears in their right hands, to gesture with.

In general the dance takes the same form, regardless of which Nguni group performs it. In the first section of the dance, the dancers enter the dance floor and sing a preparatory song, *isaga*. They usually approach in double file in a crouching position, circle the floor before sitting on the ground, and then sing the *isaga*. The first section is followed by the clan anthem (*ihubo*), which is the main accompanying dance-song. The dance leader steps forward from the ranks of one or two rows of men, depending on the number of dancers present, and signals for the first sequence to begin by stamping into the ground. The dancers sometimes throw themselves onto the ground or point with their sticks to mark the final movement. This gesture is also an expression of the dancer's exhaustion; the *ndlamu* is physically demanding.

In its heyday the dance was at its most impressive when between one thousand and two thousand men performed before the chiefs on special occasions. *Refer to Track 4.*

Amahubo: clan anthems

"The song which made Juluka famous, Impi, *is a well-known ihubo."*[36]

Equally as powerful as the *ndlamu*, but performed for different reasons, are clan anthems (*amahubo*).[37] *Amahubo* are the most sacred of all Zulu songs: they provide a channel between the ancestors and the living. The harmonious relationship between the spirits and the community is the most fundamental aspect of Zulu identity, and the Zulu use *amahubo* to 'to speak' and please their ancestors. Through this communication, song is imbued with religious significance, and is equivalent to prayer at a religious ceremony. The sacred nature of *amahubo* restricts their performances to contexts that are of high national importance, or that contain high ritual value. *Amahubo* also hold strong social significance. Each clan has its own *ihubo*, which serves to strengthen the identity of the clan, unifying it and instilling dignity and pride. These songs embody the most noble of the Zulu traditions, one of which is respect for elders. *Amahubo* are only performed by elders of the clan, in

The *igemfe* was made from two pieces of reed, one thicker than the other. The smaller reed was inserted into the larger reed so that the instrument consisted of a thick upper portion, and a thin lower portion. These whistles were always played in pairs. In a pair of *amagemfe* (plural), one was always larger than the other. The larger whistle was known as the male, and the smaller one as the female.[10]

Playing amagemfe

The ndlamu *dancers dramatically leap off the ground to land with an energetic stamp*

deference to the ancestors. In Zulu culture, men usually attain the status of elders once they are over sixteen. Wives are regarded as elders only once they pass menopause, thus junior wives are excluded from the performance. The song leader must have a high status, and is therefore usually the most senior member of a clan. Old people are respected for their wisdom and their ability to connect with the ancestors. Furthermore, the vocal qualities of an older singer, such as a slight vibrato, compliment the style of *amahubo*.

Amahubo have a very slow tempo, which is equated with dignity. The notion of power through communal as opposed to individual strength is manifested in their musical structure. They have numerous harmonies that intersect, and the chorus part and leading part are inter-dependent. *Amahubo* are still performed in most of their original contexts, but they have also become political tools used to incense and motivate people. They evoke emotional responses from both participants and listeners, and it is not uncommon to see weeping during a performance. Various musicians of today have adapted *amahubo* to include in their repertoires, as these songs transport people back to their Zulu roots, depicting and mirroring some of the nation's most important moments. As one academic asserts, "*amahubo* songs have acted as a major source of reference for those people interested in maintaining tradition or using traditional styles and symbols to resist what was perceived by the oppressed musicians to be dangers of colonising and domination."[38] *Refer to Track 5.*

Ceremonies of the past

Umkhosi: *the first fruits festival*

The original term for the Zulu anthem was *ingoma*, which referred to the royal dance song that was performed at the first fruits festival (*umkhosi*) every year. It was regarded as the most sacred of all Zulu songs, and its performance was reserved for this festival.[39] The first fruits ceremony no longer exists, and the term *ingoma* is now used to classify the broad category of Zulu recreational dance songs.[40]

The first fruits festival was held in honour of the Zulu king, and was celebrated at the beginning of the harvesting season. The entire nation gathered at the royal residence to pay homage to the king and the ancestors. Before Shaka came into power, the focus of this festival was on the ancestors. People used the festival as a forum to appeal to the ancestors for guidance and protection. When Shaka came into power, the focus shifted, with the king becoming the central figure of the celebrations, and the channel through which people could pray to the ancestors.[41] Shaka used the festival to strengthen and fortify his power by insisting that all his regiments were present and playing an active part in the ceremony.

The Zulu warrior ethic instilled in the Zulu nation by Shaka was proudly displayed through song and dance. There was no bigger spectacle than that of thousands of warriors in regimental dress, chanting an emotive war song, dancing for their king and their nation.[42] The most likely reason for

The *imbande*[11] was a flute made from a section of the leg-bone of a bird from which the marrow had been extracted. It was also sometimes made from the shin-bone of a reedbuck or goat. In the past, diviners used this instrument to immunise warriors from danger when going into battle.

The *impempe* was a small river-reed pipe that was stopped at one end. The open end served as an embouchure. Normally only one note could be obtained from the pipe. The instrument was used as a toy for boys, and also to signal for help in a fight.

war dances being performed at the first fruits festival was that wars were frequently waged after this ceremony. Thus the dances of the regiments were the focus of the ceremony.[43] When men danced they threw their entire beings into the performance. They simulated the movements of war, marching and charging, causing the ground to tremble beneath their feet. Each regiment had its own dance, but all men bowed before the king as they passed him. The men formed serpent-like lines that spiralled outwards into a circle. The king eventually joined the ranks to take part in the performance, upon which the women approached the men, chanting while advancing towards them. In some of the oldest accounts of this ceremony, there are passages describing the king's participation. Sometimes he rushed into the centre of the arena and strutted about, gesticulating with his war shield and stick, to the roaring applause of the nation. Warrior dances culminated in the frenzied, chaotic battle cries of men and women, accompanied by the wild gestures of men raising sticks and shields, and their energetic stamping onto the earth.

Other dances performed at the first fruits festival included the *isiqubulo*, a stately dance accompanied by male songs. This dance was named after the *qubulo* quilt that the men wore in this performance. The festival came to its official close when the king ordered special messengers to start playing their end-blown flutes (*imitshingo*) and reed-pipes (*amagemfe*). The playing of these instruments was a signal to the populace that they could start tasting the products of the new harvest. The whole countryside would be filled with joyful piping, which would last until the end of summer, after which the pipes were silent until the next first fruits ceremony.[44]

Nomkubulwane

Another festival that has become obsolete is one that was associated with Nomkubulwane.[45] According to Zulu myth, Nomkubulwane is the princess of heaven. Many centuries ago she was regarded as the goddess of agriculture. Her role is similar to that of the Roman corn goddess, Ceres.[46] She descended from heaven at springtime "robed with light as a garment" to watch over and guide women in their agricultural activities. She also held the power to bring rain or withhold it as she pleased. Some women reported actually seeing her, and these reports induced fear and respect for this mysterious figure. Young maidens and women gathered at an appointed time so that they could enact the rituals necessary to bless and honour Nomkubulwane. They sang to the princess, pleading for a good harvest. This festival did not have a repertoire of songs specific to the rituals performed; young girls and women borrowed the *ukubhina* songs from the girls' puberty ceremonies, and performed them when enacting the rituals.[47]

Modern ceremonies

Umkhosi womhlanga: *royal reed dance*

While some traditional rituals and festivals have fallen away, others have been created within the last century as a means of preserving Zulu heritage. The royal reed dance and Shaka Day were installed as occasions that would consciously recall the Zulu heritage through song and dance. The royal reed dance, otherwise known as *umkhosi womhlanga*, is a two-day ceremony held at the king's residence annually in September.[48] The ceremony serves to unify

Horns

The *upondo*, an ox horn, is blown when the *mpalampala*, an antelope horn, is not available. Traditionally the horn is played to signal an oncoming war and during hunting expeditions. It is also blown by a young man who has successfully courted a girl. He blows the horn to signal to other young men to accompany him to an appointed place to thank the girl. Otherwise it is blown to enliven communal occasions.

Trumpets

The Zulu possess an unusual instrument that is not found anywhere else in South Africa. Made of a length of bamboo that has been hollowed out, the *icilongo* is attached to an ox horn with its tip cut off. The instrument is blown like any other trumpet. It is generally used as a replacement for the *mpalampala* horn in boys' courting rituals, and is also used for wedding ceremonies.[12]

the nation with the king, instilling a sense of pride in all present. Girls from the entire KwaZulu-Natal region travel across the country to participate in the reed ceremony. In the stately procession led by the chief princess, the young maidens sing as they approach the palace. When they arrive they pay tribute to the king by presenting him with reeds and participating in the reed dance. The reeds are collected, and are used to repair the king's enclosures.

Shaka Day: Zulu Heritage Day

Shaka Day is primarily a celebration of Zulu nationalism. It came into being during the 1950s when the government encouraged ethnic nationalism. The performances seen on this day are generally demonstrations of power. Most of the songs are war songs associated with great leaders like Shaka who have left their imprint on Zulu history. Praise poetry is also performed during the official part of the ceremony. After King Zwelethini and Chief Buthelezi have delivered their speeches, they join the crowd to sing *amahubo* songs to acknowledge their ancestors. The texts of these songs usually refer to important historical events that have impacted on Zulu culture. The king uses such celebrations to interact with his people on an equal level. He is obliged to take part in the performances as a symbol of his connection to his people and his ancestors.

Rite of passage rituals

Thomba and ukwemula: female initiation

During female initiation, two main categories of song are performed, to correspond with the two main initiation ceremonies.[49] *Ukubhina* puberty songs are sung during a girl's private puberty ceremony (*thomba*). This ceremony takes place when the girl menstruates for the first time. Her friends and age-mates join her in seclusion in her mother's hut where she remains for one to two weeks. They sing the *ukubhina* songs, which fulfil the role of sex education. The songs are delivered through recitation as opposed to pure melodic song. This style of expression complements the texts that, according to many researchers, contain obscene sexual references. According to some

Zulu informants, the reason for the use of such language is that "firstly, the songs serve as a form of sex education, in preparing the girl for what is expected of her in marriage; and secondly, that by presenting a fearsome picture of the act of sex, the songs serve to deter the girl from indulging in pre-marital sex."[50] These songs are performed without dancing, but performers use clapping, cupping their hands to produce a hollow sound (*ukunqukuza*). In the past the songs were accompanied by the *ingungu* friction drum, but this has been replaced by the *isigubu* drum. Various writers have pointed out the symbolic significance of the use of the *ingungu* drum. It is connected with fertility rites by virtue of the sexual connotations attached to the playing technique. One writer has referred to the technique as "representing the milking of the penis during sex intercourse" because the girl slides her hands down the stick.[51] Furthermore, "the pot-drum (the trunk of an *umsenge* tree which is associated with rain and fertility was used in the old days) represents the vagina or even the womb."[52]

The second ceremony, the *ukwemula,* is used as a forum to publicly announce a girl's marriageable status a few months after the onset of puberty. The *ingcekeza* [53] is the main dance-song performed at the public celebration (*icece/umdlalo*) of the ceremony. Like *ukubhina* songs, *ingcekeza* are accompanied by a distinct style of hand-clapping and the *isigubu* drum. During the dance, the girl for whom the ceremony is being held leaves the line of female dancers and moves towards the male spectators sitting on the opposite side. She carries a spear and plants it in front of one of the men, after which she returns to the dancing line of girls. The chosen man is required to return the spear to the girl and to pin money into her hair. As he does this, he *giyas* and the other men respond by shouting praises for him. Once this is completed, the girl leaves the line once again to choose another man, and the whole process is repeated about three times. In this way, the spectators pay to watch the girls dancing and singing.

The texts of *ingcekeza* songs reflect the issues that arise with the onset of female adolescence, such as the transition that needs to be made from childhood to adulthood. One of their central themes is the father, for whom the girl holds extreme fear and respect. She reproaches him for forcing her to

Bows

The **ugubhu** is an unbraced gourd-bow with a resonator that is attached near the lower end of the instrument. While the string was traditionally made from the twisted hairs of a cow's tail and the resonator from a calabash, the string is now made from wire and the resonator sometimes from tin. The preferred calabashes are now scarce as modern dishes have taken their place in the kitchen. The instrument is held with one hand and the string is struck with a thin stick or reed in the other hand. The player can stop the string with the finger, or leave it open, producing two different fundamental notes. Men usually make the instrument, but it is played by women. The musician strikes the string with the reed while singing. At the same time, she moves the small opening of the calabash towards and away from her chest to selectively resonate the harmonics present in the sound of the string.[13]

54

leave home by getting married, and expresses her sorrow in so doing.

Ingoma dance-songs are also performed to mark the end of the female initiation ceremony. Their texts generally cover topical issues. The girls dance in a circle with one person in the middle. This dance concludes the *ukwemula* ceremony.

Thomba: *male initiation*

Pre-Shaka, boys were circumcised, but when Shaka came to power in 1816 he discontinued circumcision because it immobilised too many warriors.[54] Throughout initiation boys practise the repertoire of songs that belong to this ritual.[55] According to one source, the texts of the boys' puberty songs mainly consist of meaningless words such as *"Uye uja ho, uye uje ho eya he he."*[56] The initiate goes into seclusion to receive intensive training from older tribe members. At the end of this period, a feast is held to accommodate the ritual of escorting the boy out of his hut and the *izilo/umgonqo* dance is performed. Just before the dance begins the boy's father starts to *giya*, singing his own praises to express his pride in his son's new status in society. The boy slowly approaches the front of the group, leading them in the dance. This is the climax of the ceremony, and it is at this point that the females join the group, "shrilling or trilling in high-pitched tones to show their joy."[57]

Weddings

Of all the milestones in an individual's life, the wedding is regarded as the most significant rite of passage among the Zulu.[58] In Zulu culture, a marriage is a contract not only between two individuals but between families and clans. A wedding is thus an open invitation to the entire community to witness and to celebrate. Lasting for three days, the extended ceremony centres on song and dance. The structure of the wedding is dictated by the musical activities, and the music serves to connect each stage of the event. Music is the central core of the wedding as it is the medium through which the bride weds her groom.

Zulu weddings vary, and they have also changed over time, which means that there are variations in the musical performances at each wedding.

It is believed that the **umakhweyana** was borrowed from the Tsonga. It looks similar to the *ugubhu* bow, except that the metal string is divided by being held back near the middle, and the calabash is attached at the same point. The instrument is grasped at the calabash, with the fingers extended to allow the player to finger either segment of the string to a higher note. The other hand strikes the string with a thin stick or reed. The *umakhweyana* may be played by both sexes[14], but is particularly associated with young unmarried women who sing love songs with it. *Refer to Track 2.*

A number of songs and dances have, however, been performed over many generations, and are still performed today. The preparation for the festivities begins days in advance when the bride's family and friends arrive, practising their repertoire of wedding songs and dances. While some dance-songs are improvised during the wedding, others are carefully planned and rehearsed. Individuals who are regarded as professional composers (*izingqambi*) are commissioned to compose music for formal occasions such as weddings. They work with professionals who coordinate the words of the song with the dance moves (*indabuli*) to create a holistic performance piece.

The celebrations at all Zulu weddings follow a similar routine. The bride and her party leave for the groom's homestead the day before the wedding. As they approach, they sing a solemn chant (*ukulilizela*) which, it has been observed, might have been borrowed from the descendants of the ancient Egyptians about ten thousand years ago.[59] On arrival, the bride's party offers payment in the form of cattle so that they are accepted into the groom's home, and they sing a lively song that requests a special hut for their party. In one such song the singers are very direct in their request:

Si-Godola, ye! ye! mKwenyana; ku-maKaza, ye! ye!
mKwenyana; ye! ye! Mka-Dade; u-Qalis' ukuGanwa, we: siTsholo
(We-are-shivering-with-cold. Hi! You-bridegroom;
it-is-cold, hi! You-bridegroom; hi! You-husband-of-our-sister;
you-rejected-of-the-girls) (obviously getting married for the first time).[60]

Once their request has been answered and they are seated in the hut, they start singing a 'hand-clapping' song (*ukuNqukuza*) which holds another request – for beer. Both parties use song to indicate that the wedding has officially begun. The bride's party (*umthimba*) starts to perform the *ukugqumushela*, a special dance reserved for weddings; and the groom's party (*ikhetho*) responds with their own dance. During the course of the afternoon the groom's and bride's parties use dance competitions as a form of playful rivalry, and take this competitive spirit to the extreme by shouting insults at each other. The bantering remains friendly throughout, however, and rather than creating hostility generates a spirited atmosphere of goodwill. The performances grow progressively louder and more energetic. When the *ingungu* drum still existed, participants played the instrument during this part of the ceremony, and in combination with the enthusiastic hand-clapping, ululating, singing and dancing, created a cacophony of joy and elation.

The wedding ceremony formally opens the next day when the young girls of the bride's party walk in single file singing the *inkondlo*, an ancient dance-song which is regarded as one of the core wedding performances for a bride.[61] While the song is characterised by the use of vibrato, its accompanying dance is "slow and stately", and is characterised by 'the gesture of pointing (*ukukhomba*), in which the bride points ahead of her with a short stabbing spear (*isigindi*)."[62] The father of the bride initiates the singing of praises, directing them at his child, and praying for her wellbeing. He ends his praises when he *giyas*, dancing as if attacking an enemy in battle. The bride's male relatives follow suit, dancing *imigiyo* to affirm their masculinity and their virility, while the surrounding men sing their praises, often using praise poetry to comment on their characters. Once the praises are completed, the bridal party dances the *umphendu*, a wedding march. This dance provides light relief; it has been described as:

> "… a rather pretty and captivating performance, in which the dancers, two abreast, arranged themselves into two columns (sometimes only one), which moved dancing about the field to the tune of a spirited song, intercircling the one with the other, or sometimes approaching each other head-on as though about to clash, when the excitement and amusement would become quite thrilling; but only, at the last moment, turning each gracefully about and retracing its steps, or peacefully passing the other by, each continuing in opposite directions."[63]

Other wedding performances include the *umgqigqo*, *isigekle*, *isiqubulo* and *ingoma*. The *umgqigqo* and *isigekle* are lively dances which are characterised by hand-clapping and stamping. The *isiqubulo* is more sedate and stately than the *umgqigqo* and *isigekle*. When men perform the *ingoma* dance at wedding

The **ubhel'indhela** is played only by males. It consists of a hollow bar of bamboo fitted with a wire string and a tuning peg. A paraffin tin is attached and is used as a resonator. The instrument rests on the left shoulder of the player, and the thumb and first finger of the left hand pinch the string alternately to obtain the fundamental notes. The player holds a small hair-bow in his right hand, and bows the string with varying pressure for high or low notes.

ceremonies, they dance in lines of eight or ten, and individual dancers take turns to demonstrate their dancing skills by dancing at the front of the group while the women ululate. This dance is characterised by high-kicking, stamping steps that are performed in unison. Apart from the *inkondlo*, most of the song texts are of a light-hearted nature, referring to aspects of the marriage rituals such as the payment of *lobola*. The *inkondlo* song texts are expressions of the bride's sorrow and fear about leaving home. Along similar lines, the *isimekezo* are 'bridal laments' performed on the final day of the wedding. In this song, the bride expresses her sense of abandonment by her father and family:

Ngona ngani?	What have I done wrong?
Abasangithandi	They no longer love me
Ngona ngani kwabendlu yakwethu	What have I done wrong to those of my home?
Lokhu ubaba kamfokazane	Here is the father of a poor creature
Heya Heya	Alas, alas
Aniboyilondoloza	Have pity on her
Heya heya	Alas, alas[64]

A wedding cannot take place without the rendition of both clans' anthems (*amahubo*), which are sung at different stages.[65] *Amahubo* are performed during the ceremony to reinforce the sacredness of this social institution. By singing *amahubo*, the ancestors are invited to become part of the ceremony. When the bridal party perform their *ihubo*, the bride's father appeals to the ancestors to guide his daughter. In this case the *ihubo* is not accompanied by dance, but shields are raised as a symbol of peace.

One of the most moving moments in a wedding ceremony occurs when the bride's party sing the lullaby (*isihlabelelo*) that was sung to the bride during her childhood. In Zulu culture, every mother composes a personal lullaby for her baby. In her adolescent years, a girl hears her lullaby only on two occasions: when she menstruates for the first time and when she gets married. Her mother sings her childhood lullaby for the last time on the day of her wedding, as a symbol that her daughter is leaving behind her childhood and the life that she lived with her mother and family. Towards the end of the afternoon the groom dances for his bride, and she in return leads her team in another dance. It is a prerequisite for the bride to dance in public if her marriage is going to be formally recognised and accepted by the community. When the bride performs for her community, her suitability as a wife is judged according to her musical abilities, and her character is assessed during her performance. The bride initially sings with her party, but eventually joins the groom's group of performers to indicate that she has now switched families. Finally, on the last day of the wedding, the two parties come together to dance.

As is evident, music and weddings are inseparable. Music rather than speech is used to convey and affirm the most fundamental values behind the institution of marriage in Zulu culture. *Refer to Track 6.*

Elokubalisa: bow songs

In Zulu communities almost all individuals compose their own music while engaging in daily activities. Solo music-making is a reflective activity: individuals can roam their internal worlds freely, creating personal music. Women use the musical bow and voice to express their deepest thoughts and emotions. Bow songs stand outside community performance. The term *elokubalisa* means 'a song of brooding', which effectively captures the mood of the majority of bow songs.[66] Songs of the *umakhweyana* and *ugubhu* bows are usually played by young women, and these are most often love songs.[67] When describing the feelings expressed in her bow song, a woman might say "*Ngikhumbula insizwa/isoka*" ("I am yearning for the one I love").[68] Women also sing these songs to ponder their misfortunes.

The use of poetic language features strongly in the texts of bow songs. They are especially rich in metaphor:

Ngivutha nezikhotha   I burn with the long grass
Uthando lwangiphonsa eziweni   Love has hurled me onto the cliffs[69]

The *isitontolo*, an instrument played by men, has been adopted from the Sotho. It is made from a piece of wood that tapers on either end, so that there is a thicker piece in the centre of the bow. The string, made from twisted sinew or wire, is tied back at the centre, and is plucked on either side, with different techniques, producing four notes. The player holds the bow horizontally with the left hand in line with his face, and with one end of the thick centre portion of the stave against his mouth. He fingers the string with the left index finger, and plucks the string with the forefinger and thumb of the right hand.

Women sometimes intersperse lines of praise poetry into their songs. When other people are present while someone is performing a bow song, they might start to sing the performer's praises at any point in the performance. In terms of vocal delivery, unmarried women usually produce a higher-pitched vocal quality than married women, whose tone is much more resonant.[70]

In the past, the *umakhweyana* bow was played by unmarried girls (*izintombi*).[71] This was related to the sacred state of virginity that is expected of young Zulu maidens.[72] In Zulu culture, virginity (*ubuntombi*) is regarded as a gift from mother nature. So sacred is this gift that if a girl gives her virginity away, something in her dies. The *umakhweyana* carried the symbolism of virginity: only those who had not lost it could play the instrument. When a woman got married she put the instrument aside as a symbolic gesture of her loss. To play the bow was to celebrate the victory of feminine virtues in the battle to retain one's virginity. It was seen as a sacred and respectable exercise that perpetuated and consolidated traditional Zulu values.

In the past it was taken for granted that every Zulu woman was capable of playing musical bows. Today many of the instruments that were once considered to be vital to the existence of Zulu music have fallen into disuse and Zulu bows are only played by a few people who still uphold Zulu traditions.

Emergent music

Maskanda: *guitar music*

Despite the fact that many Zulu musical traditions no longer exist, Zulu people have continued creating music that is distinctly their own. They have borrowed from some of their most unique traditional music and appropriated it for modern contexts. The styles that have developed as a result of this innovation have put Zulu culture on the global stage. One of the most well-known Zulu neo-traditional musical styles is *maskanda* guitar music, a genre that is exclusive to men.[74] Although it might not be regarded as strictly traditional, it nevertheless draws heavily on traditional Zulu music, and has become one of the most easily recognisable Zulu musical forms. This style borrows from Western forms of music, but also refers back to Zulu traditions and strengthens the Zulu identity. *Maskanda* has its roots in various traditional Zulu instruments such as the *umakhweyana* and *ugubhu* bows, and the *isitolotolo* Jew's harp. These instruments were replaced by the guitar, violin and concertina, although nowadays the guitar is the only instrument used in *maskanda* music. The guitar was introduced to Zulu culture by Portuguese explorers as far back as the 1880s. An academic explains that one of the main reasons why the guitar is the most widely used instrument among *maskanda* musicians is because "it is on this instrument that indigenous Zulu musical principles can be most effectively realised."[75] *Maskanda* musicians have a different tuning system from that of the Western tuning system, which enables them to translate indigenous musical principles onto this instrument. The playing technique that is most commonly used by *maskanda* guitarists is *ukupika* or the 'picking style', which was popularised by Phuzushukela (John Bhengu).

Almost all *maskanda* musicians are males in their twenties and thirties, and they are usually also dancers. Apart from playing their own compositions, musicians often play traditional dance-songs. Thus, many *maskanda* styles are named after the dance-songs to which they refer. *Maskanda* musician-dancers draw heavily on the traditional Zulu *ndlamu* and *ngoma* dance styles, which are a source of inspiration for them. Other popular dance styles incorporated into *maskanda* performances include *isizulu* and *umzansi*.[76] It is interesting to note that certain parallels have been observed between the dance songs and the music of the *ugubhu* and *umakhweyana* bows. As has been asserted, "most of the structural features of gourd-bow music are clearly transferred to some of the guitar styles."[77]

Maskanda songs have a particular structure, which generally begins with an introductory section called the *izihlabo* or *intela*. In the introduction the musician establishes his personal style. This is an instrumental section, and is generally fairly fast. After the introduction the guitarist plays an instrumental

The **umqangala** is a hollow river reed with a string of ox sinew, or nowadays wire. The bow is mouth-resonated and plucked with the fingers. One end rests against the player's lips, and the right index finger plucks the string while the left hand fingers the string at the other end.[15]
Refer to Track 3.

in which two clearly disparate melody lines are established. The dynamic between two different parts represented by one instrument is typical of African instrumental music. In this instance one guitar is capable of producing both a solo and a chorus line. The musician starts singing in such a way that his vocal part reflects the instrumental part. When the song reaches its climax the musician starts reciting praises (*izibongo*). He lauds himself by identifying for the listeners who he is, where he comes from, and other important aspects of his identity. The musician often improvises, creating praises that are humorous and satirical. When the praises are completed the performer continues singing, sometimes alternating between vocals, guitar, and praise poetry. There is no fixed ending to the song: the musician stops playing when he feels the song has reached its natural end.

Maskanda songs are used as expressions of various aspects of Zulu identity and culture. Many *maskanda* texts reinforce Zulu tradition, emphasising the importance of Zulu customs and the Zulu hierarchical structure in society. *Maskanda* music has been adapted for full-band performances that include the bass guitar, guitar and drums. It is continually absorbing Western styles, but it will probably always source its inspiration from traditional Zulu music.[78]

Isicathamiya: *male acapella music*

Isicathamiya is another Zulu style that evolved in the last century and has become equally as popular today as *maskanda* music.[79] It reached Europeans initially through one representative group, the popular South African all-male ensemble, Ladysmith Black Mambazo. *Isicathamiya* is a style of male acapella music that emerged from the Natal Province in the 1920s and 1930s. It was performed in competitions held by migrant labourers who were living in all-male hostels. They performed *isicathamiya* to strengthen their sense of identity and congregate as a group during the long lonely hours in the cities. Although this style only emerged in the 20th century, some academics argue that its origins can be traced back to the end of the 19th century. They claim that *isicathamiya's* roots lie in the American minstrels and ragtime US vaudeville troupes that toured South Africa extensively from 1860.[80] It was possible that they inspired the formation of numerous Black South African groups who imitated the musical styles they were exposed to. *Isicathamiya* would have emerged from a combination of the minstrel-inspired songs and traditional Zulu music. One of the biggest influences on this genre was a song composed by Solomon Linda in 1939, the world-hit *Mbube*, which is characterised by its male acapella harmonies. Linda's song was so effective in evoking the African spirit that it roused the world's imagination and was adapted by companies like Walt Disney. Up until 2004, when issues of royalty payments to Linda arose, very few people realised that *Mbube* is in fact the original version of the western adaptation, *Wimoweh* or *The Lion Sleeps Tonight*.

The word *isicathamiya* is derived from the verb *cathama*, meaning 'to crawl like a cat'[81] or 'to walk on one's toes lightly'.[82] Labourers rehearsed late into the night in the hostels, and were forced to dance without making a noise, thus using light footsteps so that they would not wake the guards. In consequence, these dances were different from the traditional Zulu dances that were characterised by loud stamping of the feet.

An *isicathamiya* group comprises anything from eight to twenty performers. There is always a leading tenor who is supported by a falsetto soprano and an alto, while the rest of the group sings bass. The *isicathamiya* repertoire includes political, love, and other topical songs, all of which have an underlying Christian slant. The content of the songs makes frequent references to biblical texts, and the ritualistic pre-performance prayers are reminiscent of religious ceremonies. Before performances begin it is not unusual to see the choir members huddled in a circle, praying for spiritual guidance. The circle formation recalls the cattle enclosure (*isibhaya*) of a Zulu village, a sacred, powerful male space where men can feel the presence of their ancestors and pray to them. This reference might be a subconscious one, but it is evident that traditions are woven into new styles to create symbolic value in modern performance contexts. The references are often subtle, and it is particularly difficult to detect them in groups that sing renditions of modern European and American songs. *Isicathamiya*, like all other musical styles, is continually under the influence of new musical developments, and therefore metamorphoses with time.

The **umhubhe** consists either of a curved piece of wood or a hollow river reed, with a thin rod inserted in the tube. The string is made from wire or fibre. The instrument is bowed by scraping a dry reed or stick across the string, and the mouth is used as a resonator. The melody is produced by varying the size and shape of the mouth, thus selecting one of the harmonics present in the two fundamentals. The player can obtain these by playing the string open or stopping it with the thumb.

Stringed-wind

The Zulu use the name **ugwala** for their version of the Khoi **gora**[16] (see Chapter 10, page 237).

Princess Constance Magogo kaDinuzulu (1900 – 1984)

Born into the royal clan in 1900, Princess Constance Magogo kaDinuzulu was the daughter of Zulu king Dinuzulu kaCetshwayo and the mother of Gatsha Buthelezi. With a vast knowledge of Zulu culture and exceptional musical skills, she provided a link to Zulu cultural heritage. For many years she held the reputation of being the greatest authority on Zulu music, and many academics, both from within South Africa and abroad, approached her to gain insight into Zulu culture. Through her recordings and compositions, she upheld Zulu tradition and encouraged others to do so. She was first recorded by Dr Hugh Tracey in 1939. She was well known for her skill on the *ugubhu* and *umakhweyana* bows, as well as the European autoharp. The princess distinguished herself with her wide vocal range, which covered approximately three octaves, and her ability to evoke different moods with her voice.[73]

'Bombing'

'Bombing' is a musical style that is seen as a predecessor of *isicathamiya*.[83] Removed from a rural setting and adapting to different lifestyles, Zulu men developed a new style of singing to distinguish themselves from those who were still enacting Zulu traditions in rural areas. Against the backdrop of World War 2, the performers themselves came up with the term 'bombing' to identify this style, because they felt it was an apt description of the sound they produced. Bombing choirs consisted of small groups of men who created a choral yell through the vigour and power of their vocal delivery. Like *isicathamiya* groups, bombing choirs also gave themselves elaborate names. By the adoption of names such as 'The Morning Tigers', 'Evening Birds' and 'Super Dynamos', bombing performances took on mythical proportions. Competitions took place in city halls, and a white person was appointed to choose the winner. The logic behind having a white adjudicator was that he was more likely to be an impartial judge than a local.

Gumboot dancing

The Zulu gumboot dance, otherwise known as the *izicathulo* or 'boots', was developed at schools run by the missionaries as a substitute for some of the banned traditional Zulu dances.[84] Before the missionaries arrived, Zulu performers danced barefoot, but pupils started wearing shoes at mission schools. The sound produced by the shoes hitting the ground and the heels clicking became the core characteristic of the gumboot dance that was refined in later years. Wellington boots were introduced at the docks in Durban to protect the Bhaca workers' feet. It was a coincidence that the rubber boots created a good percussive sound, so the dockworkers incorporated the boots into the new *izicathulo* dance, slapping them with their hands and clapping their feet together in intricate and inventive rhythmic patterns. Scores of Zulu teams have been formed to participate in competitions. The performers most often wear trousers and coloured vests to accentuate the syncopated leg and arm movements, and the dance is sometimes accompanied by a guitar. Gumboot dancing has become a hallmark of Zulu and Baca culture, and is one of the most popular dance styles presented to tourists in South Africa.[85]

King Mswati II, the namesake of the AmaSwazi, organised the army into centralised regiments, consolidating the strength of the Swazi kingdom.

The AmaSwazi live in Gauteng, Mpumalanga, Limpopo and North West Province, and in Swaziland, one of South Africa's neighbouring countries. Swaziland is a small, landlocked kingdom nestled between South Africa in the west and Mozambique in the east. The kingdom, one of the last remaining monarchies in the world, was established by Sobhuza I of the Dlamini lineage in the early 19th century.

AmaSwazi

History of the AmaSwazi

In the late 15th century, Dlamini, founder of the royal clan of the Swazi, led the Ngwane, an Nguni clan, in its migration south from central east Africa.[1] They settled in the territory now known as Maputo in Mozambique, and lived there for two hundred years. In the late 18th century, possibly following a series of conflicts with people living in the same area, the Swazi left their home, under the leadership of King Ngwane II. He led his people along the banks of the Pongola, finally settling in Lobamba in south-eastern Swaziland. This area is regarded as the true birthplace of the Swazi and is known as Eshiselweni ('the place of burning'), a reference to the conquests of the Swazi. Ngwane's kingship is still commemorated today in Swazi rituals, and Swazi people often refer to themselves as *Bantu Baka Ngwane* ('People of Ngwane').[2]

The Swazi were forced to move further north when Sobhuza I, Ngwane II's grandson, came into conflict over land with Zidze, chief of the powerful Ndwandwe clan. Rather than clashing with an army stronger than his, Sobhuza fled with his followers. They eventually entered northern Swaziland and established the royal village at the foot of the Mdzimba mountains. Those who accompanied him are acknowledged as the 'pure Swazi' or the *Bomdzabu* ('Those who originated at Eshiselweni').[3] When they entered the mountainous territory of northern Swaziland, they came across various loosely organised Sotho and Nguni clans already there. Sobhuza demanded that they recognise his superiority and pay allegiance to him. Most people humbly submitted, and those who did not were defeated and forced to recognise Swazi authority. In the years of Sobhuza's rule, the Swazi state was slowly strengthened despite various external threats. Sobhuza prevented the destruction of his kingdom through a strategy of submissiveness to the great Zulu King, Shaka Zulu. He established ties with the Zulu nation by offering two of his daughters to Shaka Zulu as wives, and by later marrying a Zulu woman. By the time he died in the late 1830s, the foundation of the Swazi kingdom was in place.

The Swazi derive their name from Mswati II, the "greatest of the Swazi fighting kings"[4], who succeeded Sobhuza I and ruled the kingdom from 1840. Mswati emulated the Zulu warrior nation during his reign, reorganising his army into centralised 'age' regiments, and expanding his territory through combat. This centralising principle was enhanced through the creation of royal villages that served as

Two men play the intambula *drum by holding the skin in place*

Drums

The *intambula* may have derived its name from the Portuguese *tambor*. It is made from a clay beer pot (*ludziyo*) with a goat-skin stretched across the mouth. However, the goat-skin is not attached, like other drum-skins. The clay pot is placed in front of the drummer and someone else holds the goat-skin tightly over the opening of the pot. The skin is beaten with a reed stick held in the right hand. It is also possible for a single player to play this instrument. When an individual plays the *intambula* alone, he uses his legs to keep the skin in position over the pot on the ground. He holds the drum with his left hand, and beats it with a stick in his right hand. This instrument was formerly used during the initiation of a diviner and during one of the wedding dances. Nowadays it is played during exorcism rituals.[6]

Rattles

Emafahlawane are ankle-rattles made from different materials.[7] They are most commonly made from moth cocoons tied onto a pad made of fibre.

The Swazi adopted their hand-rattle, the *ligoshu*, from the Tsonga. It consists of an oval calabash filled with small stones and attached to a handle. Nowadays, the Swazi use a tin instead of the traditional calabash as a resonator. They use this rattle during exorcism rituals.

military outposts across the country. As his reputation spread, many survivors of rival kingdoms sought protection under his rule and flocked to his kingdom. Mswati allowed smaller clans to retain their chiefs under the umbrella of his rule, thus creating allies out of potential enemies. Even though he was tolerant of cultural diversity and did not impose Swazi customs and rituals on others, many of his followers started imitating the culture of the Dlamini royalty. In time, a degree of uniformity was established through intermarriage and citizenship of Swaziland.

From the 1840s onwards, white settlers increasingly passed through Swaziland, and Mswati ceded some land to them. His successor, Mbandzeni, continued granting land concessions to white settlers, and gradually Swazi power and authority started diminishing. At the turn of the century, with the defeat of the Boers in the Anglo-Boer War,

Man playing the luveve

Swaziland became a British protectorate. In 1899, during the Anglo-Boer War, Sobhuza II was born. After the death of his father Bhunu (when the crown prince was still a baby), his grandmother, Labotsibeni, assumed the regency until the king came of age. When Sobhuzo II eventually ascended the throne in 1921 and became *Ngwenyama* ('The Lion') of the Swazi nation, he sought to free Swaziland from British rule. King Sobhuza II and his council formed the Imbokodvo National Movement (INM), a political group that fought to reclaim the traditional Swazi way of life. In September 1968, Swaziland finally gained independence under King Sobhuzo II's rule.

Whistles, flutes and reeds

Luveve were whistles made from the horns of small antelopes, or from wood cut into the shape of a horn. The Swazi used these instruments for calling their dogs and as signal whistles in war and hunting. They were also played by doctors when calling the ancestors for assistance. Due to the spiritual significance attached to these whistles, laymen were not allowed to blow their *luveve* in their kraals, except to announce a hunt.

The ***umtshingozi*** end-blown harmonic flute was made from a tube of reed or the bark of a cabbage tree. A diagonal embouchure was cut at the thicker end. The size of the instrument varied: if it was large the Swazi called it the *umtshingozi* 'with the big voice'. Before the player performed, he would run water through the instrument to make it airtight. He placed the embouchure between his lips, resting the flute against his teeth on the right-hand side of his mouth. With a hollowed tongue, he blew air across the opening. He held the lower end with the right hand, and fingered the opening with the right fore- or second finger. The flute produced two harmonic ranges: one from the open tube and one from the closed tube. The player selected the pitch with the strength of his blowing. This instrument was played mainly by herdboys.[8] *Refer to Track 7.*

Boy playing the umtshingozi

Music in performance

Musical sensibility

The Swazi derive great pleasure from music that inspires and exults. Dancers aspire to perform movements that are graceful, and singers strive to produce intricate harmonies with a beauty that moves listeners and rouses participants. Those who can create this effect are admired, while those who are clumsy, awkward or inhibited are mocked. As is evident in the incident narrated in the following anecdote, people of the older generation are intolerant of those who do not understand Swazi musical aesthetics:

> "*In 1935 Sobhuza sent his four eldest daughters together with two other royal maidens to his kraal at Entonjeni in the Peak to have some lessons in the* incwala *(first fruits festival) tunes from two very ancient princesses, daughters of the King Mswati. He explained (to me) that the queens of Lobamba had not grown up in the royal atmosphere, but had come there on marriage, and the* incwala *was relatively new to them. I accompanied the young princesses; we found the old women most exacting teachers, contemptuous of the singing and general lack of knowledge of the younger generation, and the old lady was so disgusted at a rehearsal with the warriors that she walked away and vowed she would not listen to them again.*"[16]

The Swazi have a distinctive musical sensibility and style, despite the various influences they have absorbed from other cultures.[17] Their vocal harmonies are easy to distinguish and they have a unique vocal quality. When men perform their ancient songs, they employ "a slow, tremulous 'diaphragm vibrato.'"[18] In many respects, Swazi music is similar to that of its Nguni neighbours – the Zulu, and many songs have in fact been adopted from them. This can be attributed to the cultural exchange that occurred between the two cultures over many years. The Swazi have also picked up influences from the Tsonga, adapting their *mancomane* exorcism music. The *isibhaca* dance, one of the most popular performances in Swaziland today, is in fact a dance of the Bhaca people (one of the Xhosa-speaking peoples of the Eastern Cape), and was adopted by the Swazi on the South African mines. The greatest influence on Swazi music, however, is the structure of society in the Kingdom of Swaziland.

Swazi monarchy and music

The traditional system of dual monarchy in Swaziland is reflected in their two main royal ceremonies: the reed dance and the first fruits ceremony. One pays tribute to the queen mother – *Indlovukazi* ('She-elephant') – and the other to her son, the king – *Ingwenyama* ('The Lion'). The wellbeing of the nation centres around these two figures, who play an active role in national life. As a sign of respect and deference, the people refer to the king as 'The Lion', 'The Sun' and 'The Milky Way'; and to the queen mother as 'The Lady Elephant', 'The Earth' and 'The Mother of the Country'.[19] The reed dance and the first fruits ceremony are symbolic of the greatness conferred upon the royal 'lion' and 'elephant'. The songs *(tsingoma)* and dances of both ceremonies, which are central to the attached rituals, thus also function as symbols of royal power and sovereignty.

Incwala: the first fruits ceremony

> *"The warriors dance and sing at the* incwala *and so they do not fight, although they are many and from all parts of the country and are jealous and proud. When they dance they feel they are one and they can praise each other."*[20] – KING SOBHUZA

The great annual *incwala* ceremony is regarded as "the most essential event of the year"[21] among the Swazi.[22] With the king as the central figure or 'owner'[23] of the *incwala*, this ceremony celebrates and reinforces his role in the Swazi nation. As a first fruits ceremony, one of its core functions is to spiritually cleanse the king and his nation before they eat the newly harvested crops. It takes place over a three-week period during December and January. These three weeks are seen as a 'sacred period'[24] which is clearly set apart from everyday

The *livenge*, named after the plant from which it was made, consisted of a hollow stalk. Herdboys played this instrument in the same manner as the *umtshingozi*.

Horns

The Swazi's *mpalampala* is always blown by men. It is made from antelope or kudu horn and is used as a royal instrument for important ceremonies and big hunts.[9]

Bows

The *sikhelekehle* consists of an oil-tin resonator to which a stick strung with wire is attached. Players bow the string with a small cow-hair bow made from a curved twig, and create the melody by fingering the two fundamentals and varying the bow pressure to select higher or lower harmonics.

The *isitontolo* was borrowed from the Sotho. It is a braced, mouth-resonated bow made out of bamboo and a cow- or horse-hair or wire string that is tied back at the centre, dividing the string into two. With one end between the player's lips, the instrument is held in a horizontal position with the left hand and is plucked with the fingers of the right hand on either segment of the string.[10]

71

activities. Astrologers decide when the moon is in the right phase and determine the exact date of the ceremony. The ceremony is divided into two phases: the small *incwala*, which lasts two days; and the big *incwala*, which lasts six days. In preparation for the first phase, a group of national priests (*bemanti*) known as the 'people of the sea'[25] go on a pilgrimage to collect sea water, the main medicinal ingredient used to strengthen and purify the king. They wade into the sea completely naked and sing the *incwala* song as they fill their calabashes with water. On their return they sing the chief's praises (*izibongo*).

The opening of the small *incwala* ceremony takes place in the capital and all gather at the cattle kraal, the temporary amphitheatre, to participate. Standing in the formation of a crescent moon, the sacred *incwala* songs – reserved for the *incwala* ceremony and the death of a king – are chanted with great solemnity. The punishment meted out to those who dare chant them on any other occasion is severe. For the *incwala* performance people are arranged in rows according to rank, and are graded from front to back accordingly. The warriors hold their shields and sticks in their left hands and the women hold thin, long wands. As they sing, they raise these objects, causing them to quiver in time to the rhythm of the song. Their accompanying movements are dignified. The themes of the sacred *incwala* songs may be strange to those who are not familiar with Swazi culture, being about "hatred of the king and his rejection by the people."[26] According to one interpretation, the following song alludes to the king's enemies and denounces them. By virtue of his superior position, the king will always have enemies, whether within or outside the royal family. The song is thus "a national expression of sympathy for the king."[27] The words of the song have been described as 'mournful' and 'tremendously moving'.[28] By singing about the king's enemies and recognising the enmity he provokes, his people are in essence showing their loyalty and support for him:

> Shi shi ishi ishi – you hate him,
> Ishi ishi ishi – mother, the enemies are the people.
> Ishi ishi ish – you hate him
> Mother – the people are wizards.

Admit the treason of Mabedla
ishi ishi ishi — you hate him,
You have wronged,
ishi ishi — bend great neck,
those and those they hate him,
ishi ishi — they hate the king.[29]

As the sun sets, the formation of the dancers changes from a crescent into a full moon, so that they are standing in a full circle. Another type of song with a completely different mood is also performed. *Imigubo* are not sacred but they make strong historical references. The main *umgubo*, known as *lihubo*, is regarded as the national anthem and is performed to praise the king and end the evening's activities:

Here is the Inexplicable,
Our Bull! Lion! Descend.
Descend, Being of heaven,
Unconquerable.
Play like tides of the sea,
You Inexplicable Great Mountain.
Our Bull ye ye ...[30]

On the second day, the same songs are performed while people feast and drink beer. This concludes the small *incwala* ceremony. There is an interim period between the small and big *incwala* ceremonies, during which everyone anxiously awaits the full moon. People keep themselves busy by preparing for the big ceremony: they rehearse the *incwala* songs and dances for many hours a day, perfecting their performances so that they will be ready for the most important festival of their annual calendar. They also make their dance costumes, which mainly consist of animal skins and bird feathers. On the first day of the big *incwala*, branches of the sacred tree, a species of acacia (*lusekwane*), are collected by a group of young, unmarried boys to enclose the king's sanctuary in which he will be 'reborn'. They sing a sacred lullaby as they

The *ligubu* gourd-bow is regarded as "the 'classic' stringed instrument of the Swazi."[11] This bow, played only by men[12], is made from cane or from the branch of a tree with the bark removed. A calabash resonator or a cylindrical tin with a small opening is fixed near the bottom end of the instrument. The string was originally made from twisted strands of hair from a cow's tail, but this has largely been replaced by wire. The player holds the instrument in his left hand, leaving his thumb and first finger free to pinch the string to raise its pitch. The string is struck near the lower end of the bow with a thin grass or reed held in the right hand. The player varies the tone by moving the resonator towards and away from his chest.[13]

Male dancers in war attire perform the incwala *dance*

cut the branches and beat their shields against their sides in a steady rhythm that has been likened to that used by a mother to rock her baby to sleep:

We lull him, shiwayo shiwayo,
The child grows, we rock him, shiwayo shiwayo,
He who is as big as the world, shiwayo shiwayo.[31]

Some believe that this song was once sung by an exiled queen to her baby, who became the king. The boys sing this lullaby on their journey home and as they arrive in the village on the second day. The commotion caused by their return is captured in this description:

"Usually the branch-bearing men arrive at the outskirts of Lobamba in the light of the rising sun, and are welcomed by a surge of people: warriors loping, drums beating, bugles, kudu horns and whistles blowing; lines of men and women loudly chanting, clapping hands and caterwauling; children following in quiet procession, wide-eyed with wonder at the wild commotion."[32]

Celebration follows in the cattle byre, where the whole community, including the king, performs the *incwala* and *imigubo* songs. On the third day, the 'Day of the Bull', the boys sing their sacred lullaby once again while they ritually kill a bull. The fourth day is seen as the highlight of the entire ceremony: the king appears in full ceremonial attire, dancing with the warriors and eating the first fruits of the season in the company of the queen mother. Towards the late afternoon, the songs are 'wild and sad like the sea' [33] and reflect the emotional intensity of the rituals. The day is symbolic of a new beginning and people use music to express the emotion attached to this symbolism.

Wearing black plumes over his face, grass to cover his body, monkey-skins over his loins and the fat of an animal across his chest, the king performs a frenetic dance to mark the end of the great day. He holds a green calabash, known as the 'gourd of the north', which represents his people's origin. He throws the gourd at the shield of an age-mate, symbolising the discarding of the old year. On the following day the capital is silent. Painted in black ointments and smeared with animal fat, the king and royalty stay in seclusion.

On the final day of the big *incwala*, the objects used for the ceremony are burned and the king is cleaned, signifying the purification of the nation. People congregate at the cattle kraal, a space where the entire community can come together to sing as they did at the opening ceremony. People dance in the hope that the heavens will respond to their vigorous movements by opening up for the rains; the closing symbol of purification. No storm is great enough to disperse the people. They sing and dance until they are finally ready to conclude with the national chant. *Refer to Track 9.*

Umhlanga: the reed dance

The reed dance takes place in August or early September each year. It is an event which attracts young maidens from every area of the kingdom, and provides an occasion for them to honour and acknowledge the queen as the feminine role model of the nation. In paying homage to her, young Swazi girls celebrate their own femininity. The ceremony lasts for eight days and is held at the queen's residence in Ludzidzini, the capital of the Swazi people.

For the first three days, the girls, who are divided into groups according to age, collect reeds from rivers surrounding the royal residence. Each group has its own particular dance steps and songs to mark their respect for the monarch. On the fourth day the maidens gather at the queen's residence with the bundles of reeds they have collected to repair her royal hut. As they approach they perform a slow, rhythmic dance. Once they have entered the royal territory, they begin their preparation for the elaborate dances to be performed for the queen. They wear beaded skirts and drape woollen sashes adorned with woollen balls across their chests. The royal princesses are distinguished from the other young maidens by the red feathers they wear in their hair. *Refer to Track 10.*

Marriage ceremonies

Swazi weddings are elaborate affairs and there are almost as many songs as there are rituals.[34] Rehearsals start weeks before the occasion so that both

The *umakweyana* is a braced gourd-bow made from the branch of a tree with the bark removed and a string that is tied back at a point near the centre, dividing it into two segments. A calabash is fixed in the middle of the bow. The player holds the instrument vertically in one hand, with the calabash opening facing the chest. The instrument is grasped near the calabash, with the fingers extended on either side of the strings division. The other hand strikes the string with a stick. The *umakweyana* is usually played by girls as accompaniment to their singing. Married women do not play the *umakweyana* as it is believed that if they do, their children will grow up wild.
Refer to Track 8.

The *utiyane* is a mouth-bow that consists of either a curved piece of wood or a hollow river reed, with a thin rod inserted in the tube. The string is made from wire or fibre. The instrument is bowed by scraping a dry reed or stick across the string, and the mouth is used as a resonator. The melody is produced by varying the size and shape of the mouth, thus selecting one of the harmonics present in the two fundamentals. The player can obtain these by playing the string open or stopping it with the thumb.[14]

The umakweyana is played in moments of rest

parties are ready for their wedding performances. Songs in the repertoire include those that symbolically mark the acceptance of the bride's party into the groom's home. When the bride's party arrives at the cattle kraal (*sibaya*) they bend forwards as 'a sign of humility'[35] and then commence singing. They use song to ask for shelter at the homestead and to request an animal to slaughter.

Parents acknowledge the sadness of parting with their children, and the bride mourns the loss she experiences in leaving her family. Many of the songs in the ceremony reflect and dramatise the bride and her family's distress at saying goodbye. The journey of the bride's marriage party (*mtsimba*) to the groom's homestead is an emotional one. The songs often move the bride (*makoti*) to tears, and in turn affect the other women who also start weeping.

Man playing the utiyane

As the party approaches the groom's homestead, the women sing their reluctance to hand the bride over to the groom. Later in the proceedings, there is a dramatic moment when the bride stands in the groom's cattle byre and laments the loss of her childhood, pleading for her brothers to come and rescue her. She sings the song *Simekezo*:

> *Banibani buya umgikhoke (brother's name)* (come and take me out).[36]

This is followed by a mock escape where the bride and her party run away in the direction of their home. They are followed by a member of the groom's party who tempts the bride to return with the gift of a cow. The emotional turmoil mirrored in these wedding songs is a necessary component of the wedding ritual. They accentuate the tension between the two parties, and the emotion inherent in rituals of parting. *Refer to Track 11.*

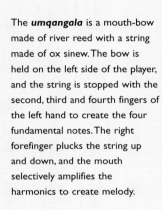

The **umqangala** is a mouth-bow made of river reed with a string made of ox sinew. The bow is held on the left side of the player, and the string is stopped with the second, third and fourth fingers of the left hand to create the four fundamental notes. The right forefinger plucks the string up and down, and the mouth selectively amplifies the harmonics to create melody.

Stringed-wind

The Swazi formerly played the **makwindi,** which is the equivalent of the Khoi *gora.*[15] (See Chapter 10, page 237).

The AmaXhosa, otherwise known as the 'Red Blanket' people, constitute the largest chiefdom of the Cape Nguni. The Xhosa-speaking people of today are not all originally from the Xhosa clan, but originated from approximately ten related Cape tribes which spoke similar dialects. Largely because of forced removals into designated areas from the mid-1950s and later through radio broadcasting in the 'Xhosa' language, many of the people in these disparate groups began identifying themselves as Xhosa. The various dialects have more or less merged into the isiXhosa spoken today, which is one of the most widely spoken languages in South Africa.

The Xhosa people inhabit the south-eastern corner of South Africa. The majority reside in the Eastern and Western Cape, especially in the cities of Cape Town, East London and Port Elizabeth.

AmaXhosa

History of the 'Red Blanket' people

Little is known about the early history of the southern Nguni. Archaeological records of the Cape are not extensive, and this has limited knowledge of Xhosa origins.[1] There is uncertainty about the date of their arrival in the region. The earliest evidence, found in accounts of shipwreck survivors who came into contact with Xhosa people in 1593, suggests that the Xhosa ancestors were already in occupation there by the mid-16th century. However, there is no evidence to prove that they had only recently arrived, and many believe that they had in fact been there for centuries. One element of Xhosa identity that has been well documented is the interrelationship between the Xhosa and the original inhabitants of South Africa – the Khoi and the San. Oral traditions as well as linguistic, social and cultural links between these peoples have provided evidence that the earlier inhabitants were assimilated into the Xhosa through intermarriage and subjugation.[2]

The most dramatic encounter in Xhosa history was with the white settlers. This changed the makeup of their society and shaped their future. The Xhosa were the first of the South African Bantu-speaking peoples to come into contact with whites while migrating from the eastern banks of the Kei River in the Cape in the 16th century. Two hundred years later, the arrival of white missionaries in the late 18th century marked one of the greatest collisions between two civilisations: Africa and Europe. This was the beginning of the ongoing conflict that was to transform the Xhosa nation. It was predominantly conflict over land that led to the frontier wars fought between 1778 and 1878, between the various clans, the British and Dutch missionaries.

During the time of the Cape frontier conflicts, a series of inter-tribal wars were fought, weakening the Xhosa peoples' resistance to foreign influence. The introduction of Christianity into Xhosa culture had caused great turmoil among rivaling Xhosa chiefs. A peculiar mixture of Christian and traditional beliefs emerged, which threw the people into disarray and tore at the very fabric of their society. At this time the Xhosa camp was split down the middle: those who believed in the teachings of the missionaries, nicknamed the 'school' people; and those who did not, nicknamed the 'red' people because they upheld their traditions such as the painting of their bodies, blankets and clothing with red ochre. The two most powerful Xhosa chiefs, Sandile and Maqoma, died around this time, and the Xhosa's military resistance was further weakened. It was around the turn of the 19th century that Ntsikana, regarded by many as the first true Xhosa Christian prophet, emerged as a man of influence. He worked hard at restoring peace among the warring factions, and is most notably remembered for writing a number of hymns still sung today. But as influential as he was, Ntsikana only managed to placate the Xhosa factions to a limited extent. The Xhosa remained divided and became increasingly disempowered as the colonists' influence grew stronger.

In 1856, after sixty years of frontier wars with both the Boers and the British, which had cost them most of their ancestral lands, the Xhosa people

Drums

The *ikawu* is a shield made from ox-skin that is beaten with a knobkierie and is slammed into the ground with tremendous force. In the past it was played during male initiation ceremonies, and accompanied a special dance performed by boys and girls (*umtshotsho*). The beating of the *ikawu* also accompanied battle cries.[3]

The *ingqongqo* is a rudimentary drum made from a stiff, dried ox hide and beaten with sticks. It has been suggested that the *ingqongqo* is based upon the hunting shield and the drumsticks on the assegai. A bull's skin is cured and tied onto a number of posts three to four feet from the ground. The instrument is played by a group of women who beat the skin with sticks (*amaqoqa*). Sometimes the skin is fastened with small loops of hide, and in this case the performers hold the *ingqongqo* in one hand while using the other hand to beat it with a stick. Alternatively, the skin is laid on the ground, and the women sit around it, beating it with sticks. This instrument is no longer found among the Xhosa, but in the past it was widely used by women during male circumcision ceremonies. It was also played during initiation ceremonies for novice diviners. This drum has been replaced by modern substitutes such as pieces of cardboard or zinc, which are beaten with sticks.

Women sitting on ground playing the ingqongqo

sought help from their ancestors through traditional means. Desperate to reclaim their independence and strength, both of which had diminished through years of foreign conquest of their land, they decided to act upon the prophecies of a young girl, Nongqawuse. She had a vision and claimed that salvation lay in the killing of all their cattle (their most prized possession), and the destruction of all their food stocks. The young prophetess said that on a certain day everything would be returned to them in greater abundance and their ancestors would rise from the sea. The herds were duly slaughtered and the food stocks destroyed. The appointed day came and went, and tens of thousands of Xhosa starved to death. The consequence of their decision was so severe that this event is regarded as their national suicide, named after Nongqawuse, the woman partly responsible for their downfall. The only option for those still struggling for survival was to turn to their enemies for help. Many moved to the white-owned farms in the Ciskei, where they were employed by farmers. This movement permanently affected the location of Xhosa people, who still live in this area today. In more recent times, the Xhosa have emerged as the political core of the struggle for South African democracy. Leaders such as Nelson Mandela, Steve Biko and Oliver Tambo all come from a predominantly Xhosa region of South Africa previously known as the Transkei, and now part of the Eastern Cape.

Music in performance

Ihlombe

A Xhosa woman once said:

> "*Speak to me about music and you bring joyous excitement to the Xhosa. People cannot help but get this feeling* (ihlombe) *when they sing; even those who listen to them shudder* (-hlasimla) *when they hear music.*"[10]

The Xhosa use *ihlombe*, a word that has no equivalent in the English language, to express the transcendental feeling induced by music. It transports people to a state of overwhelming joy in which they become so acutely moved that they are compelled to stand up and participate. The impact of *ihlombe* is most apparent when the song rises in volume and pitch, and the dancers work themselves into a frenzied trance-like state. Large-scale performances are more likely to induce *ihlombe* because the strength of the group dynamic heightens the intensity of the experience. The term *ihlombe* holds such relevance that among some Xhosa it has become a synonym for song or music. Xhosa music is traditionally defined by the term *ingoma yesiXhosa*, which encompasses music in its broadest sense, ranging from the traditional to the more modern genres.[11] *Ihlombe* can only be induced by music, which is why the Xhosa have such an intimate relationship with this artistic form of expression. The more music there is in the community, the more *ihlombe* is evoked in its people.[12]

Umngqokolo: overtone singing

Xhosa music is exceptional for its use of overtone singing, a vocal style rarely heard today. It is highly valued because it represents an integral part of the dying customs of the Xhosa.[13] Although overtone singing is heard among various peoples in Asia, where it is commonly known as 'harmonic chant', 'harmonic singing' or 'throat singing', it is not widespread in Africa. Here it is practised by a small group of Xhosa/Thembu people in the Eastern Cape and is known as *umngqokolo*. A singer who uses overtone singing produces a low, rich-sounding drone with the vocal chords, and selects different harmonics present in this sound by varying the size and resonance of the vocal and nasal cavities. The resulting sound is a hoarse, low drone with a clear, high, flute-like tone above it. Singers achieve this effect by exercising precise control over their vocal resonators and the tongue.[14]

In some cultures this style has been linked with healing rituals and ancient religious customs. Some fascinating conclusions have been drawn in relation to Tibetan monks, who have practised overtone singing for many centuries, and use it as they recite their sacred texts. Among the people of Tuva in Mongolia, throat singing is an essential part of their animistic practice: they

The origins of the *igubu* drum are thought to lie in the marching band bass drum of early European settlers. It is cylindrical and is usually made from a tin that has been cut to size with a skin tied over both ends. The drum is beaten with short, padded sticks or pieces of wood or rubber. The player sometimes attaches a leather cord or thong to the drum and hangs it around the neck, so that he or she can move while playing. This instrument is played on various occasions and for a variety of ceremonies, particularly in African independent churches.

The *igogogo* is similar to the *igubu*. It is also made from a tin and is played by male initiates to signal their hunger. Upon hearing the signal, members of the local village bring food to the boys.

The *isidiphu* is a friction drum. A stick is attached to the inside of the drum through the skin head. It is played by rubbing the stick with a wet hand or cloth, causing it to vibrate, producing a moaning or roaring sound.[4]
Refer to Track 12.

83

A group of women hold the ingqongqo *drum with one hand, and use the other hand to beat the skin with sticks*

use the voice to mimic nature's sounds. Among Xhosa people, overtone singing is known as *umngqokolo*, a word derived from the Khoisan language. Due to the strong influence of the Khoisan language and culture, many Khoisan musical techniques and songs were assimilated into Xhosa music. Various Xhosa musical terms thus have Khoisan roots or are in fact Khoisan words.[15] Xhosa overtone singing is based on Xhosa bow instruments, particularly the *umrhubhe* friction mouth-bow and the *uhadi*. Apart from producing two fundamental notes, these instruments also produce overtones. However, we cannot always hear them distinctly unless they are purposefully emphasised. The Xhosa imitate the sounds of their musical bows using their voices, and through a careful manoeuvering of the tongue and shaping of the mouth cavity, are able to create overtones above the basic notes they sing. They produce overtones by raising the tongue, thus shaping the resonance chamber. The throat muscles are tightened, which creates the low, rasping, guttural sound characteristic of overtone singing. When women use this technique, their voices sit so far below the ordinary female register that they sound like men. Overtone singing is in fact only practised by women, and it is generally the leader of a song who uses the overtone technique. Diviners commonly use overtone singing, as they believe that it enables them to speak to the ancestors. *Refer to Track 15.*

Offering an explanation on how she invented a personal style of overtone singing, a Xhosa woman asserted that she had taught herself the technique. She got the idea "from the way people (especially boys) use an insect called *umqangi*: this is a large flying beetle, which the boys impale alive on a thorn, and then hold the desperately buzzing insect within the mouth, resonating overtones derived from the sound of its buzzing."[16] Her technique came to be known as *umngqokolo ngomqangi*. Overtone singing puts a lot of strain on the voice, yet an accomplished leader is able to keep a song going in this fashion for several minutes. Despite the complexity of this technique, Xhosa people are not taught how to sing in this fashion; they learn by watching and listening.

This song is sung by thirteen women using overtone singing, about a woman who was stingy with beer. She was called Nondel' ekhaya ('Married at home')

Rattles

Imiguza are dried gourds worn around the waist as dancing rattles.

Izikunjane are tied below the knee and consist of small tins that have been filled with stones and closed on one end.

Amanqashele are rattles worn by initiates. They are tied to the ankle and made from goat-skin.

Iingcacu[5] are worn mainly by female diviners. They are made from reeds and are worn from just below the knee to the ankle.

The *iqhagi*, made from a small calabash filled with stones, was worn by boys as a penis-rattle.

Since colonisation, many other rattles have developed. People use modern materials such as bells and bottle tops to make rattles.

He! Nondel' ekhaya	Hey Nondel' ekhaya
	('Married at home')
Wath' utywala buphelile	She says the beer is finished
Yewu … ndinesizi ngamankazana	Yes … I feel pity for the
	(unmarried mothers)
… bandibambel' …	they have taken my place
bandilingen'	they were stronger than me
He! Nothobile, ma	Hey! Nothobile (a name), mother
Amandla akalingan'	you are not as strong as I am
Ho! Vedinga	Oh Vedinga (a thick brown blanket)
Andigodoli, ma	I do not get cold, oh mother
Asivani ngomthetho	We do not agree about traditional law
Hayi, ma	No, mother
Ho! lilongwe	Ho! This is the
	inside-wall-of-the-house
Khe, mntakama	yes child-of-mother
Ho! Lilongwe kulendawo	Ho! The inside-wall-of-the-house
	is this place
O hamba, ndiyanqen' uKuthetha	Oh, go away, I am tired of talking[17]

The Ngqoko Women's Ensemble

The Ngqoko Women's Ensemble is a group of traditional musicians who reside in the Eastern Cape and are some of the remaining Xhosa musicians who use overtone singing. Performing on instruments like the *umrhubhe* (mouth-bow), the *uhadi* (gourd-bow), the *ikatari* (bow-type instrument played by friction) and the *isidiphu* (friction drum), this female group has made an invaluable contribution to the preservation of traditional Xhosa music. The Ngqoko Women's Ensemble has performed extensively both locally and internationally, recording the successful CD – *Le Chant des Femmes Xhosa* – for the Musée d'Ethnographie de Geneve in 1995, and producing a number of their own CDs as well. At the 2002 Arts and Culture Trust Awards, Nofinishi Dywili, the founder of the Ngoko Women's Cultural Group, was posthumously honoured with a Lifetime Achievement Award for her contribution to traditional South African music.

because she had children but no husband. It explores the plight of sexually active unmarried women. In one line the song refers to a 'thick brown blanket'. A blanket, it is believed, is a euphemism for the female sex organs. Thus, when a woman sings "I have my blanket, I do not get cold", she means that she always has male company in bed. *Refer to Track 16.*

Other vocal techniques

"Xhosa people like to put salt into their songs."[23]

Xhosa music is characterised by a range of unusual vocal techniques, particular to the culture. These techniques often put strain on the voice, which becomes hoarser as the performance progresses. The Xhosa are unafraid to push their voices to their limits and are in fact admired if they manage to lose their voices through exhaustion. When boys perform the *umtshotsho* dance, they sing in a style called *ukutshotsha*.[18] They create deep, gruff tones by singing in a very low register and pushing the voice to the back of the throat. *Ukubhayizela*, a vocal style performed by boys during the *umbhayizelo* dance, is the modern equivalent of *ukutshotsha*.[19] The voice is used to create percussive sounds in the form of guttural exclamations. The *iintlombe* dance for young men also has its own unique vocal style. *Ukubhodla* is literally translated as 'to bring wind up from the stomach', and young men use this technique to produce a deep belching sound.[20]

Other vocal techniques that stand out in Xhosa song include humming (*ukumbombozela/imbuyo*).[21] In some songs, singers hum to imitate the sound of the rock pigeon. Other animal and bird calls are frequently evoked using the voice.[22] One of the most interesting aspects of the Xhosa voice is the use of click sounds. The clicks in the Xhosa language, directly derived from the family of Khoisan languages, have been popularised through Miriam Makeba's famous click song, *Ungqongqothwane*. One immediately recognises a Xhosa song through the distinctive, sharp, clicking sounds, which play an important role in accentuating the rhythm of the song. These create yet another layer to the music. A Xhosa woman from the Ngqoko area once commented: "Xhosa

Bull-roarers

Uvuru is the name given to the Xhosa bull-roarer or spinning disk.

87

people like to put salt into their songs."[23] She was referring to the various vocal and rhythmical techniques that add flavour to Xhosa music. *Refer to Track 17.*

Rhythm

Xhosa music is striking for its use of multiple rhythms. Cross rhythms are created on a number of levels: through different vocal parts, through dance, and through clapping. According to Xhosa sensibility, the rhythm of the clapping and the singing should in fact not follow one another directly. Performers 'add salt' to their music by creating independent intersecting rhythms. Through multi-layering or 'salting' in Xhosa songs, the music always sounds full and rich. There is a fundamental principle behind the concept of cross rhythm. The Xhosa song contains multiple layers, but these layers only work because they are placed within an overarching structure. Despite the freedom that performers are given to 'salt' their songs, they never forget that they are part of a group. As one Xhosa man explained:

> *"Actually, everyone does his own thing, but it must fit in with the others. You cannot sing just anything. A song has a certain sound* (tune), *and a beat, and all of us have to sing around that."*[24]

This notion of individual expression within the structure of the group is made tangible through the use of clapping. The "even-spaced regularity of hand-clapping"[25] imposes an overarching structure for the song and is used to remind each individual that he/she is performing with the group and for the group.[26]

Amagwijo: personal songs

The only time that individuals can truly separate themselves from the group is when they are performing what the Xhosa classify as 'personal songs' (*amagwijo*).[27] These songs are created and performed in moments of rest and relaxation, when people are free to smoke their pipes, play their bows, or sit around the fire. They stand outside of community performance and are usually performed by women for self-expression. They accompany individuals through every stage of life, reflecting their emotional, physical and mental states. This is the one category of song where there are no rules to follow or standards to meet. Songs can be vocal or instrumental, and listeners can join in if they please, provided they do not obstruct the soloist's words and melody line. This is one instance of Xhosa song-making where the words should not be altered because they contain the emotional core of the individual's thoughts and feelings. These songs are emotive, often enabling listeners to identify with and become moved by the singers message. The singing of these songs does not, however, depend on the presence of an audience. They are often sung or played in a private, introspective moment.[28] As one Xhosa woman explained:

> "You will not find anyone dancing when he listens to this music. It is played only when you sit up at night, when it is dark and you have time to think. You think deeply, too deeply, and then you play it (music). Sometimes the tears come. Sometimes it makes you think so deeply that you cannot bear it, and you want to run away forever."[29]

The two instruments most commonly used to accompany these songs are the *uhadi* and *umrhubhe* because they complement the voice. The *umrhubhe* is able to simulate the sound of crying and thus is especially well suited to this type of song.[30] In more recent times, men started composing personal songs with European instruments such as the guitar, accordion and concertina. Other songs that stand apart from community performance include lullabies (*thuthuzela*). These are usually improvised, but there is one Xhosa lullaby that has become an African standard. It has been adopted by other African peoples, and is nowadays performed as a modern lullaby. The original version of this song was *Thula umntwana* ('Be quiet, child'), and it was sometimes accompanied by hand-clapping, with the singers swaying from side to side. The modern version is *Thula baba* ('Be quiet, little baby'),[31] which has become one of the best-known African lullabies.

Whistles, flutes and reeds

The *imbande* whistle, which was normally made from the thigh-bone of an animal, was used to call important meetings.

The *ingcongolo* whistle was made from reeds and the **utwi-twi-twi** was made from the stalk of a flower.

The *impempe* was a small river-reed pipe that was stopped on one end. The open side served as an embouchure. The instrument was used to signal for help in a fight and by herdboys to signal to their cattle. It was also used as a toy.

The *ixilongo*[6] flute is made by herdboys to call their cattle into the fields. It is constructed from a variety of materials. Traditionally, it was made from the wood of the *umhlehli* tree, and sometimes from reeds. Its modern equivalent is made from a piece of metal or plastic piping.

Xhosa boys play a double whistle called **ukombe.** This whistle is modelled on the European 'police' whistle with two parallel stopped tubes of different lengths.

Today, whistles bought in shops are more common than hand-made whistles.

Umteyo *shaking dance performed by the Rose Deep team*

Communal music

The Xhosa are extremely festive and use music to celebrate at community gatherings. The largest gatherings, the *umdudo* and *umgidi*, involve an entire village.[32] Originally the term *umdudo* was used to refer to very important gatherings like weddings and war meetings, whereas the term *umgidi* was used for large feasts to honour the chief, and for other celebrations such as harvesting festivals. Today, these terms are used interchangeably. Gatherings of such a large scale cannot take place without song and dance, which feed into the communal spirit. In Xhosa society people are divided into different age groups or social sects, and each group performs the dances and songs specific to them at large feasts. The Xhosa also hold formal dancing parties for each age group, from childhood where girls arrange parties, to old age when married men and women gather at organised parties. Formerly these parties took place during winter, between the harvesting and ploughing seasons, when there was little activity in the community and people had more leisure time. Nowadays they do not occur regularly and are only kept alive in places where enthusiasts organise regional competitions.

Dance movements

Each social group has its own repertoire of song and dance, but there are certain dance movements that are common across the age spectrum. *Ukutyityimba*[33] is one of the core movements in Xhosa dance. It has been described as "a gymnastic feat peculiar to the Xhosa."[34] The dancer's entire upper body quivers, and the knees are pushed forwards and backwards. With an erect posture and minimal foot movement, the pelvis is contracted with an upward body movement and the arms are bent at the elbow in imitation of the horns of cattle. The effect is that the whole body appears to ripple as it "shakes like a river reed in the wind."[35] It is the distinguishing movement found in the Xhosa shaking dance, *umteyo*, but is also incorporated into other dances.[36] A dancer who is able to perform this movement successfully is one "who shakes so much that he shakes the skin off himself."[37] Performers often wear small bells across their chests and tin rattles filled with stones (*izikunjane*) around

Horns

In the past the Xhosa used an ox horn to summon people to the chief's private kraal (**isigodhlo**), and thus called the instrument by this name. It was also used as a signal instrument in war, and is occasionally used by boys for their amusement and by diviners.

their calves to emphasise the vibrations of their shaking bodies. Another common dance movement practised among all age groups is *ukusina*. Dancers kick their legs upwards and outwards in any direction and then stamp each foot into the ground.[38]

Dance parties

Umtshotsho: *dance parties for teenagers* – Pre-initiate teenage boys and girls enter into the social life of the community through their *umtshotsho* dance parties, the focus of which is the *umtshotsho* dance.[39] Dance parties provide a platform for young people to meet in a friendly environment and connect through the performance of song and dance. Music also makes courting easier and it is not unusual to see couples who have met at the party leaving together afterwards. From the age of five, children emulate their teenage brothers and sisters, practising the *umtshotsho* dance in anticipation of the day when they will be old enough to participate.

The teenagers are given free reign over the event and are responsible for all the planning. The party lasts a full weekend: the festivities begin on a Saturday afternoon when the boys gather their friends together by singing and blowing whistles, and ends on a Monday. Each age group has a set of rules, and participants appoint six people to take on various roles such as policemen and magistrates, to enforce the rules. For example, no one is allowed to go to sleep in the middle of the party without first asking for permission from the 'policeman', who then refers the matter to the 'magistrate'. This role-playing teaches the significance of social etiquette and is perhaps symbolic of the teenagers' preparation for adulthood.

The main performance, the *umtshotsho* dance, is divided into two sections. The first involves the preparation and 'gearing up'[40], followed by a more energetic sequence with clapping that is often double the speed and at a heightened volume. *Umtshotsho* dance-songs have different tempos, and the dancers match their movements with each song's pace.[41] The participants form two circles. The girls stand or kneel in the outward circle, clapping and singing while the boys dance anti-clockwise, making roaring sounds (*ukutshotsha*) as they move. The boys mainly use the *ukutyityimba* shaking movement as well as some improvised, sexual dance movements symbolic of their maturing sexuality. The girls only occasionally join in the dancing by breaking out of their semi-circle to dance solo, also using suggestive movements. While the teenagers express their awakening sexuality through dance, they reflect on the social customs of their culture through song.

Intlombe: *dance parties for young adults* – *Intlombe* dance parties for initiated but unmarried young men and women bear similarities to the *umtshotsho* dance parties of their younger counterparts.[42] They also provide an opportunity for people who are at the same stage in life to socialise. The format of *intlombe* dances is very similar to *umtshotsho* dances, with the women standing on the outside of the men's circle, clapping and singing, and the men dancing in the centre. The men perform the *ukutyityimba* movement in a more exaggerated fashion than the *umtshotsho* dancers, and the adults are generally more dignified and graceful than the teenagers. With their feet positioned close together, they lift their heels and use their knees to balance. The men use the *ukubhodla* vocal technique, creating belching sounds. They also use a vocal sound characterised by a hooting noise which makes this type of music easy to identify.[43]

Etywaleni: *beer parties for adults* – Sorghum beer is the Xhosa national drink[44], and people always associate the drinking of beer with a social gathering. In the past married men and women used both formal and informal beer parties as occasions to socialise.[45] Nowadays, married couples as well as single people attend informal beer parties, held by any individual who wishes to host such a gathering, and open to anyone who wishes to participate. Formal parties, on the other hand, are more like exclusive clubs with members who pay membership fees, and they are open only to married men and unattached women. Beer drinking is often the catalyst for song and dance, and thus people regard drinking and music-making as complementary. By implication, beer songs (*iingoma*

Woman playing the uhadi *bow*

Bows

The design of all Xhosa bows developed from the San hunting bow, which consists of a curved stick and an attached string.

Traditionally the **uhadi** gourd-bow is played by women and is mainly used to accompany the voice. The bow of the *uhadi* was formerly made from the *umbangandhlela* tree, but nowadays is made from any type of wood. The string is made from twisted ox sinew, cow/horse hair or wire, and the resonator is a calabash. The instrument is held in one hand and the string is struck with a reed held in the other. The player can stop the string with the finger, or leave it open, producing two different notes, a tone apart. She strikes the string with the reed while moving the small opening of the calabash towards and away from her chest. In this way she varies the resonance of the sound by selecting different harmonics that are present in it. The *uhadi* player is responsible for producing the melody line, and in most cases sings the leading part of the song. She may also produce another rhythm by beating the feet. *Refer to Track 13.*

Umteyo *shaking dance performed by the Rose Deep team*

zotywala) cannot be sung without the drinking of beer, and people cannot imagine drinking beer without song and dance. As one Xhosa man aptly commented, "where there is meat and beer, there is a party; the more meat and beer, the bigger the party."[46]

Musical performances at such occasions have a similar structure to *umtshotsho* and *intlombe* dance-songs, with women clapping and singing on the outside of a circle and men moving around slowly on the inside. The women are responsible for most of the singing and are often the song leaders. Beer-dance songs present a good opportunity for people to display their performance skills. Aside from their entertainment value, they also allow people to express themselves through the song texts. The songs usually comment on topical issues relevant to those present, and often include lighthearted criticism. Songs that stem from beer parties have been adapted for other social events, usually where beer-drinking takes place. They are performed at work parties (*amalima*), where workers drink beer at the end of their shift, using song to end the day on a high note. They are also sung on ceremonial occasions such as weddings and initiation ceremonies.

Sacred ceremonies

Divination
Many divination activities centre around music, and diviners (*amagqirha*) are reputed to be excellent musicians.[47] They have a large musical repertoire because they travel widely, acquiring new songs and absorbing foreign influences into their music-making. They continually compose music to enhance their work. When an individual is 'called' by the ancestors as a diviner and becomes ill, one of the main remedies is dancing. People believe that the ancestors have a great love for divination music, and thus novice diviners dance as often as possible to please them. The diviner's dance (*umxhentso*) consists of stamping movements for the lower body, and the shaking movement (*ukutyityimba*) characteristic of many Xhosa dances for the upper body. The dancer shakes so that the whole body convulses in sharp, sudden spasms. Eventually she falls to the ground when every last ounce of energy has

The **umrhubhe** is a mouth-bow usually played by women. It consists either of a curved piece of wood or a hollow river reed, with a thin rod inserted in the tube. The string is made from wire or fibre. The instrument is bowed by scraping a dry reed or stick across the string, and the mouth is used as a resonator. The melody is produced by varying the size and shape of the mouth, thus selecting one of the harmonics present in the two fundamentals. These can be obtained by playing the string open or stopping it with the thumb. A good player is able to produce a rich range of harmonics and also whistle them out of the corner of the mouth. *Refer to Track 14.*

been spent. It is essential that the dancer is surrounded by people who clap and sing while she performs, and the spectators are often given beer to encourage them to participate.

Diviners attending séances use music as the main channel through which they communicate with the ancestors. Séance rituals resemble formal performances in that the music is carefully prepared before the event, and the diviner draws up a programme indicating which songs are to be performed. Each song is specially designed for a particular ritual, and the song text reflects the thrust of the diviner's message. Songs are also borrowed from other contexts, and these are performed towards the end of the séance to break the tension of the divination rituals. Drumming is an essential part of séance music, and diviners usually possess a drum that has been tailor-made for them. During a divination ceremony, one drum is beaten with curved sticks or curved pieces of rubber. If no drum is available, people substitute the sound of drumming by beating the ground or cardboard boxes with sticks. The only other instrumentation used for diviners dances are reeds or ankle-rattles worn on the calves, in the case of novices; and beads worn around the ankles (*iinkaca*) in the case of fully certified diviners. These objects rub together, creating the percussion for the song. Music transports diviners into a trance-like state in which they experience the spiritual state of *ihlombe*.

Initiation

Ukwaluka: *male initiation* – A boy is only recognised as an adult member of society once he has been circumcised.[48] So highly valued is this ritual in Xhosa culture that the date of a boy's circumcision is as important as the date of his birth. After the circumcision rite is performed, the initiates (*abakhwetha*) go into seclusion for four to six weeks, but in the past this could last up to three months. The initiates remain in isolation from the rest of the community and have their food bought to them by children. They communicate with their community by blowing a horn (*isigodhlo*) to indicate that they are hungry. In the past a range of dance-songs were performed during this period, but these have fallen away.

The *umtshilo*[49] initiation dance was "one of the great occasions" in Xhosa life.[50] These dances are no longer performed, mainly because they were expensive affairs, and nowadays people do not have the time or the money to invest in them. The initiates wore grass skirts made from strips of palm leaf, which have been likened to ballet tutu skirts. They also wore lofty palm headdresses that covered their heads and masked their faces. These had stems and leaves attached on either side, creating the appearance of "grasshoppers' antennae."[51] When the dancers bent forward, the headdresses lightly touched the ground. These two items were the defining feature of this dance. With an array of bright body paints and the palm leaf outfit, this dance costume is the most widely recognised as distinctly Xhosa. The *umtshilo* dance included the now extinct *ingqongqo* drum, which was made from a large piece of animal skin and was held above the ground by a group of women, who beat it with sticks. The *ikawu*, another makeshift drum made from a shield and beaten with a knob-stick, also accompanied the dance. The men danced in single file using stiff movements because their bodies were restrained by the heavy palm-leaf skirts and headdresses. With legs far apart, they bent from the waist, creating a sharp percussive rattling sound with their skirts. Some have commented that this dance movement is apt because it mirrors the way the circumcised boys have to sit after their operation.[52] This description captures spirit of the dance:

"In his dance he paws the ground and tosses his 'horns' in clear mime of the behaviour of a vigorous and proud bull. Dancing is in line, facing the audience. Both feet are on the ground and the action involves a curious drumming of heels and a vigorous flexing of torso muscles. These combined movements cause skirts to flick, clatter and toss in hectic rhythm. The boys, lost in their dance, snort in the manner of bulls and perspire freely, causing rivulets to run down their patterned, all-over disguise of white sandstone."[53]

In this excerpt, the writer makes reference to the presence of an audience. During their seclusion period, the initiates often visited different kraals to exhibit the *umtshilo* dance. By doing so, the rest of the community could witness one of the greatest and most spectacular Xhosa performances.

The *inkinge* is virtually extinct. The stick of this bow is hollow and the string very thin. This bow was played in a similar fashion to the *umrhubhe*, except that the player used a plectrum made from animal horn to pluck the string.

Intonjane: female initiation – The seclusion period during female initiation also centres around one main dance-song that is performed outdoors.[54] The round dance – *umngqungqo* – is performed by married women, and is the exception to the Xhosa tradition of men being responsible for most of the dancing and women for the singing. The women form concentric circles and perform two main movements, both characterised by walking, swaying and balancing on the ball of the foot, then stamping the heel down. In the first movement they move clockwise, and then change directions. In the second movement they face inwards. The dancers move with grace, shaking their shoulders throughout, while their spectacular costumes of braided skirts, red blankets, colourful handkerchiefs and beaded ornaments enhance their movements. They also hold sticks in their right hands in imitation of men. Unlike the *umtshilo* dance performed during male initiation, there is no instrumentation, and the vocal parts are largely improvised.

The women's *umngqungqo* dance usually lasts for two days. Thereafter the men perform the *umdudo* dance, which lasts a further two to six days. In this performance the men form lines of about ten people. The dance opens with

Girls clapping at their initiation ceremony

the singing of *umyeyezelo*, and the beating of the now-extinct *ingqongqo* drum. When the men are ready to begin the dance, they stamp with the left foot, flex the body forward, and jump up. They return to their erect positions, and repeat this step a few times. When the leader whistles, a more energetic second movement begins which is accompanied by *Mhala's* song. The leader breaks off from the group and performs a number of steps that are copied by the other dancers. He "dashes off curvetting, prancing and making figures of eight."[55] In the third and final movement, the dancers break off into small groups, dancing individual steps that consist mainly of shaking movements (*ukutyityimba*)[56] that cause the muscles to quiver.

Emergent music

In Xhosa society, there is a split between those who adhere to traditional practices ('red people') and those who do not ('school people'). The school people have developed activities separate from those of the red people. Whereas the young men of the red people (*abafana*) hold traditional *intlombe* dance parties, the school people (*iindlavini*) have created an equivalent in their *umtshotsho* dance parties where they perform *iindlavini* music.[57] The school people have modernised some of the traditional dance parties, adopting them to suit their needs. While the red people still perform traditional Xhosa music, the school people have absorbed new styles, blending them with traditional Xhosa styles. This blend is embodied in the *indlamu* stamping dance performed at *umtshotsho* parties.[58] Some elements of traditional Xhosa song and dance are retained, such as the shaking movements of the body and the roaring vocal sounds, but the polyrhythm that is central to Xhosa music is absent, which means that there is more correlation between the rhythms produced by the vocal parts and the dance movements.

Nofinishi Dywili

The divide between the two groups is even more apparent when looking at some of the new styles that have been borrowed from foreign cultures, which the people call 'i-modern'.[59] These reflect modern values and experiences, and are strongly influenced by European music. One of the most popular styles used by the school people is known as 'sounds' (*amasawundi*). It is not exclusive to the Xhosa and is performed by most of the other black groups. Sung by adults and children, this style is used in many social, ceremonial and religious contexts. Afro-American jazz influences can be heard in the scatting technique used by singers. The influence of European hymns is also evident, which makes this style of music well-suited to church services and wedding ceremonies. One advantage of incorporating foreign styles into African music is that more people can access it. During apartheid, the use of new styles enabled black people to communicate their plight to the rest of the world. 'Sounds' were used as freedom songs during this important era in history.

The **ikatali** borrows its name from the Western guitar, and is used by boys before they are initiated. It consists of an oil tin resonator to which a stick strung with wire is attached. Players bow the *ikatali* with a small cow-hair bow made from a curved twig, and create the melody by fingering the two fundamentals and varying the bow pressure to select higher or lower harmonics.[7]

"I asked the bow player of Mackay's Nek, Mrs Nosinothi Dumiso, how she had learned to play the bow. Her answer was, she had never learned. Because of illness (she went blind in one eye), she felt called to become a diviner, and for that reason she took up the uhadi bow. But she did not learn, she just played. Further questioning brought to light that she had in fact learned how to play and make an uhadi when she was a young girl, by observing the older bow-players. Then, in 1983, Mrs Nofinishi Dywili was asked to give lessons in playing uhadi to one of the Lumko nuns. Nofinishi's method was simply to come into the room, sit down, and play for an hour, then say 'Ndidiniwe' (I am tired), and pack up and go home. No explanations or demonstrations were given. This example shows the traditional Xhosa attitude to learning. The learner is expected to have a very high level of concentration and awareness, and also a magnificent sense of hearing."[8]

– Dave Dargie

Stringed-wind

The **ugwali**[9] is derived from the Khoi *gora*, but is no longer played by the Xhosa. (See Chapter 10, page 237)

The AmaNdebele of South Africa, most renowned for their murals and beadwork, trace their origins to King Musi who, in the 17th century, led his people to the area of present-day Tshwane (Pretoria) from the Nguni heartland in present-day KwaZulu-Natal.

There are two groups of AmaNdebele in South Africa, situated in different areas. The Northern Ndebele or Nrebele are located in the Limpopo Province around the towns of Mokopane (Potgietersrus) and Polokwane (Pietersburg). The Southern Ndebele, otherwise known as AmaNdebele, comprise two main groups: the Manala and the Ndzundza, and are located in the Mpumalanga and Gauteng provinces. In the 1830s another Ndebele community called the Matabele was formed under the Zulu chieftan, Mzilikazi, and settled in Zimbabwe, where it is now the second-largest population group.

AmaNdebele

History of the AmaNdebele

The history of the Ndebele can be traced back to the 17th century when they broke away from the Nguni and migrated from the Natal province to the central highveld of South Africa.[1] Under the leadership of King Musi, they settled just north of Pretoria, but soon became fragmented following disputes over succession. Musi's five sons squabbled over inheritance when their father died, and there were two main splits in the group; one led by Manala, the eldest son, and the other led by Ndzundza. Various other sub-groups emerged and split from the two factions, but most of these were absorbed into other more-dominant surrounding groups. Today people recognise the Manala and Ndzundza as the two main Southern Ndebele groups.

"*Choral music and group dances dominate, and solo music is largely, albeit not exclusively, reserved for courting and love-making, and thus associated with the age-group of the unmarried youths.*"[2]

Drums

Ndebele drums are always played in sets of three, composed of different sizes. The largest drum is called *ingungu enkulu;* the middle drum, *umaphendula;* and the smallest, *encane.*[3] These drums have a single head of skin and are held between the player's knees in a sitting position.[4]

The *isigubhu* is a tin drum covered with animal skin and beaten with sticks. This instrument is widely used by diviners and is also played during girls' initiation.[5]

The *equde*, a single-headed tin drum, is played by girls on the first evening of their initiation, which takes its name from the drum. This instrument is not used on any other occasion.

Rattles

Amafahlakwana are leg-rattles worn mainly by women when they dance. They are made from skin or plastic filled with small stones and sewn together. They are threaded on a long piece of string and wound around the dancer's legs.[6]

Clappers

The Ndebele use *izikeyi*, wooden clappers, to create percussion in their songs. Nowadays these instruments are more commonly known as *amaplanke*, and are made from wood.

Little is known of the Manala after the major Ndebele split, except that they had made their way to Wallmansthall in Pretoria by the 1830s. While the distinctive Manala culture gradually disappeared, the Ndzundza Ndebele culture flourished over time. It has been suggested that the reason the Ndzundza managed to retain and nurture their culture was their persecution, which forced them to unify as a form of protection. Around 1840, Chief Mabhogo became king of the Ndzundza Ndebele, who had by this time almost been entirely destroyed by the *mfecane*, the upheavals of the early 19th century. He migrated with his followers in search of a fortress where he could protect his people. They settled at a place near Roosenekal in Gauteng, then the southern Transvaal, which is today commonly known as Mapoch's Caves. From this inaccessible fortress he was able to prevent attack. Over a period of thirty years, refugees from other struggling communities joined the Ndzundza, slowly introducing aspects of their own culture. The result was a hybrid culture that retained its strong Nguni influence.

Meanwhile, the Ndzundza had clashed with the Boer settlers over territorial ownership during Mabhogo's reign. The Ndzundza were at the height of their power during this period and the Trek Boers failed to take over

their territory both in 1849 and 1863. However, in the 1880s there was a shift in power. Nyabele, the reigning Ndzundza king, allowed the Pedi leader, Mampuru, to seek refuge from the Boers at his Ndebele fortress. The Boers offered him two hundred head of cattle in exchange for handing over Mampuru, but Nyabela remained loyal to his Pedi ally. In 1882, the Boers declared war, but it took until 1883 before the Ndzundza were forced to surrender. While the Pedi chief, Mampuru, was hanged, Nyabela and other members of his family were imprisoned and many of them became slaves to the Boers. Their land was confiscated and divided among the Boers, and they became a displaced people. Many Ndebele thereafter were dispersed throughout Gauteng, living as nomads as they moved from one area to another. Some managed to find more permanent homes on farms near Pretoria, which were eventually grouped together under the North Sotho 'homeland', Lebowa.

In the 1970s, under apartheid policy, the Ndebele 'homeland' of KwaNdebele was created in Mpumalanga, then the Northern Transvaal. Many who had been living in the North Sotho 'homeland' of Lebowa either chose or were forced to move to the 'homeland' that had been assigned to them. Work was scarce in the 'homeland', and like many other groups who lived in 'homelands', the Ndebele were forced to work in Pretoria and Johannesburg. During the 1980s and the early 1990s, many Ndebele recognised the Mahlangu family as the royal family, and the capital of KwaNdebele was called KwaMahlangu. The royal family was divided, however, over economic issues and the question of 'independence' for the 'homeland'. These disputes were overridden by the dissolution of the 'homelands' in 1994. Despite the hardships they had to endure throughout the apartheid era, the Ndzundza Ndebele remain proud custodians of their cultural heritage.

Music in performance

Nguni influences

The Ndebele's Nguni heritage is evident in their music. There are many striking similarities between Ndebele and Zulu music. The music of both

Whistles, flutes and reeds

Among the Ndebele, whistles are called **ifengwana**. In the past they had two sound-holes and were made from animal bone. Nowadays they are made from plastic and have only one hole.[7]

Ndebele horns are called **impalampala**. The Ndebele used horn ensembles for big ceremonies. The horns were played by boys who were undergoing initiation. Women do not play horns; instead they play pipes, especially during their initiation period and on other special occasions. These instruments are usually made from materials such as hosepipe, bicycle tuning or PVC.

In the past, the Ndebele played flutes made from bamboo in reed-pipe ensembles (**dinaka**). According to oral tradition, they acquired the flutes from the Venda. They played on occasions of rejoicing such as weddings and beer parties, and performers were rewarded with an ox. Because they were associated with celebration, people were not allowed to play their flutes for a full month after the death of a chief or the ensemble leader.[8]

The **ipandula** is a flute that was played at the chief's kraal during the first fruits ceremony as dawn approached. The first woman to hear it cried out and the flute was silenced. Everybody woke up to start dancing and the boys played their flutes.[9]

Pipes are sometimes used as musical instruments

105

groups is characterised mainly by the widespread use of choral song. The most sacred songs of their musical repertoires have similar ritualistic significance. The warrior spirit that is so evident in Zulu male singing is equally as important among Ndebele men. In a similar manner to their Nguni neighbours, the Ndebele use praise poetry (*izibongo*) in conjunction with the male war-dance step – *giya*. Once a man's praises have been chanted, he rushes forward and performs a series of dance steps in a pantomimic warfare style. He brandishes his spear, jumps and stamps, while the surrounding women ululate and applause his prowess. When it comes to female dance, the style used by Ndebele women is markedly different to that of Zulu women. Ndebele women are renowned for the heavy beading that covers almost the entire body. The length of their legs is covered with thick leg bangles and these constrict their movements to a large degree. Ndebele women thus use very small foot movements: they sway their bodies slightly, shifting their weight from one foot to the other. More focus is placed on arm movements, and women sometimes hold small painted wooden axes (*ubhanyibane*) which they thrust forwards and backwards in front of their bodies.

Sacred songs

Some of the most important and sacred moments in Ndebele life are reflected in song.

A mother composes a personalised lullaby (*susuzela*) when her child is born.[13] This song accompanies the individual through childhood, and is performed for the last time, in the case of a girl, when she marries. When an individual enters adolescence, the songs of initiation reflect the sacredness of the institution. In ancient times, certain initiation songs were considered so powerful that it was believed that when initiates performed them they could cause rain to fall. One of the most important moments in a woman's life is when she enters the cattle byre (*isibaya senkoma*) of her bridegroom's family to perform a solemn bridal dance-song.[14] The cattle byre is the most sacred place in the homestead because it is where communication with the ancestors is most likely to occur. It is for this reason that the clan anthem is performed here during a wedding ceremony and during a ritual held to 'bring home' the spirits of the dead. Numerous songs of symbolic significance are performed at weddings. *Ukuyeyezela* is a special song sung by the bride's friends and family. As they sing and ululate, the women brush the floor with brooms – a symbolic gesture of clearing the way for the new couple. It also makes reference to the bride's domestic role and responsibilities in her new home.

In the past, the most sacred ceremony in Ndebele society was the annual first fruits celebration (*luma*).[15] In one source the writer explains, "This glorious and exuberant experience enhanced the determination and will to live."[16] The whole nation gathered at the king's home in February to celebrate Ndebele heritage and identity, and to bring in the new year. They used song and dance to rejoice and praise the king. The greatest and most sacred song performed on this occasion was both a national anthem and a royal praise song. This song belonged to the entire nation and its sheer power enabled people to cast spells through its performance: the song could bring rain, fertility for the crops, and a sense of wellbeing in the nation. People were strictly forbidden to perform it at any other time, and they believed that if they disregarded this rule they would be struck with illness or death. The big dance of the first fruits festival also involved the entire nation. Surrounded by the community, the warriors danced before the king as one by one they marched past him. *Refer to Tracks 18, 19 and 20.*

Notembi Mkhwebane, the 'queen' of Ndebele music, playing the isikumero

Bows and other string instruments

The *icaco* consists of a wooden bow, a calabash fixed near the lower end, and a string of wire. The musician strikes the string with a thick stalk of thatching grass, while moving the small opening of the calabash towards and away from her chest to vary the resonance of the sound by selecting different harmonics that are present in it. The player can stop the string with the finger, or leave it open, producing two different notes, a tone apart.[10]

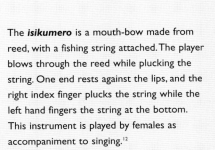

The *pone* consists of a hollow bar of bamboo fitted with a wire string and a tuning peg. A paraffin tin is attached and acts as a resonator. The instrument rests on the left shoulder of the player, and the thumb and first finger of the left hand finger the string alternately to obtain the fundamentals needed. The player holds a small hair-bow in the right hand and bows the string with varying pressure for high or low notes.[11]

The *isikumero* is a mouth-bow made from reed, with a fishing string attached. The player blows through the reed while plucking the string. One end rests against the lips, and the right index finger plucks the string while the left hand fingers the string at the bottom. This instrument is played by females as accompaniment to singing.[12]

107

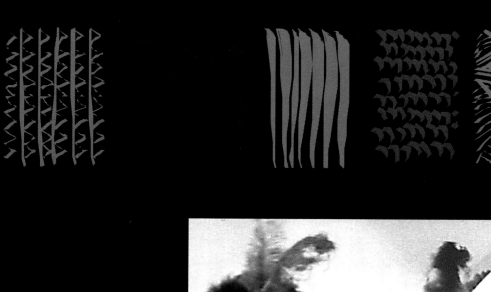

Sotho-Tswana

Basotho of Lesotho

Bapedi (Northern Basotho)

Batswana

The Sotho nation was unified under Moshoeshoe I. The great Bakoena chief offered protection and leadership to refugees who had been displaced as a result of the devastating *difaqane* raids in the early 1800s. He retreated with his followers to the mountain of Thaba Bosiu in present-day Lesotho, creating a fortress from which he prevented the annihilation of the Basotho and strengthened the nation.

The southern Sotho, otherwise known as the Basotho[1], are situated mainly in the mountainous Kingdom of Lesotho, one of South Africa's neighbouring countries. They also inhabit parts of the Eastern Cape and the Free State in South Africa.

Basotho of Lesotho

History of the Basotho

The Sotho nation is a result of the amalgamation of several clans. Their ancestors migrated south from the Transvaal to the Free State and arrived in the mountainous region of Lesotho during the 18th century.

The original inhabitants of Lesotho were the San. Through intermarriage over many years they were eventually incorporated into the Bantu peoples, among whom were the Sotho. The first Bantu-speaking people to enter the region were three Nguni groups: the Baphetla, Bapolane and Baphuti. They were soon followed by Basotho chiefdoms, the first of which, it has been suggested, were the Bafokeng who settled south-east of the Caledon River.[2]

Sotho political structures at this time were characterised by fragmentation: small clans arrived in waves, settling and then sub-dividing even further. Thus, different clans, independent of one another but sharing the land, were scattered in and around present-day Lesotho. Up until the 19th century, they lived in relative peace.[3]

At the beginning of the 19th century the peace was shattered with the *difaqane* ('the hammering'[4]). Shaka's Zulu regiments swept across the land in an attempt to expand the Zulu nation, forcing people to flee, breaking up entire groups, and leaving many homeless and desperate. The small fragmented Sesotho-speaking communities were particularly vulnerable to attack. Countless Basotho clans were destroyed, thousands were killed, and many who survived fled to the Cape colony and sought employment from white colonists. There were only a few Basotho groups that withstood the marauders and, under strong leaders, the remaining refugees were unified. One such group, the Batlokwa, lived a semi-nomadic existence during the *difaqane*, gathering people from broken communities as they moved around. Under the leadership of MaNthatisi, the group eventually established a base on two mountain fortresses near the Caledon River. The Batlokwa maintained their independence in the years to come. They were defeated in the mid-1800s by the most dominant Basotho group led by the great Moshoeshoe, and were incorporated into his kingdom, remaining near Ficksburg and also moving into the Maluti mountains.

On a larger scale, Moshoeshoe, a chief of the Bakoena clan, unified the Sotho nation by providing protection and leadership to many large groups of desperate people who had been displaced as a result of the *difaqane* raids. King Moshoeshoe managed to gain their support and established control over several groups of Sotho and Nguni people. With great skill and cunning, he used a defence strategy of withdrawing into the mountains whenever his people were under attack. He created an impregnable fortress on top of Thaba Bosiu, the 'Mountain of the Night', and this became the power base from which he was able to prevent the intrusion of invading forces. He also followed a strategy of diplomacy, settling disputes through non-aggressive means to

"Sesotho liletsa are melodic instruments whose performance is either an accompaniment to, or a substitute for, actual singing."[5]

secure peaceful relations with as many groups as possible. By 1831 Moshoeshoe was the undisputed leader of the Basotho. He had managed to fight off all enemies and had established a stable, unified nation. Over the years his reputation as one of the most powerful and brilliant African statesmen was consolidated. Many people in search of a leader were drawn to Moeshoeshoe, and his chiefdom expanded dramatically. He was remembered as a wise, enlightened man who prevented the defeat of his people. The way in which he united so many diverse groups under his leadership is regarded as "one of the most remarkable achievements of the *difaqane*."[5]

Moshoeshoe's success can be attributed to both his brilliant leadership as well as his incredible foresight. Even though he had restored a sense of peace and stability to the Sotho nation after the *difaqane*, he remained aware of potential dangers and threats to his kingdom. He had heard about the advantages of allowing missionaries to set up stations from neighbouring communities. In 1833, at Moshoeshoe's invitation, three missionaries arrived in Lesotho from the Paris Evangelical Mission and set up their first mission station at Morija. This was the start of a new relationship that was to have a profound effect on the Sotho nation. The missionaries provided protection over Moshoeshoe's land and people. In return, Moshoeshoe made some concessions by compromising some of his traditional beliefs and practices, and educating his people in the way of the colonists. He so strongly believed in incorporating British values into the culture of his people that he sent three of his own sons to be educated in Cape Town. The Basotho nation was divided in their response to the colonial presence. While some were hostile to the newcomers, others accepted their teachings and became converts.

Soon after the missionaries settled in Lesotho, another group of white people, the Boers, began arriving. Moshoeshoe foresaw danger in their presence. As they increased in number, conflict over land-ownership became more severe. The Basotho and the Boers started stealing stock from one another and the situation deteriorated. Once again, Moshoeshoe realised the urgency of aligning himself with the British colonists so that he could provide effective protection for his people. He appealed for Queen Victoria's intervention to put an end to the disputes. Between the years 1848 and 1868, Moshoeshoe struggled to gain British protection, until finally, in 1868, the Basotho were declared British subjects, and Lesotho was established as a British protectorate. In exchange, the British promised to protect Moshoeshoe and his kingdom from the onslaught of the Boers. The British lived up to their promise, helping to protect the Basotho from attack. Although they were attacked by Zulu, Matabele and Boer armies, they were never defeated. On the other hand, Sesotho culture was greatly altered by contact with missionaries, who sought to eradicate some of their traditional practices. The missionaries adopted a 'no conversion, no education' attitude. Nonetheless, in 1870 Moshoeshoe died happy in the knowledge that his people were "folded in the arms of the queen."[6]

After the death of King Moshoeshoe, divisions started to appear among the Basotho. Moshoeshoe had divided the land into three sections, one for each of his three eldest sons, Letsie, Molapo and Masupha. There was rivalry not only among the three brothers but also between Moshoeshoe's brothers and his sons. Furthermore, his sons were not as content under British rule as their father had been, and the years following Moshoeshoe's death were marked by unrest. In

1871, a year after his death, Basutoland was annexed to the Cape and a small colonial British administration set up. Moshoeshoe's three sons protested because they wanted direct rule over the kingdom. Their dissatisfaction flared up and led to the Gun War of 1880-1881, so named because of the Cape government's attempts to disarm the Basotho. The outcome was that the British government, in response to the Basotho's urgent pleas for help, transferred Basutoland from Cape rule in 1884. They set up a new administration and agreed to continue protecting the Basotho under imperial

Drums

The *moropa* drum is made out of clay or wood and the skin (usually goat-skin) is secured by means of leather strips. The player either places the drum on the ground or on her lap when playing. It is used during the girls' initiation ceremony and is played only by initiated women. Men do not play the *moropa*, but rather instead use their voices to provide the bass sounds associated with a drum.[8]

A more modern drum, the *sekupu,* is based on the European marching band or military drum. Made from a wooden or tin container, and double-headed with goat, sheep or cow hide, it is beaten with wooden sticks or rubber hoses. The drum is played at various communal functions including feasts, rituals and ceremonies.

In the mokorotlo *dance men hold knobkierrie sticks, raising and lowering them as they stamp*

114

rule. The British advised that Moshoeshoe's three divisions of the land be dissolved because they were causing inter-tribal quarrels. Letsie I, Moshoeshoe's eldest son, ruled until his death, and was succeeded in 1893 by his son, Lerotholi.

Today the Basotho still share a common allegiance to a single political authority represented by King Letsie III, the present-day monarch who was crowned in 1997. It was only in 1965 that the Basotho gained independence from their colonial rulers. The Lesotho government has never been completely financially independent of South Africa, with which it has had to maintain strong economic links, especially since the installation of the migrant labour system. The Qwa Qwa 'homeland' which borders Lesotho was created for the Basotho during apartheid. Many Sotho lived there until the South African homelands were dissolved in 1994. The Basotho people are a proud nation who work hard at restoring their days of former glory, which were marked by resilience in the face of adversity.

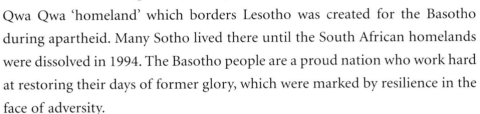

Rattles

The Basotho wear **morothlwane'** – rattles that are tied to the ankles or waist. They are made from goat-skin and are sewn into little bags containing stones or seeds. They are worn by men when performing the *mohobelo* and *ntlamo* dance, and by diviners.

Today, bells called **manyenenyene** are joined on a string and tied across the torso to provide accompaniment to dancing. They are mainly worn mainly by diviners.

A more recent ankle-rattle, the **ditjobo** is made from bottle tops that are strung together and tied around the waist, providing a percussive backing. They are used in the *litolobonya* dance.

Music in performance

The Basotho are virtually the only South African group who still play an instrument based on the Khoi *gora*.[13] This instrument is unique to South Africa – no other class of stringed-wind instrument has been found anywhere else in the world.[14] The Basotho call it the *lesiba*, meaning 'feather', after the feather attached to it. It is regarded as the Basotho's national instrument,[15] and has become a hallmark of Basotho music in the same way that the conical straw hats and blankets are characteristic of Basotho tribal dress. When tourists travel through Lesotho they are fascinated by this unique instrument and consider it a privilege to witness a *lesiba* performance. The harsh, bird-like sound the instrument produces is so well recognised among the Sotho that it is used on Lesotho radio to signal the start of the news broadcast.[16] The *lesiba* is played mostly by herdsmen and herdboys to give signals and instructions to their cattle. So important is this instrument when it comes to herding, that a herdboy without a *lesiba* is regarded as ineffective and is mocked by his friends. Herdboys believe that they are able to control the movements of their cattle by imitating bird sounds.[17] This is not an isolated example of the way the Sotho use music to control animals. According to one source, "A favourite pastime of Sotho boys is to lure field mice with song. The youths crouch on their haunches, in a circle to cut off an escape route, then lull the mice into a feeling of security with their solo-chorus singing, while other youngsters busily forage in the grass and pounce on them."[18] Sotho children have a very practical use for their bull-roarer (*sevuruvuru*), a musical instrument that protects them against dogs and animals. In many contexts, music is used as a functional tool. It is an essential part of the everyday tasks and activities that enable people to effectively fulfil their roles in society.

The gender divide

Traditional Basotho society is structured around the divide between the genders. Men and women are assigned different activities and roles in society and there is a vast difference in their lifestyles. Basotho musical practices mirror this divide. This is most evident in the style of men's and women's work-songs. These songs have developed according to the requirements of each activity. There is a strong relationship between movement (precipitated by the activity) and rhythm. Female activities, such as grinding corn, tend to involve quicker movements and their work-songs are thus generally faster, with "livelier tempos" and "irregular rhythms".[19] The movements accompanying male activities, such as stretching cow hides, are generally slower and thus their work songs have slower tempos with more-regular rhythms. Men and women also approach their music differently, according to their roles in society, and musical expression is used for diverse purposes. Many male musical performances serve to affirm the male identity and the qualities of masculinity that are admired in Basotho men. In song, masculinity is embodied in a deep, low vocal: "The songs of the men are characterised by their deep bass setting, the Sotho ear loving a deep bass sound which he compares to the sound of thunder before the rain."[20] However, in their music, women are less concerned with flaunting their feminine qualities, and are more focused on creating a sense of group solidarity. They use music to express themselves and transport their experiences from the realm of the personal to the collective. *Refer to Track 22.*

Male performances

Mokorotlo: *a war dance or 'riding' dance*

The two best-known male dance-songs exclusive to the Sotho are the *mokorotlo* and the *mohobelo*. *Mokorotlo* are dance-songs that reinforce male identity.[21] The word *mokorotlo* is derived from the verb *ho korotla* meaning 'to grumble in a low growling voice'.[22] The deep-throated choral voices beneath the high-pitched voice of the song leader complement the dance movements that capture the spirit of the song. The men, usually dressed in black trousers and white shoes, or in full war attire, dance in an L-shaped line.[23] They hold knobkierries, raising them and then bringing them down to the level of the body as they stamp to the rhythm of the song.[24] Their movements are slow, and they often simulate the actions of war as if in slow motion.[25] Women are usually present to ululate and clap, which encourages the men and enhances their bravado. The underlying poetic impulse in Sotho music is embodied in the praise poetry (*dithoko*) interspersed throughout *mokorotlo* performances. The Sesotho language lends itself to poetry, and there is a strong link between poetry and song in Sesotho culture.[26] Poetic forms, such as assonance and alliteration are a notable characteristic of Sesotho oratory. Eloquence (*bokheleke*) is highly valued in this culture, and people who display this quality are respected for their skill. Song leaders use elevated language with poetic imagery, in combination with stylised performance techniques.[27]

The praise poet, donning the conical Basotho grass hat (*modianyewe*) and extemporising with verbal finesse, is a stately figure. Strictly speaking, praise poetry (*dithoko*) is not a musical form, but is interwoven in most Sesotho songs, and is thus an important aspect of Sesotho music. The following account provides a good description of Sesotho praise poetry:

Bull-roarers

Basotho children have a very practical use for their ***sevuruvuru***. Playing it is believed to provide protection against dogs and animals.

117

The dance leader, Pamudze Chifa of the Consolidated Main Reef team, using a typical mohobelo gesture

In this movement the performers dance without their knobkierries so that they can use their hands.
The whistle around the leader's neck is used to signal to the dancers

"During the early part of our sojourn among them (the Sotho), we often heard them recite, with very dramatic gestures, certain pieces, which were not easy of comprehension, and which appeared to be distinguished from the ordinary discourse, by the elevation of the sentiment, powerful ellipses, daring metaphors, and very accentuated rhythm. The natives called these recitations praises. We soon discovered that they were real poetical effusions, inspired by the emotions of war or of the chase. The hero of the piece is almost always the author of it. On his return from war … his friends surround him, and beg him to relate his exploits. He recounts them in a high-flown manner. He is carried away by the ardour of his feelings, and his expressions become poetical."[28]

When the performer praises himself in the middle of a *mokorotlo* performance, he breaks away from the group of men and mimics the action of rushing towards an imaginary enemy with a knobkierrie or a stick. *Mokorotlo* might be classified as war songs, as their primary function in the past was to instil feelings of courage in men about to go to war. Today *mokorotlo* are performed on important occasions such as initiation ceremonies, national festivals and the king's birthday. *Refer to Track 23.*

Mohobelo: a 'striding' dance

Like *mokorotlo, mohobelo* dance-songs are performed exclusively by males, and much emphasis is placed on male virility.[29] Apart from providing entertainment, they also hold a sacred dimension. In the past they were performed as part of the rain ceremony (*molutsoane*) and at feasts. In both contexts these songs were imbued with spiritual significance because the ancestor spirits were evoked. They were also performed during communal work parties, which were arranged by the chief so that men in the community could come together to work on his land. In this context, these songs were functional because they set a consistent pace for the work. They were used to unify the work force, uplifting and energising the workers. It was not unusual to see a man become carried away during the dance, breaking out of the group of workers to perform a solo, leaping and kicking. His fellow workers cheered

Whistles, flutes and reeds

The *lekodilo* end-blown harmonic flute is made of reed and is open at both ends. The player changes the pitch by using his index finger to open and close the one hole, thus selecting either the odd- or the even-numbered harmonics of the fundamental pitch of the flute, and also by changing the force of his the breath to choose high or low notes. Herd boys made these instruments just before they were promoted from herding sheep and goats to herding cattle.

and egged him on, and when women were present, they showed their approval by ululating. According to one source, such a display of enthusiasm was witnessed by a visiting bishop, who, "when seeing the man, tearing across the land among young plants in this frantic fashion, and at intervals making certain movements like those of a proud peacock; thought the man had suddenly become insane and the women were grievously lamenting and mourning for him."[30] When the migrant-labour system was introduced, *mohobelo* was used in competitions on the mines, and nowadays is performed at national festivals as a celebration of Sotho identity.

The word *mohobelo* is derived from the verb *hoba*, meaning 'to hum, to make a noise'.[31] In addition to humming, performers also hiss, this being one of the distinguishing characteristics of Sotho song. Hissing is said to coordinate the dancers' movements and help them heighten their focus.[32] One of the most interesting aspects of the *mohobelo* is the way in which, unlike in most other Sotho songs, the role of the singer and the dancer is divided. The singers sit or stand behind the dancers, who are arranged in lines. The dance leader uses a whistle and/or gestures to initiate the moves of the dance. The *mohobelo* is commonly known as the 'striding dance' because of its characteristic striding and leaping movements. Dancers dramatically raise their legs to their chests, and then emphatically reach forward and stamp their feet to the ground to draw attention to their strength; they leap and twist through the air, showing off their agility, and simulate the gestures of attack during war, affirming their power. The *ntlamo* dance, with its emphasis on the downward stamp, is regarded as the modern equivalent of the *mohobelo*. This dance originates from the Nguni people, and hence *ntlamo* dancers often wear Nguni dance costumes. As with the *mokorotlo* and *mohobelo* dances, warfare actions are simulated and the dance consists mainly of high-leg stamp actions. *Refer to Track 24.*

Female performances

Mokhibo: *the 'knee' dance*

If *mokorotlo* and *mohobelo* are the two most popular male dance-songs, *mokhibo* is the most popular female dance-song.[33] Whereas Sesotho male songs emphasise the desirable qualities of masculinity, female songs emphasise the core characteristics of the female in her domestic environment. The *mokhibo* dance stylises movements from women's work activities, representing women's domestic roles. The word *mokhibo* is derived from the verb *ho khiba*, meaning 'to perform actions with the shoulders while kneeling'.[34] Sotho women often kneel when working, and it is not unlikely that the *mokhibo* dance-song originated while women worked in this kneeling position. This dance formation is not seen among any of the other South African peoples, who perform their dance-songs in a standing position. The women arrange themselves in lines, with the singers standing in a row behind the kneeling dancers. A leader cues the dance moves and chorus, as in the males' *mokhibo* dance. The dance starts with the women kneeling, hands placed on hips. The leader blows her whistle to indicate the start of the dance. As the tempo gets faster it builds to a climax, and it usually ends "with a whoop, body erect (but still kneeling) and arms flung upwards, fully extended."[35]

There are four main dance moves that are repeated in varying patterns during the dance. The women stretch their necks, pushing their faces forward in time with the music. They also move their heads from side to side. They shrug and rotate their shoulders, and finally, wave their arms from side to side. They also knock their knees against the floor to create percussion. Dancers sometimes move around, rotating positions and then returning to their original positions. These moves can all be performed from a more upright kneeling position. On their knees, moving in unison with short lengths of wood in their hands, and dressed in colourful costumes, the image of the *mokhibo* dancers is striking. Nowadays *mokhibo* is performed mainly at competitions or national events. *Refer to Track 25.*

The ***lekhitlane*** is a whistle made from the horns of a female blesbok. The large opening serves as an embouchure and a finger-hole is bored into the bottom of the narrow end so that two notes can be played. The instrument was traditionally used at midnight during the male circumcision dance.

Ditolobonya: *a shaking dance*

Where *mokhibo* was once an important musical feature at a special feast held in celebration of a baby's birth, it has largely been replaced by a more modern dance-song, *ditolobonya*.[36] This dance-song is performed exclusively by women of child-bearing age who have given birth to at least one child. The word *ditolobonya* refers to the backward thrusting of the buttocks, and some assert that this movement, along with other suggestive abdominal movements, is used to imitate the sexual act. In comparison to the older *mokhibo* dance, the dancers use a sexual motif more explicitly in the *ditolobonya*. This performance is a private women's affair and excludes men. As with many other modern Basotho performances, the *sekupu* drum is used to accompany the dance. The women wear waist-rattles (*ditjobo*) which enhance the rhythm of the song.

Children's performances

Moqoqopelo *and* mothonthonyane

While the three most distinctive Basotho adult dance-songs, *mokorotlo*, *mokhibo* and *mohobelo*, are still performed today, although not necessarily

Children dancing

in their original contexts, the traditional dances performed by children are rarely seen. Children's dance-songs in their original form were done away with when the missionaries took control of children's activities. These dance-songs were often performed at night, and the missionaries associated them with sexually inappropriate behaviour and therefore attempted to curb them.[37] The traditional children's dances were commonly known as *metjeko*[38], a term which is derived from the verb *ho tjeka*, meaning 'to turn, to dance'.[39] Boys and girls grouped themselves in lines on opposite sides and danced towards each other. The dance consisted of "a jerky step, the dancers either dancing independently or holding hands."[40] Other traditional children's dances include the *moqoqopelo* and *mothonthonyane*[41] which are performed by girls, but which have largely been replaced by modern dances.[42] The word *moqoqopelo* stems from the verb *qoqopa* meaning 'to vibrate',[43] which is the defining feature of the dance. The girls stand in a circle around two or more dancers. Unlike in other Sotho dances that have fixed dance moves, the dancers use individual styles, displaying their flair. The chorus consists of spontaneous exclamations that run beneath the leader's song line. The *mothonthonyane* dance is similar to *moqoqopela*. The same circle formation is held, with the leader and chorus, call-and-response format. The term *mothonthonyane* is derived from the word *thonthonya*, meaning 'little vibrations'.[44] These 'little vibrations' capture the thematic content of the songs. The girls usually sing about things in community life that occupy the thoughts of most young girls: love, romance and community gossip!

Dipina tsa mokopu: *pumpkin songs*

Another set of traditional dance-songs that have largely been replaced by modern dance-songs are girls' 'pumpkin songs' (*dipina tsa mokopu*).[45] These songs were sung by girls during autumn when food was abundant in the village. The songs celebrated fertility, and teenage girls sometimes sang these as a symbolic gesture to appeal to the ancestors to help them conceive. In a spirit not dissimilar to that of Western children trick-or-treating on Halloween – knocking on neighbours' doors in the hope of receiving sweets – Basotho girls travelled to different villages and sung their repertoire of pumpkin songs in the hope that they would receive pumpkins. They danced in a circle or semi-circle, repeating dance moves that were synchronised by the whistle of the dance leader. Traditional songs like the autumn pumpkin songs, *mothonthonyane* and *moqoqopelo*, were eventually replaced by European step dances and a modern dance style called *monyanyako*, which is performed by schoolchildren. However, the

Bows and other string instruments

Bows are the basis for many Sotho songs (*liletse*).

The *lekope* is a mouth-resonated bow made from a straight, hollow river-reed and twisted sinew, hair or fibre. One end of the stick is held against the mouth and the other end is held in the left hand. The player plucks the string with the finger or a plectrum, and uses the thumb of the other hand to finger the string towards the bottom. This instrument is played mainly by older women for personal amusement for personal amusement. *Lekope* songs are often based on *mohobelo*, *mokhibo* or *lesiba* songs. The performer sometimes dances a solo dance called *saku* as she plays.[10]

older dances are still performed at national occasions that showcase Basotho identity, as well as in rural areas where children do not attend school.

Initiation

The continued performance of traditional song repertoires depends largely on the extent to which people uphold traditional practices. The current political, social and religious climate partly determines whether people still undergo traditional ceremonies such as initiation. The disapproval of the missionaries and their endeavour to spread Christianity led to a decline in attendance of initiation schools by the Basotho from the late 19th century.[46] In the mid-20th century, however, the number of people attending initiation schools increased owing to the growth of Basotho nationalist sentiment.[47] A standard repertoire of traditional songs is sung during initiation and is central to its existence. The

At their graduation male initiates wear colourful blankets and bright beading around their necks

continued practice of initiation thus prevents these songs from falling into extinction. Every time an initiation ceremony is performed, the importance of these songs is reaffirmed. Many of the initiation songs, while retaining their traditional styles, have also absorbed modern influences, and refer to modern subject matter.[48]

Lebollo: *male initiation*

During initiation (*lebollo*), males learn the values of their culture by being taught *dikoma* songs from the highly secret *koma* teachings.[49] These are imparted by mentors, who are usually older initiated males. There are normally two or three mentors per school, but in some Basotho clans, each boy is attended by his own mentor. The mentor (*mobineli* – 'the one who sings for him'),[50] is responsible for teaching the *dikoma* songs to the initiate. The secret nature of these songs restricts their performance to the private ceremony where only the initiates are present. *Dikoma* songs are chanted slowly in a low-pitched voice and they are not accompanied by dance. The leader composes the song with the chorus supporting him, and through this performance, reinforces his new adult identity. *Dikoma* songs not only teach important values to the initiates, but also educate them about the history of Basotho culture. While the initiates are undergoing the pain of circumcision they sing *mokorotlo* songs to reinforce their masculinity and to appeal to the ancestors for strength and courage. Their cries are drowned out by the sheer power and volume of this traditional war song.

When their initiation is completed, the boys sing *mangae* songs in public. These bear a close resemblance to *dikoma* songs. The word *mangae* is derived from the verb *ho ngae* which means 'to cry out or howl'.[51] The boys use song to 'cry out' or plead to the ancestors for guidance. *Mangae* songs include content about the experiences within or outside of the lodge. They give the individual the opportunity to express his thoughts and feelings, which is an attribute the institution promotes and encourages. The subject matter of *mangae* songs ranges from the personal to the topical. Contemporary concerns are reflected in both the examples below. The first song is an expression of emotion.

The *mokhope* is an unbraced, curved wooden bow, struck with a thin stick or grass stem and played by women. The string, often made from wire, is stopped with the finger, and the mouth is used as a resonator.

125

The singer expresses his pain over the death of his father, and reprimands Adam and Eve for allowing the tragedy to happen.

Ntate of timetse tsepeng, tsa makhooa	My father died at the gold mines of the white men,
Ntate of timetse tsepeng, tsa makhooa	My father died at the gold mines of the white men
Rangoane, Adama, uena Eva	Uncle Adam, you Eve
Ntate of timetse tsepeng, tsa makhooa	My father died at the gold mines of the white men.[52]

The second song is more light-hearted:

Ke toeota, ke toeota,	It's a Toyota, it's a Toyota,
ke toeota, koloi ena	It's a Toyota, this car
Koloi e tsoeu, mabili a matso	It is white, the tyres are black
Ke toeota, ke toeota banna	It's a Toyota, it's a Toyota, men.
Ke toeota, ke toeota,	It's a Toyota, it's a Toyota,
ke toeota, koloi ena	It's a Toyota, this car
Ke ela e potela ka hará motse	There it disappears into the village
Ke toeota, ke toeota banna	It's a Toyoto, it's a Toyota, men.[53]

The initiation school culminates in the graduation ceremony, where the boys' ceremonial dress matches the weight of the occasion. Wearing bright blankets adorned with striking objects such as safety pins and mirrors, as well as heavy beading around their necks, they are called up one by one. Each initiate recites praise poetry (dithoko – an artform that he is taught at initiation school) on the acknowledgement of his achievement. Dithoko can include self-praise, recitation of family histories, important occurrences in history and chiefs' names. Given the emphasis on poetic skill and eloquence in Sotho culture, the performance of praise poetry at the graduation ceremony symbolises the boys' entry into the adult world. The most talented boys also sing *mangae* songs at this ceremony, often moving the community, their audience on this occasion, to tears:

> *"The onlookers follow these songs and choruses with keen interest and applaud at the end of each. Many of them are witty, some salacious, and a few beautiful and moving. At the end of a good recital people may be seen wiping tears from their eyes and, as often as not, the parents and friends of the boy concerned, overcome with pride and emotion, weep unashamedly."*[54]

Lebollo: *female initiation*

The majority of female initiation songs are dance-songs and their focus is more on entertainment than the male initiation songs.[55] Consequently, they are of a much faster tempo than male songs. The performances of female initiates also differ from their male counterparts because they do not include self-praise. Whereas men use their voices to provide the bass sounds associated with a drum, women use the *moropa* drum to create the bass of the song. An interesting aspect of some of the music performed during female initiation is that it parodies male behaviour. By enacting male identities, the female initiates signal the identity-shift they are undergoing. Some of their songs reflect this parody, and the girls imitate male styles of singing, such as the *mokorotlo*. They use low-pitched tones, crouching in a tight circle so that the sound is more

Woman playing the thomo

The **thomo**[11] gourd-bow has a calabash attached to the bow-stick near the bottom end. The bow is made from mountain bamboo and the unbraced string is made of twisted horse hair. The player usually sits, and holding the instrument upright in the left hand, strikes the string with a thin reed or grass. The player produces two fundamental notes by fingering the string with the forefinger and thumb of the left hand. The sound is modulated by slightly moving the resonator towards and away from the chest. The *thomo* is played by both men and women. According to one source, Moshoeshoe I composed songs that were accompanied by this instrument.[12]

127

audible to all present. These songs, much slower in tempo, stand in sharp contrast to the female songs, which are much faster.

Female initiation is divided into distinct phases, and the songs reflect the lessons the initiates learn in each phase and the experiences they have undergone. During the first phase the girls hide in the veld and are instructed in the secret *koma* teachings through the medium of *mangae* songs. These songs reinforce the importance of discipline and prepare the initiates for life's hardships. The girls crouch in a small circle and sing in a low pitch in imitation of male voices. In the next phase the girls perform dance-songs that relate to their experiences during initiation. They form a circle around two girls dancing in the centre, clapping their hands or beating them against their cow-hide or sheepskin skirts, which are pulled tight as they bend their knees. Dance-songs called *dipina tsa tantsi* are usually performed during leisure time. The dancers move into an arc with a few individuals standing in the centre. They move their shoulders and necks forwards and backwards while singing in chorus and beating their hands on their thighs or skirts.

An all-night feast is held at the end of this phase, during which the *thojane* ritual is enacted. The girls have to perform very strenuous physical tests to prove their ability to endure hardship. Their limbs are smeared with two different-coloured ochres, and the challenge is for them to stand or sit in one position for a length of time without letting the two colours smudge.

Diviner holding the sekupu *drum*

The dance-songs accompanying this ritual are often performed by men, and are accompanied by the *moropa* drum. Many of the songs used during initiation are performed to educate the girls. The *thojane* song imparts the message that without a disciplined lifestyle, females are as sinful as males:

Mamela, oee!	Oh listen!
Sefebe ke mosali	Prostitute is a woman
Mamela, oee!	Oh listen!
Sefebe ke monna	Prostitute is a man
Le mosali o joala	and the woman, also, even is
O n'a latolele monna ke'ng?	Why did she not deny the rights?[56]

In the last phase of initiation a feast is held, and the girls are re-welcomed into the community as adults. The final coming-out ceremony (*litsoejane*) is marked by a colourful, festive parade at which a slow dance called *ho tebuka* is performed.[57]

Divination

During healing ceremonies, music is used as a therapeutic tool in addition to other curing rituals.[58] Traditional healers and diviners (*matwela*) combine Nguni and Sotho healing styles in their practice.[59] When an individual is 'called' to this vocation, she (*matwela* are usually female) shows physical and mental symptoms of illness, which are believed to be sent by the ancestors. The curing rituals are always accompanied by singing and drumming. The apprentice is guided by a fully fledged diviner. The *sekupu* drum is beaten by anyone who is skilled on the instrument and the dancers respond to the drumbeats with jerky, frenetic movements. The presence of the ancestors (*balimo*) is evoked by playing the *sekupu* drum. It is believed that the ancestors communicate with the apprentice, telling her which cow to sacrifice and use for the drum-skin. Traditional healers use the *sekupu* drum, believing that the

The **sekatari** ('guitar') consists of a tube of bamboo fitted with a wire string and a tuning peg. The string is struck with a miniature bow made of wood, and hair from a cow's tail. Resin is applied in order to enhance the friction needed for bowing. The mouth was originally used as a resonator but it was replaced by the one-gallon paraffin tin. The player holds the bow with his left hand, fingering the string with his right thumb.

This instrument is often accompanied by singing and is mainly used mainly by herdboys for personal amusement.

sound of the drumbeat is therapeutic. If somebody is troubled by physical ailments, movement to the beat of the drum is believed to alleviate discomfort. The drum is used every morning and evening to pray to the ancestors, and as an expression of gratitude for their protection and guidance.

The songs performed during a diviner's initiation focus on prayers to the ancestors, as well as expressions of the initiate's mental and physical state. During the apprenticeship period, the initiate also learns a dance that is used in healing ceremonies. Dancing is part of a group-therapy session called *hlophe*, where movement and music lead to an altered state of consciousness. Furthermore, dancing is in itself 'physiological therapy':[60] it helps to alleviate physical body aches and pains. Another healing property of dance is rhythm. The dancers wear *meruthloane* rattles and *manyenyane* bells on their bodies to add textures to the music's rhythm and to heighten the impact of the music. One ethnomusicologist explained why rhythm is healing:

> *"… rhythm in music … is one of the important elements that, once set in motion and maintained, vibrates back into the correct order the part of the body that might have been losing or had lost its normal rhythmic order."*[61]

When an initiate finishes the apprenticeship, an elaborate closing ceremony takes place, so that the final ritual can be performed. The songs used on this occasion are regarded as prayers to the ancestors for the recovery of the apprentice.

Siya ba thandazela,	We shall pray for them
Ao siya ba thandazela.	We shall pray for them
O balimo ba rona,	Oh our ancestors
O beng ba lefehlo,	The ones who prepared the *lefehlo*
Siya ba thandazela.	We shall pray for them
Re kopa masedi le mahlohonolo,	We ask for guidance and blessings
Balimo ba rona.	Our ancestors
O balimo bo nkhono,	Our ancestors, our great grandmothers
Oh khomo shoe, motho o phele.	Let the cow die to restore human life.[62]
Refer to Track 26.	

A cow is slaughtered as a sacrifice to the spirits, while song-prayers are chanted. In this song, the singers respect and awe for their ancestors is evident.

Emergent music

Setapo: *the step dance*

Traditional Sotho dance-songs exerted a major influence on the modern musical styles developed at schools by the missionaries. These modern forms of music are hybrid dance-songs that blend traditional Sotho and European styles.[63] A popular dance enthusiastically adopted by the Sotho was the European step dance (*setapo*).[64] During the 19th century, migrant workers who had been exposed to this dance on the mines and farms incorporated it into Sotho culture. School children were introduced to this dance style, and it started to replace their traditional dances. In the step dance, the girls and boys perform steps in unison. Singing with two or more leader lines (*sephokoli*) and chorus lines (*libini*) overlapping, performers play a mixture of European and Sotho instruments. The male, adult version of this dance is the *diphotha*, which developed directly from the step dance. The men wear gumboots, and as in the Nguni prototype, the Zulu gumboot dance, knock their legs together, slapping them with their hands. The *diphotha* is accompanied by the concertina, a European instrument adopted by the Sotho.

Monyanyako

Monyanyako, another modern style that combines a variety of influences, emerged in Lesotho between the 1950s and 1960s.[65] The early forms of this song style originated in the mission stations in the Cape and Natal regions, and were eventually transported to Lesotho. The style developed within the context of choral competitions and concerts organised by schools. 'Action songs' and 'sounds' were the two most popular musical styles, and were the predecessors of *monyanyako*.[66] Literally translated, *monyanyako* means 'to arrange well',[67] which refers to "the organised actions and uniform appearance of the singers/dancers."[68] The blend of Sotho traditional musical styles and modern, European styles is evident in *monyanyako*. These dance-

The **setolotolo** is a braced, mouth-resonated bow made out of bamboo and cow- or horsehair or wire string that is tied back at the centre of the bamboo, dividing the string into two segments. With one end between the player's lips, the instrument is held in a horizontal position with the left hand, and is plucked with the fingers of the right hand on either segment of the string. This bow is played only by men and is generally used for entertainment when travelling.

Man playing the setolotolo

133

The lesiba *is regarded as the Basothos' national instrument*

songs were influenced by the Christian hymns introduced to Sotho culture by the missionaries, and consist of four parts, unlike traditional Sesotho songs. However, the traditional call-and-response style is used, with the choir divided into a leader and chorus part. Like traditional Sotho songs, the texts are generally short and repetitive. A conductor figure, borrowed from the European tradition, leads the choir, but also often leads the songs and performs solo "acrobatic leaps and dances,"[69] as a traditional Sotho song leader would. *Monyanyako* are sung mainly by children and have largely replaced their traditional repertoire sung during leisure time. They are often performed at song-feasts (*mokete oa lipina*) where choir groups perform in a public place and charge a small entrance fee. The audience bids to hear a certain song and the choir performs accordingly. Audience members sometimes attempt to outbid one another, and the result is a jovial, rowdy entertainment session.

Difela

Difela were developed by migrant workers.[70] These songs were composed and sung as the migrant labourers travelled to and from the South African mines. Unlike the majority of Sotho songs (*dipina*), which consist of a call-and-response structure, *difela* were male, unaccompanied solos. They were influenced by various aspects of male-initiation music such as praise poetry (*dithoko*), and they blended poetry and song. Among the Sotho, poetry is a tool of self-empowerment. The use of self-praise helped to construct male identity outside of and despite the degradation of migrant labour. One ethnomusicologist coined the term 'word-music' to describe this style. He states that "migrant men and women respond to their situation with complexly evocative word-music, creating a cultural shield against dependency, expropriation, and the dehumanising relations of race and class in southern Africa."[71]

Migrant workers who spent many hours travelling by foot developed their poetic skills and were known for their eloquence, often being referred to as *dikheleke* ('the eloquent ones'). These songs were originally sung while walking to work, but they are now performed in a stationary position. The poetic nature of the Sotho language was exploited to its full, and the texts of

Stringed-wind

So widespread is the *lesiba* in Lesotho, the equivalent of the Khoi *gora*, that it is regarded as the Sotho's national instrument, typically associated with herdsmen. (see Chapter 10, page 237).
Refer to Track 21.

these songs drew strongly on metaphor and symbolism. When the migrant-labour system was in place, the song texts usually centred on the migrant-labour experience and the theme of travel. They presented a commentary on the living conditions of the labourers and provided an outlet for men to express their longing for home. Through self-praise the performer was also able to articulate his origins and his history. Using this form of 'poetic autobiography', he was able to articulate his origins and history, and assert his

identity.[72] Like many of the other Sotho song styles, *difela* were often used competitively among men. Women who lived in urban areas also eventually started performing *difela*. They used these songs to communicate and share their experiences in urban South Africa. Whereas males did not use instruments in their *difela*, women sang to the accompaniment of the accordion and the typical Basotho home-made drum.

Famo

Another very popular song form in Lesotho is *famo*. It also developed when the migrant-labour system came into being. These songs are strongly influenced by the Sotho songs of the *setolotolo* bow. Men on their way to work would play the instrument to the rhythm of their walking. The solo voice of the singer produced the equivalent of the leader section, while the bow produced the chorus section. The musician thus alternated between the vocal and instrumental parts. When European instruments became more easily available, the concertina (*korosetina*) and accordion (*koriana*) replaced the *setolotolo* bow. The concertina was popular because it was light and easy to carry, and it also allowed the performer to sing and play the instrument at the same time. This instrument was also played in the shebeens of the mines, but the accordion was eventually preferred as it created a bigger sound which was more suited to dancing. *Famo* songs thus emerged "out of the blend of self-accompanied walking songs and the dance music provided by the accordion."[73] The term *famo* was coined from a particular type of dance that women performed at the shebeens. Women also started relocating to urban areas in search of work. They spent a lot of time in shebeens entertaining men by dancing. They danced suggestively, thrusting their bodies forward and lifting their skirts to the men. These dances became known as *famo*, derived from the term *ho re famo*, meaning to 'open nostrils or to raise garments'.[74] The dances were accompanied by the organ or the accordion, and the participants, both men and women, sang over the instrumental backing. Female *famo* singers used ululations as part of their performance, and much like the male *famo* songs, their lyrics related mainly to urban life. Women also challenged men through their songs, often resulting in a style that was "declamatory, aggressive and bluntly humorous."[75]

The ancestors of the Bapedi, also known as the Northern Basotho, broke away from the Bakgatla clan of Botswana during the 16th century, settling in what became the north-central Transvaal.

The Bapedi empire was later established in the Limpopo Province, after a powerful leader split from the original group.

Bapedi (Northern Basotho)

History of the Bapedi

The Bapedi descended from the Maroteng, a small offshoot of the Bakgatla of Botswana.[1] Around the 16th century, the Bakgatla fragmented and the Maroteng, led by Chief Tabane, migrated to present-day Schilpadfontein in Pretoria. Tabane was eventually succeeded by his grandson Motsha, whose youngest wife gave birth to a son. Some say that he was named 'Lellelateng' ('It cries inside') because Motsha's other wives claimed to have heard him crying inside the womb, which was interpreted as a bad omen. In order to prevent both child and mother from being killed, Thobela, Motsha's successor, took the mother and child with him when he broke away with a large following and founded the Bapedi nation. They settled near Steelpoort in approximately 1650.

When the Bapedi arrived in the Limpopo Province, it was already occupied by various peoples of different origins. From around 1780 to 1820, the Bapedi's power was at its zenith under the leadership of the great Chief Thulare. He built an empire by extending their territory, and conquering surrounding groups to bring them under Maroteng paramountcy. Thulare died in 1824 and was succeeded by his eldest son, Malekutu. Two years later, the Bapedi were invaded by the Matabele, led by Mzilikazi. After the recent death of their great leader, the Bapedi were ill-equipped for attack, and the damage was severe. The invaders burned the land, plundered the cattle and killed a number of Thulare's sons. Thulare's eldest surviving son, Sekwati, fled north with the remaining Bapedi survivors and took refuge amongst the Ramapulana, a neighbouring chiefdom. After four years of living in exile, Sekwati and his people returned to their land and settled at Phiring in 1828. Sekwati slowly started re-establishing Bapedi dominance by reinstating himself as paramount, forging new alliances and warding off attacks.

Around 1837, the first Voortrekkers arrived and in 1845 they were followed by a second group under the leadership of Hendrik Potgieter. Their entry into Bapedi land marked the beginning of an ongoing conflict between the two groups. Potgieter founded Ohrigstad and signed a treaty granting Sekwati the rights to this piece of land. The treaty was, however, ineffective because there were increasing accusations of stock theft and land encroachment, and the relationship between the Boers and the Bapedi quickly deteriorated. In an attempt to remove the Bapedi, the Boers attacked them in 1847 and 1852. Even though these attempts were unsuccessful, Sekwati, feeling threatened, moved to Thaba Mosego (Mosego Hill) in 1853 to the village of Dsjate. In 1857, a peace treaty between the Bapedi and the Boers was signed. The agreement fixed the Steelpoort River as the eastern boundary of Bopedi, the traditional territory of the Bapedi, and peace reigned for several years. So respected was Sekwati at this time that many people flocked to live under his rule. The chief spent his final days at Thaba Mosego, and died there in 1861.

"Nearly every Bapedi village possesses a drum and flute ensemble of 12 to 30 players which can be hired to entertain."[2]

Drums

The *moropa* drum has a wide upper end that narrows at the base. In its traditional form, the body of the drum is made from the trunk of a morula tree. The head is made from kudu, ox- or antbear-skin, and is pegged to the resonator. The instrument comes in different sizes, and is usually played in groups of four, which compose a full set. The drum is made by men but is usually played by women. It is held under the left arm or placed on the ground. The player squats and strikes the drum head with the fingertips, producing a sharp, staccato sound. The pitch of the drum is altered by applying varying pressures to the skin. In some areas, the women stand with the drum grasped between their legs, and beat the drum head in this position. *Meropa* (plural) drums are used in many contexts, and accompany most singing and dancing. Two ceremonial occasions on which they are played are girls' initiation ceremonies and exorcism rituals. The only time that men played this drum in the past was on the mines. They also occasionally played the drum during boys' initiation ceremonies.[3]

Traditional *meropa* drums are not manufactured as regularly as in the past. Those that still exist usually belong to chiefs, and are treated as sacred objects. Nowadays, modern versions of the drum made from tins are often used. These are sometimes beaten with sticks or pieces of rubber tubing. They are sometimes referred to as *kiba* (named after the dance they most often accompany).

One way of playing the moropa *drum is holding it under the left arm and beating it with the right hand*

Sekwati was succeeded by his son, Sekhukhune, but not without some rivalry from Sekhukhune's younger brother, Mampuru. Sekhukhune eventually established his legitimacy as heir through his military superiority, and Mampuru went into exile with his royal followers, thus dividing the Bapedi people. Over time many fled from Sekhukhune, who had a reputation as a cruel man and was not respected by his people. At this time, Sekhukhune's

A group of women playing a variety of instruments

followers also became divided over the presence and activities of the first missionaries. Sekhukhune initially accepted the missionaries and their influence, but his tolerance diminished as members of his own family started converting to Christianity. He felt that his authority was being undermined and started meting out severe punishment to converts.

At first, Sekhukhune's relationship with the Boers was amicable, and he hoped to strengthen his position by aligning himself with them. However, after the first few years of his rule, land and labour disputes intensified and the relationship deteriorated. The tension came to a head when the Boers declared war on the Bapedi in 1876 after hearing rumours of an impending Pedi attack. The battle continued for several months and there was no decisive victory. Finally, in 1877, Britain intervened and a peace treaty was signed between the two parties. Two months later the British annexed the Transvaal. The British demanded that Sekhukhune recognise the sovereignty of the British crown and fined him for his actions. When he refused these terms, the Bapedi were attacked, and were finally defeated in 1879. Sekhukhune was imprisoned and Mampuru, his rival, was installed as paramount chief. When the former chief was released from prison in 1881, Mampuru arranged his assassination. The Transvaal government captured him and he was hanged for murder. The Bapedi had lost their independence and have since been divided.

The **ntshomane** resembles a European tambourine and is usually about the size of a dinner plate. The hoop is made from pliable wood, and the skin, pegged to the hoop, is usually goat hide. The player holds the drum in one hand and strikes the skin with the palm, fingers, or a stick held in the other. This instrument is used in exorcism rituals.

The **moshupiane** is a friction drum in the shape of a bowl.[4] The resonator is generally made of wood and the head is made of goat-skin. This drum is made and played in secret by initiated older women during the girls' initiation ceremony. The player holds the instrument under her left arm. She sounds the drum by rubbing the head anti-clockwise with the cut ends of a bundle of corn stalks that have been tied together and wetted for the performance. When played, the *moshupiane* emits a screaming noise. Similar drums are used by the Xhosa and Zulu, as well as in western Zambia and Angola. It was introduced to Brazil via the slave trade, where it now features as the well-known *cuica*.

Music in performance

Social music: from daytime to night time

From the moment the inhabitants of a Bapedi village awake to a new day, men, women and children move off in different directions to begin their daytime activities.[15] The work each social group performs is dictated by the seasons and the weather. One might find men ploughing and hoeing the fields, women attending to household duties such as washing clothes in the river, and young boys herding goats or milking cows. All these activities are accompanied by music, which makes the long hours of work pass quickly. The singing follows the natural rhythm of the activity at hand. Men's working songs usually consist of simple melodies with only four or five notes. Someone initiates the song, thereby taking on the role of leader, and the other men respond with a chorus line. As women wash their clothes, it is not unusual for someone to step out of the group huddled by the river to play a short melody on a portable solo instrument such as the *setolotolo* or *dipela*. The music of these instruments creates a soothing background to the rhythmical scrubbing and rinsing. Herdboys blow their herding flutes as the sun sets to drive the herds back to the kraal. The landscape echoes with the music of their pipes as people slowly start making their way back to their respective kraals.

During the early evening members of the community gather around fires. After a long day's work, they spend their leisure hours singing. Adults of both sexes attend beer-drink parties, which usually take place

The player uses both hands to pluck the dipela

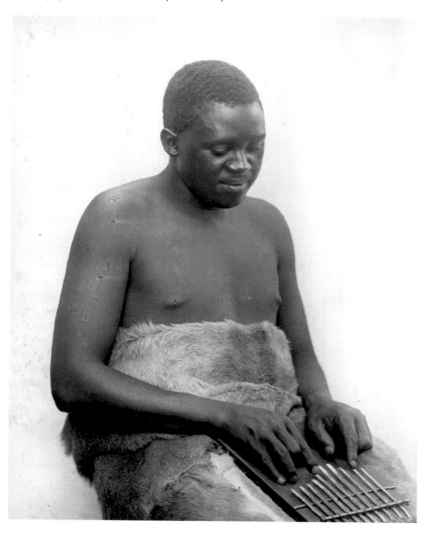

on a Saturday night. At such parties, when there is a large gathering, people break into song. One person usually initiates the dancing and singing, and eventually the music takes on its own momentum and more people join the dancing circle. On any other night, men enjoy asking each other riddles, which are often chanted. Both the question and the answer of this riddle are sung:

Bana ba Nkoto ba bina xe yena mong a bina-dikala
Nkoto's children dance when he dances
Answer: Branches: they shake when the trunk shakes.[16]

Thlwahlawadi

Men also chant praise songs (*direto*) resembling historical epics in the still of the night. They usually recall events pertaining to tribal chiefs and heroes. The poet orates a story and evokes a mood through his grand, expansive descriptions. The praise poem lends itself to interaction, and the listeners sometimes respond to the storyteller by joining in with a sung rejoinder. While men use praise poetry to narrate the past glories of the Bapedi, women use folktales to explore their world through the ancient stories that have been passed down through the generations.[17] Older women regularly spend their evenings performing folktales for children, using this medium not only to amuse and entertain them, but also to teach them morals and values. Children enthusiastically participate and interrupt the stories with a sung response.

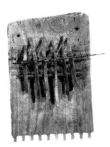

Apart from participating in folktales around the fire, children also entertain themselves at night with musical games. In a popular game called

Rattles

Thlwahlawadi are leg-rattles made of long strings of cocoons filled with sand or stones, and sewn in pairs onto a thong. A full string consists of about 140 cocoons. Women wear these rattles on their calves in a variety of dances.[5]

The ***mathotse*** is another type of leg-rattle made from the fruit of the *mathotse* tree.[6] When not available, other gourds or small tins are used. These are filled with small stones or sand, and holes are drilled at both ends so that a stick can be inserted. A number of sticks with attached gourds are bound together with thong, and the instrument is tied around the back of the dancer's calves. These rattles are usually worn in pairs – one on each leg.[7]

The Bapedi hand-rattle is called ***tshela*** and consists of a calabash, usually oval in shape, or a long, small tin. This is filled with hard berries, seeds or small stones and is attached to a handle. This rattle is played in combination with the *ntshomane* drum during exorcism rituals.

Mbiras

The ***dipela*** consists of a rectangular piece of wood to which metal tongues or keys are fixed using two metal bars, one below and one above the keys. The tongues of different lengths and sizes are arranged in a fan shape. The *dipela* is sometimes placed inside a large paraffin tin which acts as a resonator. The tin is often fitted with bottle tops to give additional vibration. *Refer to Track 27.*

Bull-roarers

The Bapedi call their bull-roarer ***kgabududu***.[8]

143

makaesana, girls and boys sit in a circle singing. Each boy takes a turn to sit in the centre of the circle where he chooses a girl to join him. She kneels in front of him, throwing her shawl over their faces, and the singing volume of the surrounding group rises. When the couple throw the shawl off their faces the singing gets softer and another boy enters the circle. *Refer to Tracks 29 and 30.*

Kiba *and* dinaka: *reed-pipe ensembles*

> *"This 'one man, one note' music is much more than the sound alone – it is an incredible web of coordination of sound and body, legs and voices, drums and rattles, players with each other, the group with its society, that is so compelling, so socially binding, that in almost every case African reed-pipe dances have become the national dances of the group playing them."*[18]

> — PROFESSOR ANDREW TRACEY

The word *kiba* is literally translated as 'to beat time or to stamp'.[19] This musical style was originally performed in the rural areas at social occasions or during competitions between neighbouring villages.[20] The performance of this music was regarded as non-ritualistic; a form of entertainment belonging to the category of games (*dipapadi*). Many of the stylistic features of the genre as it is today were developed in the migrant-labour settings when dance teams took part in competitions. There are mixed opinions as to where and how the *kiba* style originated, but it is generally agreed that it was imported from the VhaVenda. Many believe that the Bapedi adopted the Venda ensemble of end-blown pipes, changing the Venda seven-note scale to a five-note scale. The Bapedi also brought their own cultural heritage to the genre by including indigenous songs. Another significant difference between the two forms of music was that the Venda's reed-pipe music was inextricably related to political power, whereas the Bapedi used pipe music as a form of entertainment.

Dinaka, the male version of *kiba*, is the oldest Bapedi traditional form of dance, and is regarded as their national dance. Groups of *dinaka* players form orchestras composed of no less than twelve instruments. The men play *naka* pipes; and four drums of different sizes – either traditional *meropa* or their modern substitute, *kiba* – are played by three people The *dinaka* ensemble is handed down from one generation to the next. From a young age children are given a *naka* pipe and pick up the technique of playing the instrument and dancing the difficult steps at the same time, simply by listening to and watching their elders. Only once an individual has reached a certain level of skill will he take part in performances.

Dinaka performances are held on many festive occasions. Some groups make a profession out of their music by playing at weddings and other ceremonies. In most Bapedi places, *dinaka* gatherings take place weekly, usually on Sunday mornings near the chief's kraal. Competitions are also held in urban areas where Bapedi people live. Mamelodi and the other Pretoria townships support scores of *dinaka* groups. To add to the entertainment level of the performance, the performers wear ties, scarves, towels and other colourful, decorative items tied round their waists. Some wear beaded aprons and others sport ostrich-feather headbands. The most distinctive item of clothing they wear is the Scottish kilt. The adoption of the Scottish kilt is one example of the way in which the original *dinaka* dance changed in the migrant context. It was in the 1940s and 1950s that *dinaka* players saw Scottish kilts for the first time and adopted them for their dance costumes. Before this time the dancers wore a cloth garment that restricted their leg movements. The use of the kilt allowed more freedom of movement. The men developed the characteristic sway or swinging movement where they toss the kilt from side to side over the hips and buttocks. The kilt also provides an element of humour, when performers purposely lift it with a pelvic flick to expose their boxer shorts underneath.

The dance consists of three or four sequences that have a similar format. The

Boys hold their left hands against their ears when they play the lengwane

men form rows, and only start playing their pipes once the leader has indicated the beginning of the dance by blowing his *naka*. The performers stand in line and then move into a circle after several minutes. They alternate their

Whistles, flutes and reeds

Dinaka pipes are played in an ensemble of flutes, known as *kiba*. These pipes are made from reed or metal tubing (more common nowadays), and are closed at one end. They are sometimes covered with a piece of animal skin and are usually decorated with engraving or beads. Each pipe produces only one note, but the pipes are made at the different pitches of their pentatonic (five-note) scale so that they can be played in the reed-pipe ensemble. The player holds the *naka* in the palm of one hand and the open end rests against the lower lip and tongue. The loud, strident tone of the *dinaka* is achieved using a special technique, where a concentrated stream of air is funnelled down the tongue into the top of the pipe.

In the past, the **mokudietane** was made and played by warriors in times of war to give them courage and strength. The shape of this whistle is conical. It is made from hard wood and covered with animal skin. Once the skin has dried, the whistle is decorated with iron and brass wire. The player breathes across the embouchure, opening and closing the bottom of the pipe with one finger. Nowadays this instrument is played by initiated boys as they escort younger boys to their initiation school.[9]

The **lengwane** is a whistle made from the leg-bone of a goat or sheep. It has a V-shaped opening and produces a brassy, piercing tone. When a boy plays the instrument he holds his left hand against his ear. Formerly boys played the *lengwane* before they went to initiation school, and used it to mimic warfare.

direction throughout the dance, starting by dancing anti-clockwise around the drums in the centre, then facing the inside of the circle. They change direction, dancing clockwise, jumping around to face outwards and then pivoting around again to face the centre. The dance ends when they move closer to the drums with their backs turned away from them. During the dance, soloists break out of the circle to dance in the centre, using energetic body movements. It has been observed that "once the dancers get into their stride it is very difficult to stop them. They seem to gather energy as they progress from one dance to another, putting every ounce of strength into the stamping and various other movements which accompany their blowing."[21] The sharing of energy excites the performers and audience alike, entertaining them for many hours on end.

The Bapedi have a repertoire of songs that is found among most, if not all, groups of Bapedi performers from different areas, and which is used as part of the *kiba* performance. They originally included lyrics, and although they are now performed only instrumentally, some people still remember the original words. Their lyrics revolved largely around a heroic conception of the past. Qualities that were admired in men, such as warrior bravery, became important themes. The kilt, a military symbol, ties into these themes. Furthermore, the fiercely competitive nature of the dance alludes to the spirit of competition in battle. *Monti*, a regimental song, is one of the most important items in the repertoire of *kiba*. On returning from war, soldiers would enter the chief's kraal singing this song. In a contemporary context, it is used as a song of greeting, and is thus found in the introductory and concluding sections of the dance.

A female version of *kiba* was developed in the late 1970s. It was influenced by several rural styles, both from within and outside the Bapedi heartland. Although *kiba* performances usually take place in between the performances of male *dinaka* groups and share some similarities with *dinaka* music, Bapedi women have developed their own style. While both genders use *meropa* drums and employ similar rhythms in their dances, females sing songs (*dikosa*) instead of playing *naka* pipes. Their music is more sedate and has different themes to those alluded to in the men's music. Women have developed an interesting link between the past and the present through this style. Although they draw heavily on traditional music and values, they use *kiba* as a platform to comment on contemporary experiences. *Kiba* allows for the "creative transformation of older themes"[22]: fragments from older song lyrics are blended with new lyrics, so that the themes are continuously reinterpreted. The songs often approach domestic concerns and conventional female issues in a critical, comical manner; and, at the same time, they incorporate feelings of resistance and criticism of the roles assigned to women.

When women perform *kiba*, they wear layers of coloured cloth tied around the waist, embroidered cotton dresses, headcloths and leg-rattles. They also occasionally dress up for the dramatic interludes that are interspersed in their performances. They play a range of characters, often involving the audience in the performance and amusing them with the idiosyncrasies of their dramatic personae.[23] Likewise, men also dress up to play different roles, often cross-dressing to aid their exaggerated mimicry of female gestures.

Malopo: possession

Bapedi healers are responsible for helping people to drive out unwanted evil spirits and, in some cases, to receive good ancestral spirits.[24] On an appointed moonlit evening just after the harvest, when there is lots of beer and the crops are ripe, a *malopo* dance is held for this purpose. It is a gathering open to all women, whose

Man playing the tsula ya noko

presence validates and enhances the ritual. The healer, usually an elderly woman adorned with animal skins, bangles and beads; and the patient, who is induced into a trance-like state, are the focal point. A healer's status is reinforced by the band that she provides to play for the occasion. The instruments in the band include the *moropa* and *mantshomane* drums and *ditshela* hand-rattles. The band forms the backdrop to the action, namely the

Dinaka tsa lethlaka are reed-pipes that are not tuned to any particular pitch. They are relatively small and thus have a limited range of sounds. They yield only one note, but the player whistles as he inhales, and in this way produces other notes. They are made by boys and played when walking or herding from October to December, when the reeds are mature. Nowadays these pipes are often substituted with European-style police whistles.

The ***tsula ya noko*** is a type of pan-pipe made from the quills of a porcupine. Each quill functions as a stopped tube and yields different notes. When sickness broke out in a kraal the diviner would go to the top of a hill and blow this instrument to prevent it from spreading.

Bapedi diviners used a flute called ***naka ya sefako*** to ward off hailstorms. It is made from an impala horn that has been covered with leather on one side and is ornamented with a design of brass and iron wire on the surface. An ostrich feather that has been dipped in 'medicine' is kept inside the flute to keep it airtight when not in use.

A kiba *tableau*

In this dramatic performance the women do a skit on policewomen

dancing of the possessed patient. The dance has been described in the following way:

> "*The dancing appeared to consist of a great deal of whirling about in a more-or-less static position (which must have induced excessive giddiness); the stamping of the feet, hesitating frequently with one foot suspended in mid-air before bringing it down to meet the earth with a resounding thud; and abandoned body-contortions, swaying and arm-waving, indicative of despair.*"[25]

Dizziness and exhaustion help the afflicted person to enter a trance. She stands in the middle of the circle of dancers, who take turns to spin her around until she collapses. The songs that accompany the dance are also conducive to a trance state. They consist of simple, hypnotic phrases with just a few repeated notes. The healer sings a solo, chanting words of foreign origin against the background of female voices. When the healer becomes entranced it is believed that she actually transforms into one of the ancestral spirits who speaks through her in strange voices. The songs' content centres on the spirit world or the patient's illness, but at times the content is non-lexical, consisting only of onomatopoeic phrases. When the patient collapses from exhaustion and dizziness, she is given water and encouraged to get up and continue dancing. This ritual dance can be stretched out over many evenings, and ends only once the healer is convinced that the bad spirit has left or the good spirit has entered the patient. *Refer to Track 31.*

Rain songs

During periods of drought, songs are used as a medium of prayer to 'heal the land'.[26] Songs enhance the activities of rainmaking rituals. One of the main activities is the collection of water for the rainpot, when the chief sends young girls to the river:

> 'E-e-moxoxa, xoxa o tle nayo'
> E-e-drawer, draw and bring it with you.[27]

Bapedi diviners used another kind of flute – the **tsula** – which was made from the leg-bone of an eagle or wild cat and encased in the skin of a leguaan. It contained specially prepared 'medicine', which was believed to give the instrument supernatural powers. A feather kept the tube clean, and a red and black lucky bean was inserted through the opening. The *tsula* produces a shrill, sharp sound. It was used during rainmaking ceremonies as well as during burials of chiefs, so that the diviner could 'smell out' the person responsible for the death.

Transverse flutes are known as **faai**. They are made from reeds and closed at the bottom by a node. At one end a blowing-hole is cut, and towards the bottom, one, two, three or four finger-holes are bored. In the past, these flutes were played in a band of six.[10]

Once the water has been collected the diviner adds 'medicine' to the rainpot, while the women sing.

When the children sprinkle the water from the rainpot onto the land, they sing rain songs, clapping as they walk. Finally, when the rain does come, the women greet it with song, communicating their relief and gratitude through music. The children play joyfully in the pools of water and mud, dancing and singing repetitive phrases of appreciation.

Mokato: first fruits ceremony

In January, when the first crops of the harvest are ready to be eaten, the chief declares a holiday for a small celebration.[28] Everyone in the village spends the day eating, singing and dancing. An even bigger celebration is that of the great feast that accompanies the second crop of the season. On the day of this

A gathering of women at the first fruits ceremony

festival, men and women carrying pots of beer on their heads approach the chief's kraal in long rows. Once they have reached the courtyard they form a large circle, singing as they move around as a gesture of greeting. The sight of the women wearing bright ostrich feathers in their hair and the men raising and lowering their knobkierries, combined with the festive singing, enhances the carnival atmosphere. The participants are entertained with many different musical styles during the feast. Reed-pipe ensembles are performed, praise songs are chanted and any other type of song that is appropriate to the occasion is sung. Men leap in the air energetically, contorting their bodies in a show of agility; and women beat their drums with exuberance. The formal festivities last two days, but the celebrations continue in the evenings for weeks after the great feast.

Initiation

Koma/lebollo: *male initiation*

Before male initiates (*masoboro*) go to initiation school, there is a training period during which they are exposed to the strict discipline that they will be subjected to at the school.[29] They rehearse a large repertoire of initiation songs for hours on end, and are expected to know them all by rote once the school commences. Initiation is divided into two distinct ceremonies: *bodika* and *bogwera*. The name of the first ceremony, *bodika*, is derived from the verb *go dika* ('to encircle or surround someone' or 'to join in attacking someone')[30]: the initiates' strength, courage and endurance are put to the test through various devices. The second ceremony, *bogwera* ('friendship')[31], reinforces the bonds that were forged between the boys at the first school.

   Initiation officially begins with the blowing of the horn (*phalaphala*) to round up all the boys and their fathers at the headkraal (*kgoro*). As people arrive they join the loud chant that echoes through the community, signalling the opening of one of the most sacred institutions of their society. The boys are led in a solemn procession to the appointed place in the mountains where they will be circumcised. They walk in single file to the ceremonial accompaniment of the *moropa* drum, *mokudietane* flutes and *phalaphala*

Horns

Made from sable antelope horn, the Bapedi horn is called **phalaphala**.[11] Once the bony inside of the horn has been removed, a square embouchure is cut near the tip of the horn. The instrument is often decorated with strips of skin which strengthen it. It is held in both hands and the player blows it trumpet-fashion, with buzzing lips. The result is a powerful, booming sound. This instrument is played mostly by men, and every headman owns a horn. In the past, the *phalaphala* player appointed by the chief would use the horn to sound the signal for war, and the chief's men would promptly arrive bearing arms. To engage in battle, the horn-blower blew his *phalaphala*, and the enemy's horn-blower responded in like manner. If someone important was killed, members of the clan were not allowed to sound their horns to indicate victory. In a completely different context, horns were blown by herdsmen to entice their cattle into a race, which was a traditional part of the first fruits festival.[12] Horns were occasionally played by women to call female initiates to their initiation schools, to accompany them en route to the school, and to signal to the women in the village if something went wrong with one of the initiates. Diviners sometimes play horns to ward off a storm.

151

The phalaphala *horn is used as a musical instrument*

horns that are played by older, initiated boys (*mediti*). Each boy is led to a rock where his cries are deafened by a surrounding circle of shouting, singing and drumming. In the days that follow, the initiation lodge resounds with song. The initiates sing before they eat and when they enter or leave their lodges. They also sing when they go hunting so that people in the area can hear them approaching and avoid accidentally meeting them. In the early mornings, late afternoons and evenings, song is used as a medium of instruction. The secret initiation formulae are chanted by the older boys, and are learned by the initiates through repetition. They spend hours singing in this new language, until their voices are hoarse and they are mentally exhausted. Every time a boy forgets the formulae he is beaten so that he comes to understand the importance of the secret codes of manhood.

During the second month of initiation, new rituals are introduced which vary from school to school. Among some Bapedi groups, poles are erected that represent the sacred elephant, and songs are sung around this structure. The boys also sing while creating kilts out of bullrushes, which they wear when collecting food from the girls. These costumes are also worn when dancers from neighbouring clans visit to compete in performances. The dances last all night, and are a test of the boys' endurance. In most Bapedi lodges, another important activity is the preparation of stones which they use to construct cone-like structures that become monuments of the school. Two well-known Bapedi songs, the song of the salt and the song of lightning, accompany this activity. In the third month, the initiates prepare for their homecoming, and perform farewell songs. When they are finally ready to leave the school, they form a triumphant procession and are escorted to the chief's kraal where they are greeted as adults by their mothers.

The second initiation school (*bogwera*) usually takes place after a year has lapsed since the first school. With modern daytime restrictions, not all Bapedi groups hold this ceremony, and if they do, it only lasts one month. Its chief function is to help the initiated boys create lasting friendships with one another. Once again, the boys enter a lodge, but they are not completely separated from the rest of the community. During the day they receive further training in the initiation formulae. They wear disguises of grass kilts and

Bows and other string instruments

The Bapedi have two instruments that they call **lekope**. The first is played only by females and is almost extinct. It is made from a slightly curved river reed, usually bamboo, and the string is made from sinew. Before the instrument is played, the string is lubricated with the sap of a leaf or plant. The bow is held at an angle, with one tip resting in the player's mouth, which acts as a resonator. The string is stopped with the third, fourth and fifth fingers of the left hand, and is plucked near the bottom with the index finger of the right hand. Nowadays, the Jews harp or **setolotolo** is also known as the women's *lekope*. This is a very popular imported instrument which can be bought at country stores.

The other instrument known as **lekope** is made of a piece of the branch of a syringa tree, or from any other resonant wood. The string is made from sinew or wire and is tied back at the centre to give two notes, one on each side of the tie. One side is plucked with the forefinger of the left hand, and the other is plucked with a plectrum made from a thorn or a thin stick. The bow is held against the lips and the mouth acts as a resonator. This instrument is played only by initiated males, usually on a summer evening. Sometimes the instrument is charmed with 'medicine' by a diviner to help a man courting a woman, and bring him luck and strength in battle.

The Bapedi have two instruments that go by the name of **sekgapa**, which means calabash. The first instrument is made from wood with the bark removed, with the string made from twisted fibre. A calabash, which serves as a resonator, is attached to the lower end of the instrument. The player holds the bow in one hand near the calabash, leaving the thumb and first finger free to pinch the string, creating two notes. The other hand strikes the string with a piece of grass.

The second instrument is made from a thin branch of a tree. The branch is bent with the pressure of the string, which is made from ox sinew, twisted strands of hair from a cow's tail, twisted fibre from a plant or, more commonly, wire. The string is tied back in the centre and the calabash is attached in this position. The player holds the instrument vertically in one hand, with the calabash opening facing the chest. The string is struck with a thin piece of grass. Each segment of the string produces a different note, and the player can finger the string near the division to produce an additional note. He moves the calabash towards and away from the chest to vary the resonance of the sound. Both these bows are played by boys to accompany their songs.

155

masks so that their entire bodies and faces are covered, and they communicate with one another using a special whistling language. Their initiation school comes to a close when they dance for the women of the community, reciting the formulae they learnt in the first school as a statement of their new status as men.

Byale: *female initiation*

Before a girl enters initiation school, she must undergo puberty rites during which she goes into seclusion for a week, and washes in the river every morning.[32] In the evenings, the women gather in her hut, dancing, singing and drumming. While the dances are characterised by movements that represent the development of the child in the womb, the songs are characterised by a vocal style in which the women sing in unison, plucking their lower lips with their fingers. When the girl comes out of seclusion, she embarks on a period of preparation, which includes the learning of initiation songs.

The girls' passage to a secluded spot in the mountains is marked by the eerie sound of the friction drum (*moshupiane*). The drum is played by an older woman but the initiates (*byale*) are not allowed to see her or to know the source of the sound. The drummer is therefore completely concealed by the women surrounding her. The girls are told that the strange, screaming sound of the *moshupiane* is the spirit of the hills, which will guard them during their initiation. The sound of the instrument also resembles a lion's roar and is thus sometimes called 'lion's voice'.[33] Much secrecy surrounds the drum, which, according to some, is burned when the girls reach the kraal. At another point in the initiation, in the middle of the night, a dried flower stem is whirled like a bull-roarer, and also resembles a lion's roar. Gripped with terror, the girls run into the mountains to hide from the 'lions'. In this context, musical instruments are used to embody spirits and to simulate animal sounds.

The daily activities of the female initiates follow a set routine. In the mornings, after they have washed in the river and eaten breakfast, they form a single, S-shaped line, and perform a dance-song with slow movements. They have formal training sessions during which the older girls teach them the extensive repertoire of initiation songs. They learn the school's formulae, chanting the short phrases over and over as well as using mime to learn the behaviour that is expected of them as women, and the duties that they will be obliged to perform as adults. The girls create songs based on small models of animals they make to represent a range of human qualities, both desirable and undesirable. In the evenings, they perform physically strenuous exercises that challenge their strength and stamina. If the head of the school is unsatisfied with the girls' execution of the exercises, she forces them to stay awake through the night chanting, regardless of their exhaustion. When everyone is asleep, the older women beat the *moropa* drum throughout the night to ensure that strangers are made aware that the initiation school is in progress and that they should keep away.

During the second phase of the initiation school, the girls are located at the headkraal. The most important activity throughout this period is the singing that takes place in the enclosure every morning and evening. In between, the girls work in the chief's fields, or are hired out to work elsewhere. Towards the end of initiation, role-play and disguise are an important feature in their activities. In the evenings, mini-dramas are performed as a method of instruction. Disguised figures wearing reeds and leaves sing and dance for them, using symbolic gestures. In the last month of initiation, the girls are visited by a boy disguised as a bird. Every evening the 'bird' dances for the girls in the enclosure and blows a whistle to communicate certain instructions to them. On the last evening of initiation school, the girls spend the entire evening dancing and singing, and the 'bird', escorted by a group of men, leaves the school. In the closing ceremony, the girls proceed to the chief's kraal where a feast awaits them.[34] *Refer to Track 32.*

The *sekgobogobo* is also played by boys. It is a long piece of hollowed-out wood or bamboo. A single string is attached to a long tuning peg, which elevates it slightly from the wood. Where the upper end was once secured inside a calabash resonator, a paraffin tin is now used. Before the instrument is played, the string is rubbed with saliva or honey to make it sticky. The instrument rests on the player's left shoulder, and the left hand thumb or first finger presses upon the string to give three different fundamentals. The player holds a friction-bow, made from a small stick with cow hair attached, in his right hand, and rubs it up and down on the string using greater pressure to achieve high notes.[13]

The Bapedi adopted the German 'autoharp' zither, which they call *harepa*. It has a hollow wooden body with twelve to twenty or more parallel wire strings stretched over it from end to end, held in place with nails. On one end the nails are bent so that the strings can be tuned. The player sits and rests the instrument on his legs, plucking the strings with the fingers of both hands. The *harepa* and the *dipela* are used for very similar purposes, including the accompaniment of personal songs and laments. Although western in origin, the *harepa* allows "for a more effective realisation of indigenous musical principles than did the original instrument – in this case the plucked reed *dipela*, and has virtually replaced it."[14]
Refer to Track 28.

Stringed-wind

The *lesiba* is no longer played among the Bapedi. (See Chapter 10, page 237).

157

The Batswana's ancestors lived in the north-west of what is today the Limpopo Province. Their history is characterised by patterns of internal division, resulting in the existence of numerous independent chiefdoms of varying sizes.

The Batswana live in the North West Province, Free State and the Northern Cape of South Africa, as well as in the eastern and north-western regions of Botswana.

Batswana

History of the Batswana

Many centuries ago, the Batswana ancestors migrated south from the vicinity of the Great Lakes of East Africa to the highveld in three main waves.[1] The Kgalakgadi or 'Kalahari people', after whom the Kalahari Desert is probably named, arrived first.[2] When they entered the country, they encountered the San, whom they dominated by enslaving or forcing them to disperse in the desert. The Kgalakgadi were soon followed by the present Rolong and Thlaping Batswana clans, and later by larger groups of Sotho people, the most prominent being the Hurutshe, Kwena and Kgatla. Ironically, the Kgalakgadi, the first group to settle in this area, became subservient to the more powerful Sotho-Tswana clans. They were bullied into moving away from the fertile regions and spent the rest of their days as servants to others in the arid wastelands of the desert. To this day, they bow down to the more-powerful Batswana peoples. By the 17th century, the Batswana, divided into numerous sub-groups, had settled on the highveld. For the next two centuries, their history was marked by internal conflict and secession: sections of chiefdoms broke away to form new groups under new leaders, and hostility between the chiefdoms arose because of fierce competition over cattle, land and subjects.

In the 19th century, the internal fragmentation within the group was diverted by a series of external pressures. With the devastating *difaqane* upheavals of the early 19th century, the Batswana were forced to realign themselves. They did not have the military strength or fighting power of other groups like the AmaZulu because of their fragmentation, and the attacks they suffered were crushing. The two most severe attacks were by the female marauder, MaNthatisi, of the Batlokwa, and the fearsome Matabele leader, Mzilikazi. While MaNthatisi forced the Batswana to move north, leaving many starving, and forcing them to live semi-nomadic existences; the

Rattles – matlhowa

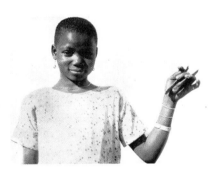

Playing marapo

Playing the seburuburu

"Instruments are not played much anymore. They have been left at the cattle post. People are too busy going to school, working, gone to the mines. They haven't got the time to practise. The coming of the gramophone took some of the interest away."[3]

Drums

The Batswana **moropa** is a wooden drum in the shape of a wooden milk jug. A skin is stretched over the wood and attached with pegs. The drum is held under the left arm or placed on the ground. The player squats and strikes the drum head with the fingertips, producing a sharp, staccato sound. The pitch of the drum is altered by pressing the skin. Performers sometimes stand with the drum between their legs. It is played only by women, and is used during female initiation ceremonies.[4]

Rattles

Batswana men wear dancing rattles, **matlhowa**, made out of moth cocoons filled with dry seeds or pebbles. These are strung on long strings and wound round the lower leg for dancing.[5]

Hand-clappers

Animal rib-bones are used as musical instruments to provide rhythmical accompaniment to singing. **Marapo** are made in pairs, are held in both hands and are struck together.

Bull-roarers

The **seburuburu** is primarily used as a child's toy.

Doctor sounding his naka

Man sounding the mokoreie

Matabele conqueror killed hundreds of people, wiping out entire groups and forcing others to regroup. By 1840, the wars had ceased and the Batswana started to rebuild their chiefdoms. They began to unify as a form of self-protection, and slowly their chiefdoms grew as the fractions among them decreased.

Lengwane

Batswana chiefdoms were also prevented from fragmenting further as European control extended. British missionaries and Boers entered Batswana territory at the beginning of the 19th century, and gradually started settling there. Unclaimed land became increasingly difficult to find, and this prevented many Batswana groups from sub-dividing and seeking new land. Eventually the government started to intervene in Batswana disputes, settling civil conflicts and hence preventing secession. Meanwhile, the Boers posed another challenge to the now-reformed Batswana groups.

Pala

The Batswana had initially welcomed the presence of the Boers, who had helped them drive away the intruding Ndebele during the *difaqane*. However, Batswana chiefdoms started clashing with the Boers who began asserting their sovereignty over them, and infringing on their territory in what was then the northern Transvaal. As a result, several clans moved across the border to Botswana, most of whom never returned.

The Boers formed the South African Republic in the second half of the 19th century. During this period, Khama III, King of the Ngwato, dominated most Batswana regions. He recognised British authority, with the understanding that the British would protect Batswana territory from the Boers. The western parts of this territory became the British Protectorate of Bechuanaland under Chief Khama. It gained independence in 1966, changing its name to Botswana. The eastern parts of Batswana territory fell within South Africa. Under apartheid South Africa, a Batswana 'homeland' – Bophuthatswana – was declared, which was dissolved in 1994.

Whistles, flutes and reeds

The *lengwane* is made from the leg-bone of a goat, sheep or small antelope, and is characterised by its V-shaped mouthpiece. The flute is sometimes decorated with engravings or with an animal's gullet, which dries hard around the bone. It was played by boys before they entered circumcision school (*bogwera*), and they used it to signal to one another. They also blew the whistle during fights to affirm their masculinity.

The *mothlatsa* is a conical whistle made from wood or ivory. Men played it when hunting elephants and to signal from a distance.[6] Young men made the *pala* from impala horn and used it as a signal whistle.[7]

The *mokoreie* is made from the stem of the *bolatsi* reed. The player binds the tube with a strip of wet cloth so that the flute is airtight during performance. The embouchure is held to the mouth and the right finger closes the hole at the end of the instrument.

Boys aged seven to twelve played a reed whistle called *lethlaka noka*. It yielded only one sound, but the player whistled as he inhaled, and in this way produced other notes. Boys played the instrument for their amusement while herding.

The *naka* was a bone whistle used by diviners to ward off lightning and hail. It was made of assorted materials, including the leg-bone of a secretary bird, a feather of a 'lightning bird', and the skin of a leguaan, with a specially prepared 'medicine' used to plug the bottom end. The instrument was also played at the sentencing of a murderer. If foul play involving the poisoning of somebody was suspected, the diviner was called in to perform a special ceremony where he blew his *naka*. The sound was believed to penetrate the heart of the murderer, causing an illness that would ultimately lead to his or her death.

Music in performance

Introduction

"Music can have a curative function. When one is very sad, too sad, it awakens the mind. It is very important. If one hears the sound of the drum just now, it is music. And if a person is too downhearted, and one plays the tune: 'La…and do-mi-so' – you wake up! So, music is a very lovely thing and should be appreciated by everybody. If you are tired and you hear someone sing, you must wake up and listen. Then you may smile by yourself and laugh by yourself. Later on, you can see things more truly with the naked eye."[17]

This attitude towards music has been passed down through many generations and seems almost inherent to Batswana sensibility. Even though many of their older instruments are no longer played, and the older songs no longer heard, the Batswana's love for music is still evident in their attitude and approach to singing.[18] Batswana music is largely choral, but unlike the Nguni, the Batswana do not use much harmony. Their enthusiasm is displayed through other vocal techniques. A good singer is someone who has a strong lively voice and sings expressively; thus the most important vocal skill is the

ability to capture the mood of the song. When women are taken in by the song they spontaneously ululate to express their appreciation of the music; when men get caught up in a song they introduce a dramatic element into their performance by acting out the song's content. In the past, when men returned from battle or a hunt, the mood of the songs they sang as they arrived home revealed either a joyful victory or a disappointing defeat.

Kubina dithlaka: the reed-pipe ensemble

The reed-pipe ensemble is traditionally performed at night when there is sufficient moonlight.[19] The chief has sole control over when and where this performance can take place, and people are strictly forbidden to perform it without his permission.

The ensemble is divided into four sets of pipes of different pitches. Three sets consist of four pipes each, while the fourth set consists of five pipes. Each contains at least one of the four notes of the scale. The names of the groups in descending order of pitch are: *motenyane, dinokwana, madumeni* and *meporo*. The instructor of the reed-pipe ensemble (*mothlabi*) is chosen for his good ear which enables him to tune the pipes and compose songs. He composes and teaches by first singing a vocal line to the group, so that they can pick up the melody. As the performers become familiar with the song, they start adding harmony to it according to well-known principles. While playing the pipes, the men move anti-clockwise in a circle using a variety of steps such as stamping, shuffling and leaping like frogs. The women and girls sometimes follow them around in an outer circle, clapping and ululating (*mogolokwane*) to encourage them. *Refer to Track 34.*

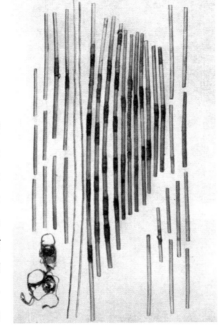

The Batswana derived their reed flutes from the Korana Khoi, and they were the first Bantu-speaking people to play reed-pipes in groups.[8] The first Batswana group to adopt the pipes were the Selaotswe, who lived in Mamusa where some of the inhabitants were Khoi Korana.[9] Their reed-pipes are called **lichaka** or **dithlaka**. They were originally made from river reed, which was later substituted with materials such as metal tubing. A complete set consists of thirteen pipes of different sizes, although this does not limit an ensemble to thirteen people, as the flutes may be duplicated. The shorter reeds are called *mepenyane* and the longer ones *meporo*. One observer likened the sound of the pipes "to the well-tuned 'latten-bells' on an English country wagon."[10] Performers of a reed-pipe ensemble are rewarded with food and thus the pipes are usually heard when there is an abundance of cattle. These instruments are played on special occasions, such as to honour a guest, or express joy at the coming of rain.

Horns

The **lepapata** is made from either sable or kudu horn and was played only by men on ceremonial occasions such as the declaration of war, during circumcision ceremonies and when hunting lion or leopard. The skin was normally given to the chief who rewarded the successful hunter with a cow.

Rain songs

So significant are rainmaking rituals in the dry Batswana country that the word for rain – *pula* – is also used to describe a state of wellbeing and is

Bows and other string instruments

The **lengope,** an instrument played only by girls, is a hollow river reed with a string of twisted sinew, hair, fibre, or wire. The bow is mouth-resonated and plucked with the fingers. It is held to the left of the player and the string is stopped with the second, third and fourth fingers of the left hand. The right forefinger plucks the string upwards or downwards. The notched end of the bow rests in the mouth, which is used as a resonator to select the harmonics present in the sound of the string.

The **nokukwane** was borrowed from the Korana Khoi, and the Batswana are the only Bantu-speaking people to have adopted this instrument.[11] Originally, a resonator made of a large tortoise shell or a dried-skin milk-sack was fixed at one end of the bow, but it was eventually replaced with a tin can. The string is made from sinew or twisted leather. The instrument is fairly heavy and the bow is large, thus the player usually sits, holding the bow against the body with the resonator resting on the ground. The string is struck with a reed, or with the left thumb. The *nokukwane* is played only by men.[12]

Man playing the segankuru

commonly shouted or exclaimed to applaud or show appreciation.[20] *Pula* is also the name of the Botswana currency. In the past the role of the rainmaker was extremely important because of severe drought in the North West Province, home to many Batswana. Batswana rain rituals were high on the scale of ritual significance. The chief was often responsible for rainmaking rites, although in some cases he hired a diviner to fulfil this role. The understanding behind the choice of the chief as rainmaker was that only the ancestors of a great chief had the power to induce rain. The chief's popularity was greatly affected by his ability to 'make rain'. He was respected as 'the controller of the weather'[21] and when rain did fall, he was acknowledged as the intermediary between the ancestors and the heavens. Reference was made in many rain songs to chiefs and their ability to bring rain.

Rain songs were a vital part of the rainmaking prayers that accompanied rituals. In one of the core rainmaking rituals that occurred annually at the beginning of the agricultural season, the chief, having specially prepared 'medicine' in a pot in the sacred rain-enclosure behind his hut, selected a group of uninitiated girls to sprinkle it on the fields. For an entire day, the girls, carrying small pots, covered the land with the 'medicine'. This ritual was accompanied by song as a form of prayer. When they returned home the girls sang to the members of their community:

Pula, pula we!	Rain, rain!
Baroka kea beao	There are rainmakers
Baroka pula ke baloi	The rainmakers, the rain and the wizards[22]
Pula pula tlagona	Rain, rain, come and fall
Pula pula we	Rain, rain!
Mama silo	Hammerhead[23]
Pula etlana	The rain will fall;
Ahae pula we!	Welcome rain![24]

Every year after the harvest, rain songs featured at a thanksgiving (*dikgafela*) festival. The festival began with a procession to the chief's kraal. The women carried baskets of sorghum upon their heads singing rain songs

The **segankuru** consists of a hollow bar of bamboo fitted with a wire string and a tuning peg. A paraffin tin that hangs over the tip of the instrument acts as a resonator. The instrument rests on the left shoulder of the player and the left thumb and first finger stop the string alternately to obtain the fundamentals needed. The player holds a small hair-bow in his right hand and bows the string with varying pressure for high or low notes. Boys play the *segankuru* during the game of hide and seek. One participant has to search for a hidden object, while another plays the instrument using changing tones and volumes to indicate whether the seeker is closer to or further away from the hidden object.[13] *Refer to Track 33.*

The **segwana** (calabash) is usually made from a branch of the *morethloa* tree and the string is made from the twisted sinew of an ox tail or, nowadays, wire. A calabash is attached to the bow. The instrument is held with one hand and the string is struck with a reed held in the other. The player can stop the string with a finger, or leave it open, producing two different notes a whole tone apart. He strikes the string with the reed while moving the small opening of the calabash towards and away from his chest. In this way he varies the resonance of the sound by selecting different harmonics. This bow is not mouth-resonated, so the performer can sing while playing. Only males play this instrument.[14]

while they walked. This music was also used on festive occasions by both men and women to celebrate *pula* – a state of wellbeing. The songs were always accompanied by clapping, a ritual gesture used when asking for something. These rituals have declined amongst most Batswana groups, largely because of missionary influence and the introduction of Christianity.[25] *Refer to Track 35.*

Initiation

Bojale: *female initiation*

Female initiates (*bonwale*) participate in musical activities throughout initiation.[26] They have to memorise secret formulae (*rupa*), which they chant. They graduate only once they have perfected the formulae, at which stage they receive incisions on the thigh. One of the main performances of the initiation school is the *radikgaratlane* dance, which is characterised by the special skins (*peeledi*) that are worn. On the last night there is a ceremonial dance (*thojane*), and when the initiates return to the council place (*kgotla*), they greet their families with songs of their return (*megolokwane*) such as the one below. Apart from the homecoming theme, the song alludes to the last days of pregnancy when a woman cannot walk properly.[27] A common concern of many female initiation songs centres on attempting to dissuade the initiates from falling pregnant before they are married. Like many songs in the repertoire of initiation music, they have a didactic function.

Koo Gae Re Etla	We are coming home
Leader: Koo gae re etla koo teng.	We are coming home.
Group: Ahe, re etla koo teng.	Yes, we are coming home.
Leader: Re etla koo teng.	We are coming home.
Group: Ahe, re etla koo teng.	Yes, we are coming home.

The song goes on: We are coming home and we'll soon arrive. We are delayed by the steep hill, the rainy day, the rushing water. We walk slowly and it is hard to breathe.[28]

Bogwera: *male initiation*

It is interesting to note that one of the main reasons the missionaries regarded initiation as immoral was because of its musical content. They saw the use of 'obscene songs' which "consist of derogatory commentaries on all qualities, features and attributes of the female sex, and in view of their relation to the imminent initiation of the candidates into their state of manhood" as arousing their sexual impulses.[29]

Initiation school is both physically and mentally challenging for male initiates (*makatla*).[30] They have to learn an entirely new vocabulary composed of secret verses that enable them to enter and leave the initiation kraal; naming verses that are particular to each individual; and numerous songs. The overseer (*kake*) and his attendants (*bokgayane*) teach the boys using songs that are integrated into the everyday rituals of the school. While their circumcision wounds are healing, the novices start to learn the secret teachings (*koma*) and the songs praising their traditions. In the past, they had to compose their own praise poems (*maboko*)[31] and learn them by heart. At the end of the ceremony they recited them for the community assembled to welcome them back.[32] *Refer to Tracks 36 and 37.*

The **setinkane** is an earlier form of the *segwana*. The only difference between the two instruments is that the *setinkane* has no calabash resonator. This instrument is struck with a thin twig. It is played by young boys and is regarded as more of a toy than a musical instrument.

The **mafata-iswaneng,** or earth-bow, is made from a pliant branch with the heavier end stuck firmly in the ground. The top of the branch is bent down by a piece of sinew attached to a membrane, which in turn is stretched over a deep hole in the ground. The instrument is held in place for the player, who strikes the string with a stick, while changing its tension for different sounds. The earth-bow makes a 'big sound'.[15]

In the past the Batswana played the Khoi **ramkie** (see Chapter 10, page 237), but the European guitar has replaced this instrument.

Stringed-wind

The Batswana adopted the *gora* from the Korana Khoi. They called it **lesiba**, which means 'feather', after the instrument's main feature. (See Chapter 10, page 237). In the past, Batswana herdboys played the *lesiba*.[16]

Initiates performing a dance at Mochudi

Swazi maidens carrying reeds on their way to the Queen's residence where they will perform the reed dance

In the San trance dance the performers bend their knees, using small, controlled leg movements

Female Zulu dancers displaying their physical prowess

A rock painting at Tabanyama depicting a San dance

Man playing the Tswana segankuru

Men performing at a Swazi independence celebration, 1968

A woman takes a break from playing the moropa drum

Basotho woman playing her mouth-bow

Venda

VhaVenda

The Venda are a small group of people whose identity was welded into a compact whole over many years. Their ancestors were a mixture of those who came with their chiefs from the north, and the locals who were already living in the Soutpansberg in the Limpopo Province of South Africa. The Venda speak their own language and have a distinctive culture that is governed by the political divide between commoners and ruling families.

When the Venda migrated from Zimbabwe they settled in the Soutpansberg mountain range of present-day Limpopo Province, naming it Venda ('pleasant place'). The majority of Venda people still live in and around the Soutpansberg mountains, in the districts of Makhado and Sibasa. Small Venda clusters also live in south-eastern Zimbabwe.

VhaVenda

History of the VhaVenda, the 'People of the World'[1]

The Venda's origin is the subject of much uncertainty and dispute among those in search of historical veracity. However, most historical accounts maintain that the Venda migrated from the Great Lakes of Central Africa over a thousand years ago. There is also evidence that the Venda chiefs arrived in Southern Africa later than the other Bantu-speaking peoples. It has been estimated that they entered the sub-continent around the late 17th century. The two migrations that have been singled out as the most significant in the history of the area are those of the Vhatavhatsinde and the Makhwinde kinsmen. They settled along the Soutpansberg mountain range among the Bangoma – a rather disorganised, passive group that was already in occupation there. It was under the powerful leadership of Dimbanyika, the Makhwinde leader, that the Venda were recognised as the superior group among those sharing the same land. Dimbanyika subjugated all the other groups in the region and placed members of his own family as chiefs in every village of the area.[2]

According to oral tradition, there are two disputed myths woven around Dimbanyika's death. Some believe that Dimbanyika met his death when he was trapped in a cave, and his son Popi took over the chieftancy. Others assert that Dimbanyika's eldest son killed his father, "boasting that although the elephant was dead, he, the head, still remained and was called Thohoyandou ('Head of the elephant')."[3] In African mythology an elephant is a symbol of strength and greatness. This symbolism has been carried through the generations, and important people in Venda society are still greeted with *'ndau ndou'*, meaning 'good day elephant'. Thohoyandou was the greatest

Venda leader and seems to have been deserving of his title. He unified the different clans in the area, and with his followers, settled in the region now known as the Dzata ruins in the Njelele valley. This was the Venda's golden age.

Thohoyandou's leadership came to an end when he disappeared on a hunting trip, never to be seen again. For many years, people clung to the belief that he would one day return to his people "to restore the Venda to their former greatness."[4] After his disappearance, the Venda were left to the devices of Thohoyandou's brothers who engaged in warfare to fight for the chieftaincy. As a result, the Venda fragmented: the four eldest brothers became chiefs of four different districts, and Thohoyandou's son, Rampofu, took over his father's chieftancy. The eventual outcome was that two main lines of royalty were formed. Tshivhase, one of the brothers, became an independent chief in the east of Vendaland.

Drums

The Venda are known for their expressive drumming. Most sets of drums consist of one **ngoma**, one **thungwa**, and two or three **murumba**. They are normally kept in the homes of chiefs and headmen. Drums are usually played by women, except in certain contexts, such as possession rituals.[7]

The largest Venda drum is called the **ngoma**. The *ngoma* is a single-headed, pot-shaped drum carved out of one piece of solid wood. The drum has distinctive handles, which are ornately carved onto the drum shell by an expert. The head is made of cow-skin that is stretched when wet over the drum body and pegged to it. Before the head is secured with pegs, a few stones (supposedly extracted from the stomach of a crocodile, the Venda's totem animal) are dropped into the drum. It is held in a slanting position and played with a single beater in the right hand. The *ngoma* is played on a number of occasions, including during girls' initiation ceremonies (*domba*). The drum was once used in war, but is now more commonly used as a 'rain-drum'. The sound of the drum is similar to thunder, and when beaten it is believed that rain follows within three days. *Ngoma* drums belonging to chiefs are usually given special names.

When Thohoyandou's eldest son, Rampofu, died, his second son, Ramapulana ('the Treacherous'), took his place. He in turn was succeeded by Makhado who was the first Venda chief to encounter the Boers. He was known as 'Lion of the North' because of his "determined stand against European invasion."[5]

The Venda were the last of the South African ethnic groups to come into contact with Europeans, and they submitted to the authority of the Transvaal Republic only in 1899. For a number of reasons, Europeans had less influence on this group than on any of the other South African peoples. During the first part of the 20th century, the Venda had begun to move away from the villages of their rulers, taking up homesteads scattered over the hills and mountains. Being situated in a mountainous region made access for outsiders difficult. Furthermore, the Sibasa district was doing well in comparison with other South African 'reserves', and thus fewer men needed to leave home to work as migrant labourers. Lastly, the Venda had been more preoccupied with their own political agendas than with external politics. In all likelihood it is the Venda's separation from the outside world that has enabled them to retain their cultural institutions and traditional musical activities. The Venda's culture still thrives in Venda, despite the more recent changes that have come with the infiltration of European culture.

The murumba *drummers sway their bodies from side to side rubbing their hands over the drum skin.*

Music in performance

Wada: a sacred drum

According to legend, the Venda chiefs who travelled to southern Africa from the north in the late 18th century brought with them a magic drum, the *ngoma lungundu*. When they played the drum, their enemies became powerless and retreated. The great leader Thohoyandou had only to beat the drum to bring instant death to any enemies who heard it.[19] The mystery of the *ngoma lungundu* is matched by the mystery of the *Wada* drum. The myth of *Wada* is one that has retained its power, impacting on the Venda's relationship with their music, and still evident in their use of drums today. In Venda culture, drums are "an integral part of the cosmology of their peoples."[20] The story of the *Wada* drum is one of mystery, magic and superstition. It is one that is subject to retelling, with community members adding their own versions and reinforcing the intrigue.[21]

The Domboni mountain is the ancestral home of a Venda clan, the Tavhatsindi, living in the Folovhodwe-Muswodi district. Regarded as a sacred place, it was the ideal location for the storage of the *Wada* drum. During the 1930s, the Venda communities living in this district were forced by the government to move further south. With no time to consult their ancestral spirits about how to transport and where to store the drum, they left it in the Domboni mountain. This mountain became a shrine that people visited every year. According to various versions of the myth, outsiders attempted to move the drum, but never succeeded. People have attributed the continued safety of the drum to their ancestors' protection over them and their sacred objects. Apart from these myths, there are also those who recall the ancestral spirits actually playing the drum. There are reports of people who claimed to have heard the sound of the drum from a distance, but on approaching it, found no one there. These stories have added to the mystery surrounding the drum. An old man spoke about the fear and awe *Wada* has provoked in the community, stating that "not even the naughtiest boys will go near *Wada*."[22] Further:

"When donkeys or goats happen to stray near the drum, they are not rounded up, but left to find their way home. People sometimes find that the spirits close the opening to the tree. An event that is still recalled involved a boy who entered the tree, only to find that he was unable to get out. Only after a prayer offered to the ancestral spirits, who, it is thought, were offended and held the

The **thungwa** is a smaller version of the *ngoma* and is also played with a stick.

The **murumba** is made from a conical wood resonator and an ox hide that is pegged onto the drum while wet. The drum is modelled on the Venda milking jug (*khamelo*). Both objects have a large handle on the side, and are held between the thighs. The drum is played with both hands and produces two different sounds. A bass sound is created when the player strikes the head near the centre with a flat palm, and the higher tones are created when the player strikes the edge of the drum-skin. In the *domba* dance of the girls' initiation, the girls sway their bodies from side to side, rubbing one hand over the drum-skin between beats. This movement is referred to as 'washing the drum with the hands'.

The **tshigubu** is a double-headed drum that is modelled on the European marching band bass drum. It is usually played with two rubber beaters.

187

Wooden slabs of the mbila *(xylophone)*

boy captive, did he manage to get out. However, the spirits put a curse on him, and he is well-known today for his short stature."[23]

The *Wada* drum was eventually moved to another tree, nearby Muswodi-Tshisimani where it is still situated today. The drum is suspended from a horizontal pole: it can never be allowed to touch the ground as it is believed that "misfortune will befall the community if this happens."[24] The practice of hanging the drum from a pole was carried through into Venda culture. Venda drums are 'ritual objects'[25] imbued with religious and spiritual symbolism. The Venda's *ngoma* drum, still played today, carries with it some of the sacred qualities of the *Wada*. In the past, the *ngoma* was given religious significance, and was regarded as the embodiment of the ancestors' spirits. Today, people still kneel in reverence to the *ngoma* drum. It is played only for sacred events that reflect the ritualistic aspects of a community. The reed-pipe dance, initiation schools and possession dances are included in this category.

Ngoma: sacred events

The word *ngoma*, apart from referring to the Venda drum, is also used to refer to rituals with a sacred dimension.[26] In Venda society, these events also have political significance, and the musical activities that accompany them are inextricably linked to the political makeup of the society.[27] Many musical activities reflect and enhance political power, and thus play an important role in upholding established political systems. In Venda society there is a strict division between commoners (*vhasiwana*) and the descendents of chiefs (*mahosi*).[28] Music is performed to emphasise and assert the importance of this socio-political structure. Chiefs determine when and how musical performances should take place, and music cannot be performed without their permission and approval. Such is the intimate relationship between music and politics that music has the power to "settle peacefully a political dispute."[29]

Rattles

Mutshakatha are leg-rattles made from the hardened shells of a hollowed-out fruit called a monkey orange (*strychnos spinosa*). Stones are placed into the round shells, which are threaded onto sticks. Once the shells have been secured, the sticks are tied together with cloth to form a complete instrument. Both men and women wear these rattles.[8]

There are two variations of **thandana** rattles. The first type consists of horns or baskets filled with beads. The second type is made from carved sticks.

Tshele are hand-rattles made from calabashes that are filled with seeds. They are used during possession rituals (*malombo*).

Bull-roarers

The Venda call their bull-roarers **tshivhilivhi**.[9]

189

Tshikona: *the reed-pipe dance*

One of the most powerful musical performances that stands as a symbol of political power "and a sonorous emblem of national pride"[30] is the Venda's reed-pipe dance – *tshikona*.[31] The performance of *tshikona* is the kind of musical event that excites and inspires the community. As one writer explained:

> *"Tshikona 'makes sick people feel better, and old men throw away their sticks and dance', it 'brings peace to the countryside', both because people leave their hoes and let the earth rest, and because it brings everyone together in fellowship and co-operation. It is* lwa-ha-masia-khali-i-tshi-vhila, *'the time when people [rush off and] leave their pots to boil over', because they are captivated by the descending scales of the reed-pipes and the stately beat of the drums."*[32]

Apart from inter-group competitions held over weekends between *tshikona* teams, the dance is performed only for important occasions that hold significance for rulers, such as the installation or death of a chief, the first fruits ceremony (*thevula*), and the inauguration of initiation schools. The *tshikona* also has a sacred dimension; it is sometimes performed as a prayer or sacrifice to the ancestors of the royal clans. In the past the dance had a practical function. The participants were young men who were trained in warfare and acted as community police. They were sent by their chiefs to collect outstanding debts or fines from the community. Given the social, spiritual and political significance of *tshikona* in its various contexts, this dance was traditionally performed only by adults. This has changed considerably over time, due to changes arising from the shifting socio-economic environment. When the migrant-labour system was in place, many Venda men in rural villages migrated to the cities in search of work. The departed men left gaps in many *tshikona* groups and it became common for teams to be comprised of boys, some as young as ten.

Another recent development has been the formation of female *tshikona* teams. One researcher gives an example of the formation of a female team in the 1980s. He explains that a group of women in the village of

Muswodi-Tshisimani had been asked to prepare a *tshigombela* (another Venda dance) team for an agricultural showday at Mutale. The women were not familiar with this dance because it had never been performed in their area. Villagers tried to organise a *tshikona* team of boys or men, but the men had left for the city and the boys did not know the dance. A group of women who still remembered the dance decided to mobilise a small team and their headman agreed. So determined were they to perform the dance that they were not deterred by the fact that there were only broken drums in their community. They made their own drums from large tins and a big iron cooking pot. The outcome was that:

"*Outsiders initially were shocked to see women performing a male dance, but came to accept their involvement as an innovative novelty. The establishment of this dance team seemed to have boosted the morale of an economically depressed community. A strong sense of community pride folllowed its enlargement, its first performances, and its subsequent fame.*"[33]

Chiefs send messengers and horn blowers from their villages to notify all dancers in the district to gather to perform *tshikona*. The practices and performances of the dance are formally organised. The men are trained by a leader (*malugwane*), who leads them during the performance. People spend many years learning and mastering the dance. It is complex, involving the coordination of dance with the playing of a single note in precisely the right place. Each dancer blows only one pipe, which represents one note in the seven-note scale. Combined, the pipes create a variety of interlocking

Xylophones

Both the Venda and the Chopi of Mozambique call their xylophone instruments **mbila**. The Venda's *mbila mutondo* is a large instrument consisting of twenty-one or twenty-two wooden slabs. The slabs are cut from the *mutondo* tree (*kiaat*) and are suspended by means of bark cords over an equal amount of calabash resonators. It is important that each resonator is sized accurately for each slab, so that it is in tune with it and gives maximum volume and clarity.

A small hole is cut near the end of the resonator, over which a piece of spider-egg membrane is stuck with wax or resin. This creates a buzzing sound each time the slabs are struck. The tuning is the same as the reed flutes that are played in the *tshikona* dance. Two men squat on the floor; one playing the lower notes with two rubber beaters, while the principal player uses three rubber beaters, one in his right hand and two in his left. In the past the Venda *mbila* was played during beer parties. There was also a spiritual element to xylophone playing – people regarded it as a form of prayer to the ancestors. This instrument is now virtually extinct among the Venda.

Refer to Track 38.

Two performers playing the mbila mutondo

melodic patterns. Being a dance with political significance, the *ngoma* drum is also included in the performance of the *tshikona*. The dance has both political and social implications. While it cultivates loyalty and respect for the chiefs of the ruling classes, consolidating their political power, it also generates social solidarity by bringing the community together to participate in a group activity that requires strong musical coordination. Here is a description of the performance of the *tshikona*:

> "*The whole community waits expectantly in the heat. Women, men and children gather at the meeting place and the atmosphere of festivity heightens as the* tshikona *dance teams arrive. The teams vary in size but one can only gauge how big they are when they enter the performance area, with four men leading the team carrying the* ngoma *drum by its ornately carved handles. The drums are set up outside the group that has now huddled together in a spiral formation. A handful of women lie with their faces and bodies against the ground, and remain in this position throughout the dance as a sign of respect. The dance begins with the sounding of one chord, which is played by the entire group. The reed-pipe played individually creates a small sound, but when played by a group of up to 200 men, the sound is large and rich. Once the starting note of the dance has been played, the men begin to move out of the compact formation in such a way that they spiral outwards to form a large circle, with the drums in the centre. Each pipe sounds a different note, and the result is the distinctive sound produced by* tshikona *reed-pipes. The music consists of twelve pulses which are repeated in a cyclical form. The men move anti-clockwise around the circle, playing the pipes while performing intricate dance-steps. There are standard steps, found in every* tshikona *dance, which represent activities that form part of the first fruits ceremony. These steps include 'gathering ground nuts' and 'sowing seeds'. The men lean forward into the circle and then turn around and step out. There are also variations among the teams, each of them portraying a unique character. The teams showcase their individual qualities through their costumes. While some teams are clothed in animal skins, others are more colourfully dressed in feathers and bright materials. During the course of the dance the circle usually grows wider*

as the team moves outwards. Towards the end of the dance, one or two men break out of the circle to dance solos around it. Finally, the dance comes full circle as the men move back into the formation presented at the beginning of the dance. The dance ends with the sounding of a final chord by the entire group."[34] *Refer to Track 41.*

Initiation

Another politically symbolic *ngoma* or sacred event that reflects the divide between commoners and royalty is initiation.[35] Initiation schools are privately owned by commoners, who pay an annual fee to the local ruler in order to hold them. Chiefs sometimes encourage commoners to run these schools because it is a source of revenue for them.[36] In return for payment, rulers show their support by banning all unrelated communal music while the schools are running.

Musevetho: *male initiation* – Young men who belong to ruling clans have no obligation to undergo initiation, and in fact cannot become rulers if they have been circumcised.[37] This is because circumcision schools are not indigenous to Venda culture. They were adopted from the Northern Sotho and were never fully accepted by the royal families.[38] In the past, Venda boys went through several pre-circumcision initiation schools: *thondo, vhuthuka* and *domba,* but these were slowly replaced with *murundu* – a school that was incorporated into Venda culture at a later stage. Initiation usually takes place outside the village, on a hilltop or a mountain, during the cold, dry winter months which assist the healing of the circumcision wound. It is in these isolated regions, where the boys are completely cut off from society, that they are taught the secret codes of manhood through music.

Music accompanies the boys in their rite of passage from the morning of their arrival when the school song, *hogo,* is performed, to the very last day when they embark on their journey home as men, singing with a spirit of accomplishment. The songs cement the lessons of the school at each stage of the initiation, helping the boys to internalise them. Once all the initiates have been circumcised, they are taught various secret codes and songs around the

Mbiras

The *mbira,* called **mbila deza** in Venda, was bought to Vendaland by the Lemba, their neighbours. It is made from a rectangular piece of wood shaped like a tray with low walls around a hollowed-out top surface. Twenty-two or more flattened tongues of iron or copper are fixed to the broad end of the slab by means of a bridge and a bar and wire, much like the *mbiras* of Zimbabwe. Another thick wire adorned with small metal tubes is attached to the end nearest the player. This serves as a rattle, adding a buzzing sound. The instrument is placed inside a large resonator made from a calabash *(deza).* Attached to the resonator are small shells, which also produce a rattling sound as the instrument is played. The keys towards the left-hand side of the instrument produce lower notes and are plucked downwards by the left thumb, while the keys to the right-hand side produce higher notes and are plucked by the right thumb and forefinger.[10] Males play the *mbila deza* to accompany songs they sing during their free time. This instrument is well-suited to the reflective, calming tunes they sing outdoors for relaxation, and to while away the time. The Lemba, on the other hand, use the *mbila deza* in their rituals, as do the Shona in Zimbabwe. *Refer to Track 39.*

fire at night, few of which are sung in the Venda language. It is interesting to note that because the institution of initiation was borrowed from the Bapedi, many of the Tshivenda initiation songs have Sesotho musical features and are in fact sung in Sesotho. Their subject matter ranges from respecting elders, to ridiculing those who have not been circumcised.[39]

At some point during the initiation period, a long pole is erected while the boys are sleeping. The Venda bull-roarer (*tshivhilivhi*), usually an instrument that is used as a child's toy, is put to unusual use during this ritual. The instrument, which sounds like 'lions whimpering',[40] is played so that the boys cannot hear the pole being erected. When they wake in the morning they are told that the pole represents their grandfather. The pole becomes the central point around which much dancing and singing takes place during the remaining initiation period. Initiates dance around and climb the pole, singing so that their voices can be heard from a great distance. During the same period, one initiate, disguised with grass and rushes, is sent to dance and

A female initiate performs the ndayo *dance*

sing before the women who bring food to the boys. This ritual, centered on the disguised initiate (*daganana*), is the cause of much excitement and commotion in the community.

Towards the end of the initiation the boys prepare to go back home, and the content of the songs during this period reflect upon their imminent journey. Finally, the site of the school is burnt and the initiates are welcomed back into the community amid spirited voices of celebration.

Vhusha, tshikanda *and* domba: *female initiation* – Girls' initiation schools are held throughout the year to accommodate the three phases of initiation: *vhusha*, *tshikanda*, and *domba*.[41] During the first two phases, singing and dancing take place mainly in the council huts of rulers. There are special songs to mark rituals such as the removal of each girl from her home, the painting of the initiate's body with clay and red ochre, and the passage of a group of girls from the council house to the river and back.

In the first phase of initiation the girls spend most of their time rehearsing the physically challenging *ndayo* dances. These are used as exercises to teach the girls certain lessons. They learn these dances by imitating the older girls, and usually suffer much humiliation and teasing before mastering each dance. The most difficult of the *ndayo* dances is one in which "the performer stands on her head, and, balancing herself on the palms of her hands, performs a series of leg movements, waving her legs in the air in time to the drums and singing, with remarkable skill and energy."[42] Girls also dance with their arms folded on their chests, standing and squatting, while kicking and shuffling their feet forwards and backwards. The communal dance of the school, in which the girls move anti-clockwise around the drums, is performed two or three times every evening. Another dance that is performed regularly is one in which the girls kneel, and, in time to the drums, move their hands across their knees from one side to the other. When the tempo of the music doubles, they sit on their haunches, shaking their heads from side to side. A striking and spectacular musical performance is that of the masked dancers (*vhahwira*) who perform for the girls. Wearing masks over their faces so that they cannot be recognised, the dancers communicate with the girls by whistling.

In order for girls to undergo the final phase of initiation, *domba*, they first have to go through *tshikanda*, which lasts for a full month. During this phase, the girls start to rehearse the python dance, the most distinctive feature of *domba*. Using theatrical techniques, they also enact the myth of *Thovhela and Tshishonge*, two Venda heroes who are considered to be the originators of their people. This performance resembles a morality play, where dance, drama and song function as effective tools to communicate moral ethics to the initiates. Once the myth of *Thovhela and Tshishonge* has been enacted, the initiates are ready for the final phase of initiation.

Domba is the only initiation school that is attended by teenagers who belong to both the ruling and commoners classes. In the past, boys and girls underwent *domba* together, but today this ritual is enacted only by girls. It is sometimes held shortly after a new ruler has come to power, and it can last for up to two years. Rulers support the *domba* initiation because they have a vested interest in it – initiates pay high fees to enter this institution.

Whistles, flutes and reeds

Venda reed-pipes (**nanga**) are always played in ensembles comprising at least one set (*mutavha*) or seven pipes (covering one octave), and often as many as three sets of different sizes (covering three octaves). A set of end-blown reed-pipes resembles dismantled pan-pipes. Each dancer blows only one pipe, which, combined with the group, creates a variety of melodic patterns. There are two main variations of reed-pipes among the Venda. They are tuned by being cut to different lengths and are made of different materials. Some of the longest pipes are up to four feet in length. *Dza musununu* are made of a species of bamboo and *nanga dza musunu* are made of river-reed. In the past, the reed-pipes were made of a special bamboo (*musonono*) found only in a small forest at Tshaulu, which was considered to be a sacred place. The instrument maker was the only person allowed to enter the sacred forest to cut the bamboo. River-reed is found in many parts of Venda and is cut exclusively by the male members of one family. Nowadays, especially in urban areas, the pipes are often made of an assortment of metal tubing, hosepipe, curtain rods, or pram handles. *Tshikona*, one of the most popular Venda dances, is accompanied by a reed-pipe ensemble (*nanga ya tshikona*) and three drums in the centre of the circle.

The master of domba *stands in the centre and sings a solo*

Commoners are willing to pay these fees as a worthwhile investment in a ritual that instils a sense of pride and belonging. The number of initiates participating affects the volume of the music, which is a reflection of the ruler's prestige and wealth. When the *domba* initiation takes place, the ruler bans all other music in the community in order to emphasise the sacredness of the ritual. The *ngoma* drum, reserved for sacred rituals, is played during the initiation.

Man playing the nanga ya davhi

The *domba* dance is renowned in the Limpopo Province for its formation, which resembles a python. In Venda culture, the python is a symbol of fertility. Along the same lines, the dance also simulates the movements of a baby in the womb. The girls, wearing loin cloths or small aprons around their waists, perform this dance daily in an open, public space. They form a chain, each holding the elbow of the girl in front, and use shuffling steps to move anti-clockwise around the drums. They drag their legs forward very slowly so that their movements as a group mimic the gliding movements of the python. The girls who play the two *murumbu* drums sway their bodies from side to side, rubbing one hand over the drum-skin between beats. The master of *domba* stands in the centre and sings a solo, usually improvising. He starts by singing *"Tharu ya mabidhighami"* ('the python is uncoiling') and the girls respond with a drawn-out *"eeee"* in a low tone.[43] The master sometimes organises spectacles for the girls that consist of performers unexpectedly appearing in disguise to entertain them.[44] *Refer to Track 42.*

Malombo: *possession*

Possession rituals reflect another dimension of the Venda socio-political hierarchy.[45] Cult groups are formed and possession dances enhance the

The *nanga ya davhi* is a wooden whistle sometimes ornamented with carvings etched with hot wire, which was once played by men.

The *dzhio* is the boys' version of the *nanga ya davhi*. This whistle is either made from wood or the bones of sheep, buck or goat.

The *nanga ya danga* is a whistle made from the wing-bone of a vulture. A wizard (*maloi*) played this instrument to warn people of the presence of a wrongdoer so that he or she could be avoided.

The *nanga ya ntsa* is a whistle made from the horn of a small antelope, and the Venda used it to call their dogs.

The *pala* is a flute made from the horn of the impala and was used as a signal whistle.

The *tshitiringo* is a three-holed transverse flute made from river-reed. It was played mainly by herdboys, although men also occasionally played the instrument.[11]

The *khumbgwe* probably originated with the Karanga people of southern Zimbabwe. This instrument was played mainly by boys, and consisted of a monkey-orange shell that was pierced on opposite ends, and a reed with three finger-holes that was inserted into the bottom hole.

After the first note has been sounded the tshikona *performers stand up and slowly spiral outwards into a circle formation*

Performers shift their weight from one foot to the next

*Tshikona dance costumes vary
from team to team*

prestige and influence of the families who belong to these groups.[46] These dances are arranged at specific times when they are unlikely to interfere with more important events. They usually last for approximately one full week, with pauses at regular intervals. The first session of the ritual, *tshele*, is named after the hand-rattles that are shaken to rouse a trance state in the person who is possessed. As the intensity of the music builds, the patient (usually a female) collapses forward and the spirit speaks through her in a mixture of Venda and Karanga.[47] Occasionally patients are possessed by numerous spirits, each of which is given a turn to enter her body. At this point, other women who have been possessed step forward, allowing the foreign voices to communicate through them.

A few months later the spirits are given the chance to surface during a public dance. The music at this performance is unusual because it does not conform to conventional Venda musical practices. This is one of the few occasions when men play drums, and the music has a much faster tempo than other Venda songs. The master drummer plays the *ngoma* drum as if he were possessed, throwing his body forwards and backwards. He alters the pitch of the drum by pressing his elbow against the drum-skin. Spectators and dancers form a semi-circle around the drums, encircling each possessed individual. When a patient is on the verge of collapse, the rattle players surround her in the hope that the spirit will enter her. If the spirit is too 'shy' to expose itself in public, the dancers and rattle shakers accompany the person into a hut and sing until she collapses – a sign that she has been possessed. *Refer to Track 43.*

Bepha: musical expeditions

The political makeup of Venda society is most evident in the musical expeditions of the Venda, known as *bepha*.[48] *Bepha* expeditions take place on various occasions, and their main purpose is to reinforce the status of rulers and chiefs. On these occasions, commoners represent their rulers by visiting neighbouring districts and performing music for their respective chiefs. These expeditions generally occur to express sympathy to the bereaved of a member of the ruler's lineage, to congratulate a headman or chief upon his

The Venda are the only indigenous group in South Africa that made use of an aerophone of the vibrating-reed class, to which instruments such as the clarinet and saxophone belong. The *sitlanjani* was made of ivory and bound by a narrow strip of buck-skin. It was used only for secret ceremonies, and when played it produced strange sounds that the people believed were the voices of the spirits.

An instrument similar to the *sitlanjani* is a vibrating reed that is played during girls' initiation. The flute, covered on one end with spider webbing, is played by the *nonyana*, a symbolic figure representing the spirits of the school. Disguised with bark and reeds, the *nonyana* plays the instrument during the ceremony, and also uses it to awaken the initiates in the mornings.

Ocarinas

The **tshipotoliyo** is made from the shell of a wild custard apple (*mutuzwa*) or a monkey orange. The centre is hollowed out and a hole for the embouchure is cut at the top of the fruit. Two smaller holes that are used for pitch are cut further down the shell. These holes, usually both the same size, are smaller than the embouchure-hole. The player breathes across the embouchure and the two smaller holes can be stopped. The ocarina can produce four notes, either with both holes open, one hole stopped, or both holes stopped with a large area of the embouchure covered by the lower lip. This instrument produces a rich sound that is often compared to the whistling of birds. Boys played the ocarina in duets, with one ocarina pitched below the other.

The tshigombela *dance is performed during musical expeditions*

Two children playing leap-frog

appointment, or to maintain good relations with neighbouring rulers. In this way, lineage ties between rulers are consolidated. Expeditions may last between one and five days, during which time the hosting chief entertains the guest team, providing them with alcohol and food. The frequency of expeditions thus largely depends upon the economic surplus, because a chief cannot be expected to provide meals for a large group of people if the surplus is low.

Musical expeditions not only consolidate political power, but also engender a sense of camaraderie among the team members and other participants in the community. The build-up to the journey forms an exciting aspect of the expedition. Weeks before it begins, there is a joyful liveliness in the community. While parents help to make special costumes and equip their children for the journey, the teams enthusiastically rehearse their performances. Through this period of intensified communal activity, the ruler secures the loyalty of his people. Young people in the community are given a chance to establish ties with their neighbours, and to develop close relationships within their teams. *Bepha* expeditions also provide a platform for a community to communicate with its ruler. For the duration of the expedition, the norms that govern the relationship between leader and commoner are suspended, and individuals are able to address their rulers directly. Other social norms, such as gender roles, are also inverted. This inversion is expressed in the 'transvestite symbolism'[49] of the dance costumes. Girls wear items of boy's clothing such as shirts and hats, and carry objects usually associated with masculinity, such as sticks and shields.

The two most-commonly performed dances on *bepha* expeditions are *tshikanganga* and *tshigombela*.[50] Both dances are performed in autumn after harvesting when there is little rain. The form of *tshikanganga* resembles the *tshikona* dance, which is also performed on *bepha* expeditions. The girls play the *thungwa* and *murumba* drums, and the boys dance anti-clockwise in a circle, producing the melody of the song with a set of end-blown reed-pipes. The dance movements are graceful and the tempo is slow.

Until the 1970s, *tshigombela* was danced only by unmarried girls and women. Since then, married women have also joined *tshigombela* teams, due to various changes in Venda society.[51] The ruler has strict control over rehearsals and performances. *Tshigombela* thus holds strong political significance and is symbolic of the ruler's authority. The dance has a fast tempo and consists of two parts. In the first part, the women dance anti-clockwise in a circle around the drums, using kicking movements. In the second part, they break off into groups of two or three. They wear decorated bead skirts, waistcoats, towels, leg-rattles and costume jewellery, which serve to accentuate and enhance their movements. *Refer to Track 44.*

Mitambo: amusements

Mitambo refers to music used for recreational activities.[52] This type of music provides entertainment and is a powerful forum for social commentary.

Nyimbo dza vhana: *children's songs*

Before children reach adolescence, they use song as an accompaniment to almost everything they do. Songs bring children together and create an effective medium for communication.[53] There are two main types of children's songs. *Nyimbo* are sung by day and at any time of the year, while *ngano* are performed in the evenings in late autumn and winter. *Nyimbo* accompany almost all children's activities. Children sing when they play games, which expands their concentration and enhances their enjoyment. Physical endurance games are always accompanied by songs, which are usually simple

Horns

The **phalaphala** is made from sable, kudu or gemsbok horn, or wood. This instrument belongs to a village rather than an individual. It is used by the chief's envoy to signal to his subjects or call dancers from various homesteads to perform the *tshikona* dance. In the past the instrument was also used to call warriors to assemble before the chief. One interesting use of the horn was for the first sighting of the morning star, Sirius, in winter. The first man to notice the star would climb a hill and blow the *phalaphala* to spread the news. The significance of this was to let the village and especially the chief know that harvesting time was about to begin. The chief offered a reward of a cow to the first man who blew the horn on this occasion.[12]

Smaller horns, **tshihoho**, are made from a variety of materials, such as wood, the horns of a small animal, or the stem of a pumpkin. They are used by boys to signal to one another.[13]

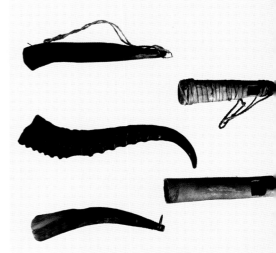

Tshihoho *horns made of different materials*

Man playing the tshihoho *made from pumpkin stem*

with repeated short phrases. For example, when girls and boys do headstands, they sing:

Ndo ima nga thoho	I am standing on my head
Nzhelele, nzhelele,	Kite, kite
Ndo ima nga thoho.	I am standing on my head.[54]

In the game *musingadi*, girls squat and hop, holding their knees together with their hands or balancing with their arms. They sing while moving about, creating a rhythm for their hopping. When children engage in an activity that involves balance, such as walking along the branch of a tree, they sing:

Dadamale! A ri kandi fhasi.	Walk carefully! We are not falling off.
Dadamale! A ri kandi fhasi.	Walk carefully! We are not falling off.[55]

Song is also an effective medium of instruction. Children learn to count through song, using their fingers and singing at different speeds. They also count limbs by sitting in a row with their legs stretched out in front of them. The counter takes on the role of the solo singer as he or she counts the legs. Another popular type of children's song is that of mockery. If a herdboy plays with the girls, he is teased with:

Tshitambana vhasidzana	Shame on you!
Ndole, ndole, tshitamba na vhasidzana!	Shame on you for playing with girls![56]

Songs that are directed towards the informal education of children are sung in the evenings when folktales (*ngano*) are told. According to one academic, "the nucleus of most Tshivenda folktales… is the song (*luimbo*)."[57] Through a combination of story and song, children become familiar with the moral and ethical fabric of their communities. The African folktale has its roots in oral tradition, where stories are handed down from one storyteller to the next. It is a form that has survived many generations and preserved many

Bows

The *lugube* bow is played by women, and is often used to convey various messages that indicate their marital status. It is a hollow reed with a string made from sinew or the hairs of a wildebeest tail. The bow is held to the left of the player, and the string is stopped with the second, third and fourth fingers of the left hand. The right forefinger plucks the string in an upward or downward direction. The notched end of the bow rests in the mouth, which is used as a resonator to select the harmonics.
Refer to Track 40.

Woman playing the lugube

cultures. Within African communities, folktales are regarded as performances involving a narrator (the performer) and listeners (the audience). Various Venda folktales incorporate song to heighten the impact of the performance. The use of song helps the narrator to hold the listeners' attention, and adds another dimension to the story. The narrator also dramatises the story through musical techniques. The voice is used to mimic and substitute the sounds produced by musical instruments, as well as the sounds of birds and animals, to bring the story to life. The narrator is someone who can capture a child's imagination as an actor, a wordsmith and a good singer.

The narrator always begins the folktale with the exclamation 'Salungano'('like a song story') and the listeners respond by echoing 'Salungano'.[58] Likewise, throughout the rest of the tale, the listeners participate

In the tshigombela *dance the women move around in a circle with the drums in the centre*

by responding with 'Salungano' after every line in the story and in the chorus of the song.[59] In another style of ngano – ngano dza bune ('songs of the game of touch') – each member of the group takes a turn to sing the solo.[60]

Mitambo: dance theatre

Mitambo is a theatrical form that arises from musical performance.[61] Venda dance theatre blends traditional dance with drama. Meaning is conveyed through mime, role-play, dance and song, and these tools are used as a form of social commentary. Social and ethical values are communicated through mitambo, and the content is largely dictated by current concerns and the way people approach them. Venda dance theatre provides opportunities for people to express their interpretations of society. Additionally, it creates a platform for people to comment upon political developments. This traditional art form has played an important role in Venda culture, particularly in the struggle for democracy. People use communal song, dance and theatre to mirror political concerns

Mitambo are spontaneous responses to social situations, and they are seldom planned. They are largely improvised performances, in which ideas are generated as the performance develops. There is no stipulated length or structure. They might occur during the length of one song, or spur inspiration for an entire evening's worth of entertainment. In some cases, mitambo are planned for more formal, structured events such as meetings and festivals. The most common forms of mitambo are reed-pipe dance theatre, dance theatre of the tshigombela female dance, and beer-song dance theatre. Beer-songs are performed at any time of the year, during any social occasion, except after a death. They are sung mainly for entertainment or during communal work-parties while workers are taking a break from their

Man playing the tsijolo

The **tshigwana** is made from a piece of wood that tapers on either end, so that there is a thicker piece of wood in the centre of the bow. This feature of the instrument has been likened to the "Indian hunting-bow with its thick hand-grip."[14] The string, made from twisted sinew or wire, is tied back at the centre, and is plucked on either side with different techniques, producing four notes. The player holds the bow horizontally, with his left hand in line with his face, and with one end of the thick centre portion of the stave against his mouth. He fingers the string with the left index finger and plucks the string with the right forefinger and thumb. The tshigwana was traditionally played by young unmarried men, and might be regarded by some as the male version of the lugube. A man used the bow to communicate his marital status. Over the years the instrument lost its traditional function and was no longer reserved solely for men.[15]

The **tsijolo** is a type of straight friction-bow played by males. It is made from soft wood and fitted with a wire string and a tuning peg. The player holds the end of the instrument with the peg in his left hand, and rests the other end against his mouth, which acts as a resonator. He rubs a small hair-bow across the string in a circular motion.[16]

205

labours. They are also adapted for certain dances, such as the *tshigombela* dance and the *domba* initiation dance. Beer is often offered as a gift between two families whose children are getting married, and the parents usually sing beer-songs when gifts are exchanged. Beer-song dance theatre is traditionally used as a forum to explore gender relations. Women might enact a love triangle between husband, wife and mistress, using basic costumes and props to dramatise the performance.

Zwilombe: wandering entertainers

Performers do not need to ask permission from rulers to play solo music and their music is not governed by the rules of any institution.[62] Some solo performers eventually acquire the status of professional musicians. In Venda culture, the wandering entertainer (*tshilombe*) is a male musician who falls somewhere between a jester and artist.[63] He is an artist by virtue of the divine inspiration he is able to transmit to the audience, and his acute sensitivity and empathy that enable him to express what others cannot. His role as a jester allows him to view society in a critical manner, using jest to expose his society's flaws and follies. There is often an underlying criticism buried beneath the humour in his comic songs. He is someone who entertains with his creative storytelling techniques and he can also be potentially insulting with his sharp wit. The wandering entertainer, who usually belongs to the class of commoners, uses his power with words and music to represent the disempowerment of other commoners who might be marginalised or neglected in society. Ironically, even though he is often regarded as a lower class, outspoken, crazy figure, his strong moral standing is reflected in his songs. In the following example, the musician takes a nostalgic glance at a lifestyle that is lost to his generation. He protests against the emptiness of the modern lifestyle:

People of old were rich indeed

But they earned only five cents

They had cattle byres, so they were rich

Nowadays we are truly ashamed

Nowadays we are truly overcome

Now even if we get money we are overcome

People of old were better off

They furthermore used to eat porridge, so they were rich

Alas, now what must we sing?

Alas, now what must we do?

Indeed, the best thing is to go and hoe

Perhaps I will become truly rich.[64]

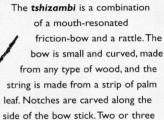

The **tshizambi** is a combination of a mouth-resonated friction-bow and a rattle. The bow is small and curved, made from any type of wood, and the string is made from a strip of palm leaf. Notches are carved along the side of the bow stick. Two or three *ntsa* pods or small calabashes are filled with pebbles and attached to a separate rattle stick, which is rubbed along the notches on the bow, causing the palm-leaf string to vibrate. The musician holds the instrument between the left thumb and fourth finger, leaving the remaining fingers free to stop the string. One end of the string is held between the player's lips, and the mouth acts as a resonator. The player rubs the rattle stick back and forth on the notches with his right hand.[17]

The *tshilombe* wanders from place to place, playing for money, beer or food, and entertaining for laughs and attention at beer houses. In strange garb and with extravagant mannerisms, he is regarded as an eccentric figure. Traditionally, *zwilombe* (plural) played mainly the *dende* and *tshizambi* bows to accompany their singing, but nowadays they often play the guitar. *Zwilombe* invest their artistic passion in their music, and often have "a remarkable mystical power which infects people and seems to send them into 'overdrive'; a type of ecstatic condition in which they submit to the music and the occasion; a condition in which singers and dancers seem to have endless energy, and instrumentalists play until the sweat pours down their faces."[65] Most of their music is sponsored by the ruler, thus these performances are associated with money and power. It is for this reason that rulers usually approve of jesters and like to have them close by. It is the musical element of the jester's criticism that makes it acceptable to the ruler. Similarly, women are able to vocalise their opinions when performing the *tshigombela* dance. As a general rule, the inclusion of music in various kinds of activities suspends certain prevailing rules in Venda society. The role of the wandering entertainer has largely fallen away as an increasing number of Western forms of societal commentary have been introduced.

The **dende** braced gourd-bow is played by male performers. It is made from the branch of a tree stripped of bark and a string that is tied back at a point near the centre, dividing it into two segments. A calabash is fixed in the middle of the bow. The player holds the instrument vertically in one hand, with the calabash opening facing the chest. The instrument is grasped near the calabash, with the fingers extended on either side of the string's division. The other hand strikes the string with a stick, thin reed or piece of grass.[18]

Stringed-wind

The Venda version of the Khoi *gora* is the **ugwala** (see Chapter 10, page 237).

Tsonga-Shangaan

Batsonga (Shangaan)

In the early 19th century the Batsonga (Shangaan) were conquered by the Nguni chief Soshangane. Their descendents became known as the Tsonga-Shangaan.

The Batsonga are concentrated mainly in the northern parts of the Limpopo Province in South Africa, as well as in parts of neighbouring Mozambique and Zimbabwe.

Batsonga (Shangaan)

History of the Batsonga

There are very few records of the early history of the Tsonga, apart from one or two Portuguese sources.[1] People have come to believe that the Tsonga clans immigrated to present-day Mozambique from the north, west and south, and that they have been in occupation there for hundreds of years. They were organised into small, independent chiefdoms, sometimes numbering a few thousand people. They did not have a central political authority, and most clans lived under headmen who had little power. They lived undisturbed for centuries until the tribal upheavals (*mfecane*) of the early 19th century. During this period, their lack of leadership made them vulnerable to invading Nguni peoples. Refugees escaping from Shaka infiltrated Mozambique, disrupting their peace.

The majority of the Tsonga were conquered by an Nguni army that had fled from Shaka in Natal. The army was an offshoot of the Ndandwe, who were under the military leadership of Soshangane at the time. He was powerful enough to subjugate the disparate Tsonga clans, and he established the Kingdom of Gaza. The descendants of some of the conquered peoples came to be known as the Shangaan (from his name – Soshangane). They were also called Thonga by the Zulu who had invaded their territory. The origin of this name probably lies in the Zulu word *ronga* which means orient. When pronounced by Zulu people, the 'r' of *ronga* becomes 'th'. The Zulu first used the name Thonga as a derogatory nickname for the captured Tsonga clans, before the people started to call themselves Tsonga. Some Tsonga or Shangaan trace their ancestry to the Zulu warriors who subjugated the armies in the region, while others claim descent from the conquered chiefdoms. Although the Tsonga were absorbed into Soshangane's Shangaan nation, they never adopted the Zulu language, and retained the majority of their customs.

In 1828, Shaka Zulu, the great Zulu king, sent an army to conquer Soshangane's army, the Ndwandwe. They failed, and it was to be Shaka's last military mission before he was killed. A few years later, in 1833, the Zulu attacked the newly formed Shangaan state, consisting of the Tsonga and Ndwandwe peoples who had now become one nation. The Zulu felt threatened by the Shangaans' control of the important trade route to Lourenço Marques (now Maputo). They seized control of Lourenço Marques, and Soshangane fled with his army to the Zambezi River in central Mozambique. Later Soshangane and his followers moved to Mosapa, south of

Music must be treated with respect because it is gives humans the power to destroy, protect or heal.

Drums

The *ncomane* is a hand-held drum shaped like a tambourine and played with sticks.[2] The head is made of goat- or buck-skin. The drum is held in the left hand and beaten with a stick held in the right. The longer fingers of the left hand press on the underside of the skin to raise its pitch. These drums are usually played together in sets of four, and are tuned to the same pitch by heating them over a fire. They are played on important occasions, such as to announce the death of a chief, to summon warriors to battle, at the end of the harvest when the *nkino* dance is performed, and, most typically, by diviners for exorcism rituals. They produce a sharp, powerful tone that helps induce a hypnotic state in the patient.[3]

The *muntshintshi* ('the big drum') is hoisted up on three legs. The skin is of buffalo, ox or antelope hide or elephant's ear. In the past it was played to call warriors to battle, but today it is used to announce a death, and for various musical performances. It is an instrument clouded in myth and mystery. While some people believe that a bullet is stored in the drum, others believe that the skull of a hostile chief was once placed inside it.

The *shikolombane* ('the son of the big one') is smaller than the *muntshintshi* and has no legs. This drum has a high-pitched sound and was used to accompany the horn ensemble. The *muntshintshi* and *shikolombane* bear a strong resemblance to the Venda *ngoma* and *murumba*, and there is evidence that the Tsonga adopted these instruments from the Venda.

the Zambezi. He managed to convince the Shona-speaking Ndau of Zimbabwe and Mozambique to join his forces. He eventually built up a realm that stretched from the Zambezi River to Delagoa Bay (at present-day Maputo). He named it the Gaza Kingdom, after his grandfather.

Meanwhile, under Soshangane's rule, many Tsonga who were unwilling to submit to his rule fled south of the Limpopo to South Africa between 1835 and 1840. They settled among the North Sotho Kaha and Lovedu in the western Lowveld, and in the Soutpansberg and Drakensberg mountains. Soshangane died in 1858, and ten years of conflict ensued as his two sons fought each other for ascendancy. During this period of unrest more Tsonga fled to the northern areas of South Africa. Muzila eventually prevailed and he was succeeded in 1884 by his son, Ngungunyane. Ngungunyane, the last of the independent Ngoni kings, was overthrown by the Portuguese in Mozambique, which led to yet another wave of Tsonga fleeing southwards.

Music in performance

Music and magic

The Tsonga believe that music has special powers to change, protect or destroy.[10] When certain work-party songs are performed, an agricultural pest known as *nunu* is killed. During exorcism rituals, the patient wears *mafowa* rattles, the sound of which protects her. Likewise, people are protected from lightning when they play a small flute made from an eagle's femur. Another type of flute is played when a possessed patient dies. When the family play the flute near the grave, the evil spirit responsible for the death is destroyed. Music has as much power to destroy as it has to heal. Communal vocal music cannot be sung in an area where beer is being brewed: the sound of singing is said to turn the beer sour. Spirits are believed to continue to play music once they have reached ancestor status. The ancestors 'speak' through *marhonge* leg-rattles on occasion. They also 'speak' by singing, dancing and playing horns when they are pleased. Music must be treated with respect because it is gives humans the power to destroy, protect or heal. It is an essential part of the Tsonga belief system and philosophy, and a vital aspect of communal life.

Bunanga: the horn ensemble

The Tsonga's traditional use of the musical horn was unique. In addition to its functional role as a signal instrument, it was played in an ensemble of horns known as *bunanga*.[11] The term *bunanga* is derived from the word *nanga*, meaning horn. There is a possibility that the Tsonga horn ensemble was modelled on the Venda reed-pipe ensemble. The ensemble consisted of ten horns, each tuned differently, and two drums. The horn players formed a ring around the two drummers, moving in time to the drumbeat. The tempo of the drumming fluctuated and the dancers changed their pace accordingly. Players formed teams and used the horn ensemble in competitions. Traditionally, the individual who announced the winner beat the trunk of a tree with an axe to finalise the decision, and then ran away to avoid complaints and insults from the losing team and supporters! The Tsonga no longer play in horn ensembles.

The role of drums in the community

Drums are an essential feature of important rituals and social institutions in Tsonga society. There are four kinds of drums, played mainly by women to accompany singing and dancing. They are played at drumming and initiation schools, and are included in exorcism rituals and beer-parties. The *ndzumba*, *mancomane* and *ngoma* drums are treasured heirlooms because they are rarely made any more, and are not played as regularly as the *xigubu* drum, which is used daily in many contexts.[12] Drum rhythms are closely linked with the dance steps and routines of rituals.

Xigubu *drumming school*

Boys are introduced to drumming at a young age through the *xigubu* drumming school: an institution that takes its name from the drums used for instruction.[13] This school is attended mainly by pre-circumcision boys and

The *ndzumba* has a conical or goblet shape with a single membrane. It is often paired with a smaller drum, the *ndzumbana*, and is played in sets of two at the girls' initiation school (*khomba*). One of the taboos associated with this drum is that women are forbidden to look inside the open bottom end.

The *xigubu* drum has a double goat-skin membrane and a cylindrical metal body. The shells that are attached to the drum are made from various materials such as bottle tops and oil tins. The size of the *xigubu* drum varies according to the requirements of the player. It is made in all Tsonga villages, and is more commonly used than other drums.

Borrowed from the Venda, the *ngoma* drum is used for beer-parties as an alternative to the Tsonga *xigubu*.

213

People gather to watch a xigubu drumming performance

usually lasts for up to a month at a time. A local musician is appointed as an instructor (*muqambhi* – the 'song-maker').[14] Students are taught skills related to drum-making and performance. They learn various drum formulae and rhythms and become familiar with a wide range of drumming techniques used for different occasions. They learn through clapping – encircling their instructor, clapping the rhythm of the songs and swaying their bodies. They also learn the *xigubu* drum-and-voice conversations, which centre on the call-and-response pattern between drum and voice. These conversations "reinforce the 'talking' aspect of dance-drumming."[15] This pattern of dialogue or call-and-response is found throughout Tsonga and other African music. The boys also learn the repertoire of *xigubu* songs that go with dances. In return for their instruction, they make small payments of beer.

Once the boys have graduated they become acknowledged drummers (*mabangoma*), and are able to accompany the *xigubu*-songs. The two main dances connected with the *xigubu* drumming school are *ku wamikapa* and *xifase*. Girls are allowed to take part in both of these performances. *Ku wamikapa* takes place in a circle around the *xigubu* drums, and dancing couples take turns in the centre. *Xifase* is danced competitively by neighbouring *xigubu* school teams. The teams form separate lines, and individuals dance towards each other, choosing partners by brushing hands with them. *Xifase* consists of one basic dance step in which the dancer transfers weight from one foot to another, repeating the phrase '*swirhendze swi ta pfimba!*' ('your heels will be sore!').[16] Performers wear leg-rattles and blow whistles in both these dances.

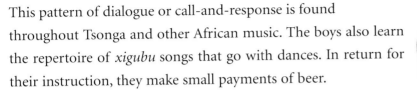

Mancomane: *exorcism*

In the first phase of the exorcism ritual, the diviner beats his drum.[17] Participants understand that this is a signal for them to start playing their *mancomane* drums and *ndjele* rattles. The power of the very first drumbeat is

Rattles

The Tsonga use cocoon and fruit-shell leg-rattles that are mounted on strips of skin and wound round the leg. These are called **mafowa**.

Tsonga fruit-shell leg-rattles, **marhonge**, are worn by women during exorcism rituals, because the sound they make is believed to represent the voices of the spirits. They are also worn around dancers' calves at initiation schools. They are treasured possessions and may be handed down to one's children.

Hand-rattles, **ndjele**, are made from an oval calabash with stones inside, with holes bored through to let the sound out. These are used during exorcism rituals.

Hand-clappers

Spagane is a hand-clapper made from a flat slab of wood with a leather strap for holding it. It is used in pairs.

electrifying and puts a halt to all activity as the whole community rushes to the site of the ritual:

> *"In the calm quiet of the evening air the first blow is struck. It reverberates, and is heard from afar on all sides; it penetrates the thickets and reaches the neighbouring villages, where it inspires a strange emotion, a transcendent delight born of curiosity, malice and I know not what feeling of unconscious satisfaction. All rush in the direction of the well-known sound; each one hurries to the hut of the possessed; all desire to take part in this struggle, this conflict with the invisible world."*[18]

Exorcism takes place nightly during the summer months, and the entire community usually participates. The ritual takes its name from the *ncomane* drum – the defining feature of exorcism. The diviner (*dzwavi*) possesses a set of four *mancomane* drums, which are a symbol of his or her authority.[19] They produce a sharp, powerful tone and are instrumental in inducing the hypnotic state of the patient. They are beaten with a stick (*rikhokho*) very close to the patient's eardrums. According to one source, "this is to create a disturbing sound that induces a reaction in the nervous system."[20] They are usually played with the big *ngoma* bass drum adopted from the Venda. Hand-rattles (*ndjele*) are also shaken, and dancers wear leg-rattles (*marhonge*), which are thought to be "repositories of Tsonga ancestor spirits."[21] Patients are individuals who have been possessed by an undesirable Zulu or Ndau spirit.[22] There are three drum rhythms used to expel different evil spirits: *mandhlozi* for Zulu spirits, and *xidzimba* and *xiNdau* for Ndau spirits.

The songs are in Zulu or Ndau, depending on which spirit is being expelled. Those possessed use the language of the spirits to communicate with the evil spirits they wish to expel. Similarly, participants attempt to cajole the spirits by flattering them with praise. Songs consist of repetition of short vocal refrains with melodies that have a "persistent, incisive, penetrating character."[23] Singing contributes to the hypnotic, trance-like state of both the patient and the community at large:

"That which is most essential is the singing, the human voice, the chorus of exorcists, a short refrain. Following on is a still shorter solo, repeated a hundred or a thousand times, always with the same object in view, toward which all strive seriously and persistently, namely to compel the spiritual being, the mysterious possessing spirit which is present, to reveal itself, and declare its name, after which it will be duly overcome. These songs are at the same time both simple and poetic. They address the spirit in laudatory terms, trying to cajole it by flattery, to get on the right side of it, and thus induce it to grant the signal favour of a final surrender." [24]

Beer-drinking music

Beer drinking is part of many social situations, and is usually accompanied by music.[25] At a typical traditional beer-drink gathering, the old men sit on the shaded platform that runs along the outside of the Tsonga hut. They sing responsive lines in low voices. Just below them, the old women rest on goat-skins spread on the ground, swaying and clapping to the rhythm of the music. The young men and women stand: the men dancing energetically and the women singing in high voices, ululating from time to time. The drummers, usually young women, rest against the walls, inclining the drums towards them. Both men and women contribute to beer-songs (*tinsimu nta le byalweni*), and they are thus rich in vocal harmony. They are always accompanied by dancing and clapping, and usually by the *xigubu* and/or *ngoma* drums. The singers use these songs to explore a range of human experiences that people in the community can relate to. While some songs reflect on Tsonga traditions and customs, others are more personal.

Four main dance styles are performed at beer parties. The men's *xichayachaya* dance is characterised by the way in which two leading dancers enter the circle. The dance leader (*ngayila* – 'the clever one') performs 'trotting-like' steps and the other dancer (*nsini* – 'the expert dancer') "humorously jerks his shoulders up and down."[26] In the women's *xilala* dance,

Mbiras

The *mbira*, known as the **timbila** among the Tsonga, is not indigenous to them. They claim that they borrowed one type from the Pedi and Lovedu, and the other from the Ndau. A *timbila* may have up to twenty or more metal keys fixed onto a piece of wood, and is tuned to either the Pedi five-note or the Ndau six-note scale. The music is polyrhythmic, with the two thumbs playing different rhythms.

Xylophones

The Tsonga **mohambi** is modelled on the Tswa and Ndau/Shanga xylophones as played in Mozambique. The body consists of ten or twelve keys made of hard wood that are attached to a wooden frame with leather lacing. The Tsonga do not have their own exact system of tuning for the *mohambi*. Beneath each key is a resonator made of the shell of the monkey orange. The instrument is played by two people, with the left-hand player at the bass end, playing the four left-hand slats. The players squat on the floor, on the same side of the instrument. The *mohambi* is made only by males.[4]

their heavy bangles play a significant role in creating the rhythm of the song. The cross patterns of the foot movements and the singers' voices create interlacing rhythms. Women use beer-dance-songs to vocalise their experiences as females. In one *xilala* dance-song the women sing:

Ku lava ku tekiwa loko a ndzi Lo
Tshama ka mhani, hinkwaswo leswi
I nge ndzi nga swi vonangi

If only I had stayed at home without experiencing all this anguish![27]

This song refers to an experience that is common to many women living traditional lifestyles. When a woman marries and moves to her husband's village, her workload is heavy, and she has to adjust to a new life. The song reflects the hardships associated with the traditional roles of women.

Another dance style used in the context of beer-drinking is that used for adult competitive team dances (*rhambela phikezano*). Dance teams visit neighbouring villages, usually in April and May. Each team consists of four male dancers, a female dancer and a clown (*phuphula* – 'the simple one'). The clown entertains the audience with his acrobatics (*tinxangu* – 'cleverness'). His performance is measured in an unusual way:

"… his skill is measured by the amount of dust he stirs up. The team's supporters refer to this dust as tlhutlhuma *(froth of the beer), because it symbolises the beer portions that will be theirs if the dust 'froths high'."*[28]

Muchongolo is regarded as the Tsonga national dance, and is performed at beer-parties and occasionally during exorcism rituals, where it provides light relief from the intensity and frenzy of the exorcism dances. The word *muchongolo* is derived from the verb *kuchongola*,

In the muchongolo *dance the performer holds a baton and points it upwards*

meaning 'to stamp', which is the defining movement of the dance. The men and women hold batons, pointing and swinging them towards the audience or the sky, as if chasing birds away, while stamping slowly. The dance begins when two soloists enter the circle with their batons, singing energetically and using improvised words. Strong coordination is required for the performers to swing their batons in time to the *xigubu* drumbeat.

This dance was also performed at the mines as a form of entertainment. In this setting it resembled the Nguni *indlamu* dance. One drummer playing the *xigubu* drum led the team of dancers. The dancers formed a line, swaying their shields and beating them with sticks, while performing a sequence of stamping steps. Halfway through the dance the drummer joined the rest of the team, later returning to his original position in front to end the performance with drumming.

Children's music

Children's songs impart Tsonga mythology and ancient folktales.[29] Many are characterised by responses that are sung or spoken in unison by the chorus. Every folktale begins with the phrase *'Garingani wa garingani…'* ('Once upon a time …'), and the audience responds with *'Garingani'*. When children use songs in their games, they are often required to give quick, short responses. Some of these songs are borrowed from the Venda.

The performance of children's songs is largely governed by the seasons. Boys do not sing their herding songs just after the harvest when the cattle graze on their own, and folktales are not performed during the harvesting season when people retire early. In some cases certain children's songs are restricted to a fixed time during the day. Folktales should not be told before dark, and children are warned that "horns might grow from their heads"[30] if they disobey this rule.

The songs in Tsonga folktales are often invested with supernatural powers; they are able to change the direction of the story or cause something miraculous to happen in the narrative. Most folktales centre around bird or

Whistles, flutes and reeds

The **shitloti** is a transverse flute made of river-reed or metal piping. There are three holes at the lower end of the flute, with the blow-hole at the upper end. Sometimes the lower end is plugged by a mielie cob, and the player opens and closes the upper end with the palm of his left hand, humming and grunting loudly.[5]

A whistle, known as the **'flute of heaven'**, is used by diviners to drive away lightning. It is made from a five-inch hollow bone, usually from the *ndlati* or 'lightning bird', and is covered with leguaan- or lizard-skin. It is made with three seeds of the lucky bean, which supposedly intensifies the instrument's sound, enabling the music to penetrate heaven. On seeing an approaching thunderstorm, the diviner attempts to defy the lightning by standing on a hilltop and blowing his whistle.

Man playing nanga *flute*

Nanga is a flute usually made from the tibia of a goat and produces two notes. It was played by herdboys tending their animals out in the fields.

Another instrument played by herdboys in the past was the **ndjwebe**, a flute made from bone.

219

animal characters that are personified. A common figure that is often referred to in folktale songs is the master hare. He is a symbol of cunning and children like to weave stories around this legendary character.

Children take part in seasonal competitive dances (*rhambela phikezano*). The chief organises competitions where dance teams of boys and girls travel within his territory to represent him. These events depend upon the availability of beer and meat, because the dance teams are always rewarded with refreshments.

Initiation ceremonies

Music is used as an educational tool in institutions attended by teenagers. Boys are educated through the songs that they learn at the *xigubu* drumming school and initiation school (*murhundzu*). Girls are educated through their pre-initiation school (*musevetho*) and initiation school (*khomba*) music. These schools are not indigenous to the Tsonga but were imported from the Pedi. The music included in these rituals has also been influenced by the neighbouring Venda.

Murhundzu: *male initiation*
Boys' initiation schools are organised by a visiting Pedi doctor and take place every four to five years.[31] Boys who have previously been initiated are obliged to attend the school to

The story of the *ndlati* bird and the 'flute of heaven'

"In Tsonga, lightning is called lihati and is said to be caused by a bird called ndlati. The thunder is attributed to either the bird itself, or more frequently, to heaven. The proper expression for 'it thunders' is 'tilo dji djuma' (heaven roars). In the northern clans, those who practise magical arts add many other particulars to the story, some of which may have been borrowed from the Pedi musicians, who seem to possess a more complete explanation of the phenomenon. According to them, the ndlati is a bird of four colours – green, red, black and white – that lives in the mountains at the confluence of rivers. When a thunderstorm breaks, the bird flies into the clouds to heaven. While there may be scores of these birds, only one will cause death. It rushes down to the ground, striking a tree on its way, tearing off its bark and its wood, and throwing it down; or it falls upon a hut and burns it; or on a person, and kills him or her.

Happily, this dreadful bird can be prevented from killing and burning by magical means. The Thonga Makasane possessed the enchanted flute, by which they could force heaven – or the bird of heaven – to spare them. It is made of a hollow bone five inches long, covered with skin, filled at its larger extremity with a black wax-like substance. Inside, to keep it clean, is a vulture's feather. The bone is said to have been taken from the ndlati bird; and the wax substance was made from powder obtained by pulverising a little of the heart, the eye, the bones, the feathers, and the flesh of the bird. Three seeds of Abrus precatorius, the 'lucky bean', are embedded in the wax. The lucky bean is well known in South Africa: it is a round seed of a splendid coral colour with a black spot, widely used in Thonga magic. The addition of the lucky bean intensifies the sound of the flute and enables it to reach heaven. The diviner, seeing the thunderstorm approaching, climbs up the hill fearlessly, blows in his flute and shouts, 'You! Heaven! Go further! I have nothing against you! I do not fight against you!' He may add in a threatening tone: 'If you are sent by my enemies against me, I will cut you open with this knife of mine.' The thunderstorm will then pass over!"[6]

220

help those being circumcised and to supervise the instruction of the initiation songs. The first of these is *hogo*, a song borrowed from the Venda. This is sung as the boys march to the area where they will be initiated. The word *hogo* is "a term much used in circumcision songs, obscene, often taken to mean copulation, shouted derisively at females seen by initiates."[32] Most of the music performed at initiation is composed of musical formulae (*tingoma*). These are short musical phrases that the boys whisper in hoarse voices.

The only instrument played during circumcision school is the doctor's ceremonial whistle. Because of the secrecy surrounding initiation, drums are excluded so that attention is not drawn to the chosen location. The only time that drums are heard is when the circumcision school comes to a close. They are played as the boys are greeted by their relatives in their coming-home ceremony. *Mayiwayiwane*, one of the most important dances in the boys' rite of passage, is performed at this ceremony. *Mayiwayiyane* are masks made from woven palm leaves that cover the head and upper body. They resemble helmets which protrude like beaks. The challenge is for the boys to wear them while dancing without stumbling or allowing the masks to fall off, thus exposing their identity to the spectators. This is particularly difficult because the dance consists mainly of high jumps. The texts of these and other 'coming-out' songs represent the change that the boys have undergone in order to become men. In the following song, the verbs 'cut' and 'shake off' suggest "separation from the old and transition to the new".[33] 'Ones-with-feet' probably refers to the dances performed at this stage of initiation:

Tsema hlamfi, mayiwayiwane

Hi lava taku

Mandembye sungwi

Wa nga hlakahla

Hi lava milenge

Cut branches, circumcised ones

Here they come

Ocarinas

The **shiwaya** is made from the shell of a *nsala* fruit. It is pierced with three holes: two finger-holes and a mouth-hole. The player breathes across the embouchure while opening and stopping the two holes with his fingers.

Horns

The **mhalamhala** is a side-blown antelope horn. The bone is removed and a mouth-hole is made near the closed end. This horn is blown during the girls' initiation school and in the past was also used in a horn ensemble.

Girls playing the sekgapa

From the Mandembye circumcision lodge
Shake off yourselves
The Ones-with-feet[34]

When the boys first enter the circumcision lodge, they smear their bodies with white ochre, which is symbolic of the death of their childhood. At the end of this rite of passage, they smear red ochre on their bodies, symbolising their birth into manhood. The concept of changing colours is reflected in the chameleon procession as the boys make their way towards the chief's residence. Through dance, the boys imitate a chameleon's movements: "They advance slowly, bowed to the ground, stretching out first one leg and then the other, with a sudden brisk motion, trying to imitate the gait of the chameleon, the wise, the prudent."[35] *Kanya-kanya*, another 'coming-out' song, explores the concept of change through its imagery of the chameleon:

Kanya-kanya Nwa-Rimpfani!
Hundzuka mavala

Step, step, Child-of-the-Chameleon!
Change your colour[36]

Khomba: *female initiation*

At the opening ceremony of the annual girls' initiation, all the females in the community march in long lines towards an appointed area, chanting as they walk.[37] The formation of the line represents the Tsonga social hierarchy, with the most important women near the front, and those with lower social standing, such as pre-initiate girls, further back. Each line is led by a headman's wife who blows a horn, followed by a village elder who balances a *ndzumba* drum on her head. When the procession has reached the centre of the village, the elders gather around the *ndzumba* drum. The most common rhythms played on this instrument are called *nanayila* and *xisotho*. A dance circle is formed and they sing *ku khana* songs ('joy-dancing'), one of which is called *nanayila* ('to move slowly'). The participants blow whistles while

Bows and other string instruments

The *xizambi* is a combination of a mouth-resonated friction-bow and a rattle. The bow is small and curved, made from any kind of wood, and the string is made from a strip of swamp grass called *nala*. Notches are carved along the side of the bow stick. Two or three *ntsa* pods or small calabashes are filled with pebbles and attached to a separate rattle stick, which is rubbed along the notches on the bow, causing the palm-leaf string to vibrate. The musician holds the instrument between the thumb and fourth finger of the left hand, leaving the remaining fingers free to stop the string. One end of the string is held between the player's lips, and the mouth acts as a resonator. The player rubs the rattle stick back and forth on the notches with his right hand. Young males play the *xizambi*, and often use it to court women. They sometimes use the instrument to accompany their singing, in which case the sound is slightly altered because the mouth no longer acts as a resonator. The Tsonga are the most skilled *xizambi* players in South Africa.[7]

The *xidende* is a braced gourd-bow made from a bent branch of the *morethloa* tree with a calabash or tin resonator attached near the centre. The string is made from the twisted fibre of the *mulala* ground palm tree or copper wire, and is divided at the centre. The bow is made from a branch stripped of its bark, or of cane. The instrument is grasped near the calabash, with the fingers extended to allow the player to finger either segment of the string to a higher note. The other hand strikes the string with a thin stick or reed. This bow is not mouth-resonated, which means that the player can and usually does sing while playing. It is fairly easy to play, and musicians often dance while playing. The *xidende* is sometimes played by a wandering entertainer (*xilombe*).[8]
Refer to Track 45.

223

moving around the drum, swaying forwards and then leaning backwards. In another dance, *managa*, the girls wear palm-leaf skirts (*xidundo*) and the dance movements emphasise the swishing motion of the skirts.

Once these dances are completed, the girls are ushered to the riverbed where they are undressed, their nakedness symbolising their rebirth. While their clothes are being removed, the older initiates sing to them, encouraging an emotional response and sometimes instructing them to cry. Many of the riverside rituals take place around a palm-leaf mat and drums. When a girl lies on the mat, it is a gesture of respect and she is said to humble herself. In one ritual, the initiate lies on the mat, curled up in an infantile position while another initiate is led to a drum to play a particular rhythm. Many of the songs that are performed around the *ngoma* drum focus on instructing and advising the girls in their role as women. They use dance to mime various female activities such as childbirth, where they simulate the birth process. As in the women's *xilala* dance performed at beer-parties, the girls also use bangles in some of their dances. The initiates sometimes transfer bangles from one wrist to the other, making them the focal point of the dance. They also wear leg bangles which jangle and create a percussive sound as the girls move.

The initiation ends with a 'coming-out' ceremony, where the community performs 'greeting-back songs' (*ku vuyisa*). In the following example, the metaphor of a ship crossing a river depicts the girls' transition from adolescence to adulthood.

At the riverside the girls lie on the ground in an infantile position while the ngoma *drum is played*

224

Call:	I khombile n'wananga
	A xikepe a xi le ntsungeni
	Eka Mulamula
Response:	Iye, iye o ka nga hume
Call:	Huma, huma Mthavine
Call:	She is mature, my child
	The ship lies on the far bank
	Of the river
	At Mulamula
Response:	Iye, iye, go home
Call:	Go home, go home, Mthavine.[38]

Xichaya: Solo music

Bows belong to the category of solo-instrument playing and are usually unrelated to Tsonga social institutions.[39] They can be played by an individual at any time. The bow most commonly played by professional musicians is the *xizambi*, an instrument that requires great musical skill. It can be played in several ways. The musician can sing and play simultaneously, using the instrument to accompany the voice. In both Venda and Tsonga society, there is a class of professional musicians who play the role of wandering entertainer (*xilombe*). The Tsonga *xilombe*, like his Venda counterpart, also plays a bow. He travels from village to village, playing in return for food, beer or shelter. More distinguished are entertainers who are connected to the chief and are given the opportunity to contribute to court life, for instance by entertaining the chief's guests. Occasionally a wandering entertainer is stigmatised as a recluse (*nwarimatsi*), and is ostracised from his community. *Refer to Tracks 46, 47 and 48.*

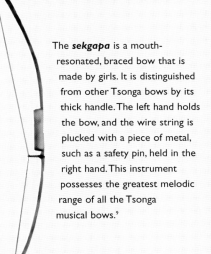

The **sekgapa** is a mouth-resonated, braced bow that is made by girls. It is distinguished from other Tsonga bows by its thick handle. The left hand holds the bow, and the wire string is plucked with a piece of metal, such as a safety pin, held in the right hand. This instrument possesses the greatest melodic range of all the Tsonga musical bows.[9]

The **umqangala** was most likely borrowed from the Zulu and Swazi. The stave is made from a hollow reed and the string is made from fishing line. The bow is mouth-resonated and plucked with the fingers. One end rests against the player's lips and the right index finger plucks the string while the left hand fingers the string at the bottom. This instrument is usually played by older men.

225

Over the last century the Khoi have been almost entirely destroyed or assimilated into other cultures. No Khoi remain in South Africa, although many so-called Cape Coloureds can trace their ancestry through Khoi lines of descent.

When the Dutch settlers arrived in South Africa, they found the Khoi spread throughout the south-westerly regions of the Cape.

Khoi-khoi

History of the Khoi, the 'men of men'

There is much debate as to where the Khoi lived before they entered southern Africa and who they were.[1] Archaeological findings suggest that they lived further north towards East Africa, and bought their cattle with them when they migrated south over 2 000 years ago. However, many historians have used the genetic and linguistic similarities between the Khoi and San to argue that they were originally part of the San race of southern Africa, but acquired domestic animals from the Bantu-speaking peoples moving southwards, and split off from the hunter-gatherers, developing their own culture to suit their new economy. What is commonly agreed is that by roughly 2 000 years ago, groups of nomadic pastoralists were living in southern Africa in the coastal regions of South Africa. Their way of life was different in many respects to that of the San. They herded cattle and sheep, returned annually to semi-permanent settlements, and were organised into clans headed by chiefs. They used the name Khoi-khoin, 'men of men' or 'the real people' to distinguish themselves from the San, whom they regarded as inferior. They asserted their dominance over the San by forcing them to work as their servants and driving them off the fertile land they were competing for.

Woman playing the /khais

The Khoi spoke closely related languages. Four main dialects were spoken by four corresponding groupings: the Cape Khoi, the Eastern Khoi, the Korana and the Nama. The Eastern Khoi were the first to come into contact with Bantu-speaking people along the South African south coast, and were largely absorbed into the Bantu tribes. By the 17th century, the Cape Khoi had made their home in the Western Cape. They had been trading with foreign ships passing through the Cape since the early 1500s, but the foreigners had never posed a threat to them. In 1652, however, a Dutch trading company entered the region under Jan van Riebeeck and formed a colony: present-day Cape Town. Men from the company set themselves up as farmers and tradesmen and slowly started flourishing.

The Khoi suffered the same fate as the San under the control of the colonists. As more foreigners settled in South Africa, the indigenous people lost their grazing lands and herds, which were taken over or stolen by the colonists. Without their traditional livelihood, they were forced into positions

It is **"with the Khoi that the history of known music in South Africa may be said to have begun."**[17]

Drums

The Khoi drum was called **/khais** but was known among the Dutch colonists as the *rommelpot*[2] – the name of a friction-drum played by children in the south of Holland. They probably used this name because the Khoi instrument, made from a pot and animal skin, resembled the Dutch instrument. The */khais* is made of a wooden jug or pot used for storing milk (*//hoes*)[3] and sheep, buck or goat, which is stretched over the top and secured with a piece of riem. Women made and played this drum to accompany men's dancing. Performers drummed in a sitting position, striking the skin with the flat palm of the right hand. They played this instrument during a dance that came to be known as the 'pot-dance' among Europeans.[4]

Rattles

The Khoi copied the San by tying cocoons, */xororokwa*, from the swart hak tree (*!noeb*), around their ankles when dancing.

Bull-roarers

The Khoi called their instrument **burubush**.[5]

of dependency. Many fought back, refusing to become labourers on the colonists' farms, and stealing cattle from the farmers, but their resistance was ineffectual. While hundreds of Khoi were captured and enslaved around Cape Town, many died in the smallpox epidemics of 1713 and 1755. Disempowered and few in number, the remaining Khoi were absorbed into the dominant societies around them, both African and European. Slavery was endemic to the Cape towards the end of the 17th century, and large populations of labourers were brought in from all over the world. There was much mixing between the Khoi and different races, and this resulted in the Coloured population.

Men blowing their reed-pipes

Some Khoi groups managed to flee the Europeans between the late 17th century and mid-18th century, moving inland. The Kora were among them, and they formed the nucleus of the Korana. However, the pure Korana race eventually disintegrated as a result of racial mixing with whites and the Bantu-speaking groups. The Namaqua lived in South Africa and Namibia. They were overcome by quarrels with neighbouring peoples and were eventually also assimilated into other races through interbreeding. Those who had lived among the settlers spoke Dutch and their culture was highly influenced by Dutch culture. Among Europeans, the Khoi were collectively known as Hottentots, a term which acquired a derogatory slant over time. Some believe that the term 'Hottentot', from the Dutch word *hûttentût*, meaning 'stutterer' in Dutch – is a reference to the click sounds in their language.

In the 1840s, the existence of the Hottentots, as they were called at the time, became known to the world through Baartman, the famous 'Hottentot-Venus'. Baartman was a Khoi woman who was exploited by being exhibited in Europe as a specimen of the Khoi race. The exhibit enhanced negative perceptions around the Khoi and created outrage among those who protested against the inhumane treatment of, and racial prejudice towards, Baartman. The history of the Khoi's subjugation was bought to the fore in 2002 when Baartman's remains were returned to her country of origin.

Music in performance

Reed-pipe ensembles

"The dance has such an irresistible attraction for the Hottentots that any group of dancers rapidly grows in size. Mothers with babies on their backs, women returning to the kraal with firewood or other burdens, attach themselves to the ring; even old matrons whose sight is failing become as if electrified when they hear the dance music, and dance like energetic flappers!"[15]

Among some groups of Khoi, the reed-pipe ensemble was the most important musical feature of their social life. It brought the community together, binding it in group activity, and added excitement and festivity to communal life.[16] All initiated young men were taught how to play reed-pipes by a bandmaster. Those who excelled were recognised and favoured by the girls, who showed their admiration by singing praises to them.

The dance usually started at about four in the afternoon, and often continued through the night until the following morning. It sometimes had a sacred slant, and was performed to invoke the new moon, thunder or rain. It was also used on festive occasions, to celebrate the visit of a stranger to the kraal, or on completion of a girl's puberty-seclusion rite. When Vasco da Gama landed on South African soil on 2 December 1497, a group of Khoi greeted him and his crew with a reed-pipe dance. It is thus "with the Hottentots that the history of known music in South Africa may be said to have begun."[17]

Whistles, flutes and reeds

A signal whistle made from the shin bone of a springbok or the leg bone of an ostrich was called *llaren!as*. A piece of riem was attached so that it could be hung from the performer's neck. The player held it against his hollowed tongue and when he blew it produced a shrill, powerful sound. It was used primarily by the chief's headmen to summon the clan.

Both the Nama and Korana Khoi played reed-pipes to accompany their dances. The flutes were usually made from reed, but the bark from acacia roots was occasionally used as a substitute when the land was dry. Bark pipes generally gave lower-pitched sounds than reed-pipes. The pipes were made in different sizes and produced different pitches in a tetratonic (four-note) scale. Chewed plant fibre was rolled into a ball and inserted into one end of the pipe to act as a plug. The player tuned the instrument by moving the plug up and down the pipe with a thin stick (*llkxaehaib*)[6] or a piece of wire. The pipes were given different names among different Khoi groups.

Among the Nama, reed-pipe ensembles were known as ≠ati, and among the Korana they were known as ≠adi. Women never played reeds, but they participated in the reed dance. Boys were only allowed to join the ensemble once they had been initiated. Performances with reed-pipes usually involved at least four performers, and took place at night. They were held on various sacred and ceremonial occasions.

Horns

The Khoi used the kelp horn as an instrument.[7]

231

In the reed-pipe dance the men formed an inner circle (*nama*) and, with knees and bodies slightly bent, played their pipes while dancing anti-clockwise. They moved forwards and backwards by hopping up and down on both legs with a 'leaping movement'.[18] The women formed an outer circle, singing wordless tunes and clapping (*inna //am*)[19], while dancing in the opposite direction to the men's circle. They used small, graceful steps, sometimes rolling and shaking their buttocks (*!hare khwedi*).[20] The musical director or master of ceremonies stood in the centre, enclosed by both circles, conducting the music with a stick. He was generally also the leader (*!khona! !kausab*)[21] of the dance and played the highest-pitched flute in the performance. He was responsible for initiating the dance and accompanying song, after which the men and women surrounding him took his lead and began dancing and singing. Each man carried a tuning stick, which he sometimes used to attract attention to himself. He would lay the stick on the shoulders of a girl whom he had singled out.

There was a strong element of drama in the performance. According to one source, reed-pipe dances consisted of 'miniature dramas' or *'singspiele'*.[22] The theme of the songs, rather than articulated, were often acted out by the performers. In many dances they mimicked animals. Some of the sacred songs contained more text and were used as prayers, praises or invocations.

Occasionally the reed dance was used as part of a friendly competition (*/hous*)[23] between different kraals. The hosts provided a feast for their visitors, and this was reciprocated when the hosting community visited its neighbours on another occasion. The women of one kraal joined the dancing men of another, socialising with them, and according to some sources, engaging in orgies. Whether this is true or not, the missionaries believed this supposedly 'immoral' behaviour justified their objections to the reed-pipe ensembles.[24]

Women dancing

Song and dance

In many Khoi songs and dances, performers imitated animals and hunting. One typical skit represented a hyena slinking around a sheep kraal.[25] The men and women formed two semi-circles facing one another. The circle represented the sheep kraal and the women represented the sheep. One of the men, 'the hyena', crouching to create the impression of slinking, approached the 'sheep kraal' and the 'sheep'. Three other men left their circle to follow the hyena. Their mimes were very detailed and skilled. They 'rode' on 'horses' towards the sheep kraal, tying their animals up so that they could search for the hyena tracks. Once they had spotted the animal, they mounted their 'horses' to chase it from the sheep kraal. The hyena was eventually captured and killed in the chase. Throughout this thrilling performance the women sang "≠Hĩ-ra-se, kxoïn xũn gye, ≠go-be-se, kxoïn xũn gye", meaning "Hyena, this (the sheep in the kraal) is the property of men!"[26]

Many songs and dances represented scenes from important historical incidents. One performance was based on the murder of the Kora leader Jan Jonker, by Hendrik Witbooi.[27] The performers formed two groups of men, one wearing red headbands (Jonker's camp), and the other, white (Witbooi's party). Jonker's men, unaware of any

The kha:s *is played in a sitting position*

Bows and other string instruments

The Khoi did not use the bow as a weapon or a musical instrument until they came into contact with the San, after which they imitated the San's use of the bow.

Kha:s was the name given by the Khoi to the hunting bow. The stave was constructed from a branch of *besjebos*. It was forced into a semi-circular form once a twisted sinew had been attached. The *kha:s*, a woman's instrument, was usually played in a sitting position. One end of the bow rested against a bag of skin or an overturned wooden vessel, which acted as a resonator. The right foot held this end of the bow in position, while the other end rested on the left shoulder. The instrument was struck with a thin piece of wood or reed held between the right thumb and first finger. The player used a staccato action to strike the string, which produced a ringing tone. Variations of playing the instrument included lightly touching the middle point of the string with the finger while striking it with the piece of reed or wood, and pressing upon the string with the chin. This playing technique was characteristic of the Khoi. In addition to singing while playing the bow, performers used the rhythm of their playing to imitate the gait of various animals.[8]

Fig. I.

The **!gabus** was based on the *kha:s* or hunting bow, but was far slenderer than its prototype. It was made from a piece of *besjebos* stripped of its bark. A sinew from the back of an ox was fitted into a groove cut into one end of the stave. One end of the instrument was resonated in the mouth, while the left hand grasped the other end. The string was plucked with the right forefinger.

The **gabowie** was an instrument that resembled a guitar, with four or five strings stretched over a piece of hollow wood and a long handle. A traveller's account describes an interesting aspect of the performance of this instrument:

"In this rude sort of guitar, which they called a gabowie, *was inserted a piece of looking-glass, of which they are immoderately fond. It was fixed in the centre of the board; and the young woman who played kept steadfastly looking at herself in it; and grinning with great complacency at the beauty of her round hunched figure."*[9]

Man playing the gora

danger, started the dance, with their women dancing in a circle around them. Out of the darkness the Witbooi group danced towards Jonker's camp. When Jonker's men noticed their enemies approaching, the women, representing the cattle, stood aside and took over the melody, continuing to clap. The men meanwhile formed a line, and in a crouching position, played their reed-pipes. The Witbooi men also formed a line, so that the two parties now faced one another. They sent a 'messenger', who approached the Jonker line of men, hopping up and down, playing his reed-pipe. A performer representing Jan Jonker then moved towards the Witbooi line, and, blowing his pipe, shook the strangers' hands. Meanwhile the 'cattle' were being inspected by a man from the Witbooi party. The murder of Jonker was then enacted, and the dance ended with the Witbooi party leaving with Jonker's cattle. Through performance, the Khoi re-enacted the past and reflected on the present.

Over time the Khoi absorbed European influences into their music, but their musical sensibility stayed intact. Their reed-pipes were eventually replaced by the mouth organ, guitar and concertina, and they started singing Dutch folk ditties and church hymns.

Boy playing the ramkie

The **ramkie**[10] is of Portuguese origin. The name of the instrument was derived from the Arabic *rebec* violin. The lower part of the instrument consisted of a resonator made from a calabash or wild pumpkin with a skin stretched over half of it. A stave was secured to the calabash. Three strings were fastened to one end of the stave and wound round tuning pegs on the other end. The strings were plucked with the fingers.[11]

The **tamboer** consisted of a flat piece of wood, shaped like a violin and covered with a piece of goat-skin with a hole cut in the centre. Four strings were attached to the lower end and secured to tuning pegs. Like a violin, the *tamboer* was bowed with a friction-bow made of horse-hair.[12]

Stringed-wind

The Khoi are the originators of the **gora**, an unbraced mouth-resonated bow.[13] The *gora* is unique because it is a stringed instrument that is played by blowing. It derives its name from the bird whose feather was originally used as part of the instrument. It is made of a straight, slender stick or reed. A short piece of flattened quill is attached to the player's end of the instrument. The quill in turn is attached to the string, which is stretched to the other end of the bow. The player holds the *gora* in both hands, with the quill between his lips, so that the stave does not touch his face. By inhaling and exhaling over the quill, he causes the string to vibrate. The *gora* was sometimes played in an unusual position -- the player lay on his back and supported the bow with his left hand. The instrument produces a powerful buzzing sound and the *gora* player can imitate the call of any bird on his instrument. Vocal sounds, such as humming or grunting, accompany some performances. The *gora* is always made and played by males and is generally used while herding cattle. The Southern Sotho of Lesotho regard the *lesiba*, their version of the *gora*, as their national instrument.[14]

The San are the original and oldest inhabitants of South Africa. While few have managed to reclaim their traditional hunter-gatherer lifestyle, and the ancestral lands from which they were expelled, others are forging new lives as farmers and labourers in South Africa and remote regions in southern Africa.

Thousands of years ago the San were spread over a vast region, from the fertile areas of South Africa to the arid regions of Namibia. Due to displacement and subjugation, their numbers have dramatically dwindled, and they are now found only in very small communities in the Kalahari desert region of the Northern Cape and North West Province in South Africa, and in isolated regions in Namibia, Botswana, Zambia and Zimbabwe.

San (Bushmen)

History of the San, southern Africa's hunter-gatherers

Evidence suggests that in very early times the San lived in tropical East Africa and moved southwards, eventually entering southern Africa where they have lived for thousands of years.[1] Some authorities have connected the San of today to the Florisbad fossil finds of 40 000 years ago. Organised into bands of varying sizes, they roamed freely as nomadic hunter-gatherers, leaving behind traces of their presence in the form of rock paintings and engravings. They spoke and still do speak a variety of languages, all characterised by click sounds. Their languages can be divided along three main geographical lines: The Northern San comprise the !Kung in the north of Botswana and Namibia, and the south of Angola; the Central San are those such as the Nharo and /Gwi of central Botswana, the western Caprivi and the eastern part of Namibia; and lastly the southern San include groups such as the now-extinct /Xam who occupied southern Botswana and South Africa.

The San's peaceful lifestyle in the isolated sub-continent was severely disrupted with the arrival of various groups of people, the first of whom were the Khoi about 2 000 years ago. They were followed by the Bantu-speaking people from the 16th century onwards, and later by the arrival of the white colonists and settlers. Each group successively subjugated the San, pushing them into the most remote, arid regions of the continent, and driving them to the brink of extinction. The history of the original hunters of southern Africa can be unraveled through a study of the terminology that was used to name them, and in essence, to disempower and dominate them. When the pastoralist Khoi started sharing the land with the San, the Khoi immediately claimed superiority over the original inhabitants. The two groups competed for land, but the Khoi outnumbered the San and had the advantage of a consistent food source in their cattle and sheep. The Khoi condescendingly called them San/Sonqua/Soaqua, words which originally meant 'aborigine'[2], but which acquired negative connotations and came to mean 'people different from ourselves'.[3] The San were regarded as inferior because they did not possess livestock and were accused of stealing from the Khoi. Nonetheless, the San played an important role in the lives of the Khoi. Bands of San gradually became servants, working for them. They were employed as rainmakers and hunters, and were usually paid for their services with grain or sheep. While some maintained peaceful relationships with their masters, others experienced great conflict with them, stealing livestock in response to their mistreatment. Some were ruthlessly killed and those who survived were driven onto inhospitable lands. There were also those who were slowly assimilated into Khoi society.

A similar process of absorption and/or displacement occurred when the Bantu-speaking races entered southern Africa in search of fertile land. It is believed that when the first of these people arrived, they co-existed peacefully with the San. However, over time, as more people arrived and pressures over land-occupation increased, the original inhabitants were overpowered and

"Musical instruments are seldom used to accompany the dances, although several different kinds are found."[6]

Drums

There is no record of San drums in the earliest accounts or observations. This is probably due to their nomadic lifestyle, which made it difficult to transport large instruments.[7] The few drums that the San later played were borrowed from other groups. The first reference to a San drum was in 1801 at the Orange River.[8] On this occasion they played a drum that was made from a clay pot and covered with skin. It appeared to have been borrowed from the colonists, who called the Khoi version of the drum the *rommelpot*, meaning 'rumblepot'. It is unknown what the San named this drum, but it was later observed by another traveller, who called it the water-drum. According to his description, the drum consisted of a jug filled with a little water so that the player could invert the object to wet the skin from time to time. The player moistened and stretched the skin over the edges of the jug with one hand, and used the index finger of his other hand to beat the rhythm. The pitch was regulated by pulling the skin with the index finger and thumb of the left hand. The San played this drum during thunderstorms and on moonlit nights to accompany their singing and dancing.[9]

In the past, /'Auni San women used the hide of an animal, called **dou**, as a temporary dancing platform. They laid the hide over hollow patches on the ground and wore ankle-rattles as they danced on it, which created a percussive sound.

Another drum, called **!kwa,** was also played by the San at a later stage. This drum is made from springbok skin that is stretched over a pot. Only women make and play this instrument. In performance, a woman beats the drum while the men dance.

became subservient to the Bantu-speaking peoples. They were either assimilated through slavery or intermarriage, or fled to the drier, more remote regions of southern Africa to escape subjugation. Through many years of living in close proximity to the San, the Bantu were influenced by many aspects of San culture and language. The San were particularly influential over the Nguni peoples, who adopted aspects of their click languages; and the Batswana, who adopted many aspects of their culture. However, in later years, with the arrival of the colonists, the Bantu-speaking peoples helped the white foreigners to destroy San bands.

During the 17th century, when the first Europeans settled in southern Africa, the San were enslaved to work on farms, and many fell victim to genocide at the hands of the colonists. The term 'Bushmen' came into existence with the arrival of the Dutch settlers during this period. They called the San 'Bushmen' or *'Bossieman'*, a derogatory term to imply their lower class status and inferiority.[4] The Dutch also used the term *vaalpens* ('greybellies') to describe the nomadic lifestyles the San lived: they slept out in the open near their fires, with the result that their stomachs were covered with ash and their bodies sometimes blistered by the flames.[5] The relationship between the San and the white colonists was that of master and slave. Many San who resisted domination were captured and killed. Survivors were drawn into colonial society and deprived of their traditional lifestyles.

By the beginning of the 1870s the culture and language of the southern San had been almost completely decimated. A minority of the remaining San have retained their culture, inhabiting remnants of their ancestral lands. Of the four groups of San once inhabiting South Africa, only one remains. The late 20th century saw a rekindling of the San community with the revision of land rights which enabled displaced, fragmented groups to re-enter and reclaim their ancestral lands. The land rights of the ≠ Khomani San of the Cape were finally recognised in 1994 with the introduction of a new land-reclamation law, and they were allocated land in the Kalahari Gemsbok National Park. Similarly, the Ju/'hoansi of Namibia have re-entered their ancestral lands in the Nyae Nyae region. Other groups have not been as fortunate and are still engaged in the struggle to win back their land. The //Gana and G/wi of

Botswana lost their land through forced removals in 1997. The majority have had to embrace the changing world and live in more permanent dwellings, which has had a huge impact on their fragile culture. Some work as farm labourers, but many are unemployed and live poverty-stricken lives, with the continuous threat of disease and discrimination. Communities have been broken apart and many San have turned to alcohol. Various organisations are working hard at restoring peace and revitalising the ancient culture of the San.

Music in performance

Vocal music

San music is largely vocal and is characterised by yodelling, a style in which singers move with flexibility from lower voice ranges produced in the chest, to falsetto ranges produced in the head. In some travellers' accounts from the early 1800s, it was noted that the San singers used vowel sounds such as 'Aye O, Aye O'[23] when they sang, which were probably to facilitate the yodelling technique. San vocal quality is also influenced by their click language, which consists of "harsh nasal, guttural or croaking sounds."[24] When singing in a group, singers often enter with their vocal lines at different points in the song. Their melodies and voices interweave, and, with the percussive backing of hand clapping and dancing rattles, they are able to create cross-rhythms. The San very rarely compose songs with words that fit verses. Most songs have very few words and consist mainly of vowel sounds without meaning[25], although from time to time short phrases or single words are incorporated into the song. Musical instruments are generally only played by individuals as a form of self-amusement and self-expression.[26]

The San express mainly domestic themes in their songs. Unlike the Bantu people, there are very few songs that focus on history and war.[27] The San also compose songs that are inspired by nature and animals. People communicate with the stars by singing and talking to them, and with animals through their praise-singing. Their praise poems are completely different to those of

Hand-clappers

The San use sticks and shoes as hand-clappers, which they strike together when they want the sun to shine.

Rattles

The San are known to be expert dancers. They tie ankle-rattles onto their feet and legs to aid their performances. They make a variety of ankle-rattles from natural materials such as wild fruits, seed shells and cocoons. The /'Auni San call their ankle-rattles *!kale*. These are made from cocoons filled with ostrich-shell fragments and strung together with leather.

The most unique type of rattle found among the San is called *!keriten*. The ear of a springbok is filled with a hard indigenous berry, fragments of ostrich shell or small pebbles, and then sewn up. Up to four ears make up a rattle. Women make these rattles, and men wear them on their lower legs while dancing. They were first observed in 1812, and later in 1905, and they were described by European observers as 'Bushmen bells'.

Bull-roarers

The San bull-roarer is known as the *!goin!goin*. People likened the sound of this instrument to the buzzing of bees, which was used to attract insects for honey production.

Children dancing while playing a game

societies with military and political structures. The San chant animal names, celebrating their co-existence with them. In naming through song, ancient bonds with animals are reaffirmed, and their social, economic and spiritual value is confirmed. The chants are stylised and the effect is the conjuring of "a dream landscape dotted with an impossible plenty of kudus …elands … giraffes…"[28]

Many observers have placed emphasis on San musicality. People who have come into contact with San individuals have admired the ease with which they are able to pick up foreign styles of music.[29] The San have been exposed to Bantu and European music and are able to mimic elements from both cultures. As one academic observed:

> "*Their mimicry extended even to a vocal imitation of a European or Coloured dance band of violins and guitars, including the bass part. The girls had apparently seen such a band play at some remote farm, for they occasionally imitated the movements of performers on the instruments. One girl actually produced deep bass notes by bringing her pharynx into action!*"[30]
> *Refer to Track 52.*

Dance

Much of our knowledge of early San culture is derived from the research conducted by one or two dedicated researchers and the San informants who shared their culture with them. In most of the writings on San dance, it has been observed that in many performances, men danced and women provided accompaniment by clapping and singing.[31] This is also true of the accounts of the San trance dance. Dances generally took a circular formation, with the men moving around the circle in single file using shuffling, stamping steps, and the women standing and sitting to one side of the circle. While certain dances were performed in specific contexts and for specific purposes, such as after a successful hunt; after the first storm of the rainy season; and at the initiation of medicine men, others were purely recreational, and took place on a moonlit night after a meal. As one writer who travelled through

Whistles, flutes and reeds

The San possessed a whistle called ≠*gi*, which was made from the quill of an ostrich feather, and was used to send signals. They also played whistles made from duiker and springbok horn, which were called *!garras*.[10]

The San played signal whistles made from the tibia or shin-bone of small antelopes. These produced a 'sharp and shrill'[11] sound and could be heard from a great distance. A whistle worn around the neck, the *umbaendi,* was made from animal bone.

/'Auni San females played an ocarina which they called *!!nasi !khosike*. It was made from the fruit shell of a wild cucumber. Two openings were pierced on either end of the shell, and the player blew across one of the holes while stopping the other with the palm of her hand.

The San borrowed their reed-pipes and reed-pipe ensembles from the Khoi. Pipes made of reeds were cut to different lengths to obtain a variety of notes. Several performers played at the same time, each producing one note, with a harmonising effect. Each flute had an individual name, also borrowed from the Khoi.

A rudimentary form of the Jew's harp, called the *-!!ku!!kx'a˜si* among the /'Auni San, consisted of a thin grass stalk. The performer held one end of the stem against his mouth, inhaling and exhaling, and simultaneously plucked the loose end forwards or backwards with his fingers. The instrument was sometimes used to mimic the sounds of animals moving.

Namaqualand observed: "Supper being over, the women with their children and the young men set themselves to dance during the first watches of the night."[32] He also noted the use of a drum in the form of "a small earthen pot covered with the skin of a gazelle."[33]

The imitation of animals features strongly in certain San dances. This idea is taken to its extreme by medicine men who claim to transform themselves into animals in a trance or out-of-body experience.[34] The San hold a unique relationship with animals. In the realm of mythical time, the boundary between humans and animals did not exist.[35] By imitating animals in their dances, the San evoke a past where humans and animals were one, refreshing their fascination with animals by studying and then mimicking their movements and behaviour. The San draw on the human qualities they see in animals to merge the animal and human in dance. When the San still lived in their natural environment they used their surroundings as a creative pool for inspiration. So central were animals to San culture, that many dances were named after animals that possessed qualities they admired.

Boy playing he hunting bow

The dancers use various materials to aid them in their representation of animals. They wear ankle-rattles to emphasise the rhythm of an animal's movements and make theatrical costumes to add another dimension to the performance. They create headdresses of feathers to represent birds, and use horns, paint and animal skins to heighten their performances. These enhance the mimicry, which is performed with utmost focus, precision and energy. During the jackal and wolf dance, male dancers break into two groups. One group imitates hyenas feeding on a carcass, and the other group represents jackals attempting to get close to the carcass. When the second group gets too close, the 'hyenas' scare them away and the 'jackals' jump back. In the horse dance, the men gallop around in a circle, with the women clapping their hands to simulate the sound of a horse. Similarly, the *kloo-rou-o*, a frog dance, involves the imitation of a frog's movements by squatting, leaping and rolling, and in the *t'oi* or bee dance, the voice is used to simulate the buzzing of a swarm of bees.[36]

Dances of animal mimicry are also included on important occasions. The eland dance is performed at girl's puberty ceremonies. When a girl menstruates for the first time, she goes into seclusion in a hut for the duration of her menstrual cycle. Every day during this period, a repertoire of 'eland' songs is performed around the hut. Some women clap and reproduce the sound of the animal trotting, while others dance to imitate this movement. Sometimes older men of the girl's family join in the dance, and it develops into a chase, where the males pursue the females. Girls use this dance to imitate the sexual behaviour of these animals.[37] The eland is one of the most powerful animals in San culture and is seen as a symbol of potency. It is thus fitting that it is used in activities with ritual significance. On various other special occasions such as high festivals, people participate in a masquerade, taking on the characteristics of an animal or bird.[38]

Whereas in most cultures games are regarded as children's activities, among the San they are enjoyed by everyone. People usually incorporate song and dance into their games to heighten their enjoyment of them. In one ball game, women arrange themselves in a line, clapping and singing while each person takes a turn to dance in the opposite direction, and throw the ball, usually a melon, to the player at the end of the line. In another game, players skip over a rope, matching their jumping with the rhythm of an accompanying song.[39] In the ostrich game, two boys dance towards each other. When their bodies meet one player bends down and the other swings his leg over the player's bent back. This movement resembles two ostriches fighting or mating. While the boys take turns to jump over each other, they make rhythmic sounds such as *'he he hi, he he he hi'*.[40] *Refer to Track 53.*

Bows and other string instruments

All South African musical bows originate from the San hunting bow. The discovery of the musical possibilities of the hunting bow occurred naturally. The bow gives a musical note when the string is released while shooting. The hunter also used to tap his bow string with an arrow to pass the time. According to one source, "the bow was the precursor of all other stringed instruments and has had a basic influence on the tone systems of San and other African peoples."[12] The /'Auni San called their hunting bow *Ikhou*. The stave is made from wood and the string from sinew. The player holds the instrument in a horizontal position, grasping the stave in the middle with the left hand. With one tip of the bow laid between his lips, he plucks the string or strikes it with a piece of twig or stalk. The performer usually squats or sits when playing this instrument but also occasionally lies on his back and supports the stave with his bent knee.

The **'kan'gan'** is a mouth-resonated braced bow: the string is tied back at the centre of the bow. The instrument rests against the player's mouth and the string is plucked with the forefinger of the right hand.
Refer to Track 49.

The **nxonxoro** bow, made from thin wood, is bent into a semi-circle by the tension of a string made of grass or palm leaf. A number of notches are cut into the wood along the middle of the bow. It is sounded by rubbing a stick across the notches, which causes the string to vibrate. The bow is held in the crook of the arm and the mouth acts as a resonator.
Refer to Track 50.

245

Southern African San trance dance

"You dance, dance, dance, dance. Then n/um *lifts you in your belly and lifts you in your back, and then you start to shiver. N/um makes you tremble; it's hot. Your eyes are open but you don't look around; you hold your eyes still and look straight ahead. But when you get into !kia[41], you're looking around because you see everything, because you see what's troubling everybody … Rapid shallow breathing, that's what draws* n/um *up … then* n/um *enters every part of your body, right to the tip of your feet and even your hair."[42]*

Central to San philosophy is the idea that humans are continually in search of something beyond themselves; something that will enable them to transcend the everyday, and experience altered states of consciousness.[43] This state is reached by activating an energy called *n/um* (among some San) that resides in 'the pit of the stomach'.[44] Much fear surrounds the mystery of trance and the pain of *n/um.* Trance is feared because it is symbolic of the unknown. People fear that they will lose themselves to this state and never return to the earthly realm. Furthermore, it is an intensely emotional experience because, in a sense, it is a miniature death and rebirth. It is also feared because it is extremely physical. When it is activated people experience a severe burning pain in the diaphragm and spleen. Despite the overwhelming fear that is associated with these experiences, the San submit themselves to this state because of its healing properties, both on an individual and communal level.

Among the San, the main channels through which a trance state is reached are song and dance. Singing awakens and triggers the boiling energy that leads to trance, and in turn 'awakens their hearts'.[45] Dancing is vital to 'heating up' the energy so that it can start to boil. Once this has happened, the heat travels through the dancer's body, through the spinal cord, exploding in the head and

The **'kopo** bow is made from solid wood or cane, and the string is made from twisted hair, sinew, leather or wire. A calabash or tortoise-shell resonator is attached to one end. It is struck with a thin stick, reed or grass.

The San borrowed some of their musical bows from the neighbouring Bantu. The **!gawu-kha:s** was borrowed from the Tswana. Some sources refer to this instrument as a 'one-stringed violin'.[13] In its original form it was mouth-resonated, but later a tin resonator was used, and the !Kung San called the instrument the tin-can bow.[14] It is made from a length of hollowed wood and is strung with a twisted sinew that is fastened around a tuning peg. The tin can is attached over the top end of the stick. It is played with a tiny hair-bow that is moistened with the lips and rubbed against the string in a circular motion. Sometimes the player sings while performing.[15]

The San and Khoi used the European fiddle as a model for their own version of the instrument. Unable to afford European violins, they constructed violin-type instruments out of old paraffin tins and wooden cocoa boxes.

The San **ramkie,** a plucked lute, was influenced by the Portuguese. It is likely that the Khoi were the first of South Africa's inhabitants to play the instrument, and to pass it on to the San. The lower half of the body consists of a calabash resonator over which a piece of skin is stretched to serve as a resonator. A plank of wood with strings attached from the top to the bottom of the instrument serves as the neck. The number of strings varies from three to six. The *ramkie* is regarded as the equivalent of the Western guitar, which has now largely replaced it.[16]

247

is eventually exuded from the body through sweat. It is at this point that the individual enters a trance state and transcendence becomes possible. Among different groups of San there are variations in healing dances, but they are most commonly and generically referred to as trance or medicine dances. Despite these variations, song and dance have the same fundamental properties in the context of healing. Through their inextricable connection with the religious experience of transcendence, singing and dancing are imbued with the weight of religious activities in San society. Most research on San trance dances have focused on the healing practices of the !Kung of Botswana. There is evidence, however, that the majority of San peoples did practise the trance dance. A central theme in San rock paintings is that of the shamanic activities of the sorcerer, particularly the trance dance. Evidence of this also exists in some of the /Xam interviews conducted by Bleek and Lloyd in the 1870s, where the informants identified the subject matter of rock paintings as referring explicitly to trance dances.

In most San communities, certain individuals receive inspiration from a deity and create songs and dances with healing properties. The !Kung San of Botswana believe that their god creates the medicine songs and then 'gives' them to certain people as a special favour through their lesser god, //Gauwa.[46] These are then shared freely with the rest of the community, and the songs travel from group to group. There are numerous legends around the origin of medicine songs and dances, and the people who originally 'received' them.

Here is one version of a !Kung woman's inspiration:

"A woman named Be was alone one day in the bush.[47] She saw a herd of giraffes running before an approaching thunderstorm. The rolling beat of their hooves grew louder and mingled in her head with the sound of sudden rain. Suddenly a song she had never heard before came to her, and she began to sing. //Gauwa (the great god) told her it was a medicine song. Be went home and taught the song to her husband, /Ti!kay. They sang it and danced to it together. It was indeed a song for trancing, a medicine song. /Ti!kay taught it to others who passed it on."[48]

Here is another account of someone who 'received' medicine songs from //Gauwa:

"Old N≠isa, very full of herself, smiling, pleased to be asked, told us how //Gauwa had come to her in the days when she was young and fresh. He had appeared beside her while she was sleeping and had said, 'You are crying for singing. Why do you not get up and sing?' She got up and sang with him, imitating him and learning. He taught her in a kindly way and said, 'Now, do not stay quiet as you used to do. Go and sing. Sing for the people as I have taught you.' She was glad. When he left, she slept again. In all, he came to her in this way five times, in both the cold and the heat of the year. People said they thought she had received this exceptional attention from //Gauwa because she was so good at singing."[49]

These accounts illustrate the way in which an inspired individual can affect almost the entire San population. Individuals share their revelations and the community enthusiastically accepts them. Shamans, also known as medicine men or sorcerers, can be either male or female. They are important figures in San society, initiating healing activities in their communities and contributing to the survival of their people.

In the past the healing dance occurred regularly among certain San groups, and was seen as a vital part of San culture. It usually took place at night and could last an entire evening.[50] Its role in San communities today has diminished and it is uncertain how widely it is practised.

The energy of each individual is contagious and people display incredible stamina when participating. The dance usually begins informally. Seated around a fire, the women start singing and clapping, creating a backing music that persists throughout the dance. The women's musical skills are highly developed and their clapping has been likened to "a group of well-played percussion instruments."[51] They are able to create music as a group because

The *//gwashi* is a pluriarc, a type of stringed instrument that the !Kung San borrowed from the Ambo people of Ovamboland (who play the ovambo guitar). There are two variations of this instrument. The five-stringed *//gwashi* is played by males and the four-stringed version is played by females. There is a legend about a man named K"ao N//ai, who made the first *//gwashi*:

"His wife had left him and gone with her own people to the north. He followed her to try to persuade her to return to him. She and her people shot at him and drove him away. On his sorrowful return journey, he passed through a mangentti forest. There he stopped and made the first //gwashi out of mangentti wood."[17]

//Gwashishi (plural) are traditionally made from mangentti, a pliable wood, and the strings are made from sinew or plant fibre. A log of mangentti is hollowed and four or five holes are burned into one end, so that thin, smooth sticks can be inserted. The strings are wound around the sticks and are tuned by tightening or loosening them. Nowadays a tin can is commonly used as a resonator. The player plucks the strings with the thumb and forefinger. *//Gwashi* music is usually accompanied by singing. The singing often consists of pure humming without words, but occasionally a few words are incorporated into the song. This type of music is very popular among the San, which is reflected in their large repertoire of *//gwashi* songs.
Refer to Track 51.

250

they are focused on listening to and watching one another. The women sing a range of different songs that correspond to the different phases of the dance. The dancers' movements, however, remain consistent throughout.

The men slowly start to dance around the women in a circle – a formation which symbolises inclusiveness. They wear rattles made from dried cocoons around their lower legs to accentuate the rhythm of the music. Their foot movements are characterised by a controlled stamp and hop, changing their weight from foot to foot. The image of the small, controlled movements of their legs has been compared to the movement of millipedes.[52] Their postures are characterised by slightly bent knees and erect upper torsos that lean slightly forward. So controlled are their postures that their bodies are like "statues being carried by dancing legs."[53] They move their upper bodies ever so slightly at times: sometimes they swing their torsos from side to side; sometimes they bend them very low so that they are in line with their thighs. They usually start by moving anti-clockwise, and change direction after a short while. The main role of the women is to clap and sing, but this does not prohibit them from dancing. When the mood seizes her, a woman might stand up and move to a spot slightly outside of the circle. She performs a step composed of "two or three small, rapid stamps, followed by a sideward fling of a foot; the arms, bent at the elbow, pumping back and forth."[54] She may also join the dancing line of men for a few moments, shuffling forward "as if she were floating."[55]

At some point, dancers begin to enter a trance. They start to shriek and howl as the pain and intensity of the experience increases. In an attempt to heat their bodies more quickly, they sometimes pick up coals from the fire or even throw themselves into the fire. There have been many reports that people in a trance can withstand fire.[56] Nonetheless, fieldwork reports assert that individuals who attempt to throw themselves into the fire are usually prevented from doing so by those sitting close by. The element of mutual support is one of the most essential principles of the dance. The women show their support for the dancers by heightening the intensity of their clapping and singing in moments of climax. Throughout the dance, there are always people to support those who are entranced. Trance is terrifying for some, but

The *Ika/ kanasi* is an ancient instrument that was made and played by older /'Auni San women. It consisted of a string made from sinew, a knobkerrie, a cocoon, dry buck hide, and a length of riem. The player sat down with the stick in front of her legs. She looped the string round the stick, passing one half of it between the big toe and second toe of her left foot, and the other half along the side of her right foot. The two ends of the string were then secured to the cocoon through one tip, and a piece of riem was threaded through the other. She passed the riem across her chest and tied its two ends behind her back. Finally, the hide was placed between the cocoon and her chest to serve as a resonator. By leaning forwards and backwards, the player could alter the tension of the string, lowering the pitch by loosening it and raising the pitch by tightening it. The player also sometimes plucked the two halves of the string with her thumbs. Percival Kirby, who recorded the music of the San described this stringed instrument as one of the most remarkable he had ever seen.

Stringed-wind

Contrary to popular belief, the San were not the originators of the *gora*[18], but borrowed it from the Khoi.[19] (see Chapter 10, page 237).

they are able to overcome their fear because they are never alone. Guardians physically hold a person when he is on the verge of collapse. When someone needs to cool down because his body has overheated, a member of the group gives him water, helping him to lie down and rest. Healers in a trance state move around the circle, laying their hands on people to withdraw any illness. They use their own sweat to massage and heal others in the circle.

Through the course of the evening the energy of the performers rises and falls. In moments when the energy of the group is at its peak, the tempo of the music is at its fastest, the singing at its loudest and the dancing at its most urgent. At other moments, when people are exhausted from the sheer exhilaration and physical energy they have invested in the dance, the music eases and shifts into another gear. It slows and quietens as people drift off to rest or chat so that they can revive themselves before the next spurt of energy. The highest peak usually coincides with the arrival of the sun at dawn, as people start to sing the 'sun' song. The San like to end the performance on a

high moment, so that they walk away feeling energised and exhilarated. The dance ends in a more formalised fashion than it begins. One man faces the women and conclusively stamps his feet. The other men follow his lead and start stamping. In response, the women clap a specific pattern and the dancing ends.

Trance music is regarded as an ally against illness, misfortune and death.[57] It is the primary means of healing in a culture that continually seeks to heal and better itself. Emphasis must be placed on the healing of the community, as opposed to the individual.[58] While individual healing is important, healing across the group is essential. This is most evident in the way the San use music to help each other heal. The women clap and sing to help the dancers reach a trance and to enhance the powerful, electric mood necessary for healing. Dancers physically support those who are entranced and on the verge of collapse. Music also fulfils a social function. The trance/medicine dance is a 'rite of solidarity'[59] – it brings a community together, reinforcing the values that bind people. According to one source "Nothing but a medicine dance assembles all the people into a concerted activity."[60] At most dances in the past, everyone in the vicinity was present, even if only as observers watching from the sidelines. If there is any hostility or tension among a group, the dance eliminates it by encouraging participation and group activity. One of the most vital functions of the healing dance is to create cultural continuity and to preserve tradition. With the gradual erosion of the San culture, these dances have become particularly significant as a means of renewing and reaffirming San values. With the increase in poverty, malnutrition and spiritual deprivation among the remnants of a broken society, healing in the traditional San style has great value. It affirms the San identity by bringing the community together, focusing the group's energy on spiritual upliftment and empowerment, and resulting in a cathartic experience. *Refer to Track 54.*

Mbiras

It has been estimated that the !Kung San first started playing the *mbira* around the 1960s, and that it was subsequently adopted by other San communities.[20] Although many of their Bantu neighbours had been playing the instrument long before then, the San probably adopted it when metal became available to them. The instrument is played mainly by younger people.[21]

Some interesting research has been conducted involving the use of the *mbira* as a tool for trance in certain areas. Jack, as he is commonly called, lives in north-western Botswana and is known over a large area as one of the oldest *mbira* players and as a composer of *mbira* music.[22] Jack fell ill and was the victim of accidents and misfortunes on various occasions through his life, but playing the *mbira* cured him every time. Jack believes that he is an instrument of God's will. God speaks to him through his music and relays important messages that are shared with the community. On a personal level, Jack prays to God through the channel of his music. He also uses his music as an outlet for his feelings. He is unique because he is one of the few players who sings while playing the instrument, and is able to enter a trance through his music. He is also innovative. He introduced the idea of playing duets using the *mbira*. He taught his wife to play it so that they could play together.

Comparative table of instruments

ZULU	SWAZI	XHOSA	NDEBELE	SOTHO	
DRUMS					
	Intambula				
		Ingqongqo			
Ingungu		Isidiphu			
Isigubu		Igubu	Isighubu	Sekupu	
				Moropa	
			Ingungu enculu		
		Ikawu			
		Igogogo	Equde		
RATTLES AND SHAKERS					
Iselwa	Ligoshu				
		Amanqashele	Amafahlakwana	Morothlwane	
Imifece	Emafahlawane				
		Imiguza			
Khenqekhenqe					
Amafohlwane		Iingcacu			
		Izikunjane	Amafahlakwana	Ditjobo	
				Manyenenyene	
		Iqhagi			

PEDI	TSWANA	VENDA	TSONGA	KHOI	SAN
				/Khais	!Kwa
Ntshomane			Ncomane		
Moshupiane					
Kiba		Tshigubu	Xigubu		
		Ngoma	Ngoma		
Moropa	Moropa	Murumba			
			Ndzumba		
					Dou
			Muntshintshi		
			Shikolombane		
		Thungwa			
Tshela		Tshele	Ndjele		
					/keriten
Thlwahlawadi	Matlhowa		Mafowa	/Xororokwa	/Kale
Mathotse		Mutshakatha	Marhonge		
		Thandana			

ZULU	SWAZI	XHOSA	NDEBELE	SOTHO	
HAND CLAPPERS					
Amatambo			Izikeyi		
FLUTES, WHISTLES AND REEDS					
	Luveve				
				Lekhitlane	
			Ifegwana		
Imbande		Imbande			
			Ipandula		
Igemfe		Ingcongolo			
		Ukombe			
Impempe		Impempe			
			No name		
Umtshingo	Umtshingosi	Ixilongo		Lekodilo	
	Livenge	Utwi-twi-twi			
TRUMPETS					
Icilongo					
HORNS					
Mpalampala	Mpalampala		Impalampala		
Upondo		Isigodhlo			
BULL-ROARERS					
Mampembe		Uvuru		Sevuruvuru	

PEDI	TSWANA	VENDA	TSONGA	KHOI	SAN
	Marapo		Spagane		No name
		Nanga ya ntsa			/Garras
Naka ya sefako	Pala	Pala			
Lengwane	Lengwane		Nanga	//Aren!as	
		Dzhio	Ndjwebe		Umbaendi
Tsula	Naka	Nanga ya danga	'Flute of heaven'		
Tsula ya noko					
Mokudietane	Mothlatsa	Nanga ya davhi			
Dinaka tsa lethlaka	Lethlaka noka				≠Gi
Faai		Tshipotoliyo	Shitloti		
Dinaka	Dithlaka	Nanga		No name	No name
	Mokoreie				
		Sitlanjani			
		Khumbgwe			
			Shiwaya		//Nasi /khosike
					-//Ku//kxa-si
Phalaphala	Lepapata	Phalaphala	Mhalamhala		
		Tshihoho		Kelp horn	
Kgabudubudu	Seburuburu	Tshivhilivhi		Burubush	!Goin!goin

ZULU	SWAZI	XHOSA	NDEBELE	SOTHO	
XYLOPHONES					
MBIRAS					
BOWS					
Ughubhu	Ligubu	Uhadi	Icaco	Thomo	
Umakhweyane	Umakweyana				
Umhubhe	Utiyane	Umhrubhe			
Isintontolo	Isitontolo			Setolotolo	
Ubhel'indhela	Sikhelekehle	Ikatali	Pone	Sekatari	
Umqangala	Umqangala	Inkinge	Isikumero	Lekope	
				Mokhope	
STRINGED-WIND					
Ugwala	Makwindi	Ugwali		Lesiba	

PEDI	TSWANA	VENDA	TSONGA	KHOI	SAN
		Mbila mutondo	Mohambi		
Dipela		Mbila deza	Timbila		Mbira
					/Khou
	Nokukwane			Kha:s	
Sekgapa	Segwana				Kopo
Sekgapa		Dende	Xidende		
Lekope		Tshigwana	Sekgapa		'Kan'gan
Sekgobogobo	Segankuru	Tsijolo			!Gawu-kha:s
Lekope	Lengope	Lugube	Umqangala	!Gabus	
		Tshizambi	Xizambi		Nxonxoro
	Ramkie			Ramkie	Ramkie
					//Gwashi
					Fiddle
				Tamboer	
				Gabowie	
	Setinkane				
					/Ka/kanasi
	Mafata-iswaneng				
Lesiba	Lesiba	Ugwala		Gora	Gora

259

Glossary

abafana – young Xhosa men of the red people
abakhwetha – initiates
aerophones – wind instruments
amagqirha – diviners
amagwijo – personal songs
amahubo – clan anthems

balimo – ancestors
bepha – Venda musical expeditions
bogwera – male initiation
bojale – Batswana female initiation
bonwale – Tswana female initiates
bunanga – Tsonga horn ensemble
byale – Pedi female initiation

chordophones – string instruments

domba – phase in Venda female initiation

emafahlawane – ankle-rattles
equde – single-headed tin drum
etywaleni – beer parties for adults

ifengwana – whistles
igemfe – reed-pipes
iindlavini – Xhosa school people
iingoma zotywale – beer songs
iinkaca – beads worn around the ankles
ikatari – bow-type instrument played by friction
ikawu – shield made from ox-skin
ikhetho – groom's party
imbongi – praise singer/poet
impalampala – horns
impempe – river-reed pipe
ingqongqo – rudimentary drum made of ox hide
ingungu – friction drum
inkondlo – ancient dance-song
intlombe – dance parties for young adults
intonjane – female initiation

ipandula – flute
isibaya senkoma – cattle byre
isidiphu – friction drum
isigodhlo – Xhosa chief's private kraal; blowing a horn
isibhaya – cattle enclosure
isihlabelelo – lullaby
isikumero – mouth-bow
isikunjane – tin rattles filled with stones
isinqindi – short stabbing spear
isiqubulo – stately dance accompanied by male songs
izaga – battle cries
izibongo – praise poetry
izicathulo – gumboot dance
izigiyo – chants
izikeyi – wooden clappers
izimtonbi – unmarried girls
izingqambi – professional composers

kgoro – headkraal
kgotla – council place
khomba – Tsonga female initiation
koma/lebello – Bapedi male initiation
kubina dithlaka – Batswana reed-pipe ensemble
lebollo – Basotho male initiation
lekhitlane – whistle made from female blesbok horns
lekope – Basotho mouth-resonated bow
lengwane – Tswane leg-bone flute
lethlaka noka – reed whistle
ligoshu – hand-rattles
lipina tsa mokopu – pumpkin songs
lithoko – Basotho praise poetry
litjobo – waist-rattles
litolobonya – shaking dance
litsoejane – coming-out ceremony
ludziyo – clay beer pot; first fruits celebration
lusekwane – species of acacia
luveve – whistles
malombo – possession
malopo – possession

mampembe – bull-roarers

mancomane – exorcism

marapo – Tswana hand-clappers

marimba – xylophone

matlhowa – Tswana dancing rattles

mbira – thumb or hand piano

membranophone – drums

mitambo – dance theatre

modianyewe – Sotho grass hat

mohobelo – 'striding' dance

mokato – Pedi first fruits ceremony

mokhibo – 'knee' dance

mokoreie – reed flute

mokorotlo – Basotho war dance or 'riding' dance

molutsoane – rain ceremony

moqoqopelo – Basotho traditional dance performed by children

moropa – wooden drum

mothlatsa – conical whistle made of wood or ivory

mpalampala – antelope horn

muntshintshi – Tsonga big drum

murhundzu – Tsonga male initiation

musevetho – Venda male initiation

mutshakatha – leg-rattles

naka – flutes; bone whistle to ward off lightning and hail

nanga – Venda reed-pipes

ncomane – Tsonga hand-held drum

ndlamu – stamping dance

ngoma – Venda rituals with a sacred dimension

Nomkubulwane – princess of heaven

nyimbo dza vhana – Venda children's songs

ocarinas – round or oval-shaped instruments with finger-holes and a mouth-hole

pala – impala horn whistle

peeledi – skins

phalaphala – Pedi horn

setapo – step dance

setolotolo – mouth-bow

sevuruvuru – Sotho bull-roarer

sibaya – cattle kraal

susuzela – lullabies

thojane – Tswana ceremonial dance

thuthuzela – lullabies

tshigubu – double-headed drum

tshikanda – phase in Venda female initiation

tshikona – Venda reed-pipe dance

tshivhilivhi – Venda bull-roarer

ubhanyibane – small painted wooden axes

ubuntombi – virginity

ugubhu – unbraced gourd-bow

uhadi – gourd-bow

ukubhina – female puberty song

ukugqashula – female solo

ukumbombozela/imbuyo – humming

ukunqukuza – hand-clapping song

ukutyityimba – shaking movements

ukwaluka – male initiation

umkhosi – first fruits festival

umkhosi womhlanga – royal reed dance

umngqungo – round dance performed by married women

umrhubhe – mouth-bow

umteyo – Xhosa shaking dance

umthimba – bride's party

umtshingozi – end-blown harmonic flute

umtshotsho – dance parties for teenagers

umxhentso – diviner's dance

upondo – ox horn

uvuru – Xhosa bull-roarer or spinning disk

vhusha – phase in Venda female initiation

wada – a sacred drum

xichaya – solo music

zwilombe – Venda wandering entertainers

Bibliography

Books

Ashton, *The Basuto*, Oxford University, Press, London, 1952.

Barnard, *Hunters and Herders of Southern Africa*, Cambridge University Press, Cambridge, 1992.

Becker, *Trails and Tribes in Southern Africa*, Hart-Davis, Mac-Gibbon, London, 1975.

Berens et al, *The Cape Herders: A History of the Khoi Khoi of Southern Africa*, David Philip, Cape Town, 1996.

Biesele, 'Anyone with Sense Would Know: Tradition and Creativity in !Kung Narrative and Song' in *Contemporary Studies on Khoisan 1*, Vossen and Keuthman (eds), Helmut Buske Verlag, Hamburg, 1986.

Binns, *The Warrior People*, Howard Timmins, Cape Town, 1974.

Blacking, 'Music of the Venda-speaking People' in *South African Music Encyclopaedia*, Malan (ed), Oxford University Press, Cape Town, 1982.

Blacking, *Venda Children's Songs*, Witwatersrand University Press, Johannesburg, 1967.

Bleek and Lloyd, *Specimens of Bushmen Folklore*, George Allen, London, 1911.

Breutz, *The Social and Political System of the Sotho-Tswana*, P.L. Breutz, Ramsgate, 1947.

Broster, *The Thembu*, Purnell, Cape Town, 1976.

Bryant, *The Zulu People*, Shuter and Shooter, Pietermaritzburg, 1949.

Casalis, *The Basutos*, Nisbet, London, 1861.

Coplan, *In the Time of Cannibals*, Witwatersrand University Press, Johannesburg.

Dargie, *Xhosa Music: Its Techniques and Instruments with a Collection of Songs*, David Philip, Cape Town, 1988.

Davenport, *South Africa: A Modern History*, Macmillan, Johannesburg, 1987.

De la Harpe et al, *Zulu*, Struik, Cape Town, 1998.

Dornan, *Pygmies and Bushmen of the Kalahari*, Struik, Cape Town, 1975.

Elliot, *Sons of Zulu*, Collins, Johannesburg, 1978.

Elliot, *The Magic World of the Xhosa*, Charles Scribner's Sons, New York, 1970.

Engelbrecht, *The Korana*, Maskew Miller, Cape Town, 1936.

Hammond-Tooke, *The Bantu-speaking Peoples of Southern Africa*, Routledge and Kegan Paul, London, 1974.

Hammond-Tooke, *The Roots of Black South Africa*, Jonathan Ball Publishers, Johannesburg, 1993.

Hansen, 'Bushman Music: Still an Unknown' in *Miscast: Negotiating the Presence of the San*, Skotnes (ed), University of Cape Town Press, Cape Town, 1996.

Huskisson, 'A Note on the Music of the Sotho' in *South African Music Encyclopaedia*, Malan (ed), Oxford University Press, Cape Town, 1982.

Huskisson, 'Music of the Pedi (Northern Sotho)' in *South African Music Encyclopaedia*, Malan (ed), Oxford University Press, Cape Town, 1982.

James, A. *The First Bushman's Path*, University of Natal Press, Pietermaritzburg, 2001.

James, D. *Songs of the Women Migrants: Performance and Identity in South Africa*, Edinburgh University Press, London, 1999.

Johnston, 'Notes of the Music of the Tswana' in *South African Music Encyclopaedia*, Malan (ed), Oxford University Press, Cape Town, 1982.

Junod, *The Life of a South African Tribe*, Vol. 1 and 2, Macmillan, London, 1927.

Katz, 'Education for Transcendence: !Kia-Healing with the Kalahari !Kung' in *Kalahari Hunter-Gatherers*, Lee and DeVore (eds), Harvard University Press, Cambridge, 1976.

Katz, *Boiling Energy*, Harvard University Press, Cambridge, 1982.

Kirby, 'The Musical Practices of the /'Auni and = Khomani San' in *Bushmen of the Southern Kalahari*, Jones and Doke (eds), Witwatersrand University Press, Johannesburg, 1937.

Kirby, 'The Musics of the Black Races of South Africa' in *South African Music Encyclopaedia*, Malan (ed), Oxford University Press, Cape Town, 1982.

Kirby, *The Musical Instruments of the Native Races of South Africa*, Witwatersrand University Press, Johannesburg, 1968.

Krige, *The Social System of the Zulus*, Shuter and Shooter, Pietermaritzburg, 1936.

Kuper, *A South African Kingdom*, Holt, Rinehart and Winston, New York, 1963.

Kuper, *An African Aristocracy*, Oxford University Press, London, 1947.

Lee and Devore (eds), *Kalahari Hunter-Gatherers*, Harvard University Press, Cambridge, 1976.

Magubane, *Vanishing Cultures of South Africa*, Struik, Cape Town, 1998.

Marshall, 'The !Kung of Nyae Nyae' in, *Kalahari Hunter-Gatherers*, Lee and DeVore (eds), Harvard University Press, Cambridge, 1976.

Marwick, *The Swazi*, Frank Cass and Co, London, 1966.

Maylam, *A History of the African People of South Africa: from the Early Iron Age to the 1970s*, David Philip, Cape Town, 1986.

Moitse, *The Ethnomusicology of the Basotho*, Institute of Southern African Studies, Lesotho, 1994.

Mokhali, *Basotho Music and Dancing*, Mazenod Book Centre, Lesotho, 1967.

Monnig, *The Pedi*, J.L van Schaik Limited, Pretoria, 1967.

Powell, *Ndebele: A People and Their Art*, Struik, Cape Town, 1995.

Rycroft, 'The Music of the Zulu and Swazi' in *South African Music Encyclopedia*, Oxford University Press, Cape Town, 1982.

Rycroft, *Say it in Siswati*, London University, London, 1976.

Schapera, *Praise Poems of Tswana chiefs*, Oxford University Press, London, 1965.

Schapera, *The Bantu-Speaking Tribes of South Africa*, Maskew Miller, Cape Town, 1966.

Schapera, *The Khoisan Peoples of South Africa*, Routledge and Kegan Paul, London, 1930.

Schapera, *The Tswana*, International African Institute, London, 1953.

Smith et al, *The Bushmen of Southern Africa: A Foraging Society in Transition*, David Philip, Cape Town, 2000.

Soga, *The Ama-Xhosa: Life and Customs*, Lovedale Press, South Africa, 1931.

Stayt, *The BaVenda*, Frank Cass and Co, London, 1968.

Thomas, *The Harmless People*, Secker and Warburg, London, 1959.

Tracey, *African Dances of the Witwatersrand Gold Mines*, African Music Society, Johannesburg, 1952.

Tracey, *Zulu Paradox*, Silver Leaf Books, Johannesburg, 1948.

Tyrrell, *Tribal Peoples of Southern Africa*, Books of Africa, Cape Town, 1968.

Wells, *An Introduction to the Music of the Basotho*, Morija Museum Archives, Lesotho, 1994.

West and Morris, *Abantu*, Struik Publishers, Cape Town, 1967.

Journals

Biesele, 'Song Texts by the Master of Tricks: Kalahari San Thumb Piano Music' in *Botswana Notes and Records*, 7, 1975.

Blacking, 'Musical Expeditions of the Venda' in *African Music*, 3 (1), International Library of African Music, Grahamstown, 1962.

Brearley, 'A Musical Tour of Botswana' in *Botswana Notes and Records*, Botswana Society, Botswana, 1984.

Clegg, 'The Music of the Zulu Immigrant Workers in Johannesburg: A Focus on Concertina and Guitar' in *Papers Presented at the Symposium on Ethnomusicology*, International Library of African Music, Grahamstown, 1980 and 1989.

Cook, 'The Inqwala Ceremony of the Swazi' in *Bantu Studies*, 4, University of the Witwatersrand, Johannesburg, 1930.

Dargie, 'Some recent discoveries and recordings in Xhosa music' in *Papers Presented at the Fifth Symposium on Ethnomusicology*, International Library of African Music, Grahamstown, 1985.

Dargie, 'Umngqokolo: Xhosa overtone singing and the song Nondelékhaya' in *African Music*, 7 (1), International Library of African Music, Grahamstown, 1991.

Davies, 'Aspects of Zulu Maskanda Guitar Music' in *Papers Presented at the Tenth Symposium on Ethnomusicology*, International Library of African Music, Grahamstown, 1995.

Dornan, 'Rainmaking in South Africa' in *Bantu Studies*, 3, Witwatersrand University Press, Johannesburg, 1927-30.

England, Bushman Counterpoint in *Journal of the International Folk Music Council*, 19, 1967.

Gildenhuys, 'Musical Instruments of South West Africa/Namibia' in *Papers Presented at the Second Symposium on Ethnomusicology*, International Library of African Music, Grahamstown, 1982.

Honore, 'Some Observations on Xhosa Dance in the 1980s' in *Papers Presented at the Sixth Symposium on Ethnomusicology*, International Library of African Music, Grahamstown, 1988.

James, 'iKe rena baeng/We are visiting: The Evolution and Spread of Kiba, Performance Style of the Northern Transvaal Migrants' in *Papers Presented as the Tenth Symposium on Ethnomusicology*, 1991.

Johnston, 'Children's Music of the Shangana-Tsonga' in *African Music*, 6 (4), International Library of African Music, Grahamstown, 1987.

Johnston, 'Shangana-Tsonga Drum and Bow Rhythms' in *African Music*, 5 (1), International Library of African Music, Grahamstown, pp60-63, 1971.

Joseph, 'Zulu Women's Music' in *African Music*, 6 (3), International Library of African Music, Grahamstown, 1983.

Kirby, 'A Study of Bushman Music' in *Bantu Studies*, 10, Witwatersrand University Press, 1936.

Kruger, 'Some of Them are Foolish, Some of Them are Good: On the Contradictions of Artistic Experience in Venda Musical Culture' in *Papers Presented at the Tenth Symposium on Ethnomusicology*, International Library of African Music, Grahamstown, 1991.

Kruger, 'Introduction to the Social Context of Two Venda Dances: Tshikona and Tshigombela' in *Papers Presented as the Seventh Symposium on Ethnomusicology*, International Library of African Music, Grahamstown, 1989.

Kruger, Singing 'Psalms with Owls: A Venda Twentieth Century Musical History' in *Journal of African Music*, 8 (1), Forthcoming.

Kruger, 'Mitambo: Venda Traditional Dance Theatre' in *Papers Presented at the Symposium of Ethnomusicology*, Number 15, International Library of African Music, Grahamstown, 1999.

Kruger, 'Singing Psalms with Owls: A Venda Twentieth Century Musical History' in *African Music*, 7 (4), International Library of African Music, Grahamstown, 1999.

Kruger, 'Wada: Story of an African Drum' in *Papers Presented at the Eighth Symposium on Ethnomusicology*, International Library of African Music, Grahamstown, 1995.

Marshall, 'The Medicine Dance of the !Kung Bushmen' in *Africa*, 39 (4), 1969.

Muso, 'Thojane' in *Papers Presented at the Symposium on Ethnomusicology*, Number 13, International Library of African Music, Grahamstown, 1997.

Ndlovu, Scathamiya: 'A Zulu Male Vocal Tradition' in *Papers Presented at the Eighth Symposium on Ethnomusicology*, International Library of African Music, Grahamstown, 1989.

Netshitangani, 'The Songs of Venda Murundu School' in *Papers Presented at the Symposium in Ethnomusicology*, Number 13, International Library of African Music, Grahamstown, 1997.

Ntsihlele, 'The Musical Essence in Tshivenda Folktales' in *Papers Presented at the Symposium on Ethnomusicology*, Number 13, International Library of African Music, Grahamstown, 1997.

Ntsihlele, 'Work Songs: Stylistic Differences Based on Gender in Basotho Adult Songs' in *Papers Presented at the Symposium on Ethnomusicology*, Number 13, International Library of African Music, Grahamstown, 1997.

Peddema, 'Tswana Ritual Concerning Rain' in *African Studies*, Witwatersrand University Press, Johannesburg, 25, 1, 1966.

Ralushai, 'The Origin and Social Significance of Malombo' in *Papers Presented at the Fifth Symposium on Ethnomusicology*, International Library of African Music, Grahamstown, 1985.

Rycroft, 'The Zulu Bow Songs of Princess Magogo' in *African Music*, 5 (4), International Library of African Music, Grahamstown, 1975/6.

Rycroft, 'Zulu Male Traditional Singing' in *African Music*, 1(4), International Library of African Music, Grahamstown, 1957.

Rycroft, 'Zulu Melodic and Non-Melodic Vocal Styles' in *Papers Presented at the Fifth Symposium on Ethnomusicology*, International Library of African Music, Grahamstown, 1985.

Thembela, 'A Socio-Cultural Basis of Ethnic Music with Special Reference to the Music of Ladysmith Black Mambazo' in *Papers Presented at the Symposium on Ethnomusicology*, Number 13, International Library of African Music, Grahamstown, 1997.

Tracey, 'Recording Tour' in *African Music*, International Library of African Music, Grahamstown, 1959, 2 (2).

Wells, 'Report on Research in Lesotho' in *African Music*, 7 (2), International Library of African Music, Grahamstown, 1992.

Wells, 'Sesotho Music: A Contemporary Perspective' in *African Music*, 7 (3), International Library of African Music, Grahamstown, 1996.

Wood, 'A Study of the Traditional Music of Mochudi' in *Botswana Notes and Records*, 8, Botswana Society, Botswana, 1976.

Wood, 'Observing and Recording Village Music in the Kweneng', unpublished article, 1978.

Xulu, 'The Zulu Wedding as a Musical Event: A Musical Realization of Social Ideas' in *Papers Presented at the Eighth Symposium on Ethnomusicology*, International Library of African Music, Grahamstown, 1989.

Xulu, 'Some Aspects of Tradition and Change in Zulu Music: An Ethno-Historical Perspective' in *Papers Presented at the Symposium on Ethnomusicology*, Number 13, International Library of African Music, Grahamstown, 1997.

Xulu, 'The Revitalisation of Amahubo Song Styles and Ideas in Zulu Maskanda Music' in *Papers Presented at the Tenth Symposium on Ethnomusicology*, International Library of African Music, Grahamstown, 1995.

Xulu, 'The Social Significance of Zulu Amahubo Songs' in *Papers Presented at the Eighth Symposium on Ethnomusicology*, International Library of African Music, Grahamstown, 1989.

Theses

Chabalala, D. *Role and Functions of Traditional Music in Spirit Possession Healing amongst the Tsonga People of South Africa*, unpublished PhD thesis, University of the Witwatersrand, 2003.

Fokwang, *Chiefs and Democratic Transition in Africa: An Ethnographic Study in The Chiefdoms of Tshivhase and Bali*, Masters dissertation, University of Pretoria, 2003.

Hansen, *The Music of the Xhosa-speaking People*, unpublished PhD thesis, Grahamstown, 1981.

Huskisson, *The Social and Ceremonial Music of the Pedi*, unpublished thesis, University of the Witwatersrand, Johannesburg, 1958.

James, *Mmino wa setso: Songs of Town and Country and the Experience of Migrancy by Men and Women from the Northern Transvaal*, unpublished PhD thesis, University of the Witwatersrand, 1993.

Johnston, *The Music of the Shangana-Tsonga*, unpublished PhD thesis, University of Witwatersrand, Johannesburg, 1971.

Mapaya, *Aspects of Contemporary Transmission of Sepedi Culture Through Music: Its Perpetuation Within and Beyond the Region of Ga-mmalebogo, Limpopo Province South Africa*, University of the Witwatersrand, Johannesburg, unpublished thesis, 2004.

Mthethwa, *Zulu Songs from South Africa* in www.lyrichord.com/refw/ref7401.html, Lyrichord Catalogue 7401 (Lyrichord Discs Inc., New York, 1986).

CDs

Dargie, *Zulu Bow Songs: The Rich Heritage of Bow Songs of Maphophoma and Nongoma*, Munich and University of Fort Hare, 2003.

Laade, *Music of Man Archive: Zimbabwe – The Ndebele People*, Jecklin and Co, Zurich, 1991.

Olivier, *Namibia: Songs of the Ju'hoansi San*, Ocora Radio France, Paris, 1997.

Websites

www.era.anthropology.ac.uk/Era/VendaGirls/VendaMusic/Mu1

www.nationmaster.com/encyclopedia/zulu-language

www.zululand.kzn.org.za

Appendix – CD tracks

Zulu chapter

1. Dukathole
– *Umtshingo*
A herdboys' tune from the district of Mhlabatini.
Performed by Mxabaniseni Buthelezi at Chief Buthelezi's Kraal, Mhlabatini District, KwaZulu-Natal.
From *Sound of Africa Series*, Hugh Tracey, International Library of African Music, Rhodes University, TR10, 1955.

2. Akasa ngi baleli (He does not write to me anymore)
– *Umakhweyana*
This is a typical love song by a young girl wondering when she will see her boyfriend again. He has gone to work in the city, far from their home in KwaZulu-Natal and he does not writes to her.
Performed by Nomatheko Zungu, Mahlabatini District, KwaZulu-Natal.
From *Sound of Africa Series*, Hugh Tracey, International Library of African Music, Rhodes University, TR10, 1955.

3. We! Mkhize
– *Umqangala* mouth-resonated bow
From *Zulu Bow Songs 1*, Dave Dargie, 1981.

4. Ukuqala
– *Ndlamu* dance
The singers stand behind the double line of dancers, introducing clapping with the accompaniment of a brass drum before the dancers begin their movement.
Performed by Zulu men from Masinga, KwaZulu-Natal.
From *Music of Africa Series 13: African Dances of the Witwatersrand Gold Mines*, Part 2, Hugh Tracey, International Library of African Music, Rhodes University.

5. Kuyashisa e Mqhobo (It is hot at the river Mqhobo)
-*Ihubo* (clan anthem)
The words to this song refer to the marriage between Constance Magogo of the House of Dinizulu (mother of the present chief Buthelezi) and the then Chief Buthelezi. The River Mqhobo marked the boundary between the Buthelezi lands and those of the Royal House.
Performed by the community at Chief Buthelezi's Kraal, Mahlabatini District, KwaZulu-Natal.
From *Sound of Africa Series*, Hugh Tracey, International Library of African Music, Rhodes University, TR12, 1955.

6. Sim'thi wakla (We applaud him)
– *Isigekle* (wedding song)
This is performed during the wedding ceremony after a song called *Indudumela* and was composed by one of Chief Buthelezi's ancestors. It is accompanied by stamping and clapping. 'We shower plaudits on him.'
Performed by the community at Chief Buthelezi's Kraal, Mahlabatini District, KwaZulu-Natal.
From *Sound of Africa Series*, Hugh Tracey, International Library of African Music, Rhodes University, TR12, 1955.

Swazi chapter

7. Ungabo phinduzibize Ngami
– *Umtshingozi*
Tune played on the *umtshingozi* end-blown flute.
Performed by Loshisa Dlamini, Emkhuzweni, Swaziland.
From *Sound of Africa Series*, Hugh Tracey, International Library of African Music, Rhodes University, TR72, 1958.

8. Ngoneni ngoneni bakithi (What have I done in Mataffin?)
– *Umakweyana*
A self-delectative song on the *umakweyana* bow.
Performed by Rosalina Ndhlole and Juana Nkosi, Mataffin, Nelspruit.
From *Sound of Africa Series*, Hugh Tracey, International Library of African Music, Rhodes University, TR72, 1958.

9. Incaba no Ncofula (Come out of your cave, Ncofula)
– *Umgubo* (regimental song) performed at the *Incwala* (first fruits ceremony)
Performed by large group of Swazi men, Entonyene, Pigg's Peak, Swaziland.
From *Sound of Africa Series*, Hugh Tracey, International Library of African Music, Rhodes University, TR70, 1958.

10. Babe kasenankomo (Father has no cattle left)
– *Umhlanga* (reed-ceremony song)
The words of the song imply that father has gone to court for various reasons so often that all his cattle have been attacked.
Performed by Masitsela with two boys and three girls, Lobamba, Mbabane, Swaziland.
From *Sound of Africa Series*, Hugh Tracey, International Library of African Music, Rhodes University, TR68, 1958.

11. Kuyashisa kunemikhobo laphekhaya (It is hot here at home)
– Wedding song
Performed by a royal bride's party at a wedding. The implication of the words is that the bride must accept her new way of life with all its trials.
Performed by five women and men of the Queen mother's village.
From *Sound of Africa Series*, Hugh Tracey, International Library of African Music, Rhodes University, TR68, 1958.

Xhosa chapter

12. Amabandla
– Diviner's song with *isidiphu* friction drum and *igubu* drum.
Performed by Nofenitshala Mvotyo and others.
From *Ezona Ngoma Zengqoko*, Dave Dargie, 2002.

13. Inkulu into Ezakwenzeka (Something very bad is going to happen)
– *Uhadi* bow song
The *uhadi* can be heard providing the basic harmonies from which Nontwintwi composed her melody. She uses the Xhosa heptatonic scale derived from the *uhadi*.
Performed by Nontwintwi, Kingwilliamstown, Eastern Cape.
From *Sound of Africa Series*, Hugh Tracey, International Library of African Music, Rhodes University, TR13, 1957.

14. Imothokali
– *Umrhube* whistling song
This track is a good example of the way in which the performer whistles while playing the instrument.
Performed by Madosini.
From *Hidden Years Archives*, produced by Almon Mamela, 3rd Ear Music and Mamela, 1975.

15. Umnqgokolo Duet
– *Umngqokolo* (overtone singing)
Aside from the overtone technique, another feature of Xhosa singing that can be heard in this example, is the use of polyphony (multi-layered voices/instruments).
Performed by Nowayilethi Mbizweni and Nofirst Lungisa.
From *Umngqokolo*, Dave Dargie, 1983.

16. Holilo

– *Umngqokolo ngomqangi* (special overtone singing technique)
Performed by the Ngqoko Women's Ensemble, led by Nowayilethi Mbizweni, University of Fort Hare.
From *Ezona Ngoma Zengqoko*, Dave Dargie, 2002.

17. Ndakutsala ngomlenze (I'll pull you by the leg)

– *Umbhayizelo* dance
This dance is characterised by the distinctive accompanying growling vocals particular to Xhosa boys and men. One can hear the sound of bells as the dancers shake their torsos strung with lines of bells. The dancers' legs, strung with leg-rattles, also quiver.
Performed by a group of young Xhosa men and boys, Kentani District, Eastern Cape.
From *Sound of Africa Series*, Hugh Tracey, International Library of African Music, Rhodes University, TR60, 1957.

Ndebele chapter

18. Vula Siyangena
Performed by Abomma Be – Kameelrivier Stadium
Composed by S. Masilela, Tequila Publishing 2.
From *African Renaissance Volume 5*, Tequila Records, 2000.

19. Indodo Ehle Ngu-Mabasa
Performed by Abomma Be – Renosterkop
Composed by Joana Mahlangu, Tequila Publishing 2.
From *African Renaissance Volume 5*, Tequila Records, 2000.

20. Sikhulele Emahlathini
Performed by Abomma Be – Kameelrivier Stadium
Composed by S. Masilela, Tequila Publishing 2.
From *African Renaissance Volume 5*, Tequila Records, 2000.

Sotho chapter

21. Khajoane (The mountain eagle)
– *Lesiba*
Composed by Theko Moshesh, Matatiele, Eastern Cape.
From *Sound of Africa Series*, Hugh Tracey, International Library of African Music, Rhodes University, TR64, 1957.

22. Ha Molelle (Molelle's place)
– Grinding song
'Far far away, at Molelle's place
Where is the train going?
He has been away at the mines too long now.
I, poor child, always say that
I have lost my relatives and have nobody
to tell me what to do.
You, Nohela women, you do not give me sufficient support.
I speak rudely in the presence of other people.'
Performed by Malebaka Moroke, Upper Qeme, Maseru District, Lesotho.
From *Sound of Africa Series*, Hugh Tracey, International Library of African Music, Rhodes University, TR104, 1959.

23. Ho ba bacha (To the youth)
– *Mokorotlo* song
This song is interrupted by several very long *lithoko* praises with whistling and ululation.
Performed by men of Koali's village, Berea District, Lesotho.
From *Sound of Africa Series*, Hugh Tracey, International Library of African Music, Rhodes University, TR102, 1959.

24. Mocholoko (The novice)
– *Mohobelo* dance
Performed by Mokoto Tsoeliane and group of Koali men, Koali's village, Berea District, Lesotho.
From *Sound of Africa Series*, Hugh Tracey, International Library of African Music, Rhodes University, TR102, 1959.

25. Mora Matlole (Matlole's son)
– *Mokhibo* dance
'Son of Matlole I am a girl who does not like (not fall in love with) uncouth people.
Her people's cattle will all die.
Goats are all killed by brack deposits.
I want to listen to what my heart tells me and think it over.'
Performed by Mahlapane Qoalike and a group of women, Tebang, Mafeteng District, Lesotho.
From *Sound of Africa Series*, Hugh Tracey, International Library of African Music, Rhodes University, TR104, 1959.

26. Ea ema nthodona matsetsela (Up stands the great one)
– Divination song
With small *isikupu* drum and bells. This song was performed to exorcise a spirit from someone who had been bewitched.
Performed by Jacob Mpalehane, Rosa Mpalehane and a group of pupils, Chief Sibi's location, Matatiele District, Eastern Cape.
From *Sound of Africa Series*, Hugh Tracey, International Library of African Music, Rhodes University,TR18, 1957.

Pedi chapter

27. Dipela
– *Dipela*
Performed by Johannes Nkoko.
Composed by K.J. Motijoane, Tequila Publishing 2.
From *African Renaissance Volume 5*, Tequila Records, 2000.

28. Adiyo jaxo kxaja nkwe (You cannot kill a leopard with a stone)
– Autoharp
With two small drums and a rattle.
'If you stone a leopard, it will kill you.
Who are we going to dance with?
There is nobody who can stone a leopard,
Everybody says so.'
Chorus: …'Adiyo.'
Performed by Frans Ncha, Gasebila, Leydsdorp, Limpopo Province.
From *Sound of Africa Series*, Hugh Tracey, International Library of African Music, Rhodes University, TR195, 1960.

29. Ke ke mmela ke ke (The sound of sneezing)
– Pounding song
With mortar and three pestles.
In the song they say that the district is plagued by men who come home from employment elsewhere, eat the food of their relatives until it is all finished without helping with the work, and then disappear again, leaving their families to starve.
'*Ke ke mmela ke ke*
Motla re tulang mobu
Ke tulela ba ditedu
Ba xotla ka go kokobetsha ditedu.'
'The day we pound earth
Pounding it for the bearded
Those who come in putting their beards in the food.'
(i.e. doing no work to produce it, but eating it.)

The meaning behind this song is that lazy men deserve only pounded earth, not good grain to eat.
Performed by four women, Chief Mashego, Thabakgolo, London Farm, Bushbuck Ridge, Mpumalanga.
From *Sound of Africa Series*, Hugh Tracey, International Library of African Music, Rhodes University, TR195, 1963.

30. Adya moreyana
– Drinking song
With two drums and a rattle.
'Mapolwane wa kolobe
O phela ka go ja leraga
Mpinelele ke rayile
Thabakgolo ke kgosi ya gokwala
O philiye ka yona kosa yoni.'
'A piglet lives on mud.
Sing that I may dance.
Thabakgolo is a great chief,
He lived through this song.'
Performed by a group of eight Pedi women and two men, Chief Mushego, Thabakgolo, London Farm, Bushbuck Ridge, Mpumalanga.
From *Sound of Africa Series*, Hugh Tracey, International Library of African Music, Rhodes University, TR195, 1963.

31. Makwidi ('Toppie' – a bird, the red-eyed bulbul)
– Divination song
The shrieking and general noise all contributes to the pleasurable hysteria associated with this kind of activity.
'Makwidi tswara bolepu ketlo tanya'
'Bulbul perch on the bird lime so I can catch you.'
Performed by a group of men and women, Motlamogale, Bushbuck Ridge District, Limpopo Province.
From *Sound of Africa Series*, Hugh Tracey, International Library of African Music, Rhodes University, TR194, 1963.

32. E kenia matsolo
– Girls' post-initiation song
With two drums, leg-rattles and whistles.
They sing this song after the initiation rituals are over. They wear animal skins, small mirrors and dance in the village asking for presents.
Performed by a group of ten female initiates, Chief Mashego, Thabakgolo, London Farm, Bushbuck Ridge, Mpumalanga.
From *Sound of Africa Series*, Hugh Tracey, International Library of African Music, Rhodes University, TR195, 1963.

Tswana chapter

33. Pina eaa badisa (A herdboy's song)
– *Segankuru* bow
Performed by Kgosietsile Mokgosi and Seyedi Merafe, Disaneng, Mafeking District, Western Cape.
From *Sound of Africa Series*, Hugh Tracey, International Library of African Music, Rhodes University, TR111, 1959.

34. Godumaduma gwa mosadi
– Reed-pipe ensemble
Played on four sets of pipes, with four pipes in each set.
Performed by a group of men at the Consolidated Main Reef Mine East Compound, Maraisburg.
From *Sound of Africa Series*, Hugh Tracey, International Library of African Music, Rhodes University, TR117, 1948.

35. Sekokodia pula wee (We humbly implore rain)
– Rain song
'Sekokodia pula wee
He helele hele sekokodia pula wee
Pula e kana helele sekokodia pula.'
'We humbly implore rain
Oh may it rain!
If it rains we shall rejoice.'

Performed by a large group of women, Kanye, Bangwaketse Reserve, southern Botswana.
From *Sound of Africa Series*, Hugh Tracey, International Library of African Music, Rhodes University, TR109, 1959.

36. Khakha si khudu (The big and the small tortoise)
– Male initiation song
'*Khakha si khudu ke-e*
A e e bannen
Re otetse khakha
E are tha re otile re be re otetse
Sebete sa khudu
Khudu si khakha si a e e bannen.'
'The great and the small tortoises are of the same family.
When we men are lean, it's because we lack the liver of a tortoise.
Here's a big tortoise, here's a small one.
Take them to the big men!'
Performed by Chief Bathoen II and a large group of men, Kanye, Southern Botswana.
From *Sound of Africa Series*, Hugh Tracey, International Library of African Music, Rhodes University, TR109, 1959.

37. Maboko (Praises)
– Praise poem
An example of Tswana praise poetry.
Praises for Chief Kgosi Sechele II.
Performed by the chief's praiser, Molepolole Bakwena Reserve, southern Botswana.
From the *Sound of Africa Series,* Hugh Tracey, International Library of African Music, Rhodes University, TR109, 1959.

Venda chapter

38. Mulovhidzana
– *Mbila mutondo*
One player begins with a repeated melody and then the other player joins, varying the melody.
Performed by W. Ravele and Mrs K. Ravele near Thoyandou in 1988.
From *New World, Ancient Harmonies*, Dave Dargie, 2003.

39. Mohodo (order or credit)
– *Mbila deza*
A drinking song played on a 23-note *mbira*.
'*Wamalicha wontanganya toho*
Mohodo wa di sherene
Naririra ngawo.'
'*Wamalichi* adds to their worries by asking for credit for ten shillings when no one has any such money to play with.'
Performed by Barangalani Mudzanani and two friends, Sibasa, Venda.
From *Sound of Africa Series*, Hugh Tracey, TR193, 1959.

40. Lugube
– *Lugube*
From *Tshivenda Music**

41. Tshikona
– Reed-pipe ensemble
The men play single *nanga* reeds and one large single-headed *ngoma* bass drum. Performed by eleven men in Sibasa, Vendaland, Limpopo Province.
From the *Sound of Africa Series*, Hugh Tracey, International Library of African Music, Rhodes University, TR193, 1957.

42. Domba
– *Domba* dance
From *Tshivenda Music* *

43. Malombo
– *Malombo* performance
From *Tshivenda Music* *

44. Tshigombela
– *Tshigombela*
From *Tshivenda Music* *

Tsonga chapter

45. Tshigombela
– *Xidende* braced bow
The performer was well known in the district as a wandering entertainer and beggar.
Performed by Elias Mtungwa, Thabakgolo, London Farm, Bushbuck Ridge, Mpumalanga.
From *Sound of Africa Series*, Hugh Tracey, International Library of African Music, Rhodes University, TR195, 1963.

46. Famba gathle Changani
– Pre-marriage song.
'Go well to Portuguese East Africa (Changani). Tell your relatives to take two knobkierries. We shall arrive at sunrise by the morning bus.'
Performed by Makahani Mubombeni and a group of Tsonga girls, Mwamitwa, Tzaneen, Limpopo Province.
From *Sound of Africa Series*, Hugh Tracey, International Library of African Music, Rhodes University, TR193, 1963.

47. Hola hola wambilo (Be still my heart)
– Love song
'*Hola, hola wamlilo*
Hola ngeletelo
Sawana mbilatelo wamilio sawana.'
'Be still, my heart
Be still, free from anger
Pain, from the gossip of others, pain.'

Performed by Mpepo Koza at Mwamitwa, Tzaneen, Limpopo Province.
From *Sound of Africa Series*, Hugh Tracey, International Library of African Music, Rhodes University, TR193, 1963.

48. Pounding song
– Work song
Performed by two women going about their day's labour of grinding corn. The mortar used was made from a fig tree and the pestle was of black ebony wood. Performed by two women in the Kruger National Park.
From *Music from the Roadside Part 1*, Hugh Tracey, International Library of African Music, Rhodes University.

San chapter

49. Hungry man
– Duet on '*kan'gan*' mouth-bow.
!Ngubi played this tune when he could not feed himself. The music would be their food.
Performed by !Ngubi Tietie.
From *!Ngubi Tietie: Bushmen of the Kalahari*, Musical Energy Loud Truth, 2002.

50. Likua Kambembe
– *Nxonxoro*
From *We Tell Our Old Stories with Music: Kulimatji Nge*, 2004, !Xun Traditional Council, Double Storey Books, Cape Town.

51. I wish to be a lucky hunter
– *Gwashi*
This song was performed on a four-string //*gwashi*.
Performed by !Ngubi Tietie.
From *!Ngubi Tietie: Bushmen of the Kalahari*, Musical Energy Loud Truth, 2002.

52. Solo woman's song

– Lullaby

This is a lullaby about how to handle a baby. The characteristic San yodelling technique can be heard in this song.

Performed by Musuva Fulai.

From *We Tell Our Old Stories with Music: Kulimatji Nge*, 2004, !Xun Traditional Council, Double Storey Books, Cape Town.

53. Chameleon

– A game using dance

'Chameleon' is a game performed by young San girls in which the lead dancer dresses to look like a chameleon while the others dance as if they are trying to trap or catch a reptile.

Performed by Angelika Mungabaputa and Marcella Igubi.

From *!Ngubi Tietie: Bushmen of the Kalahari*, Musical Energy Loud Truth, 2002.

54. Healing trance song

– Trance song

Song calling to the spirits for strength to heal the sick person.

Performed by Meneputo Mnunga and women singers.

From *We Tell Our Old Stories with Music: Kulimatji Nge* 2004, !Xun Traditional Council, Double Storey Books, Cape Town.

Endnotes

Preface

[1] Wells, *African Music*, 7, International Library of African Music, Grahamstown, p 69.
[2] Smith, *African Music*, 6, International Library of African Music, Grahamstown, 1983.
[3] Tooks, p37.
[4] www.1upinfo.com/country.guide-study/south-africa/south-africa49.html.

Overview of Instruments

[1] Information on musical instruments drawn from Bebey, *African Music: A People's Art*, Lawrence Hill Books, New York, 1975; Jones, *Making Music: Instruments in Zimbabwe Past and Present*, Academic Books Ltd, Harare, 1992; Kirby, *The Musical Instruments of the Native Races of South Africa*, Witwatersrand University Press, Johannesburg, 1968, Nketia, *The Music of Africa*, W.W. Norton, New York, 1974.
[2] Bebey, p92.
[3] Kirby, p193

AmaZulu

[1] www.nationmaster.com/encyclopedia/zulu-language
[2] www.zululand.kzn.org.za
[3] Sources used for Zulu history include Elliot, *Sons of Zulu*, Collins, Johannesburg, 1978; Davenport, *South Africa: A Modern History*, Macmillan, Johannesburg, 1987; De la Harpe et al, *Zulu*, Struik, Cape Town, 1998; Krige, *The Social System of the Zulus*, Shuter and Shooter, Pietermaritzburg, 1936.
[4] www.zululand.kzn.org.za
[5] Davenport, p15.
[6] Ibid, p14.
[7] Rycroft, 'The Music of the Zulu and Swazi' in Malan (ed), *South African Music Encyclopedia* Oxford University Press, Cape Town, 1982, p316.
[8] Information on instruments drawn from Kirby, *The Musical Instruments of the Native Races of South Africa*, Witwatersrand University Press, Johannesburg, 1968, and Krige, pp336-340.
[9] This instrument is also known as *ivenge* (Kirby, 1968, p293).
[10] This instrument is also known as *igemxe, igerre or igexhle* (Ibid).
[11] This instrument is also spelt *imbhande* (Ibid).
[12] This instrument is also spelt *ixilongo* (Ibid).
[13] This instrument is also known as *gubuolukhulu, inkohlisa, ugumbu* (Ibid).
[14] Kirby, 1968, states that the instrument is played by both sexes. Other academics suggest that the *umakweyana* is only played by females Joseph, 1983, and Rycroft, 1975/6.
[15] This instrument is also known as *umqengele, ulugibane* (Ibid, and Krige, p337).
[16] This instrument is also known as *unkwindi* (Krige, p337).
[17] Tracey, *Zulu Paradox*, Silver Leaf Books, Johannesburg, 1948, p49.
[18] Ibid.
[19] Ibid, p50.
[20] Information on singing styles used in battle cries, puberty and wedding songs is drawn from Rycroft, 'Zulu Melodic and Non-Melodic Vocal Styles' in *Papers Presented at the Fifth Symposium on Ethnomusicology*, International Library of African Music, Grahamstown, 1985, pp13-28.
[21] Song translated in Rycroft, 1985, p15.
[22] For further reading see Rycroft, 'Zulu and Xhosa Praise-Poetry and Song' in *African Music*, 3(1), International Library of African Music, Grahamstown, 1962, pp79-85.
[23] Joseph, 'Zulu Women's Music' in *African Music*, 6(3), International Library of African Music, Grahamstown, 1983, p78.
[24] Ibid, pp78-79.
[25] In her article on Zulu women's music, Joseph outlines the fact that 'praise poetry has been generally regarded as a male preserve' (Joseph, p77). She states that in the past there was little awareness or recognition of the performance of praise poetry by women in Zulu society. Joseph differentiates between the art of male and female praise poetry by stating that women's praise poetry is more secular: 'the subject matter of the *izibongo* is intensely personal, referring to a woman's character, personality and the important events in her life' (Joseph, p80).
[26] Mthethwa, 'Zulu songs from South Africa' at www.lyrichord.com/refw/ref7401.html, Lyrichord Catalogue 7401, Lyrichord Discs Inc., New York, 1986.
[27] Krige, p340.

[28] Ibid.
[29] Bryant, *The Zulu People*, Shuter and Shooter, Pietermaritzburg, 1949, p488.
[30] Tracey, p67.
[31] Distinction between the terms *ukusina* and *ukugiya* from Joseph, pp61-62.
[32] Bryant, p230.
[33] Joseph, p79.
[34] Ibid.
[35] Information on *ndlamu* drawn from Tracey, pp67-68.
[36] Xulu, 'The Social Significance of Zulu *Amahubo* Songs' in *Papers Presented at the Eighth Symposium on Ethnomusicology*, International Library of African Music, Grahamstown, 1989, p80.
[37] Information on *amahubo* drawn from Xulu, 1989, pp76-80 and Bryant, p231-232.
[38] Xulu, 'Some Aspects of Tradition and Change in Zulu Music: An Ethno-Historical Perspective' in *Papers Presented at the Symposium on Ethnomusicology*, Number 13, International Library of African Music, Grahamstown, 1997, pp43-45.
[39] Krige, p339.
[40] Bryant observed that the last festival took place in 1879 when Cetshwayo was king (Bryant, p513).
[41] Binns, *The Warrior People*, Howard Timmins, Cape Town, 1974, p121.
[42] Description of first fruits festival dances drawn from Krige, pp340-344.
[43] Breutz, *The Social and Political System of the Sotho-Tswana*, Ramsgate, P.L Breutz, 1947, p213.
[44] For a detailed account of the first fruits festival see Binns, pp121-144 and Krige, pp249-260.
[45] Information on Nomkubulwane drawn from Krige, pp197-200 and Elliot, p130.
[46] Elliot, p130.
[47] For extra reading on Nomkubulwane see Bryant, pp664-668 and Binns, pp108-120.
[48] The Swazi also practise this ceremony.
[49] Information on girls' initiation drawn from Binns, pp184-190; Krige, pp100-104 and Joseph, pp64-67.
[50] Joseph, p67.
[51] Joseph quoting Krige, p67.
[52] Ibid.
[53] Elliot calls this dance *cece*, which is in fact the name of the public celebration (Elliot, p162).
[54] Elliot, p142.
[55] There are very few resources referring to the musical activities of the Zulu male initiates. This is probably because circumcision was banned by Shaka as early as 1816, and most of the literature on the Zulu was written after this date. Information presented is drawn from Binns, pp174-179 and Krige, pp87-100.
[56] Krige, p95.
[57] Ibid, p98.
[58] Information on weddings drawn from Binns, pp204-218; Bryant, pp542-557; Joseph, pp68-75; Krige, pp137-155; and Xulu, pp71-75.
[59] Bryant, p546.
[60] Ibid.
[61] Each reference on the Zulu wedding records the programme of music in a slightly different way. According to Joseph, 'The sequence of wedding songs performed by the *umthimba* consists of the *umgqigqo, isigekle, inkondlo* and *umphendu* dance-songs, followed by the performance of *ingoma* dance-songs', Joseph, p69. She observes that the first dance, the *umgqigqo*, is performed as the bridal party approaches the dancing ground. It is only once the *inkondlo* is sung that the bride reveals herself.
[62] Ibid, p71.
[63] Bryant, pp227-228.
[64] Joseph, p74.
[65] For more information on weddings and clan anthems see Xulu 'The Zulu Wedding as a Musical Event: A Musical Realization of Social Ideas' in *Papers Presented at the Eight Symposium on Ethnomusicology*, International Library of African Music, Grahamstown, 1989, pp71-75.
[66] Joseph, p63.
[67] Kirby, 1968 states that the *umakweyana* was played by men and women. Other researchers such as Rycroft, 1975/6 and Joseph, 1983, refer only to women's bow songs. The practice of bow playing may have changed over time. Where it was once an instrument played by both sexes, it seems to be exclusively a women's instrument in certain areas. At the 18th Symposium of Ethnomusicology at ILAM, in October 2004, Len Zulu from the University of KwaZulu-Natal spoke about the *umakweyana* bow as a female instrument.

[68] Joseph, p63.
[69] These two lines are extracts from two different bow songs quoted in Joseph, p83.
[70] See Joseph, pp53-89, for a description of all categories of women's music.
[71] Joseph, p81.
[72] This explanation was presented by Len Zulu in his paper, 'Symbolism of the Zulu bow – uMakweyana, in the area Emphaphala, outskirts of Eshowe, KwaZulu Natal' at the 18th Symposium on Ethnomusicology in Grahamstown, in October 2004. This paper will be published in the 18th Symposium on Ethnomusicology.
[73] For more reading see Rycroft, 'The Zulu bow songs of Princess Magogo' in *African Music*, 5(4), International Library of African Music, Grahamstown, 1975/6, pp41-97.
[74] Information on *maskanda* drawn from Davies, 'Aspects of Zulu Maskanda Guitar Music', pp29-39 and Xulu, 'The Revitalisation of Amahubo Song Styles and Ideas in Zulu Maskanda Music', pp170-173 in *Papers Presented at the Tenth Symposium on Ethnomusicology*, International Library of African Music, Grahamstown, 1995.
[75] Davies, p29.
[76] Other styles include *isishameni, isibhaca* and *isikhuze*. For more information on styles see Clegg 'Towards an Understanding of African Dance: the Zulu *Isishameni* style' and 'An examination of the *Umzansi* dance style' in *Papers Presented at the Symposium on Ethnomusicology*, International Library of African Music, Grahamstown, 1981 and 1984.
[77] Davies, p30.
[78] For general reading on *maskanda* see Clegg, 'The Music of the Zulu Immigrant Workers in Johannesburg: A focus on Concertina and Guitar'; and Koppers, 'Jabulani Buthelezi: Profile of a Zulu Troubador' in *Papers Presented at the Symposium on Ethnomusicology*, International Library of African Music, Grahamstown, 1980 and 1989.
[79] Information drawn mainly from Ndlovu, 'Scathamiya: A Zulu Male Vocal Tradition' in *Papers Presented at the Eighth Symposium on Ethnomusicology*, International Library of African Music, Grahamstown, 1989, pp45-48; and Thembela, 'A Socio-Cultural Basis of Ethnic Music with Special Reference to the Music of Ladysmith Black Mambazo' in *Papers Presented at the Symposium on Ethnomusicology*, Number 13, International Library of African Music, Grahamstown, 1997, pp35-36.
[80] Ndlovu, p45.
[81] Ibid.
[82] Thembela, p36.
[83] Information on 'bombing' drawn from Rycroft, 'Zulu Male Traditional Singing' in *African Music*, 1(4), 1957, pp33-35.
[84] Information on gumboot dancing drawn from Tracey, *African Dances of the Witwatersrand Gold Mines*, African Music Society, Johannesburg, 1952, p7.
[85] For a detailed analysis of gumboot dancing see Muller and Fargion, 'Gumboots, Bhaca Migrants, and Fred Astaire: South African Worker Dance and Musical Style' in *African Music*, 7(4), 1999, pp88-109.

AmaSwazi

[1] Information on history drawn from Kuper, *An African Aristocracy*, Oxford University Press, London, 1947; Kuper, *A South African Kingdom*, Holt, Rinehart and Winston, New York, 1963, p29; Marwick, *The Swazi*, Frank Cass and Co, London, 1966, p81.
[2] Kuper, 1947, p12.
[3] Ibid, p13.
[4] Kuper, 1963, p8.
[5] Marwick, p81.
[6] Information on instruments drawn from Kirby, *The Musical Instruments of the Native Races of Southern Africa*, Witwatersrand University Press, Johannesburg, 1968; Marwick; Rycroft, *Say it in Siswati*, London University, London, 1976; and Rycroft, 'The Music of the Zulu and Swazi' in *South African Music Encyclopaedia*, Oxford University Press, Cape Town, 1982.
[7] These rattles are also spelt *emafahlawane* (Rycroft, 1982, p320).
[8] This instrument is also spelt *umtshingoze* (Marwick, p82).
[9] This instrument is also spelt *impalampala* (Rycroft, 1976, p169).
[10] This instrument is also known as *sidolandi* (Ibid).
[11] Kirby, p201.
[12] Kirby states that this instrument is only played by men, but Marwick states that it is 'a great refuge of lovelorn youths and maidens' (Marwick, p82).
[13] This instrument is also spelt *ligubhu* (Rycroft, 1982, p321).
[14] This instrument is also known as *ipiano* (Kirby, p290).
[15] This instrument is also spelt *makhwindi* (Rycroft, 1976, p169).
[16] Kuper, 1947, p206.
[17] Rycroft, 1982, p315.
[18] Ibid, p322.
[19] Kuper, 1963, p29.
[20] Kuper quoting King Sobhuza (Kuper, 1947, p224).
[21] Kuper, 1947, p197.

[22] Information on the *incwala* ceremony is drawn from: Becker, *Trails and Tribes in Southern Africa*, Hart-Davis, Mac-Gibbon, London, 1975, pp115-120; Cook, 'The Inqwala Ceremony of the Swazi' in *Bantu Studies*, 4, 1930, p205-210; Kuper, 1947, pp197-225; Kuper, 1963, pp68-72.
[23] Kuper, 1963, p68.
[24] Ibid, p68.
[25] Ibid, p69.
[26] Kuper, 1947, p206.
[27] Ibid, p207.
[28] Ibid, p206.
[29] Ibid, p204.
[30] Ibid, p205.
[31] Ibid, p210.
[32] Becker, p117.
[33] Kuper, 1947, p217.
[34] Information on weddings based on Marwick, pp101-129.
[35] Marwick, p105.
[36] Ibid, p110.

AmaXhosa

[1] Sources used for history include Elliot, *The Magic World of the Xhosa*, Charles Scribner's Sons, New York, 1970; Hammond-Tooke, *The Bantu-speaking Peoples of Southern Africa*, Routledge and Kegan Paul, London, 1974; Magubane, *The Vanishing Cultures of South Africa*; West and Morris, *Abantu*, Struik Publishers, Cape Town, 1976.
[2] The Xhosa language has at least 6 000 words of Khoisan origin.
[3] Information on instruments drawn from Dargie, 'Some recent discoveries and recordings in Xhosa music' in *Papers Presented at the Fifth Symposium on Ethnomusicology*, International Library of African Music, Grahamstown, 1985, pp29-35; Dargie, *The Music of the Xhosa-speaking People*, Unpublished PhD Thesis, Grahamstown, 1981, pp167-195; Kirby, *The Musical Instruments of the Native Races of South Africa*, Witwatersrand University Press, Johannesburg, 1968.
[4] This instrument is also known as *umasengwane*, derived from the fact that it is played with a milking action.
[5] These rattles are also spelt *iingcaca* (Dargie, 1988, p43).
[6] This instrument is also known as *impempe* (Kirby, p292).
[7] This instrument is also sometimes called *inkinge*.
[8] Dargie, 1985, p29.
[9] Alternative spellings for this instrument are *igwali* and *ugwala* (Kirby, 1968, p292).
[10] Hansen quoting a Thembu woman (Hansen, p24).
[11] Music in Xhosa is also commonly known as *umculo*, which also refers to hymns sung in church.
[12] Information on *ihlombe* drawn from Hansen, pp24-27.
[13] Information on overtone singing mainly drawn from Dargie, 1988, p56-60; Dargie, 'Umngqokolo: Xhosa overtone singing and the song Nondelékhaya' in *African Music*, 7(1), International Library of African Music, Grahamstown, 1991, pp33-47; and Hansen, pp127-130.
[14] www.scena.org/lsm
[15] For more reading on Khoisan influence see Dargie, 1991, pp33-34.
[16] Dargie, 1991, p45.
[17] Traditional Xhosa song originating in the Ngqoko village, performed by Nowayilethi Mbizweni and other people of Ngqoko, and recorded and transcribed by Dargie (Dargie, 1988, p164).
[18] Dargie, 1988, p56 and Hansen, p130.
[19] Information on *ukubhayizela* drawn from Dargie, 1988, p36, p56 and Hansen, pp130-131.
[20] Hansen p131.
[21] Dargie, 1988, p60. According to Hansen, p132, humming is called *ukumemelela*.
[22] Ibid.
[23] Dargie, 1988, p81.
[24] Hansen quoting the leader of a Bhaca young men's dance group (Hansen, p40).
[25] Dargie, 1988, p82.
[26] Ibid, p41.
[27] Information on personal songs drawn from Hansen, pp27-32, pp98-99.
[28] Ibid, pp98-99.
[29] Hansen quoting No-orange Lizo, a Thembu woman (Hansen, p28).
[30] Ibid, p31.
[31] Ibid, p262, p263.
[32] Information on *umdodo* and *umgidi* drawn from Dargie, 1988, pp33-34.
[33] According to Dargie, the term *ukutyityimba* is synonymous with the term *ukugaja*. It is a

dance performed at the young men's *intlombe* (Dargie, 1988, p37).

[34] Soga, *The Ama-Xhosa: Life and Customs*, Lovedale Press, South Africa, 1931, p238.

[35] Hansen, p43.

[36] For additional reading on *umteyo* see Tracey, *African Dances of the Witwatersrand Gold Mines*, African Music Society, 1952, pp9-10.

[37] Hansen, p404.

[38] Ibid, p45.

[39] Information on *umtshotsho* drawn from Broster, *The Thembu*, Purnell, Cape Town, 1976; Dargie, 1988, pp34-35; Hansen, pp296-316; Honore, 'Some Observations on Xhosa Dance in the 1980s' in *Papers Presented at the Sixth Symposium on Ethnomusicology*, International Library of African Music, Grahamstown, 1988, pp16-18.

[40] Honore, p17.

[41] Dargie comments that there are special types of *umtshotsho*. There are separate *umtshotsho* for older boys and girls. The songs are the same at both gatherings but sometimes the older teenagers are given beer at their *umtshotsho* (Dargie, 1988, p34).

[42] Information on *intlombe* drawn from Dargie, 1988, pp33-35; Hansen, pp359-376; Honore, p18.

[43] Hansen, p374.

[44] Elliot, p40.

[45] Information on beer parties, songs and dances drawn from Hansen, pp423-453.

[46] Hansen, p481.

[47] Information on divination music drawn from Hansen, pp563-594.

[48] Information on boys initiation and its accompanying music from Becker, *Trails and Tribes in Southern Africa*, Hart-Davis, MacGibbon, London, 1975, pp134-137; Hansen, pp491-513; and Soga, pp247-260.

[49] This dance was also known as *kwetha* (Becker, p134, and Soga, p256).

[50] Soga, p256.

[51] Ibid.

[52] Hansen, p507.

[53] Tyrrell, *Tribal Peoples of Southern Africa*, Books of Africa, Cape Town, 1968, p190.

[54] Information on girls initiation drawn from Dargie, 1988, p36; Hansen, pp529-562; Honore, p18; Soga, pp216-223.

[55] Soga, p220.

[56] Soga uses the word *um-tyulubo* for this movement (Soga, p220).

[57] For more reading on *iindlavini* music and *umtshotsho* dance parties see Hansen, pp389-404.

[58] Information on *indlamu* drawn from Hansen, pp394-401.

[59] Information on *i-modern* drawn from Hansen, pp458-484.

AmaNdebele

[1] Information drawn from Magubane, *Vanishing Cultures of South Africa*, Struik, Cape Town, 1998; Powell, *Ndebele: A People and Their Art*, Struik, Cape Town, 1995; West and Morris, *Abantu*, Struik, Cape Town, 1976.

[2] Laade, *Music of Man Archive: Zimbabwe – The Ndebele People*, Jecklin and Co, Zurich, 1991, p22.

[3] These instruments are played by the Zimbabwean Ndebele. It has not been ascertained whether the South African Ndebele play them.

[4] Information on instruments drawn from Kirby, *The Musical Instruments of the Native Races of Southern Africa*, Witwatersrand University Press, Johannesburg, 1968; Laade; Nothembi Mkhwebane and Sarah Mahlangu at 'Something out of nothing' in Mpumalanga.

[5] This instrument is also known as *ingungu* (informant at 'Something out of nothing').

[6] These rattles are also known as *amahlwayi*. According to one source, *amahlwayi* are made from *ilala* palm leaves (Laade, p26).

[7] This instrument is also known as *ipembhe* (Nothembi Mkhwebane).

[8] None of our informants recalled reed-pipe ensembles being used in Ndebele culture. However, Kirby recorded their use amongst the Ndebele. Perhaps it is a tradition that was once part of the culture, but has been obsolete for many years.

[9] None of our informants recognised this instrument, but it was recorded in Kirby. This ceremony no longer occurs in Zimbabwe or South Africa among the Ndebele.

[10] While some informants did not know this instrument, others said that it was called *igobogobo*. The Zimbabwean Ndebele know it as *icaco*.

[11] None of our informants knew this instrument, but it was recorded by Kirby.

[12] Among the Zimbabwean Ndebele, this instrument is known as *umqangala* and the string is made from cow sinew or vegetable fibre (Laade, p24).

[13] According to Laade, among the Zimbabwean Ndebele the lullaby is called *isihlabelelo* (Laade, p29).

[14] According to Laade, among the Zimbabwean Ndebele this performance is the spear dance, which is also performed by Zulu brides (Laade, p37). Our South African Ndebele informants

told us that this dance is not performed by the South African Ndebele.

[15] Among the Zimbabwean Ndebele the ceremony was known as *inxwala* (Laade, p19).

[16] Laade, p21.

Basotho

[1] The term Basotho only emerged in the 1820s when Moshoeshoe unified the nation. People have given different interpretations of the term Basotho. While some say that it means 'black people' in Western Tswana, others assert that the Nguni term *-shunta* (knotted) is a precursor of *-sotho* (*Abashantu*: Basotho), and refers to the knotted loincloth (*tseha*) worn by those men whose descendents now speak Southern Sotho. (Wells, *An Introduction to the Music of the Basotho*, Morija Museum Archives, Lesotho, 1994, pp19-20). Nowadays the South Sotho are more commonly referred to as the Basotho.

[2] This is not an established historical fact, but according to Wells, Fokeng clan members are always the first to be circumcised in recognition of their historical precedence (Wells, 1994, p22).

[3] Sources used for Basotho history include Ashton, *The Basuto*, Oxford University Press, London, 1952; Hammond-Tooke, *The Bantu-speaking peoples of Southern Africa*, Routledge and Kegan Paul, London, 1974; Maylam, *A History of the African People of South Africa: From the Early Iron Age to the 1970s*, David Philip, Cape Town, 1986; Schapera, *The Bantu-Speaking Tribes of South Africa*, Maskew Miller Limited, Cape Town, 1966; Wells, 1994; West and Morris, *Abantu*, Struik Publishers, Cape Town, 1976.

[4] Hammond-Tooke, *The Roots of Black South Africa*, Jonathan Ball Publishers, Johannesburg, 1993, p32.

[5] Maylam, p58.

[6] Ashton, p4.

[7] Ibid.

[8] Information on instruments drawn from Kirby, *The Musical Instruments of the Native Races of South Africa*, Witwatersrand University Press, Johannesburg, 1968; Mokhali, *Basotho Music and Dancing*, Mazenod Book Centre, Lesotho, 1967, pp1-5; Moitse, *The Ethnomusicology of the Basotho*, Institute of Southern African Studies, Lesotho, 1994, pp98-109; Wells, 1994, pp135-172.

[9] This instrument is also spelt *merutlhoane* (Moitse, p104).

[10] According to Wells, '*Saku* involves slight foot and leg motion, and neck, shoulder and back gestures similar to those in the women's dance *mokhibo*' (Wells, 1994, p152).

[11] This instrument is also spelt *tuomo* (Kirby, p288).

[12] Wells, 1994, p145.

[13] Ibid, p152.

[14] Kirby, p171.

[15] Huskisson, 'A Note on the Music of the Sotho' in Malan (ed), *South African Music Encyclopaedia*, Oxford University Press, Cape Town, 1982, p376.

[16] Wells, 1994, p152.

[17] Ibid, p155.

[18] Huskisson, 1982, p375.

[19] Ntsihlele, 'Work Songs: Stylistic Differences Based on Gender in Basotho Adult Songs' in *Papers Presented at the Symposium on Ethnomusicology*, Number 13, International Library of African Music, Grahamstown, p26.

[20] Huskisson, 1982, p375.

[21] Information on *mokorotlo* drawn from Ashton, pp95-96; Mokhali, pp8-9; Moitse, pp56-61; Wells, 1994, pp58-63.

[22] Moitse, p56.

[23] Ibid.

[24] Huskisson, 1982, p375.

[25] Wells, 1994, p63.

[26] Ibid, p5.

[27] For more reading on the poetic tradition in Sotho culture see Wells, 1994, pp5-9.

[28] Casalis, *The Basutos*, Nisbet, London, 1861, pp328-9.

[29] Information on *mohobela* drawn from Ashton, pp96-97; Mokhali, pp7-8; Tracey, *African Dances of the Witwatersrand Gold Mines*, African Music Society, Johannesburg, 1952, pp11-12; Wells, 1994, pp64-71.

[30] Mokhali, p8.

[31] Wells, 1994, p64.

[32] Ibid, p66.

[33] Information on *mokhibo* drawn from Ashton, pp97, Wells, 1994, pp99-110.

[34] Wells, 1994, p99.

[35] Ashton, p96.

[36] Information on *ditolobonya* drawn from Moitse, pp86-91; Wells, 1994, p110.

[37] Wells, 1994, p118.

[38] According to Ashton, *metjeko* is a term which is applied not only to children's dances but

which 'covers all dances in which men and women take part' (Ashton, p96).

[39] Wells, 1994, p116.

[40] Ashton, p96.

[41] Information on *moqoqopelo* and *mothonthonyane* drawn from Mokhali, pp6-7, and Wells, 1994, pp119-123.

[42] In Mokhali's study of Basotho music, she observes that the *moqoqopelo* is a dance performed by boys and girls, whereas Wells' states it is performed exclusively by girls. If the dance changed over time then this would explain the discrepancy between the two versions. In Mokhali's version, the dance is described as a type of courting game in which the boy dances towards the girl of his choice in the circle.

[43] Wells, 1994, p119.

[44] Ibid, p120.

[45] Information on 'pumpkin songs' drawn from Wells, 1994, pp123-127.

[46] Ibid, p41.

[47] Ibid.

[48] Ibid p42.

[49] Information on male initiation drawn from Ashton, pp46-57; Moitse, pp45-66; Wells, pp41-58.

[50] Ashton, p49.

[51] Moitse, p51.

[52] This song was composed by an initiation instructor at the Koma-koma village in Roma and recorded by Moitse in 1988 (Moitse, p52).

[53] Wells recorded this song at a graduation ceremony of a male initiation school near the King's village of Matsieng in 1992 (Wells, 'Sesotho Music: A Contemporary Perspective' in *African Music*, 7(3), 1996, p71).

[54] Ashton, p54.

[55] Information on female initiation drawn from Ashton, pp57-61; Moitse, pp66-79; Muso, 'Thojane' in *Papers Presented at the Symposium on Ethnomusicology*, Number 13, International Library of African Music, Grahamstown, 1997, pp98-99; Wells, 1994, pp85-99.

[56] This song appeared in Muso, p98.

[57] Contrary to Moitse, Wells states that there is no dancing or singing at the graduation and describes *ho tebuka* as a 'slow orderly walk' (Wells, 1994, p98).

[58] Information on divination drawn from Moitse, pp26-44 and Wells, 1994, pp227-261.

[59] According to Wells, *matwela* have only become widespread in Lesotho in the last century. Before the mid-19th century, the two main categories of Sotho diviners were known as *selaoli* and *senohe*. There are other types of healers in Lesotho, such as herbalists, and *matwela* represent only one type of traditional healer. The general name for all healers is *ngaka* (doctor). We have decided to focus on *matwela* because their rituals include more music than those of other Sotho healers.

[60] Wells, 1994, p239.

[61] Wells quoting ethnomusicologist Mwesa Mapoma, p239.

[62] Recorded by Moitse in 1988 and appeared in Moitse, pp 38-39.

[63] For a comprehensive study on the blend of old and new musical styles in Sotho culture see Wells, 1996, pp67-75 and Wells 'Report on Research in Lesotho' in *African Music*, 1992, 7(2), International Library of African Music, Grahamstown, pp126-127.

[64] Information on *setapo* drawn from Wells, 1994, pp128-131.

[65] Information on *monyanyako* drawn from Wells, 1992, pp126-127 and Wells,1994, pp209-221.

[66] For additional reading on 'action songs' and 'sounds' see Wells, 1994, pp209-212.

[67] Wells, 1994, p212.

[68] Ibid.

[69] Ibid, p214.

[70] Information on *difela* drawn mainly from Wells, 1994, pp279-265, and Coplan, 1994.

[71] Coplan, *In the Time of Cannibals*, Witwatersrand University Press, Johannesburg, p8.

[72] Wells citing Coplan, 1994, p275.

[73] Ibid, p290.

[74] Ibid, p291.

[75] Ibid.

Bapedi

[1] Information on Pedi history drawn from Hammond-Tooke, *The Bantu-speaking peoples of Southern Africa*, Routledge and Kegan Paul, London, 1974; Maylam, *A History of the African People of South Africa: from the Early Iron Age to the 1970s*, David Philip, Cape Town, 1986; Monnig, *The Pedi*, J.L van Schaik Limited, Pretoria, 1967; Schapera, *The Bantu-speaking Tribes of South Africa*, Maskew Miller, Cape Town, 1966; West and Morris, *Abantu*, Struik Publishers, Cape Town, 1967.

[2] Huskisson, 'Music of the Pedi (Northern Sotho)' in Malan (ed), *South African Music Encyclopedia*, Oxford University Press, Cape Town, 1982, p367.

[3] Information on instruments drawn from Huskisson, *The Social and Ceremonial Music of the Pedi*, Unpublished thesis, University of the Witwatersrand, Johannesburg, 1958; and Kirby, *The Musical Instruments of the Native Races of Southern Africa*, Witwatersrand University Press, Johannesburg, 1968.

[4] This instrument is also spelt *mosupiane, mosupjane* and *mashupyane* (Ibid, p17).

[5] Kirby calls these rattles *dichela*, but Huskisson, whose research was done at a later stage, asserted that the people actually called them *thlwahlawadi*.

[6] These rattles are sometimes called *makgoro* (Huskisson, 1958, p18).

[7] Kirby wrote that *mathotse* are hand-rattles but in Huskisson's research she states that *mathotse* are leg-rattles.

[8] This instrument is also called *kgabudubudu* (Kirby, p287).

[9] This instrument is also known as *naka ya makoditsane* and *naka ya phatola* (Kirby, p287) and (Huskisson, 1958, p34).

[10] These flutes are also commonly referred to as *dinaka* (Huskisson, 1958, p64).

[11] This instrument is also spelt *phalafala* and is also known as *lepapata* and *photwane* (Huskisson, 1958, p50).

[12] Breutz, p212.

[13] This instrument is also known as *setsegetsege, botsorwane* or *botsorane* (Huskisson, 1958, p74).

[14] James, 'iKe rena baeng/We are visiting: The Evolution and Spread of Kiba, Performance Style of the Northern Transvaal Migrants' in *Papers Presented at the Tenth Symposium on Ethnomusicology*, 1991, p114.

[15] Information on social music drawn from Huskisson, 1958, pp87-137.

[16] Ibid, p93.

[17] For more reading on Pedi folktales see Makgamatha, *Characteristics of the Northern Sotho Folktales*, Perskor, Johannesburg, 1991.

[18] Tracey, Prof. A., (Unpublished) programme for the Grand Jamboree at the 18th Symposium on Ethnomusicology, International Library of African Music, Grahamstown, 2004.

[19] James, *Mmino wa Setso: Songs of Town and Country and the Experience of Migrancy by Men and Women from the Northern Transvaal*, Unpublished thesis PhD, University of the Witwatersrand, 1993, p3.

[20] Information on *kiba* and *dinaka* drawn from Huskisson, 1958, p27, pp101-105; James, 1991, pp75-86; James, 1993a; James, Mmino wa Setso Traditional Music: Ethnomusicological Perspectives on Migrant Culture, *Papers Presented at the Eleventh Symposium on Ethnomusicology*, International Library of African Music, Grahamstown, 1993, pp74-93.

[21] Huskisson, p27.

[22] James, 1993a, p110.

[23] For more information on *kiba* see James, *Songs of the Women Migrants: Performance and Identity in South Africa*, Edinburgh University Press, London, 1999.

[24] Information on possession drawn from Huskisson, 1958, pp117-123. Mapaya, *Aspects of Contemporary Transmission of Sepedi Culture through Music: Its Perpetuation Within and Beyond the Region of Ga-mmalebogo, Limpopo Province South Africa*, University of the Witwatersrand, Johannesburg, Unpublished thesis, 2004, pp67-70.

[25] Huskisson, 1958, p120.

[26] Information on rain songs drawn from Huskisson, 1958, pp148-152.

[27] Ibid, p148.

[28] Information on first fruits festival drawn from Huskisson, 1958, pp152-154.

[29] Information on male initiation drawn from Huskisson, 1958, pp159-196; and Monnig, pp112-124.

[30] Monnig, p113.

[31] Ibid, p122.

[32] Information on female initiation drawn from Huskisson, 1958, pp197-218 and Monnig, pp126-128.

[33] Breutz, p130.

[34] For additional reading on male and female initiation see Harries, *The Laws and Customs of the BaPedi and Cognate Tribes*, Hortors Limited, Johannesburg, 1929, pp63-78.

[35] Huskisson (1958), p55.

Batswana

[1] Information on history drawn from Becker, *Trails and Tribes of Southern Africa*, Hart-Davis, MacGibbon, London, 1975; Hammond-Tooke, *The Bantu-speaking peoples of Southern Africa*, Routledge and Kegan Paul, London, 1974; Magubane, *Vanishing Cultures of South Africa*, Struik, Cape Town, 1998; Maylam, *A History of the African People of South Africa: from the Early Iron Age to the 1970s*, David Philip, Cape Town, 1986; Schapera, *The Bantu-speaking*

Tribes of South Africa, Maskew Miller, Cape Town, 1966; Schapera, *The Tswana*, International African Institute, London, 1953; West and Morris, *Abantu*, Struik, Cape Town, 1976.

[2] According to Schapera, research shows that the Kgalagadi's language is sufficiently distinct to be classed separately to that of the Tswana language. They are in fact classified as a separate people in the broader Sotho-Tswana family (Schapera, 1966, p14).

[3] Wood quoting Mr Amos K. Pilane, a Tswana historian of Mochudi, in an interview about Tswana music. (Wood, 'A Study of the Traditional Music of Mochudi' in *Botswana Notes and Records*, 8, Botswana society, 1976, p196). Through her in-depth fieldwork, Wood concludes that Tswana instrumental music has almost disappeared.

[4] Information on instruments drawn from Kirby, *The Musical Instruments of the Native Races of Southern Africa*, Witwatersrand University Press, 1968; Wood, 1976; and Wood, *Observing and Recording Village Music in the Kweneng*, 1978.

[5] These rattles are also spelt *matlhou, matlhoo, mathlo* and *makkow* (Wood, 1976, p211) and (Kirby, p282.)

[6] This instrument is also spelt *mohlatswa* (Wood, 1976, p216).

[7] This instrument is also known as *lenaka la phala* (Ibid, p216).

[8] Kirby, p147.

[9] Kirby, p150.

[10] Kirby, p147.

[11] Ibid, p213.

[12] This instrument is also spelt *nkokwane* (Wood, 1976, p213).

[13] This instrument is also known as *sefinjolo, setinkane, sebinjole, serankuru* and *segaba* (Kirby, p282) and (Wood, 1976, p214).

[14] This instrument is also spelt *segwane* (Wood, 1976, p212).

[15] Ibid, p195.

[16] This instrument was also known as *kwadi* (Kirby, p282).

[17] Wood quoting Mr Amos K. Pilane, Tswana historian of Mochudi, in an interview about Tswana music. (Wood, 1976, p196).

[18] Wood, 1978, p19.

[19] Kirby wrote the most detailed account on the reed-pipe ensemble, and the information presented on this subject in this chapter is based on his writings (Kirby, pp147-153).

[20] Information on rainmakers and rainmaking ceremonies and songs compiled from the following sources: Breutz, *The Social and Political System of the Sotho-Tswana*, P.L Breutz, 1947, pp193-200, Peddema, 'Tswana Ritual Concerning Rain' in *African Studies*, Witwatersrand University Press, Johannesburg, 25, 1, 1966, pp181-195; Dornan, 'Rainmaking in South Africa' in *Bantu Studies*, 3, Witwatersrand University Press, Johannesburg, 1927-30, pp185-195, Schapera, 1953, p22, p60.

[21] Breutz, p193.

[22] This means that the rainmakers will defeat the wizards by bringing rain.

[23] This is a bird associated with rain and storms.

[24] Song example from Peddema, p184.

[25] Schapera states 'The normal rainmaking ceremonies have now been abandoned, but in many tribes there is an annual Church 'day of prayer for rain', originally introduced by the missionaries.' (Schapera, 1953, p22). Other writers on this topic have verified this.

[26] Music attached to Tswana initiation is very similar to that of the Southern Sotho (Basotho) and the Northern Sotho (Bapedi). Information on female initiation drawn from Breutz, pp128-136; Johnston, 'Notes of the Music of the Tswana' in Malan (ed) *South African Music Encyclopedia*, Oxford University Press, Cape Town, 1982, p26; Wood, 1976, pp197-206.

[27] Wood, 1976, p198.

[28] Traditional song by a group of women in Mochudi and translated into English in Wood, 1976, p201.

[29] Breutz, p120.

[30] Information on male initiation drawn from Breutz, pp115-128; Johnston, p376.

[31] The term for praise poems, *maboko*, is derived from the verb '*boka*', meaning to 'honour by giving titles to a person in poems; sing the praises of' (Schapera, *Praise poems of Tswana chiefs*, Oxford University Press, London, 1965, p1).

[32] Praise poems were also performed at beer-drinking parties, working parties and wedding feasts.

VhaVenda

[1] According to the German missionary Beuster, Bavenda means 'people of the world' which is derived from Venda ('land' or 'world'). Stayt, *The BaVenda*, Frank Cass and Co, London, 1968, p12.

[2] Sources used for Venda history include Blacking, *Venda Children's Songs*, Witwatersrand University Press, Johannesburg, 1967; Fokwang, *Chiefs and Democratic Transition in Africa: An Ethnographic Study in The Chiefdoms of Tshivhase and Bali*, Masters Dissertation, University of Pretoria, 2003; Hammond-Tooke, *The Bantu-speaking peoples of Southern*

Africa, Routledge and Kegan Paul, London, 1974; Stayt; West and Morris, *Abantu*, Struik Publishers, Cape Town, 1976.

[3] Stayt, p12.

[4] Ibid, p13.

[5] Ibid, p16.

[6] Blacking, 1967, p19.

[7] Information on instruments drawn from Blacking, 1967, pp19-21; Kirby, *The Musical Instruments of the Native Races of South Africa*, Witwatersrand University Press, Johannesburg, 1968, and Stayt, pp316-320.

[8] These instruments are also known as *thuzo* (Kirby, 1968, p291).

[9] These instruments are also known as *luvuvu* (Kirby, p292).

[10] This instrument is also known as *sansa* (Ibid).

[11] This instrument is also known as *tshitiringha* (Stayt, p317).

[12] This instrument is also known as *kwatha* (Ibid, p75).

[13] This instrument is also known as *mfuhlulu* (Ibid, p291).

[14] Ibid, p229.

[15] This instrument is also called *tshivhana* (Ibid, 1968, p292).

[16] This is instrument is also spelt *tshijolo* (Stayt, p318).

[17] This instrument is also spelt *tshizambo* (Ibid, p319).

[18] This instrument is also known as *tshikala* (Kirby, 1968, p292).

[19] Stayt, p13.

[20] Kruger, 'Wada: Story of an African Drum' in *Papers Presented at the Eighth Symposium on Ethnomusicology*, International Library of African Music, Grahamstown, 1995, p37.

[21]. In his paper on *Wada*, Kruger investigates the history of *Wada* and its role in Venda culture. The information presented in this chapter about *Wada* is drawn from Kruger, whose documentation provides a fascinating in-depth exploration of this myth.

[22] Ibid, p39.

[23] Ibid.

[24] Ibid, p38.

[25] Ibid, p36.

[26] Kruger, 'Singing Psalms with Owls: A Venda Twentieth Century Musical History' in *African Music*, 7(4), International Library of African Music, Grahamstown, 1999, p125.

[27] Blacking, 1982, p423.

[28] Ibid, p424.

[29] Blacking, 1968, p23. John Blacking, the renowned ethnomusicologist, made a major contribution to the field of Venda music in his book on Venda children's songs.

[30] Blacking, 1982, p500.

[31] Information on *tshikona* drawn from Blacking, 'Musical Expeditions of the Venda' in *African Music*, 3(1), International Library of African Music, Grahamstown, 1962, p56; Blacking, 1982, pp492-500; Kruger 'Singing Psalms with Owls: A Venda Twentieth Century Musical History' in *Journal of African Music*, 8(1), forthcoming; and Kirby, pp155-162; pp268-269. See also Kruger 'Introduction to the Social Context of Two Venda Dances: *Tshikona* and *Tshigombela*' in *Papers Presented at the Seventh Symposium on Ethnomusicology*, International Library of African Music, Grahamstown, 1989, pp28-31.

[32] Blacking, 1982, p500.

[33] Kruger, forthcoming, p6.

[34] The Drumcafé went on a fieldtrip to Vendaland in 2003 to attend the launch of the indigenous music project at the University of Venda. The author wrote this description so that the memory of the dance would remain vivid.

[35] Section on initiation based on writings of Blacking, 1982, pp471-474, pp482-492; Blacking (www.era.anthropology.ac.uk/Era/VendaGirls/VendaMusic/Mu_1.); Stayt, pp101-141; and Netshitangani, 'The songs of Venda *Murundu* School' in *Papers Presented at the Symposium in Ethnomusicology*, Number 13, International Library of African Music, Grahamstown, 1997, p13-19.

[36] Stayt, p127.

[37] Blacking, 1982, p471.

[38] Ibid.

[39] On the subject of the songs lyrics, Netshitangani comments that 'Some of the words have been distorted and lost their real meaning or diction because the songs were foreign. Therefore many of the songs are too difficult to translate because nobody knows their meaning' (Netshitangani, p14).

[40] Stayt, p134.

[41] Blacking did extensive research covering girls' initiation. This research can be easily accessed in his article placed on the following website: www.era.anthropology.ac.uk/Era/VendaGirls/VendaMusic/Mu_1. The article includes photographs, musical transcriptions and video clips.

[42] Stayt, p109.

[43] Stayt, pp115-116.

[44] For additional information on girls initiation see Blacking, 'Initiation and the Balance of Power: The *Tshikanda* Girls' Initiation of the Venda of the Northern Transvaal' in

Ethnological and Linguistic Studies in honour of W.J. van Warmelo, Government ethnological publications, Pretoria, 1969, pp21-38; Blacking, 'Songs, Dances, Mimes and Symbolism of Venda Girls' Initiation Schools' in *African Studies*, 28(1-4), 1969, and Blacking 'Movement, Dance, Music and the Venda Girls' Initiation Cycle' in Spencer (ed) *Society and the Dance: The Social Anthropology of Process and Performance*, Cambridge University Press, Cambridge, 1985.

[45] Information on possession drawn mainly from Blacking, 1982, pp474-482. See also Ralushai 'The Origin and Social Significance of Malombo' in *Papers Presented at the Fifth Symposium on Ethnomusicology*, International Library of African Music, Grahamstown, 1985, pp2-7.

[46] Blacking, p23.

[47] Blacking states that Karanga is 'the language of the group in Rhodesia from whom the cult seems to have been derived' (Blacking, 1982, p478).

[48] Blacking was responsible for the research done on the subject of the Venda's musical expeditions. He conducted his fieldwork between May 1956 and December 1958. See Blacking, 'The Musical Expeditions of the Venda', *African Music*, International Library of African Music, Grahamstown, 1962, 3(1), pp54-78.

[49] Blacking, 1962, p56.

[50] For more information on *tshigombela* and *tshikanganga* see Blacking, 1967, pp25-26; Kruger, 1989, pp28-31; Kruger, 1999, pp122-146.

[51] Kruger, 1999, p128.

[52] Kruger, 'Mitambo: Venda Traditional Dance Theatre' in *Papers Presented at the Symposium of Ethnomusicology*, Number 15, International Library of African Music, Grahamstown, 1999, p68.

[53] Information drawn from Blacking, 1967. For further reading see Kruger, *Venda lashu*, Potchefstroom, 2004.

[54] Recorded and translated in Blacking, 1967, p43.

[55] Ibid, p44.

[56] Ibid, p66.

[57] Ntsihlele, 'The Musical Essence in Tshivenda Folktales' in *Papers Presented at the Symposium on Ethnomusicology*, Number 13, International Library of African Music, Grahamstown, 1997, p104.

[58] For more reading on folktales with musical transcriptions see Stayt, pp330-361.

[59] Blacking, 1967, p24.

[60] Ibid.

[61] The information provided in this section on *mitambo* is drawn from Kruger, 1999, pp28-33.

[62] Blacking, 1982, p442

[63] The information provided in this section on *tshilombe* is drawn from Kruger 'Some of Them are Foolish, Some of Them are Good: On the Contradictions of Artistic Experience in Venda Musical Culture' in *Papers Presented at the Tenth Symposium on Ethnomusicology*, International Library of African Music, Grahamstown, 1991, pp88-95.

[64] Song written by Daniel Luambo. (Kruger, 1991, pp89-90).

[65] Ibid, p90.

Tsonga-Shangaan

[1] Information on Tsonga history drawn from Hammond-Tooke, *The Bantu-speaking peoples of Southern Africa*, Routledge and Kegan Paul, London, 1974; Magubane, Vanishing Cultures of South Africa, Struik, Cape Town, 1998; Schapera, *The Bantu-speaking Tribes of South Africa*, Maskew Miller, Cape Town, 1966; West and Morris, *Abantu*, Struik, Cape Town, 1976.

[2] This instrument is also known as *tsomane*. (Johnston, *The Music of the Shangana-Tsonga*, Unpublished PhD thesis, University of Witwatersrand, 1971, p17).

[3] Information on instruments drawn from Johnston, 1971; Kirby, *The Musical Instruments of the Native Races of Southern Africa*, Witwatersrand University Press, Johannesburg, 1968, and Junod, *The Life of a South African Tribe*, 2, Macmillan, London, 1927.

[4] For more reading on xylophone (*mohambi*) music see Johnston, 'Mohambi Xylophone Music of the Shangana-Tsonga' in *African Music*, 5(3), 1973/4, pp86-93.

[5] This instrument is also known as *xitiringo* and *shitiringo* (Johnston, 1971, p24).

[6] Junod, 2, pp313-315.

[7] This instrument is also spelt *zambi* (Johnston, 1971, p25).

[8] This instrument is also spelt *shitendje, xitende* and *xitendzande* and is also known as *nkaku*. (Junod, 2, p278); (Kirby, p290) and (Johnston, 1971, p30).

[9] This instrument is also known as *xipendana* and *istontolo* (Johnston, 1971, p35).

[10] Information on music's special powers drawn from Johnston, 1971, pp40-41.

[11] Information on horn ensemble drawn from Kirby, pp84-87, and Junod, p431, vol.1.

[12] Johnston, 1971, p59.

[13] Information on *xigubu* drumming school and *xigubu* dance-songs drawn from Johnston, 1971, pp192-210 and Johnston, 'Shangana-Tsonga Drum and Bow Rhythms' in *African Music*, 5(1), International Library of African Music, Grahamstown, pp60-63, 1971.

[14] Johnston, 1971a, p9.

[15] Ibid, p442.

[16] Johnston, 1971b, p63.

[17] Information on exorcism mainly drawn from Chabalala, Dunisani, *Role and Functions of Traditional Music in Spirit Possession Healing Amongst the Tsonga People of South Africa*, Unpublished PhD thesis, University of the Witwatersrand, 2003; Johnston, 1971a, pp292-324 and Junod, 2, pp482-488.

[18] Junod, 2, p484.

[19] Johnston, 1971a, p10.

[20] Chabalala, p36.

[21] Ibid, p309.

[22] Johnston comments that there is evidence of the Tsonga's historical contact with both the Zulu and the Ndau. In the early 19th century the Tsonga were subjugated by Soshangane – a Nguni chief. They came into contact with the Ndau at one point when they fled from the Zulu (Johnston, 1971a, pp294-295).

[23] Chabalala, p38.

[24] Junod, 2, pp484-485.

[25] Information on beer-drink gatherings, songs and dances drawn from Johnston, 1971a, pp233-291.

[26] Johnston, 1971a, p237.

[27] Traditional song, performers/composers unknown, recorded in Johnston, 1971a, p239.

[28] Ibid, p240.

[29] Information on children's songs drawn from Johnston, 'Children's Music of the Shangana-Tsonga', *African Music*, 6(4), International Library of African Music, Grahamstown, 1987, pp126-143 and Johnston, 1971a, pp78-112.

[30] Johnston, 1971a, p93.

[31] Information on boys' circumcision school drawn from Johnston, 1971a, pp210-232 and Junod, pp71-94(1).

[32] Johnston quoting Cuenod (Johnston, 1971a, p219).

[33] Johnston, 1971a, p220.

[34] Traditional song, performers/composers unknown, recorded in Johnston, 1971a, p220.

[35] Junod, 1, p93.

[36] Traditional song, performers/composers unknown, recorded in Johnston, 1971a, p221.

[37] Information on girls' initiation drawn from Johnston, 1971a, pp113-191 and Junod, pp176-178.

[38] Traditional song, performers/composers unknown, recorded in Johnston, 1971a, pp151-152.

[39] Information on solo music drawn from Johnston, 1971a, pp333-433.

Khoi-khoi

[1] Information on history drawn from Barnard, *Hunters and Herders of Southern Africa*, Cambridge University Press, Cambridge, 1992; Berens et al, *The Cape Herders: a History of the Khoi Khoi of Southern Africa*, David Philip, Cape Town, 1996; Engelbrecht, *The Korana*, Maskew Miller, Cape Town, 1936; Schapera, *The Khoisan Peoples of South Africa*, Routledge and Kegan Paul, London, 1930; www.scienceinafrica.co.za; www.library.thinkquest.org.

[2] This instrument was also known as *seckoa* (Kirby, *The Musical Instruments of the Native Races of South Africa*, Witwatersrand University Press, Johannesburg, 1968, p284).

[3] This is the name of the Korana wooden jug. The Nama name for this object is *bambus* (Kirby, 1968, pp18-19).

[4] Information on instruments taken from Engelbrecht, pp170-174; Kirby, 'The Music and Musical Instruments of the Korana' in *Bantu Studies*, 6, 1932, pp183-204, Kirby, 1968, Kirby, 'The Music of the Black Races of South Africa' in Malan (ed), *South African Music Encyclopedia*, Oxford University Press, Cape Town, 1982, pp281-282.

[5] This is the name of the Korana instrument. The Griqua called their bull-roarer *bur-burs* (Engelbrecht, p171).

[6] This was a term used among the Nama.

[7] The use of horns as instruments among the Khoi is not reported in the majority of writings on Khoi music. Kirby states that 'the Hottentots do not appear to have made any systematic use of horns such as the Bantu did' (Kirby, 1968, p84).

[8] This instrument is also known as the *kxab* among the Nama (Schapera, p401).

[9] Kirby quoting Captain Percival (Kirby, 1968, p251).

[10] There are various names for this instrument. It is also known as *rabekin, rabouquin, ramgyib, ravekinge* and *!gutsib* (Ibid, p284).

[11] According to Kirby, the *ramkie* is unknown to the Korana. It was thus most probably played by the other Khoi tribes (Kirby, 1932, p195).

[12] This instrument is also spelt *t'guthe* or *xguthe* (Ibid, p284).

[13] Alternative names and spelling for the *gora* are *gom-gom,!gora, gorah, gorra, goura, gowra,*

kora, //kora, t'goerra, t'gorrah (Kirby, 1968, p284).

14 For additional reading on the *gora* see Mugglestone, 'The *Gora* and the 'grand' *Gom-Gom*' in *African Music*, 6 (2) International Library of African Music, Grahamstown, 1982, pp94-115.

15 Schapera (1930), p403.

16 Information on reed-pipe ensemble drawn from Engelbrecht, pp171-174 Kirby (1968), pp135-147; Kirby, 1932, pp185-191; and Schapera, 1930, pp402-404.

17 Kirby, 1982, p281.

18 Kirby 1932, p189.

19 This is a Korana word.

20 This is a Korana word.

21 This is a Korana word.

22 Kirby, 1968, p137.

23 This is a Korana word.

24 Kirby, 1932, comments that the missionaries objected and attempted to eradicate any music that was indigenous to the people they were attempting to convert.

25 Description of this performance based on Schapera's account (Schapera, 1930, p404).

26 Ibid.

27 Description of this performance based on Schapera's account (Schapera, 1930, pp404-405).

San

1 Information on history drawn from Barnard, *Hunters and Herders of Southern Africa*, Cambridge University Press, Cambridge, 1992; Lee and Devore (eds), *Kalahari Hunter-Gatherers*, Harvard University Press, Cambridge, 1976; Smith et al, *The Bushmen of Southern Africa: a foraging society in transition*, David Philip, Cape Town, 2000; Schapera, *The Khoisan Peoples of South Africa*, Routledge and Kegan Paul, London, 1930, p206.

2 Dornan, *Pygmies and Bushmen of the Kalahari*, Struik, Cape Town, 1975, p42.

3 Smith et al, p2.

4 Ibid.

5 Dornan, p75.

6 Schapera, p206.

7 Gildenhuys, 'Musical Instruments of South West Africa/Namibia' in *Papers Presented at the Second Symposium on Ethnomusicology*, International Library of African Music, Grahamstown, 1982, p30.

8 Kirby, *The Musical Instruments of the Native Races of South Africa*, Witwatersrand University Press, Johannesburg, 1968, p12.

9 Information on instruments drawn from Kirby, 'A Study of Bushman Music' in *Bantu Studies*, 10, Witwatersrand University Press, 1936; Biesele, 'Song Texts by the Master of Tricks: Kalahari San Thumb Piano Music' in *Botswana Notes and Records*, 7, Botswana Society, Botswana, 1975, pp171-188; Brearley, 'A Musical Tour of Botswana' in *Botswana Notes and Records*, 16, Botswana Society, Botswana, 1984, pp45-57; Kirby, 1968; Gildenhuys, 1982, pp28-33; Kirby, 'The Musical Practices of the /'Auni and ≠ Khomani San' in Jones and Doke (eds), *Bushmen of the Southern Kalahari*, Witwatersrand University Press, Johannesburg, 1937; Kirby, 'The Musics of the Black Races of South Africa' in Malan (ed) *South African Music Encyclopedia*, Oxford University Press, Cape Town, 1982, pp275-280; and Marshall, 'The !Kung of Nyae Nyae' in Lee and DeVore (eds), *Kalahari Hunter-Gatherers*, Harvard University Press, Cambridge, 1976, pp363-381.

10 This instrument is also spelt /garris (Kirby, 1968, p282).

11 Ibid, p93.

12 Marshall quoting England (Marshall, 1976, p365).

13 Marshall, 1976, p369; Gildenhuys, p31.

14 Marshall, 1976, p369.

15 This instrument is also known as *n!ao* and *segaba* (Gildenhuys, p31, and Brearley, p52).

16 This instrument is also known as *raamakie* (Kirby, 1968, p281).

17 Marshall, 1976, pp370-371.

18 This instrument is also known as //ha or t'ha (Kirby, p281).

19 Kirby explains that Burchell, an explorer who came across San playing the *gora* in the early 1800s and published a book on his travels, illustrated his description of the instrument. The illustration led to the assumption and misconception by most that the San were the first peoples to play the *gora*.

20 Hansen, 'Bushman Music: Still an Unknown' in Skotnes (ed), *Miscast: Negotiating the Presence of the San*, University of Cape Town Press, Cape Town, 1996, p299.

21 This instrument is also known as *dongu, dengu, sitengena*, and *!goma* (Biesele, 1975, p172).

22 Information on Jack and his *mbira* music is drawn from Biesele, 1975, pp171-188.

23 Kirby, 1937, p18.

24 Dornan, p62.

25 England, 'Bushman Counterpoint' in *Journal of the International Folk Music Council*, 19,

p59, 1967 and Marshall, 1969, p368.

26 Information on San song drawn from James, *The First Bushman's Path*, University of Natal Press, Pietermaritzburg, 2001; Kirby, 1937, pp17-49; Kirby, 1982, pp275-278; Schapera, 1930, p206.

27 Kirby, 1982, p277.

28 Ibid.

29 Dornan, p138; Gildenhuys, p30; Kirby, 1982, p278.

30 Kirby, 1982, p278.

31 Information on San dance drawn from Barnard, *Hunters and Herders of Southern Africa*, Cambridge University Press, New York, 1992; James, Kirby, 1936; Olivier, *Namibia: Songs of the Ju'hoansi San*, Ocora Radio France, Paris, 1997, pp16-17; Schapera, 1930.

32 Kirby, 1936, p215.

33 Ibid, p216.

34 James, p214.

35 Ibid.

36 Examples of dances drawn from Schapera, 1930, pp202-205.

37 Information on eland dance and girls menstruation drawn mainly from Olivier, pp16-17.

38 Schapera, 1930, p204.

39 Examples drawn from Schapera, 1930, pp204-206.

40 Thomas, *The Harmless People*, Secker and Warburg, London, 1959, p73.

41 *!kia* is the !Kung word for trance.

42 Katz quoting Bo, a !Kung Bushman who at the time of research was living in a camp at Xaixia, in 'Education for Transcendence: !Kia-Healing with the Kalahari !Kung' in Lee and DeVore (eds.) *Kalahari Hunter-Gatherers*, Harvard University Press, Cambridge, 1976, p286.

43 General information on trance healing drawn from Biesele, 'Anyone with Sense Would Know: Tradition and Creativity in !Kung Narrative and Song' in Vossen and Keuthman (eds) *Contemporary Studies on Khoisan 1*, Helmut Buske Verlag, Hamburg, 1986; Katz, 1976; Katz, *Boiling Energy*, Harvard University Press, Cambridge, 1982; Marshall, 1976; Marshall, 'The Medicine Dance of the !Kung Bushmen' in *Africa*, 39(4), 1969; and *Smith et al*.

44 Katz, 1976, p286.

45 Marshall, 1976, p352.

46 For more information on Gauwa and the great god see Marshall, 1969, p350.

47 Be is a real person who Marshall met. She lived in Namibia. She was apparently still alive in the 1970s.

48 Biesele, 1986, pp99-100.

49 Old N≠isa was a !Kung Bushman living in the Nyae Nyae region whom Marshall interviewed (Marshall, 1969, p366).

50 According to Marshall, even though the dances usually take place at night, there are no rules preventing them from taking place during the day (Marshall, 1969, p360).

51 Marshall, 1969, p366.

52 Ibid, p362.

53 Ibid, p363.

54 Ibid, p365.

55 Ibid.

56 Ibid, p358.

57 Katz, 1976, p288.

58 According to Marshall, if an individual is ill, a 'special curing' dance is arranged for him/her. The community is not involved in this rite. It is a private gathering and the healing is performed by one or more medicine men (Marshall, 1969, p354).

59 Smith *et al*, p78.

60 Marshall, 1969, p349.

Index